TURN OF
THE STORY

TURN OF THE STORY

CANADIAN SHORT FICTION ON THE EVE OF THE MILLENNIUM

Edited by

JOAN THOMAS and HEIDI HARMS

Published in 1999 by
House of Anansi Press Limited
34 Lesmill Road
Toronto, ON M3B 2T6
Tel. (416) 445-3333
Fax (416) 445-5967
www.anansi.ca

Distributed in Canada by
General Distribution Services
325 Humber College Blvd.,
Etobicoke, ON, Canada M9W 7C3
Tel. (416) 213-1919
Fax (416) 213-1917
E-mail Customer.Service@ccmailgw.genpub.com

CANADIAN CATALOGUING IN PUBLICATION DATA
Main entry under title.
Turn of the story : short fiction on the eve of the millennium
ISBN 0-88784-637-8
1. Short stories, Canadian (English).* 2. Canadian fiction
(English) — 20th century.* 1. Thomas, Joan (Sandra Joan).
PS8321.T87 1999   C813'.0108054   C98-933055-9
PR9197.32.T87 1999

Printed and bound in Canada

*House of Anansi Press gratefully acknowledges the Canada
Council for the Arts, the Government of Canada through
the Book Publishing Industry Development Program (BPIDP), and
the Ontario Arts Council for their support of our publishing program.*

Contents

Introduction

Turn of the Story: Canadian Short Fiction on the Eve of the Millennium is a book of new stories by many of Canada's best writers. It seizes on a momentous point of time to honour an exciting national literature that hardly existed a half-century ago. Think of it as the literary equivalent of a national display of fireworks. Or as a time capsule: twenty artifacts, twenty perspectives on this fascinating, uneasy age.

But *Turn of the Story* is really intended for readers, not archivists. It's a book, to use Alice Munro's words in accepting the Giller Prize in 1998, "for all those who are still hooked on the short story." There's a touch of defiance in Munro's words — a suggestion that short fiction is somehow at odds with the times. From a writer's point of view, short stories are a testament to pure aesthetic impulse. No one (almost no one) gets rich writing them. And if you're a reader standing in a bookstore, furtively dipping into this book, you may have the sense that you're committing a radical act. We've been advised of the forms that define popular culture at the end of the second millennium, and short stories are fundamentally different from most of them. Short stories are not, for example:

a) *Sound bites*: Back when fiction was subject to rules, and Edgar Allan Poe was clarifying them, Poe declared that a short story had to be of a length that could be read at one sitting. This used to be a comment on the shortness of stories, but it now calls attention to their length. You should be sitting.

b) *Novels*: Novels, as a form, have adapted well to a relativistic age. They're big enough to comprise everyone's take on a subject: the point of view of the heroine as a child and as an old woman, the thoughts of the hot-dog vendor who watched her board a bus one day, the notes of the psychoanalyst who listened to her talk for eight years. Short stories offer one sampling cut through the core of a life, make of it what you will. Some short-story writers are ingenious enough to subvert the authority of the voice they do adopt, and some manage to squeeze in more than one point of view. There are limits, though, to what one story can carry in its narrative arc. Stories are not novels, but they are long enough for a life to unravel, as Bonnie Burnard demonstrates in "Evening at the Edge of the Water."

c) *Electronically interactive*: Short stories, at least the ones in this volume, end one way and not another. They do not invite you to click on alternative plot paths, or to read the paragraphs in random order. Between the covers of *Turn of the Story*, you get human experience distilled in black ink on white paper. This is not ephemeral text floating in cyberspace — it's hard copy, a form that lends itself to exploring finalities. No matter how shrewdly he has prepared himself for every eventuality, the infirm old man in Margaret Atwood's "The Labrador Fiasco" is moving towards disaster as surely as the hapless explorers he reads about, huddled in a frozen forest boiling their moccasins.

Readers invited to select a plot path according to their appetite for sensation, or their longing that things should always turn out right in the end, are left with their solipsism unchallenged. They've missed tasting the devastating and non-negotiable effects of contingency in a life they briefly experience as real. Electronic participation seems a thin sort of interactivity, in any case, if you compare it with the collaboration between the reader's and writer's imaginations that reading requires.

d) *Pictures, moving or otherwise*: Images, one could argue, are a better approximation of experience than prose, and so might make better art. Visual media immerse us in sensation. Things happen all at once. Writers, on the other hand, work word by word, and have few options but to order things in a linear (and, we might say, artificial) fashion. This is a problem that has preoccupied twentieth-century writers, and some have been fabulously successful in approximating the unfiltered barrage of sensuous and emotional data that constitutes experience. Interestingly, although we may admire this kind of writing, it's an acquired taste, and not the daily bread of most people's reading. Stories as stories suit the naive realist in our brains, the part that experiences time as linear, and inexorable. The young man and woman in Leo McKay's "The Wedding Ring" are flirting with the idea of splitting up when they are embroiled in a shooting in a bar. The tragedy they witness is final, something is lost to them forever, and that's the essence and power of the story.

The emergence of postmodernism and metafiction has made us more aware of the fact that realism in fiction is a literary convention like any other. But this hasn't dimmed our passion for stories, a passion that grows from the way we use narrative, every day, to shape our experience. "Where are we without our plots?" Atwood asks in "The Labrador Fiasco." In Dionne Brand's "Tamarindus Indica," a young Caribbean man named Sones has been nurtured on false and damaging dreams. Eventually he creates a fiction himself, an invention about his great-great-grandmother holding a tamarind seed in her mouth throughout her forced journey across the ocean. Sones, whose life circumstances offer little but dislocation and humiliation, forges a sense of family continuity through narrative.

If the formal experiments that began in the 1960s have not dislodged narrative, they have made stories a fresher, livelier, more poetic and fluid negotiation between actuality and artifice.

They've opened the door to Mark Jarman's allusive, manic prose, and to Greg Hollingshead's layered redefinition of the sentence. Steven Heighton's "Finals," a perfect gem of the traditional short-story form (although it is, interestingly, a novel excerpt), exploits a limited point of view with an assurance that is distinctly contemporary, expertly fusing external action, physical sensation, emotion, and thought. Other pieces in *Turn of the Story* are ordered by devices we don't immediately recognize as plot. In "Dresses," Lise Bissonnette uses three gowns as the through line for a wonderful study in contrasts between the conventional female preoccupation with clothes and the reality of a girl's intellectual appetite and hunger for experience. In Janice Kulyk Keefer's "Dreams: Storms: Dogs," a dismally mismatched wife and husband gaze at two different paintings in a Venetian museum, and their reflections on the images they see connect them in surprising ways. Lisa Moore's "Mouths, Open" is about the excruciating moment before the end of love, a story readers trace through a montage of freeze-frame images of transformation.

e) *Documentaries and saturation reports*: In an age preoccupied with information, stories have a greater interest in emotional truth than in fact. A magazine feature imparts a different kind of knowledge about the effects of an untimely death than a story like Michael Winter's "The Pallbearer's Gloves" does. Reading this story, we experience the sad banality of the way death plays out in reality. It's not that we learn something specific about how families deal with bereavement; instead, we are invited into an event that can be recreated but not described.

A few years ago, when Heidi Harms and I began to float the idea of a millennium anthology to publishers, one of the things that motivated us was a notion in the air at the time that fiction was losing out to information and analysis. Non-fiction books were taking up a larger share of the review space in many Canadian publications; fiction was lumped in many minds with entertainment, a quaint, pale alternative to movies. In as short a time as two years, this sense has receded — partly because of the extraordinary success of Canadian fiction in the last few years, and because books such as Anne Michaels's *Fugitive Pieces* demonstrate so powerfully the essential role literature plays in helping us look at the overwhelming realities of the world at the end of the second millennium.

Here we are now, flipping our calendars to a date out of an old science-fiction movie, a little spooked, like the people in Carol Shields's "Our Men and Women," at the prospect of "that swift plummeting fall towards what [we] believe must be the future." No doubt the road will flatten as we move up it, the way a hill does when you begin to climb; no doubt the apocalypse will fail to live up to its advance billing. Still, anxiety would appear to be the sane response, especially given that we have no reliable way of predicting the future, having, as a society, divested ourselves of many of the mechanisms (such as religion, tradition, propriety, a certainty in the vitality of nature) that would ensure that life will carry on the way it always has.

In interesting times, it's not analysts and commentators who deliver our lives up to us in a form we can comprehend; for someone to hold a mirror up to nature (and society), we look to artists. In *Six Memos for the Next Millennium*, Italo Calvino reminds us that to understand this metaphor and all it implies, we have to turn back to the Greek story of Perseus, the hunter who succeeds in killing the Gorgon. If you remember, the sight of the writhing hair of Medusa paralyzes everyone who makes an effort to approach her, until, in an inspired moment, Perseus realizes the potential of the indirect gaze — he can approach and slay the Gorgon by catching her reflection in his bronze shield. Art is a mirror, not only because it reflects us back to ourselves, but also because it offers the possibility of looking obliquely at realities that would otherwise turn us to stone.

The writers represented in this volume were not asked to write social commentary, and would no doubt have declined to do so, but there is, inevitably, a striking *fin-de-siècle* flavour to *Turn of the Story*. Carol Shields's "Our Men and Women" comprises four fables of ordinary people struggling with intimations of disaster and working hard "to understand the topography of the real." While they're awake, they can mobilize enough bravado, wit, and denial to assert some sort of order in their existence, but the dread of plague, earthquake, and flood seeps through from their dreams.

What several of the stories capture is the heightened significance we ascribe, in millennial times, to anything out of the ordinary. A dancing fish brings an apocalyptic message in "Mad Fish," Olive Senior's magic-realist tale of cocaine and cultural intrusion in the Caribbean; in other stories, the apocalypse raises its gargoyle head in the form of natural disaster and technological nightmare. In "Banana Chaudfroid" by Monique Proulx, a devastating ice storm calls everything into question for Gabrielle, a hip, urban writer. When Gabrielle opens her home to strangers, Proulx asks whether old habits of neighbourly interdependence can be resurrected. And something shifts in Gabrielle's view of nature, something is shattered — her assumption that nature will continue to submit to its own laws.

Kent Nussey's "Summer" is an allegory of the double faces (solution/scourge) of modern science. The summer that Hicks's mother endures chemotherapy, hornets invade Hicks's crawl space like visible pulses of electricity, like malignant cells. Chemicals are Hicks's weapon, as they are his mother's. But when Hicks holds up a glass of carrot juice and smells pesticides, Nussey reminds us that the cure and the contamination are one. The dead scuba diver on the forest floor in Mark Jarman's "Burn Man on a Texas Porch" embodies our dread so accurately that he's become a part of urban myth. Tricked out with all technology can offer him, he's still ended up out of his element.

Many of us find that the number of documentaries or feature articles we can take in about the disappearance of forests and animal species, the genocide of ethnic minorities, child prostitutes on decaying city streets is limited. Call it grief overload, fear fatigue. But the fiction in this volume, although it may explore difficult subjects, opens a window for human response. Connie

Gault's "Leonard Dobie's Condition" recounts a man's encounter with three nurses, during three illnesses that span the century. The story traces the way the treatment of illness has evolved through the century — has become, for all its gains, dehumanizing — but what we feel as we read is Leonard Dobie's wholeness in the face of all that threatens to fragment him. Olive Senior looks at the persistence of the self in the face of another kind of assault — linguistic and cultural domination. The narrator in "Mad Fish" insists on reshaping the story of a character she considers crude and inarticulate, but the voice and spirit of Joshua (a.k.a. Radio) come through.

One of the great pleasures of compiling and editing an anthology has been, of course, the chance to put together the sort of book we love to read ourselves. The best stories set their own criteria, and Heidi and I find that we can identify our requirements only by looking back at what we did select. We chose stories for the flash of recognition we feel reading about things we've never experienced — stories that extend our peripheral vision, articulating what lies just beyond the boundary of consciousness or memory. Like Greg Hollingshead's "Born Again," which takes us into the fierce, dark, wonky morality of childhood, to the moments when self-consciousness emerges. We discovered in ourselves a decided appetite for stories with an edge (as hard as that is to define) — for quirkiness, irony, mordant humour, idiosyncrasy. For stories of competing insanities, like Guy Vanderhaeghe's "The Jimi Hendrix Experience," which hooked us firmly from Vanderhaeghe's description of the narrator's father, a night janitor: "A vampire who sleeps while the sun is up, sinks his teeth into my neck at the supper table, goes off to work with a satisfied, bloody, grey smile on his lips."

Reading the manuscript over, we're struck by the artlessness of the stories, by the sense that they do not sound constructed but are nevertheless scrupulously crafted. Like Elisabeth Harvor's "Down with Heartbreak," where Harvor's craft speaks in the precision of every line, in the way every image evokes Kay's vulnerability and hope, and in the canny reference in the last passage to the dentist's miniature tools of torture. The short stories we selected are neither reality, nor an escape from it. They are, in a term used by the American novelist Richard Ford, hyper-reality. In our own lives, we are almost never this lucid.

Many of the writers who are responsible for Canada's global reputation are in this volume — and so is an exciting line-up of emerging writers, such as Lisa Moore, Michael Winter, Leo McKay, Kristen den Hartog, and Lynn Coady. Both den Hartog and Coady tell incisive stories about families: den Hartog's "Too True" delicately traces the emotional fallout of losing a father, twenty years after the fact. In Coady's "Play the Monster Blind," a young woman gets an education in the overt and subtle uses of power within a family. "Emerging writers" may not be the accurate term for this new generation of Canadian writers, for some of them have catapulted straight from their first book to awards, major publishing contracts, and foreign sales, and so many of them seem to have emerged full-blown as accomplished writers. Their craft, originality, and vision suggest a brilliant literary future for Canada.

Heidi Harms and I are thrilled to offer you this cross-section of Canadian writing at a vibrant point in its evolution. There are writers from across Canada in *Turn of the Story*, although we don't claim to be providing a complete literary map of such a large and complex country. We invited widely, and then picked the best of the stories that came in. Behind this book, imagine two or three "shadow anthologies" made up of the fine stories we had to send back for lack of space, the work of writers who were too busy with other projects to submit to this anthology, and stories by writers the two of us haven't discovered — for the time has passed when an active reader can expect to be familiar with most of the interesting writing in Canada. What is astonishing is that many Canadian readers can still remember a time when such a thing was possible.

We want to acknowledge and thank, for their generosity and vision, all the writers who sent us stories; Matt Cohen for his translation of Monique Proulx's "Banana Chaudfroid" and Sheila Fischman for her translation of Lise Bissonnette's "Dresses"; Martha Sharpe, House of Anansi Press's publisher, who offered us the perfect balance of autonomy and support; and friends and family who advised, encouraged, and helped in numerous ways, among them Mark Morton, Susan Rempel Letkemann, Andris Taskans, Bonnie Burnard, Erica Ens, Gemma Gervais, Gordon Lang, Connie Cohen, Jacqueline Remillard, Caitlin Thomas Dunn, Bill Dunn (whose suggestion prompted this project), and Sara Harms.

Joan Thomas, Winnipeg, March 1999

Margaret Atwood

The

Labrador

Fiasco

It's October, but which October? One of those Octobers with their quick intensities of light, their diminuendos, their red and orange leaves. My father is sitting in his armchair by the fire. He has on his black-and-white-checked dressing gown, over his other clothes, and his old leather slippers, with his feet propped up on a hassock. Therefore it must be evening.

My mother is reading to him. She fiddles with her glasses, and hunches over the page; or it looks like hunching. In fact, that is just the shape she is now.

My father is grinning, so this must be a part he enjoys. His grin is higher on the left side than on the right: six years ago he had a stroke, which we all pretend he's recovered from; and he has, mostly.

"What's happening now?" I say, taking off my coat. I already know the story, having heard it before.

"They've just set out," says my mother.

My father says, "They took the wrong supplies." This pleases him: he himself would not have taken the wrong supplies. In fact, he would never have gone on this ill-advised journey in the first place, or — although he was once more reckless, more impetuous, more sure of his ability to confront fate and transcend danger — this is his opinion now. "Darn fools," he says, grinning away.

But what supplies could they have taken, other than the wrong ones? White sugar, white flour, rice; that was what you took then. Peameal, sulphured apples, hardtack, bacon, lard. Heavy things. There was no freeze-drying then, no handy packaged soups; there were no nylon vests, no pocket-sized sleeping bags, no light-weight tarpaulins. Their tent was made of balloon silk, oiled to waterproof it. Their blankets were of wool. The packsacks were canvas, with leather straps and tumplines that went across the forehead to cut the strain on the back. They would have smelled of tar. In addition there were two rifles, two pistols, 1,200 rounds of ammunition, a camera, and a sextant; and then the cooking utensils and the clothing. Every pound of it had to be carried over each and every portage, or hauled upriver in the canoe, which was eighteen feet long, wood-framed, and canvas-covered.

None of this would have daunted the adventurers, however; or not at first. There were two of them, two young Americans; they'd been on camping expeditions before, although at warmer lati-tudes, with fragrant evening pipes smoked before cheerful blazes and a fresh-caught trout sizzling in the pan while the sunsets paled in the west. Each would have been able to turn a neat, Kiplingesque paragraph or two on the lure of wild places, the challenge of the unknown. This was in 1903, when exploration was still in vogue as a test of manliness, and when manliness itself was still in vogue and was thought to couple naturally with the word *clean*. Manliness, cleanliness, the wilderness, where you could feel free. With gun and fishing rod, of course. You could live off the land.

The leader of the expedition, whose name was Hubbard, worked for a magazine dedicated to the outdoors. His idea was that he and his chum and cousin — whose name was Wallace — would penetrate the last unmapped Labrador wilds, and he would write a series of articles about their adventures, and thus make

his name. (These were his very words: "I will make my name.")
Specifically, they would ascend the Nascaupee River, said to flow
out of Lake Michikamau, a fabled inland lake teeming with fish;
from there they could make it to the George River, where the
Indians congregated every summer for the caribou hunt, and from
there to a Hudson's Bay post and out to the coast again. While
among the Indians, Hubbard planned to do a little amateur
anthropology, which he would also write up, with photographs
—a shaggy-haired hunter with an old-fashioned rifle, his foot on
a carcass; a cut-off head with spreading antlers; women with bead
necklaces and gleaming eyes chewing the hide, or sewing it, or
whatever they did. *The Last Wild People.* Something like that.
There was a great interest in such subjects. He would describe
the menus, too.

(But those Indians came from the north. No one ever took the
river route from the west and south.)

In stories like this, there is always — there is supposed to be —
an old Indian who appears to the white men as they are planning
to set out. He comes to warn them, because he is kind at heart and
they are ignorant. "Do not go there," he says. "That is a place we
never go." Indians in these tales have a formal manner of speaking.

"Why not?" the white men say.

"Bad spirits live there," says the old Indian. The white men
smile and thank him, and disregard his advice. Native super-
stition, they think. So they go where they've been warned not to,
and then, after many hardships, they die. The old Indian shakes
his head when he hears of it. Foolish white men, but what can
you tell them? They have no respect.

There's no old Indian in this book — he somehow got left out
—so my father takes the part upon himself. "They shouldn't have
gone there," he says. "The Indians never went that way." He
doesn't say *bad spirits*, however. He says, "Nothing to eat." For
the Indians it would have been the same thing, because where
does food come from if not from the spirits? It isn't just there, it
is given; or else withheld.

Hubbard and Wallace tried to hire several Indians to come with them, at least on the first stages of the journey, and to help with the packs. None would go; they said they were "too busy." Really they knew too much. What they knew was that you couldn't possibly carry with you, in there, everything you would need to eat. And if you couldn't carry it, you would have to kill it. But most of the time there was nothing to kill. "Too busy" meant too busy to die. It also meant too polite to point out the obvious.

The two explorers did do one thing right. They hired a guide. His name was George, and he was a Cree Indian, or partly; what they called then a breed. He was from James Bay, too far away from Labrador to know the full and evil truth about it. George travelled south to meet his employers, all the way to New York City, where he had never been before. He had never been to the United States before, or even to a city. He kept calm; he looked about him; he demonstrated his resourcefulness by figuring out what a taxicab was and how to hire one. His ability to reason things through was to come in very handy later on.

"That George was quite a boy," says my father. George is his favourite person in the whole story.

Somewhere around the house there's a picture of my father himself — at the back of a photo album, perhaps, with the snapshots that haven't yet been stuck in. It shows him thirty years younger, on some canoe trip or another — if you don't write these things down on the backs of the pictures, they get forgotten. He's evidently crossing a portage. He hasn't shaved, he's got a bandana tied around his head because of the blackflies and mosquitoes, and he's carrying a heavy pack, with the broad tumpline across his forehead. His hair is dark, his glistening face is deeply tanned and not what you'd call clean. He looks slightly villainous — like a pirate, or indeed like a northwoods guide, the kind who might suddenly vanish in the middle of the night, along with your best rifle, just before the wolves arrive on the scene. But like someone who knows what he's doing.

"That George knew what he was doing," says my father now.

Once he got out of New York, that is; while there, George wasn't much help, because he didn't know where to shop. It was in New York that the two men bought all the necessary supplies, except a gill net, which they thought they could find up north. They also failed to purchase extra moccasins. This may have been their worst mistake.

Then they set out, by train and then by boat and then by smaller boat. The details are tedious. The weather was bad, the meals were foul, none of the transportation was ever on time. They spent a lot of hours, and even days, waiting around on docks and wondering when their luggage would turn up.

"That's enough for tonight," says my mother.

"I think he's asleep," I say.

"He never used to go to sleep," says my mother. "Not with this story. Usually he's busy making up his list."

"His list?"

"His list of what he would take."

While my father sleeps, I skip ahead in the story. The three men have finally made it inland from the bleak northeastern shore of Labrador, and have left their last jumping-off place, and are voyaging in earnest.

It's the middle of July, but the short summer will soon be over, and they have five hundred miles to go.

Their task is to navigate Grand Lake, which is long and thin; at its extreme end, or so they've been told, the Nascaupee flows into it. The only map they've seen, crudely drawn by an earlier white traveller some fifty years before, shows Grand Lake with only one river emptying into it. One is all the Indians have ever mentioned: the one that goes somewhere. Why talk about the others, because why would anyone want to know about them? There are many plants that have no names because they cannot be eaten or used.

But in fact there are four other rivers.

During this first morning they are exhilarated, or so Wallace records. Their hopes are high, adventure calls. The sky is deep blue, the air is crisp, the sun is bright, the treetops seem to beckon them on. They do not know enough to beware of beckoning treetops. For lunch they have flapjacks and syrup, and are filled with a sense of well-being. They know they're going into danger, but they also know that they are immortal. Such moods do occur, in the North. They take pictures with their camera: of their laden canoe; of one another — moustached, be-sweatered, with puttee-shaped wrappings on their legs and things on their heads that look like bowler hats — leaning blithely on their paddles. Heart-breaking, but only when you know the end. As it is they're having the time of their lives.

There's another photo of my father, perhaps from the same trip as the one with the portage; or he's wearing the same bandana. This time he's grinning into the camera lens, pretending to shave himself with his axe. Two tall-tale points are being made: that his axe is as sharp as a razor, and that his bristles are so tough that only an axe could cut them. It's highjinks, a canoe-trip joke; although secretly, of course, he once believed both of these things.

On the second day the three men pass the mouth of the Nas-caupee, which is hidden behind an island and looks like shoreline. They don't even suspect it is there. They continue on to the end of the lake, and enter the river they find there. They've taken the wrong turn.

I don't get back to Labrador for more than a week. When I return, it's a Sunday night. The fire is blazing away and my father is sitting in front of it, waiting to see what will happen next. My mother is rustling up the baking-powder biscuits and the decaffeinated tea. I forage for cookies.

"How is everything?" I say.

"Fine," she says. "But he doesn't get enough exercise." *Everything* means my father, as far as she is concerned.

"You should make him go for a walk," I say.

"*Make* him," she says.

"Well, suggest."

"He doesn't see the point of walking just to walk," she says. "If you're not going anywhere."

"You could send him on errands," I say. To this she does not bother even to reply.

"He says his feet hurt," she says. I think of the array of almost-new boots and shoes in the cupboard; boots and shoes that have proliferated lately. He keeps buying other ones. If only he can find the right pair, he must think, whatever it is that's causing his feet to hurt will go away.

I carry in the teacups, dole out the plates. "So, how are Hubbard and Wallace coming along?" I say. "Have you got to the place where they eat the owl?"

"Slim pickings," he says. "They took the wrong river. Even if they'd found the right one, it was too late to start."

Hubbard and Wallace and George toil upstream. The heat at midday is oppressive. Flies torment them, little flies like pinpricks, giant ones as big as your thumb. The river is barely navigable: they have to haul their laden canoe over gravel shallows, or portage around rapids, through forest that is harsh and unmarked and jumbled. In front of them the river unrolls; behind them it closes up like a maze. The banks of the river grow steeper; hill after hill, gentle in outline, hard at the core. It's a sparse landscape: ragged spruce, birch, aspen, all spindly; in some places burned over, the way forward blocked by charred and fallen tree trunks.

How long is it before they realize they've gone up the wrong river? Far too long. They cache some of their food so they won't have to carry it; they throw some of it away. They manage to shoot a caribou, which they eat, leaving the hoofs and head behind. Their feet hurt; their moccasins are wearing out.

At last Hubbard climbs a high hill, and from its top he sees Lake Michikamau; but the river they have been following does not go

there. The lake is too far away; they can't possibly haul their canoe
that far through the forest. They will have to turn back.

In the evening their talk is no longer of discovery and exploration. Instead they talk about what they will eat. What they'll eat
tomorrow, and what they'll eat when they get back. They compose
bills of fare, feasts, grand blowouts. George is able to shoot or
catch this and that. A duck here, a grouse there. A whisky-jack.
They catch sixty trout, painstakingly one by one, using a hook
and line because they have no gill net. The trout are clear and
fresh as icewater, but only six inches long. Nothing is nearly
enough. The work of travelling uses up more energy than they
can take in; they are slowly dissolving, wasting away.

Meanwhile, the nights become longer and longer and darker
and darker. Ice forms on the edges of the river. Hauling the canoe
over the shallows, through the rushing, stone cold water, leaves
them shivering and gasping. The first snowflurries fall.

"It's rough country," says my father. "No moose; not even
bears. That's always a bad sign, no bears." He's been there, or near
it; same sort of terrain. He speaks of it with admiration and
nostalgia, and a kind of ruefulness. "Now, of course, you can fly
in. You can cover their whole route in a couple of hours." He
waves his fingers dismissively. So much for planes.

"What about the owl?" I say.

"What owl?" says my father.

"The one they ate," I say. "I think it's where the canoe dumps,
and they save their matches by sticking them in their ears."

"I think that was the others," says my father. "The ones who
tried the same thing later. I don't think this bunch ate an owl."

"If they had eaten one, what sort of owl would it have been?"
I say.

"Great horned or boreal," he says, "if they were lucky. More
meat on those. But it may have been something smaller." He gives
a series of thin, eerie barks, like a dog at a distance, and then he
grins. He knows every bird up there by its call; he still does.

"He's sleeping too much in the afternoons," says my mother.

"Maybe he's tired," I say.

"He shouldn't be that tired," she says. "Tired, and restless as well. He's losing his appetite."

"Maybe he needs a hobby," I say. "Something to occupy his mind."

"He used to have a lot of them," my mother says.

I wonder where they've all gone, those hobbies. Their tools and materials are still around: the plane and the spirit level, the feathers for tying dry flies, the machine for enlarging prints, the points for making arrows. These bits and pieces seem to me like artifacts, the kind that are dug up at archaeological sites, and then pondered over and classified, and used for deducing the kind of life once lived.

"He used to say he wanted to write his memoirs," says my mother. "A sort of account; all the places he's been. He did begin it several times, but now he's lost interest. He can't see too well."

"He could use a tape recorder," I say.

"Oh, help," says my mother. "More gadgets!"

The winds howl and cease, the snow falls and stops falling. The three men have traversed across to a different river, hoping it will be better, but it isn't. One night George has a dream: God appears to him, shining and bright and affable, and speaks in a manner that is friendly but firm. "I can't spare any more of these trout," he says, "but if you stick to this river you'll get down to Grand Lake all right. Just you don't leave the river, and I'll get you out safe."

George tells the others of his dream. It is discounted. The men abandon their canoe and strike out overland, hoping to reach their old trail. After far too long they do reach it, and stumble along it down the valley of the river they first ascended, rummaging through their former campsites for any food they might have thrown away. They aren't counting in miles, but in days; how many days they have left, and how many it will take. But that will depend on the weather, and on their own strength; how fast they can go. They find a lump of mouldering flour, a bit of lard, a few bones, some caribou hoofs, which they boil. A little tin of dry mustard; they mix it into the soup, and find it encouraging.

In the third week of October, this is how things stand:

Hubbard has become too weak to go any farther. He's been left behind, wrapped in his blankets, in the tent, with a fire going. The other two have gone on; they hope to walk out, then send help back for him. He's given them the last of the peameal.

The snow is falling. For dinner he has some strong tea and bone broth, and some boiled rawhide, made from the last of his moccasins; he writes in his journal that it is truly delicious. Now he is without footgear. He has every hope that the others will succeed, and will return and save him; or so he records. Nevertheless, he begins a farewell message for his wife. He writes that he has a pair of cowhide mittens that he is looking forward to cooking and eating the next day.

After that he goes to sleep, and after that he dies.

Some days farther down the trail, Wallace too has to give up. He and George part company: Wallace intends to go back with the latest leavings they've managed to locate — a few handfuls of mouldy flour. He will find Hubbard, and together they will await rescue. But he's been caught in a blizzard, and has lost his bearings; at the moment he's in a shelter made of branches, waiting for the snow to let up. He is amazingly weak, and no longer hungry, which he knows is a bad sign. Every movement he makes is slow and deliberate, and at the same time unreal, as if his body is apart from him and he is only watching it. In the white light of day or the red flicker of the fire — for he still has fire — the patterns on the ends of his own fingers appear miraculous to him. Such clarity and detail; he follows the pattern of the woven blanket as if tracing a map.

His dead wife has appeared to him, and has given him several pieces of practical advice concerning his sleeping arrangement: a thicker layer of spruce boughs underneath, she's said, would be more comfortable. Sometimes he only hears her; sometimes he sees her as well. She's wearing a blue summer dress, her long hair pinned up in a shining coil. She appears perfectly at home; the poles of the shelter are visible through her back. Wallace has ceased to be surprised by this.

Even farther along, George continues to walk; to walk out. He knows more or less where he's going; he will find help and return with it. But he isn't out yet, he's still in. Snow surrounds him, the blank grey sky enfolds him; at one point he comes across his own tracks and realizes he's been walking in a circle. He too is thin and weak, but he's managed to shoot a porcupine. He pauses to think it through: he could turn around, retrace his steps, take the porcupine back to share with the others; or he could eat all of it himself and go forward. He knows that if he goes back it's likely that none of them will get out alive; but if he goes on, there's at least a possibility, at least for him. He goes on, hoarding the bones.

"That George did the right thing," says my father.

———————————

While sitting at the dinner table my father has another stroke. This time it knocks out half the vision in each eye, his short-term memory, and his sense of where he is. From one minute to the next, he has become lost; he gropes through the living room as if he's never been in such a place before. The doctors say this time it's unlikely he'll recover.

Time passes. Now the lilacs are in bloom outside the window, and he can see them, or parts of them. Despite this he thinks it's October. Still, the core of him is still there. He sits in his armchair, trying to figure things out. One sofa cushion looks much like another unless you have something to go by. He watches the sunlight gleaming on the hardwood floor; his best guess is that it's a stream. In extreme situations you have to use your wits.

"I'm here," I say, kissing his dry cheek. He hasn't gone bald, not in the least. He has silvery white hair, like an egret frozen.

He peers at me out of the left sides of his eyes, which are the ones that work. "You seem to have become very old all of a sudden," he says.

As far as we can tell, he's missing the last four or five years, and several blocks of time before that as well. He's disappointed in me: not because of anything I've done, but because of what I've failed to do. I've failed to remain young. If I could have managed that, I could have saved him; then he too could have remained as he was.

I wish I could think of something to amuse him. I've tried recordings of bird songs, but he doesn't like them: they remind him that there's something he once knew, but can't remember. Stories are no good, not even short ones, because by the time you get to the second page he's forgotten the beginning. Where are we without our plots?

Music is better; it takes place drop by drop.

My mother doesn't know what to do, and so she rearranges: cups and plates, documents, bureau drawers. Right now she's outside, yanking weeds out of the garden in a bewildered frenzy. Dirt and couch grass fly through the air: that at least will get done! There's a wind; her hair is wild, blown up around her head like feathers.

I've told her I can't stay long. "You can't?" she said. "But we could have tea, I could light a fire . . ."

"Not today," I said firmly.

He can see her out there, more or less, and he wants her to come back in. He doesn't like it that she's on the other side of the glass. If he lets her slip away, out of his sight, who knows where she might go? She might vanish forever.

I hold his good hand. "She'll come in soon," I say; but *soon* could be a year.

"I want to go home," he says. I know there's no point telling him that home is where he now is, because he means something else. He means the way he was before.

"Where are we now?" I say.

He gives me a crafty look: Am I trying to trip him up? "In a forest," he says. "We need to get back."

"We're all right here," I say.

He considers. "Not much to eat."

"We brought the right supplies," I say.

He is reassured. "But there's not enough wood." He's anxious about this; he says it every day. His feet are cold, he says.

"We can get more wood," I say. "We can cut it."

He's not so sure. "I never thought this would happen," he says. He doesn't mean the stroke, because he doesn't know he's had one. He means getting lost.

"We know what to do," I say. "Anyway, we'll be fine."

"We'll be fine," he says, but he sounds dubious. He doesn't trust me, and he is right.

The story related within this story may be found in its original version in The Lure of the Labrador Wild, *by Dillon Wallace, published in 1905 by Fleming H. Revell Company and reprinted by Breakwater Books, Newfoundland, in 1977.*

Margaret Atwood's short stories, poetry, novels, and criticism have come to represent Canadian writing to the world. Among Atwood's five collections of short fiction are Wilderness Tips *(McClelland & Stewart, 1991) and* Bluebeard's Egg *(McClelland & Stewart, 1983). Atwood has published nine novels with McClelland & Stewart, including* Cat's Eye *(1989) and* The Robber Bride *(1993). In 1990 her novel* The Handmaid's Tale *was the basis of a Volker Schlondorff film, with a screenplay by Harold Pinter. Her most recent novel,* Alias Grace, *was awarded the Giller Prize for 1996 and was shortlisted for the Booker Prize.*

Steven Heighton

FINALS

Sevigne "the Machine" Torrins lost a close fight in April, but Hogeboom chose him as one of his boxers for the North Ontario high-school finals, at home in the Soo. It was his last month of school, for one thing. He won an easy bout in the light-middleweight quarters, then won his semi against a good fighter who had been battling a cold and fell apart in the third round, Sevigne scoring three points in the final minute to win. Or had the guy just wanted to avoid meeting Carmine LaStarza in the finals? Sevigne had not thought facing LaStarza would be an issue — no one expected him, Sevigne, to survive the semis. For the past year Hogeboom had been raving about LaStarza — a terrific prospect, he was bound for Detroit in the fall, they were giving him a tryout at the Kronk Gym.

Best not to be afraid of things, Sevigne's father once told him, what you fear most has a knack of finding its way to you. Good enough. But this makes it worse, having Torrins there in the front row waiting, swilling prominently from a zinc flask, Eddy and Sylvie and others of their gang trying not to stare but staring all right as Torrins stops Sevigne, on his way into the ring, to mumble advice — "Keep your chin tucked in and your hands up, boy, please" — the strong smell of rye on his breath not masking the brassy stink of fear.

Physically LaStarza is unremarkable — medium height and build, muscles undefined, the chest under his black fishnet singlet a bit sunken. What frightens is that long narrow lupine face, unshaven, the Roberto Duran look, his dense black stubble setting off pale eyes of Husky blue. What frightens is that cool ferocity — how he does not need to flex and preen and posture in his corner, only fix you with those terrible eyes. Hogeboom insists he be shaved, the stubble counts as intimidation, it's an amateur rule, but the ponytailed Ojibwa ref points at his watch, says the meet's running way late, forget it.

The bell unchains LaStarza who charges out of his corner meaning to end it fast, while Torrins starts yammering instructions from his seat as if the flurry of words itself might ward him off. "Work that jab, boy! Step right, step right!" Sevigne jackknifes over as LaStarza storms in, taking the first flurry on his shoulders and back and the top of his head, trying to hook LaStarza to the body. He lands one left to the belly with decent force and feels something he's never felt before: no give at all, no weakness: like punching the stump of an oak. LaStarza shoves him back and glides in snapping out beautiful jabs Sevigne can hear whizzing past his ducking head like fastballs and each in time with the man's grunting exhalations: *ooss ooss ooss*. Sevigne's own jab is his prize punch but LaStarza is a beat faster and steals the point every time. Doesn't feel like a jab when it lands, feels like a stiff right. "Letting your head come up, boy!" Torrins is yelling, slurring so that a deeper flush flames into Sevigne's face already red from the blows and bleeding now too, he feels and tastes the hot salt flux under his nostrils just as LaStarza tags him with a right lead, a slap in the face to any boxer, *I can land anything I want* it means, and *Shut up* Sevigne is thinking *Shut the fuck up, Dad,* and then his father yelling "If the bastard leads right again lay him out with a cross!" and Sevigne *Shut the fuck up Dad please*

and his father "Nice hook there Sev but you're *mailing* it" and
with a wave of rage Sevigne plants a jab full on LaStarza's nose,
lucky, the blue-eyed boy *like yours* got careless *Dad* cocky, Sevigne
feels the punch down to his toes and LaStarza's head lashes back,
a silver cross spilling out from under his singlet, and sweet to see,
all of it, the release of it, but now his father is hollering "BRAVO!
BRAVO, BOY!" and peripherally Sevigne — backing off as LaStarza
comes on firing furious triple, quadruple jabs — Sevigne sees
Torrins has leapt to his feet with both hands raised as if he's in
the ring. Maybe thinks he is. The crowd around him is frozen,
numb. "Stop," Sevigne thinks aloud, tears welling, "Jesus, stop,"
and LaStarza's wolfish eyes narrow, sharpen, *Thinks I mean him.*
The ropes like an electric fence touch Sevigne's back, sending a
jolt through him, and he ducks low and lands two, three good
hooks to the steel hull of LaStarza's gut, useless, though the last
one draws a grunt. "Bravo, more hooks boy! You're tiring him out.
Like Clay with Foreman." Sure. Right. LaStarza lands a low hook
to his temple and Sevigne, dazed, hooks high, misses but twists
off the ropes firing short rapid jabs as he backs away. "Now stand
your ground, boy!" Damn it. Fuck it. Like to see you in here. See
you in here now. *You and me.*

The round is over faster than any he can recall and he's slumped
on the stool in the corner, Hogeboom swabbing his face with a
towel and massaging his shoulders with clammy palms. "You're
holding your own, lad. I've never seen you fight so hard. Stay
careful and you'll last the full three."

The referee is leaning over the ropes having words with Torrins,
who has the dazed, wildly aggrieved air of a battered fighter being
forced to stop against his will. "What the hell's your problem
here, mister? I've always accorded respect to you people. I've got
no animus there. This land was yours a hell of a long time before
we ever . . ." For a moment Sevigne, watching with growing
horror, forgets about LaStarza. Then the bell goes and his bowels
refill with ice water, his knees are soggy as he stands and Hogeboom pats him on the rump, gently urging him out.

The second round is the first round over — Sevigne fighting gamely but being pushed around the ring by LaStarza, while his old man in the peanut gallery makes asses of them both. Fear for his son hasn't sobered him, the adrenaline is working in him like an extra shot of rye, a double, that one too many there's no going back from. From this. There's no going back from this. A sharp combination from LaStarza: Sevigne, drained and wobbling, takes a standing eight-count but his father's inane babble during the count refuels him and right afterwards he goes for LaStarza, throwing six crisp jabs in a row. Now for the first time he truly feels the animal come alive inside him. Towards the end of the round LaStarza is visibly frustrated, he's not used to going more than one, he's eager to put Sevigne away before the bell and it makes him sloppy so Sevigne lands a left hook, more a slap, to the side of his face, then a good straight right and LaStarza in a rage flails out wildly driving him back towards his corner as the bell chimes: LaStarza freezing with his right hand raised: wincing with the strain of not letting fly.

"Lad, that nose doesn't look too good."

"Don't throw it in on me, sir. Please, sir. I've got to finish this."

"Let's have a look at that eye."

Suddenly Torrins is there beside Hogeboom, his hand groping through the ropes for his son's shoulder. Sevigne will not turn to face him. Strong fingers dig painfully into his flesh.

"BRAVO, BOY! Looks fucking great in there, doesn't he, Leo?"

"Well, Sam," Hogeboom says gently.

"I'm getting *creamed* in there, Dad. Jesus."

"Turn this way, boy, let me see your face. That nose. Looks more like mine now, eh — less like Mart's. You ever meet Mart, Leo? My wife. Turn this way, boy! You take one in the ear or something?"

Sevigne sits stiffly, shoulders heaving, eyeing LaStarza.

"Thinks I'll worry for him," Torrins tells Hogeboom in a seismic whisper. Then with sudden force: "THINKS I'VE NEVER SEEN A GODDAMN BLOODY NOSE ERE TODAY! WELL AS A MATTER OF EMPIRICAL FACT, BOY —"

"Better have a seat, Sam, the bell's coming."

Torrins turning away, slumped and muttering. "Tolling's the word, Leo." Sevigne sees he's missed two of the back beltloops with his belt. "Amen."

In the last round when LaStarza finally corners him to open up with his full arsenal and Torrins, as if being hit himself, starts braying in a pained shuddery voice, Sevigne feels again that surge of nightmare disbelief that while the two of them are ringed by adults — the custodians of order, the good cops of childhood — and both are being beaten to a pulp, just boys, *nobody is going to do a thing to stop it.* So it seems to him now. Adults and their polite, safe civilization, it's all a lie, a promise he has clung to despite the evidence — in the end they will stand quietly watching, eyes rapt, as the lions lope from the forum pens. The world is carnivorous and there's no court of appeal. Exhausted, Sevigne keeps throwing weak hooks, just enough to keep the ref from calling the fight, while he absorbs LaStarza's slowing punches and his father's endless blow-by-blow. Then when he knows it can't go on a second longer, Hogeboom will towel the fight or the ref will step in, his father's voice surges louder, closer, my God he's approaching the ring, bellowing "That's it, I've had it, if you're looking for a fight you stubbly son of a bitch I'll give you one!" and Sevigne comes out of his tuck and hooks hard swinging free of LaStarza and planting himself in open ground. LaStarza lurches towards him, eyes coldly furious, while behind him like a coach or some bloated shadow, gripping the ropes with huge veined fists, looms Torrins. As Sevigne and LaStarza begin trading blows, four meet officials converge behind Torrins. LaStarza reaches inside with a right to the heart then a hook to the liver that doubles Sevigne over wheezing yet something pulls him back up punching feebly but *punching* and over LaStarza's shoulder his father being gently pulled, then tugged, then dragged off the ropes — "Leave me the fuck alone you sons of bitches you want to try me out try me one on one" — and every word is a blow to the chest far harder than LaStarza can land. The bell knifes through a haze of red beating sounds the smells of sweat and soaked leather the iron taste of blood, eyes scalded with sweat and blood, his father lost in the blur only his voice roaring on above the crowd which anyway is silent, deathly still, and over the referee's sharp warnings *Break it up now boys enough enough!* Sevigne and LaStarza toe to toe in the heart of the ring still swinging wildly.

In the change room cursing through swollen lips he pitched his bloody handwraps and shoes and mouthpiece into the trash barrel. Later, by the river under the bridge to the States, where he sat gazing up at the underbellies of cars, trucks, and Greyhounds whining over high spans while tears salted his cuts, he thought better of it; but when he went back to pick them out, they were gone.

Steven Heighton's first short-story collection, Flight Paths of the Emperor *(Porcupine's Quill, 1992), was a Trillium Award–finalist, and his second collection,* On earth as it is *(Porcupine's Quill, 1995), was chosen by the* Toronto Star *as one of the best books of the year. Both recently appeared in Britain with Granta Books. He has also published three poetry collections, most recently the Governor General's Award–finalist* The Ecstasy of Skeptics *(Anansi, 1994), and a book of essays,* The Admen Move on Lhasa: Writing and Culture in a Virtual World *(Anansi, 1997). His first novel,* The Shadow Boxer, *from which "Finals" is excerpted, is forthcoming with Knopf Canada and Granta.*

TOO TRUE

For so long there were three of them, Hannah and Vivian and their long-haired mother, Darlene. The ghost of their father hovered like a transparent umbrella. There but not there. He's still hovering years later when, out of the blue, Darlene announces she's getting married. Not to on-again, off-again Tim, but to Reg Sinclair, Shoe Store Man. Hannah shuts her eyes to call up pictures. Behind her closed lids is the shoe store, glitzier than other stores in town. A band of mirror running low along the fake wood walls so that everywhere you walk you can see your feet. Reg Sinclair measuring Hannah's foot with a foot-shaped ruler, sliding its metal knob to cup the place a bunion has since grown. From him, Darlene bought Hannah sandals in summer, school shoes in fall. Once patent-leather shoes that smudged when she touched them, showed the print of a finger. Then they would never have guessed he would marry their mother.

Hannah can picture Darlene at the shoe store, pumiced foot on the foot ruler, red toenails gleaming. She'd have a skirt on, probably, and let it slide high on her tanned thighs, insisting Reg Sinclair measure both feet just to check that all was as it should be. Darlene always liked to measure everything, especially herself. "Most people have one side a little bigger than the other," she'd say, laying the soft cloth measuring tape on Hannah's arm, shoulder to fingertip. "Not me, though. Not you either, Girly. Not Vivvy." The yearly measurements are recorded on the wall in the back room by the hair-washing sink. Darlene's height, the circumference of her head, chest, waist, hips, biceps, wrists, thighs, calves, and ankles. The length of each arm and leg. Year after year the numbers the same. Beside is a column for Vivian, and beside that, Hannah's.

In her rusty vw Bug, a convertible, Hannah drives home for the wedding. As she turns off the Trans-Canada and into town, sickness sweeps hotly through her and then is gone again. The water tower with its missing letters seems small now, but it's true a boy once jumped from it. There is the shoe store, Sorry! We're Closed. And beside it the snack bar, still called the Snack Bar. Kids she can't know lurk outside, leaning against bicycle racks, smoking.

Hannah weaves through the town that is too familiar, the river that took her father always visible. She turns onto her old street, where she first learned to tell left from right no matter which way she was facing. Past the stop sign, which faces the other way. The tree in Darlene's front yard dwarfs the For Sale sign and now blocks most of the picture window. A stupid place to put a tree. Surely Hannah's father planted it, but Darlene probably picked the spot. "Right here," she would have said. She would have trampled the grass with her smooth feet to mark the chosen place. Held her slim arms out at each side, tree-like. "It's gotta go right here, Sweet Boy."

Darlene had made him cry, and he had made her cry too. That was love. For him, Darlene had cried until her eyes were raw, stuck shut, and Hannah had felt the sting in her own eyes. People were soft and bruisable. But what could you do with a heart once it landed in your hands? It seemed unlikely that Darlene might ever sob and break down over Reg Sinclair.

Hannah pulls into the driveway and parks over an oil splotch, years old from her father's Alfa Romeo, and before she has turned off the engine Darlene emerges, screen door banging behind her.

"Girly!" she squeals, reaching in, hugging.

Hannah hasn't unbuckled her seat belt. She keeps her foot on the brake and hugs back, breathing in the scent of Darlene's thick hair and also Darlene's own secret fragrance — lavender, sweat, mandarin oranges.

Inside there are boxes all over.

"Most of it's going to charity," says Darlene. "Reg has pretty much everything we'll need."

Hannah carries her bags down the hallway, and with her toe softly pushes open the door to her room. In here old sorrow hangs heavy in the stale air. The room is pink, the colour of Pepto Bismol, always unsettling. Pink wallpaper. Pink paint. How badly Hannah had wanted blue.

"Pink's cheerier," said Darlene at the time. "Blue would only bring you down. That's why they call it the blues." Darlene soaked her roller in the pool of pink and spread it on. "See?" she said. "Gorgeous!" She dipped her finger in the paint and touched it to Hannah's nose.

On-again, off-again Tim was in charge of the wallpaper. Because the big pink flowers turned this way and that, it was hard to tell which way was up, causing Tim to roll one panel on upside down. No one noticed right away. Not until the end, late in the day, when Vivian came in and pointed at it.

There was a silent moment.

"Oops," said Tim. He bent and picked at a stuck-on corner.

Vivian laughed out loud at Tim, and Darlene glared at her. Hannah stared at the mismatched flowers and at Tim's hand touching them.

"It doesn't matter," said Darlene. But it was plain that it did. Her cheeks flushed their own shade of pink and she slapped Tim's hand away from the seam, a long length that now glowed in a way the rest of the room did not. "You'll never notice it," she said to Hannah. "Not after a while, anyway."

Which was untrue. There was rarely a day she didn't notice it, maybe never a day. She even noticed it in bed, in the dark, when she herself was in a way upside down. She ran her hand along it, feeling its wrongness. It is the first thing she notices now, so many years later. The pink matches the paler pink bedspread, but not the cowboy curtains, which she loves, which billow in the breeze. Now with the door open the breeze also moves the air in the room, stirring up sadness. Some of Hannah's things are packed into give-away boxes and others are where they always were. Tucked into her mirror frame is a square school picture of her grinning self, high pigtails in plastic happy-face baubles, small teeth, big teeth, one tooth missing.

Vivian rides to town in her old blue Dodge, wide like a boat. She drinks expired chocolate milk, not lumpy but sweet and sour, and watches the trees grow thicker as she nears the valley. Town is five minutes from here. A stretch of black pine trees, then the water tower, which always reminds her of the boy who thought he could fly. She rumbles past the dairy and the fluorescent gas station where now you can rent movies. Then onto the road to town, downhill, towards the river, black too. At Darlene's she parks behind Hannah's car and turns the engine off and for a moment the Dodge keeps running, then shudders to a stop. The key is under the pot of chives, along with shiny brown ants and grey-lined beetles. Vivian turns the key in the lock and a heaviness sets in. She can smell all of them in here, and also fruity shampoo from the uncapped bottle on the hair-washing sink. She can hear Hannah and Darlene sleeping. Recognizes their breathing the way she would their voices, a yawn, or a sneeze. In the darkness she runs her hand along the measurement wall and moves in silence to her room.

He is here too; she can feel him. Before he died, he left them, which is something Hannah sometimes forgets but Vivian always remembers. She doesn't blame him. Most likely he left because Darlene was ridiculous. And once he was gone, even though he was only downtown, everything changed. For a long while they ate wieners every night, sometimes with buns, sometimes without. Darlene stopped combing her hair, and Vivian's too, though by then Vivian was old enough to comb her own hair and chose not to. Hannah's hair hung in a long knotty ponytail from which the bauble would have to be cut free.

When Aunt Alice suggested dating, Darlene, true blue, blew out a long sigh and said she never wanted another man.

"I love my husband," she told Alice, and she blinked her puffy eyes slowly.

Alice said she should at least come to a beach party for Uncle Charlie's work. A man named Tim would be there. It wouldn't be like a date. She could bring a jellied salad. She could bring Hannah and Vivian and just see.

Darlene perked up as the days passed. She took Hannah and Vivian to the shoe store and bought them each new shoes, platform wedgies for herself that tied high on her calves, and for Hannah and Vivian, stiff black-patent shoes with buckles, all wrong for the beach.

"These have more class than a flip-flop," said Darlene, and Reg Sinclair, who owned the shoe store, agreed. He said they could wear them to church as well, and Darlene said, "True enough," though they had never been to church in all of Vivian's life.

In the days leading up to the beach party, Darlene bought three new perfumes, one thickly musky, one sweet and berryish, one like squeezed lemons. Fragrant clouds wafted as she walked the halls to break in her new sandals. Hannah walked too, to soften the leather, taking gentle steps to avoid cracking.

"You should break those in, Vivvy," said Darlene, but Vivian's distaste for the shiny shoes was enormous.

On the day of the party they walked to the beach. Darlene felt the extra time in the sun would give them that healthy glow.

"We'll have a bit of an edge on the others," she said.

But during the walk, a blister quickly grew on Vivian's foot and throbbed and throbbed. All around the watery bubble was pink, achy skin. Vivian sank down in the sand, twisting her leg so that her heel touched air only. Darlene struggled on, holding Hannah's hand, not noticing, and when finally she turned she was so far away that Vivian could feel but not see her green eyes narrow.

"Come on, Viva! Vite-vite!" she sing-songed. She let go of Hannah's hand and wobbled a step closer to Vivian.

"I can't," whined Vivian. "It hurts." She watched Hannah kick sand and saw the sun briefly glinting on her patent shoes.

"Just a bit farther, Sweet Pea! You can do it!" Darlene stood with her hands shading her eyes. Her wraparound sunglasses rested on top of her head, holding her hair in place.

Vivian shook her head. She looked at her blister, now throbbing so intensely that even the air around it hurt.

"Vivvy!" called Darlene less musically. "Come on!"

Again Vivian shook her head. It was hard to know if dipping her foot in the river might make it feel worse or better. She spread out on the sand. She could sense Darlene moving quickly towards her.

"Get up," hissed Darlene. "Now." She leaned over Vivian and the freshly trimmed ends of her hair brushed Vivian's cheek. Darlene's eyes darted back and forth, looking together into one of Vivian's, then the other. She tightly grabbed Vivian's arm above the elbow and pulled, but Vivian pulled back and away. "Get up," she said again, and she spelled out "n-o-w" to show she meant it.

"N-o," said Vivian, knowing as she spelled it she'd gone too far.

Darlene's eyes widened, then squinted. She sat in the sand in her blue wrap skirt and grabbed Vivian's ankle in one hand, new hard shoe in the other. Her face tightened as she crammed the shoe on, slapping the base of the heel with her palm. Vivian felt the full blister burst and the slippery water ooze out. Her foot and her heart and the backs of her eyes stung. Darlene's face softened. She lowered Vivian's foot onto the sand and rubbed her calf. Then she put her hand in Vivian's and pulled her up.

"Come on, Viva. The party's starting."

Vivian took in Tim. He was not a strapping man. His hair was dark greasy brown and his skin had a pale yellowy cast. Today he would burn in the sun. His shoulders sloped and black hair grew on them. There was hair on his chest and back too, the blackness a contrast. He had breasts. Small, true, but unmanly. Big nipples pointing. Darlene lapped him up. She sprawled beside him on the sand, one leg crossed over the other, foot swaying in its new wedgie sandal. She laughed so often, so loudly, that hot shame bled into Vivian's face and neck.

Uncle Charlie roasted wieners.

"No," Vivian said boldly when he offered one. "It's all my mother ever cooks."

She ate three buns slicked with mustard. Looked at the jellied salads with their trapped, suspended fruit and shreds of carrot. She ate a devilled egg. Eggs were abortions, she had read that. She picked up another and tongued the red-sprinkled yellow and placed the firm white back on the platter. Inside her shoe was sand and raw skin. Water would wash it away. Water would soften the shoes, like with buffalo sandals. She limped to the shore and walked along it, stepping on soft dead minnows. She let the blistered foot slip in, and after three steps heard Darlene's high false laugh.

"Viva!" Sing-songy. "You'll ruin those shoes!"

A pause. A giggle. What was funny? Cool water swished between Vivian's toes.

"Come out please, Sweet Pea."

Vivian turned and stepped the other way, letting the right foot slip in, because now that heel was raw too.

"*Vivian.*"

There.

With each step, her shoe made a splurching noise. Darlene's

wedgie sandals beside them now, water splashing up around them, the canvas wet. Polished toenails peering out.

"*Get those shoes out of the water.*"

Top teeth and bottom teeth clenched together, all lined up.

"*You're making a fool of me.*"

Hands around Vivian's wrist like an Indian sunburn, then long fingernails pinching the fat part of her arm. Now unpretty red face close to Vivian's, sweet breath and too many mingled perfumes. Strangers and the man named Tim sat staring. Aunt Alice stared. Uncle Charlie stared. Hannah's cheeks hot blotches.

Hannah ran from the beach in her sandy broken-in shoes. From here she wasn't sure of the way to her father's place, but if she had to she could find him from smell. She was made from him. Soon she would be sitting on his blue plaid chesterfield watching the blobs of the lava lamp that moved the way the blobs inside her did when things went wrong. They were moving now. Swelling and deflating in her stomach with the wieners. He would set a place for her at the marbly red table with chrome legs, laying down the plastic placemat that said HANNA, spelled wrong in flowers, and he would pour lemonade and not ask questions, even if she kept crying, which she wouldn't, not if she was there.

But in his apartment there was nowhere to go. The kitchen was in the living room and the bedroom was in there too. There was a big window but only the small bottom part of it opened, and so the air that came in was like someone blowing on you, nice but not enough. Where could she go? She stood on the sidewalk and watched the cars go by. She was wearing just her orange swimsuit and shiny new shoes, which rubbed on one heel. Her foot and her heart and the backs of her eyes stung. She looked at her legs, now starting to marble with sunburn. She pressed a finger to her thigh and made a white spot that quickly reddened again. The sand had scratched her shoes. She licked a finger and squatted, rubbed at the scratches. The scratches would not rub off and now there were smear marks too. She could see a blurry version of herself in each shoe, pieces of her missing near the toes, where the cut-out diamond shapes were. She had stopped crying. Even her stomach had settled. She would return to the beach because they would be worried. Perhaps they'd already called the police and were hunting for her. A special police dog sniffing her left-behind dress.

But no one had noticed. She slipped her shoes off and wiggled her feet into the sand. Vivian was far out, swimming, washing the fight off. The man named Tim was spreading lotion on Darlene's back, pressing hard like kneading dough. No one had noticed she had gone.

Vivian moves to the living room and lies in the dark on the sofa. She glances at the stacked boxes marked with Darlene's loopy writing. Kitchen. Fragile. Charity. The window to the backyard is open and the orange curtains billow. The orange curtains and the orange shag carpet may be sold with the house, like the trailer. "A little added bonus," Darlene had said on the phone, and Vivian had thought of the swarming centipedes they'd once found in the folds of the trailer's canvas, a different sort of bonus.

Eyes adjusted, she rises from the sofa and moves down the hallway. In Hannah's room she sits on the bed.

"Hey, Banana," she says, waking Hannah.

Next evening they drink wine while packing, and Hannah feels nostalgia well up. She'll take home the faded cowboy curtains and the A-to-Z fridge magnets. Darlene gives them their baby books, a touching moment until she adds, "I can't hang on to all this stuff — Reg just hasn't got the room."

Vivian lifts an eyebrow. "Reg," she says, "must have a very small place."

Which makes Hannah think of Tim and his square-box house outside of town. "How is Tim?" she asks.

Darlene shrugs. "Tim's Tim," she says. "He'll be okay."

But to Hannah this seems unlikely. She pictures Tim's sad face.

The yellowy whites of his puffy eyes.

"He drives a pick-up now," says Darlene, brightening. "He's offered to move my stuff to Reg's." She makes a clucking sound with her tongue. "Sweet man."

Hannah runs her hand over the marbly pink book, which says on the cover, in scripted gold, Our Baby. She was born at 8:50 p.m., and she came out so quickly and easily that the doctor arrived afterwards. She was nine pounds, two ounces, huge and healthy. Her hair was red-gold — there's a curved lock of it taped to the page, and also there's the scab from her booster. "I couldn't just throw it away, Girly," Darlene has said. "That scab's a part of you — a milestone." Throughout the book there are more locks of hair, changing from red to blonde and back again. Darlene clipped the locks regularly, from underneath so no unevenness would show. It was comforting to pull on the hidden short piece. "Pull too hard and you'll pull it right out," Darlene would say, gently slapping Hannah's hand. "Bald spots aren't pretty."

The curves of hair remind Hannah that once a bat flew towards light through a rip in the screen and a cat, dirty white, followed him through the hole. Suddenly trapped, the bat hid behind the bureau, wedged the back half of his tiny body between the floor and the baseboard and screeched. Hannah and Vivian and Darlene, in bare feet and nightgowns, screeched too, bending to look beneath the bureau, alarmed, pale-faced. "Get sheets!" cried Darlene, and Vivian did, pulling a crisp white, a floral blue, a soft worn flannel from the closet. Thinking ahead and grabbing also three clothespins with which to fasten the sheets, cloak-like. A bat's wings could get stuck in your hair, Darlene said, and he'd just flap and screech there until you cut him loose, chopping a big chunk of your hair, and maybe by then he'd have bitten you and you'd get rabies and foam at the mouth and then die.

Wrapped, they bent in unison, kneeling and peering. The bat screamed wildly at them. Writhed but could not break free. The dirty white cat peered too, even stretched forth a paw as if to swat, but didn't. Colour appeared on Darlene's face, a circle of red on each cheek. She covered her hand with a corner of the sheet and stretched it forward, panting as if she were in labour or on a high bridge. When her hand closed around the quivering body of the bat, she gave a quick tug and screamed, but the bat remained stuck and screeched louder as though a limb had been broken or a muscle had been pulled. Touching him unnerved Darlene so much that she stood and ran and so did Vivian, sheets trailing behind them.

Hannah stayed, wrapped and watching, and the cat stayed too.

"Ssshhh," she said. "Ssshhh." She said it over and over for a long time and then she reached forward and slowly pulled, holding her breath, hoping his legs wouldn't be left behind, still wriggling and bleeding at the breaking point.

When finally he came loose, he screeched and writhed so much that Hannah felt her heartbeat in the tips of her fingers, but still she held him wrapped in her hands. She walked him outside to set him free in the darkness, and the cat walked too, wending around and in between her legs in meowing figure eights and almost tripping her. When the cool of night touched her exposed parts — her circle of face, her feet and ankles — she wanted to fly with that bat on brittle wings. Opening her sheeted hands, she wondered what it sounded like inside when you flew. If the wind was like the ocean in a seashell.

Vivian laughs. She refills their glasses. "That was me," she says. "Not you. *You* ran with Mom to the kitchen. You were petrified. It was pathetic! *I* took the bat outside. And as for a cat, I don't remember any cat at all."

"Too true, Banana," says Darlene, clinking her glass to Hannah's. "Viva wore the pants that day."

"And I didn't set it free," says Vivian, grinning. "I squished it with a rock. I can still remember the June-bug crunch it made."

In the night Hannah wakes half-drunk, her pink room spinning. She slips a foot out from under the sheets and presses it onto the cool floor. She can hear the lilting murmur of Darlene's voice in the hall. A man's voice too, and the sound of an engine running in the driveway. She crawls to the end of her bed and peers out the door. Darlene in her red kimono is wrapped in Tim's curly-haired arms. Tim clings and sobs, kissing the top of Darlene's head, kissing her eye and cheek, her forehead, and Darlene holds him up. His sloping shoulders slope more with the weight of his sadness, a sadness Hannah can feel across the top of her chest and in her throat too. Darlene slides her hands up inside Tim's T-shirt, squeezing him hard. She pulls away a little and touches his face, placing a finger at the top of his forehead, where lines now show, running it slowly down his gloomy profile, along the large bumpy nose, over lip and lip and stubbled chin. She turns her finger and lifts his head. "Hey," she whispers. "Chin up, Sweet Boy."

Hannah lies back in bed, suppressing the sweep of sickness that might just be the wine. It was Tim who taught her to grow an avocado tree from the pit, propping the pit up on toothpicks in a glass of water. The plant grew up out of the pit like a weed in a sidewalk crack. Each day the stem curved taller and a new leaf unfolded.

In the front row on Darlene's side, Hannah stands with Vivian, turning to see Darlene approach in her georgette dress. The church aisle is not carpeted and even though the organ is loud, Hannah hears grit crunch beneath Darlene's specially dyed shoes. Dog-eyed Tim in a rumpled suit leans into the aisle and snaps photos with Darlene's Instamatic.

The look in Darlene's eyes is convincing — her lids heavy, hooded. She blinks slowly, peering in a sultry way at Reg and Reg only. Hannah has seen the look before. With her own father, certainly with Tim, and even with Darrin — Derek? Darwin? — who appeared one Labour Day weekend and disappeared shortly thereafter.

"Do you, Darlene Miranda Oelpke, take Reginald Joseph Sinclair to be your lawful wedded husband, to have and to hold from this day forward, forever and ever, amen?"

"I do," says Darlene, and then, whispering, leaning closer, "I really do, Sweet Boy."

As Vivian heads out of town, the Dodge emits low rumbles and also a faint burnt-rubber smell. Her father always drove cars that were falling apart. Even though his cars were often dented or missing pieces, he maintained that a car was a thing of beauty. It took you places you might not go without it, and it gave you the freedom to go anywhere you wanted on your own. The Alfa had been rusty. Had had a tied-on muffler and leaked oil, leaving a trail wherever it went. The wipers were broken, and in winter he scooped snow from the side of the road to clean the spotty windshield. He rubbed the shiny wood steering wheel as though he cherished it. The steering wheel of Vivian's Dodge is cracked plastic, covered in fake blue bath-mattish fur. The lit-up numbers of the radio glow green, but no sound comes out. The Alfa had no radio. Just a dark hole where the radio should have been. When Vivian and Hannah complained, he rolled down his window and bellowed made-up arias that both embarrassed and delighted them.

Hannah drives up to the highway. Away from home, back home. She passes the population sign, which faces the other way, and then the no-name road that leads to Tim's. She passes a school bus heading into town, loaded with wild bus kids. Faces pressed against the tiny top windows. Tongues swirling spit on the glass. Just briefly she sees a red-haired boy with a finger in each nostril, his eyes bugged open as though the fingers are pushing them out, and then the bus is gone, visible only in the rearview.

There was that time after he died and the Alfa was brought back to them, oil staining the driveway. Hannah sat in the driver's seat, stretched to reach the pedals. In there it smelled of him, so strong it hurt to breathe. She could see just her cowlick in the rearview. Tiny baby hairs that don't grow, dipping down on her forehead.

Still when she thinks of him her stomach turns over, even though she knew him for only eight years.

Kristen den Hartog's story "Too True" is part of a novel-in-progress called Flutterby. *Related stories have appeared in* Prairie Fire, Other Voices, *and the* Journey Prize Anthology 9. *Other work has also been published in* B & A New Fiction, Event, *and the* Antigonish Review. *She lives in Toronto.*

Connie Gault

LEONARD
DOBIE'S
CONDITION

Miss Lind

It was always winter at the sanitorium, that's how I remember it, always snow on the hills, the roads like zippers, snow bunched like heavy cloth either side along their length. From the second-floor balcony Leonard and I could see the few cars that made the journey into the valley with chains on their tires, a delivery van or two, sometimes horses and drays. Sleighs. Out on the lake, the ice fishermen huddled on stools by their huts while Leonard shivered under heavy blankets, reading books with gloves on, turning the pages with his nose so he wouldn't rip them with his clumsy woollen fingers. That was on good days.

On bad days he trembled with fever, didn't know his name. We kept him in his private room. I bathed him to bring his temperature down. Listened to his delirium. He was on the roof, he was always on the roof of his house, not knowing how or why he came to be there, clinging to the shingles, afraid to fall.

I'm here, I said to him. You're not alone, I'm here beside you.

I can't hold on, he said. I can't keep holding on.

His face glowed a frantic pink, his bedclothes were drenched with sweat. I held both his hands. I said, You can't fall. I'm here, I'm holding onto you.

But he wrestled his hands from my grip, tossed his head back and forth. No, no, I'm slipping, I'm falling, he said.

Finally I discovered the way to ease the fear. I curled his fingers around the metal rails at the head of his bed. He gripped them, pulled himself up against them, and crouched there, panting. While he crouched there, I said: Leonard, you are in your bed, you have a fever. You're in your white bed and I'm here beside you. Do you see me? I'm in my white uniform, white as snow; think of snow, Leonard, the valley filled with cold white snow. We're out there in the valley, where the air is cold and the snow stretches as far as you can see, white snow as far as you can see, and the sky is black, blue-black, winter black, and the stars are shining cold and far away. You're safe with me, in your bed in the snow.

I talked and talked until the roof disappeared from under him and he found himself in bed again.

And this is what I said to him when he was himself again: The cure is an idea. Not a medicine in a bottle, not a surgery, not a procedure, but a way of life.

I had my ideals; I wouldn't deny my idealism, my sense of mission, my need to do some practical good. My pleasure in the idea of a way of life that would become a cure. I would walk to work in the morning, marching in the middle of my friends; we would march through the early morning, through the long infirmary corridors. Our uniform skirts flapped. Our white oxfords thumped the polished fir floors. We were young women with side parts and permanent waves under our caps, healthy, wholesome young women in head-to-toe white. We sounded efficient.

It was 1936. I was the youngest nurse to work in the infirmary and I thought I was the best nurse. I thought: The Cure is an idea and the idea is in me. I was such a *Saturday Evening Post* girl.

I can see myself marching between my friends, rounding the corner, marching on, up the stairs. Miss Lind.

Come on, Lind, you know he likes you, one of my friends said.

Everyone likes me, I said.

Aren't you chipper? my other friend said. He's awfully cute.

He's married, I said. I was carrying a letter for Leonard. The day before, the mail had arrived too late to be delivered to the patients. I held out the envelope to show them as we strode on.

Is it from her?

Is it?

Shh, I said. We were on our ward. We bustled into the nursing station. The night staff looked at us and sighed.

But nobody died? Not this morning? Not this morning, when if I could have told the truth I would have admitted my heart had sunk when I'd first seen the letter addressed to him, and then had bounced back up like a balloon to make me lighter because it was from his sister. His wife hadn't written for months.

No, nobody died. The night staff were tired women; that was fine. You get used to being tired.

Go home to bed, girls, one of my friends said.

You get used to being tired. You don't get used to patients dying. Twenty percent of the patients died, and most of them died in the infirmary. And you never got used to it, any of us would have said that.

And you never got used to the smell of the place. We took it home with us at the end of every shift, that cool and clammy, clinging odour. Eau de infection. Evening in the San. It wasn't something we would have told an outsider, how we smelled it again when we stripped off our uniforms and our bras and garter belts and stockings and pitched them onto chairs in the corners of our small rooms in residence.

We got used to being tired, and we got used to the coughing. Wheezing and hacking and barking. The sound of strangling. That chorus. A hundred different variations on a theme. You had to get used to that.

Better save some energy, one of the orderlies said. It's going to
be a hot one.

If it was a hot one outside, it would be a hot one inside. The
patients slept with their windows open if the weather didn't allow
them to sleep outside on the balconies. As soon as they'd had their
breakfasts and their washes, they were wheeled out onto the
balconies, even if it was thirty below, even if it was a hundred
above. It had been a hot one for days, for weeks, for months. It
was going to be hot everywhere. Who needed X-rays? Didn't
Leonard Dobie? Oh good. X-ray was in the basement.

I took Leonard his letter on his breakfast tray. He was in a
private room. He had large cavities in both his lungs; his sputum
was consistently positive. After two years at the san, two years of
pneumo and diathermy twice to cut the adhesions so at least one
of his lungs could collapse, he was slated for thoracoplasty, but
first he needed six months of complete bed rest. That day he was
beginning month five.

Leonard looked up when I walked into his room, and he turned
his radio off. He had been lying on his bed with his hands folded
on his stomach, his head at a tilt on two pillows, and his eyes
half-closed, his eyes on the radio world, like all of them, that
listening look on his face. Then I walked in and he turned the
radio off.

Letter for you.

He was not handsome in a pretty way, or in that bullish way of
some men. He was handsome in his expressions. His face crinkled
in ways you liked to see. His eyes said things. What? There you
are. His eyes said: There you are, Miss Lind. The older nurses
warned about those kinds of looks that created heavy air between
a nurse and patient. An odd thing about these patients: many of
them possessed an unusual intensity. Looks like passion, the older
nurses said, but it's fever.

But his eyes also said: How capable you are, Miss Lind. I had
been his nurse for four months, ever since he'd been moved to
the infirmary.

I always kept in mind the fact that he had a wife.

When I came back after breakfast to wash him, he wasn't listening to the radio, he was staring at the ceiling, but he smiled at me. Not as quickly as usual, I thought.

That was a letter from my sister.

I soaped his legs, rinsed them, and patted them dry.

Franny said they had the rain.

That's good.

We'd had a thunderstorm in the valley, too, that week. The thunder had echoed through the hills. Though they weren't really hills, Leonard said; they weren't elevated above the prairie. The prairie just ran along in its usual flatness, then fell off into the valley, and there the Qu'Appelle River and the lakes had formed. Creeping glaciers had gouged the land on their retreat north.

I lathered the cloth and ran it up one arm and then the other.

What does Franny do?

She works at the store, for our father. Lives with him above the store. She's twenty-seven, still single.

Older than me, I thought, and I pictured a woman older than myself, with thick arms, standing in the partial shade of a caragana hedge, holding a tabby cat.

Does she like cats?

Yes, I think so.

I washed his chest and his armpits.

Nice to get news from home.

Yes. It was mostly about the storm.

They need the rain.

Yes, but they got as much dust as rain. Franny had to wash the windows at the front of the store.

I sat him up and moved around to his back, his poor back that the doctors wanted to cut into, removing ribs. You had to accept whatever the doctors ordered, but most of the nurses weren't convinced about that surgery. It would leave a hollow and a scar. It rested the lung, but it wasn't a cure.

I suppose there were sounds, while I washed his back. A bird nattering outside the window and a truck driving by making that friendly crackle of wheels on gravel. Our breathing is the only sound I truly remember, our breathing together. Sooner or later I must have tossed the washcloth into the basin and told him to take over.

I must have left his room, distributed hot water to patients who could do their own baths. Likely I was back in two minutes.

Roll over, I would have said. He stretched out on his stomach, his arms above his head, his fingers cradling the white-painted metal rails at the head of his bed. I poured the alcohol into my palm to take off the chill, then rubbed him down.

It was always spring when I thought about his wife. Spring on the farm where his wife was the farmer while he was away. In his heavy old overcoat, she crossed the yard to the barn, to the chicken house, to the shed, to do the chores. He didn't tell me about her wearing his overcoat; it's what I would have done.

Susannah was his wife's name but everyone called her Suzy.

In town, where his sister lived, it was always summer; the dandelions rimmed the sidewalks, their yellow heads the only surfaces not coated with dust. In her letter Franny said there was not enough rain in the storm to do any good. It was noise and flying dirt with a few spatters of wetness to stick dirty dots to the windowpanes, a mockery of raindrops to be scrubbed off the next day. She had washed down the windows at the front because there was such a film on them when she came downstairs to open the store, she couldn't see outside. The glass was the colour of mud.

Standing on a stepladder, with her bucket on a chair beside her, she went over the panes with a sponge and warm water first. No use wasting soap, the water — I could see — was already a thick brown soup. When she switched to soap and ammonia, the cleaning was almost pleasure, the water warm, suds sliding down the outside of her hand, along her thick arm, past the elbow, and into her rolled-up sleeve. She shoved the sponge to the top of the pane, her left arm up along the glass for balance, and her breasts lifted. She felt the tug all through and closed her eyes, resting on the glass. In her mind she heard gravel shift, footsteps on the street behind her, and if she opened her eyes she would see in the plate glass the reflection of a man walking toward her, his eyes on her. He would not be anyone she knew in town; he would be a stranger.

Right at the moment I wanted Franny to open her eyes and see the stranger, it came to me that it was not Franny I was picturing, it was Suzy, washing her windows at the farm, about to envision Leonard walking up behind her. I saw Suzy with the sun on her, on her fair hair (I was sure she would be fair), and I saw the sun lighting up the unpainted siding of the old farmhouse and the streaked window and I could almost see Leonard's reflection there. I remember I looked down at my hands on Leonard's back. Rosy from the alcohol. Fingers radiating toward his ribs. I remember my pelvis pressed into the mattress at his side.

Time to go out, I said. I held open his pyjama top.

He did his buttons up.

It was nothing, I told my friends at lunch in the cafeteria. Only a letter from his sister.

From his sister.

That's about as exciting as the meat loaf.

After cure hour, I took Leonard down to X-ray. You always had to wait in the basement corridor for a while. That day the air was only a little cooler in the basement; mostly it felt muggy, enervating. I rested my elbow on Leonard's stretcher and my head on my hand.

What had we been talking about? Nothing. The heat, the humidity after the storm, then immediately it was dry again. All of May and June, hot and dry, and the crops withering — and I wanted him to say: But remember how it was in the winter. Because it was winter when he came to the infirmary; I hadn't known him all the time he'd spent in the men's pavilion. It was the first of March he came, and everyone was complaining about the weather. The harshest winter on record. And we had a game, Leonard and I, that we liked the winter. We loved the winter.

Every day we played our game. God, what a beautiful morning
—when he woke up with frost on his eyebrows. Another blizzard?
More snow! Hurrah! Nothing's getting through, no mail, no
meat? Wonderful, we live in a wonderland. More snow, give us
more snow. We annoyed everyone. We laughed and laughed. So
I wanted him to talk like that again.

There we were in the basement corridor, where there was nothing to look at and the sounds around us were only the usual
wheels and doors and footsteps and low voices in the distance.
I didn't see how it could be wrong to be close to him if it was
only talking.

My wife had a baby, Leonard said. That's why Franny wrote.

His wife had a baby, my mind repeated. Was that what he said?

The night of the storm. Alone on the farm.

I am sitting here, I thought, on a chair in the basement corridor.
I can hear Jack Montgomery in X-ray teasing Bobby McCaig.

There's a joke going around town, he said. That she found it on
the doorstep.

She had the child alone, the letter said. Called no one from town
to help her. As if we didn't all know she was pregnant, Franny
wrote. As if the event could be secret. Franny didn't say whether
Suzy had a boy or a girl. She must have thought it wouldn't matter
to Leonard.

After a minute, he said, I hope it's a boy. We have two little
girls, you know. It would be nice for Suzy to have a son.

On Friday nights all the staff went to the show. That night it
was Gary Cooper in *A Farewell to Arms*. There weren't many Gary
Cooper stand-ins at the san. All of the doctors on staff were
married. The only eligible men on the grounds were the orderlies,
and one of them said the title of the movie was a quote from the
Venus de Milo. That was about the standard they set.

After the show a few of the nurses went out walking with the
available orderlies. Most of us strolled back to the residence in
threes and fours; we had a curfew anyway. We made cinnamon
toast in the kitchen; we soaked the bread with butter, then spread

the brown sugar half an inch thick. We had a pot of tea steeping
in a big brown Betty. It was only the younger nurses remaining;
the older ones who lived in residence couldn't stay up so late any
more when they were on days. You girls burn the candle at both
ends, they said. Someday you'll be old like us.

Someone began in a sing-song voice to say: Leonard and Lind,
Leonard and Lind. It was one of the girls who worked in Children's.
Several of them joined in the silliness, lying back with their feet
up, chanting like school kids. Some of them were prone to this
sort of thing at the end of the day. Leonard and Lind, Leonard
and Lind. It was all desultory. Their grins were half-hearted.

I picked up the teapot and threw it against the wall. It was a
stupid thing to do and it wasn't a help, though the teapot smashed
spectacularly and tea spewed out and crockery flew in our faces.
It was more fun for the others. They hadn't had such a commotion
since the last time a bat got into the building. I went to my room.

The next morning I left for the infirmary early and crossed the
grass from the residence alone. The mail had been late again and
I'd picked it up on my way after breakfast. A parcel for one of
the teenagers on the south balcony, a couple of letters, including
a letter from Leonard's wife. In a slender, hard-slanting-to-the-
right script, in the left-hand corner: S. Dobie, and her general
delivery address.

I won't remark on the letter, I thought when I took in his tray.
And when I came back, he had put it away. Once or twice during
the day, which was an ordinary day of meals and bathing and cure
hours and nothing out of the ordinary happened, he seemed
about to speak to me, then didn't. Or was it my imagination? On
the balconies you could hear the summer people out on the lake
having their weekend fun; the sound carried over the water.
Maybe it was only in listening to their distant shouts of laughter,
once in a while, that I'd thought I felt him getting ready to speak.

The next morning, walking over to the infirmary, I decided I
would ask Leonard about his wife. He'd told me about the baby,
after all.

They were mowing the grass early, before the heat of the day; the air was full of the smell of cut grass and weeds, and I could smell sage, too, coming down from the hills. There I was, with a beautiful lake glimmering at the bottom of the grounds and the hills on three sides around me, rising up to meet the prairie horizon, their outlines softly smudged with grey-green sage and shrubs. You could see the valley had been hacked out of the open plain, but then nature and time had healed the wound. Someone smart had built the sanitorium so it would be pocketed in the enclosure.

I stepped on pineappleweed that grew at the edge of the gravel road. Here it hadn't fallen under the mower. The dwarf plants stood up around my oxfords. They were pretty things. I hadn't really ever noticed them before. Bright green ferny leaves and little chartreuse heads. I picked a sprig and rubbed it between my fingers. It did have a pineapple smell, a clean sweet chamomile smell. I carried it to Leonard's room.

His bed was empty. Stripped of bedding. I opened his locker. Nothing of his was in the locker. Stupidly, I went to his balcony and of course he wasn't there; no one was there. Only me and the lake and the hills. Thunder began rolling about; with all the heat, the air was often unstable. A green light quivered over the lake. I couldn't go on standing there.

I went to the nursing station to check my charts. But I wasn't ready to face anyone and when I heard some of the others coming, I stepped into the washroom just off the station. I stayed there, leaning with my back against the door, and looked at myself in the mirror.

I heard somebody say, Where's Lind? Does she know Leonard went home?

Oh I think so, another of the girls said. I went to find her because I saw her go into his room, but she'd left.

She didn't walk off the ward?

Poor Lind.

I was his nurse; I was the youngest nurse in the infirmary, and at night I came to him in my white uniform like a ghost in his

dark room and took him out into the snow-filled valley. I took
the head of his bed by the metal railing and I glided with him
through the halls as if his bed were as light and pushable as the
lightest of light stretchers and he himself weighed no more than
a dream. Through the grey halls where the smell of sickness
shadowed every breath, I skated him and his bed; we left everyone
else behind, the quiet wards, the not so quiet, the private rooms
where the most ill lay, and when at last we came to a window, we
passed through the glass.

This is what I said to him as we rolled on the icy crust of the
snow down one side of the valley and up the other to see what
was on the other side (flat land blue-glazed then the black sky):
The cure is an idea. Not a medicine in a bottle, not a surgery, not
a procedure. The cure is an idea.

He breathed the scent of snow, his fever cooled. Some nights
we had a little fun with stars. Neither of us was any good at
naming them, which was the object of the game. But that didn't
matter. It didn't matter one bit what we named them. It was only
a game, only a ruse to prolong my belief.

I often think of Leonard. And of his wife, too. I think of him
returning home that day. Oh he would have been tired. But Suzy
would have been waiting for him; he would have telephoned to
say he was coming. I can see her standing on the doorstep, where
her neighbours said she must have found the baby, watching the
road for his arrival, the sun shining down on her. Fair hair like a
halo. Eyes the colour of wild blue flax. Beautiful, she'd be. Standing on the doorstep with that baby in her arms.

Miss Love

First you lay out the newspaper, then unpack the dressing kit.
Check to see it contains everything you need. I remember more
of it than you'd think. And I remember Mr. Dobie. He was my
last patient, the last person I looked after before I quit. A memorable day. I quit nursing and Neil Armstrong took a big leap for

mankind too. Seriously, I am certain I did the world a favour by ridding the halls of hospitals of my incompetent presence. But it wasn't an easy decision. And it had to be made that day. Mrs. Thompson, my own particular nemesis, had decreed it. I'd made a mistake in someone's medication. I'd forgotten to give it, and Mrs. Thompson had reported me. I had until the next day to write a big essay on "The Importance of the Timely Administration of Drugs," or quit.

Mr. Dobie slept while I unpacked the kit and set the stuff on his bedside table. I wasn't being quiet either, and still he was sleeping. I checked my student's version of his chart, the recipe card with the information my instructors considered relevant. Mr. Leonard Dobie. Fifty-nine. Bowel obstruction. Emergency cecostomy. Former TB patient. What does that say to you, Miss Love? Nothing? I'm stupid? Breathing, Miss Love. Breathing.

Lucky for me he was in a semi-private room and his roommate had gone to the solarium to watch the coverage of the *Apollo 11* on TV. I didn't need any extra witnesses to my state of mind. I drew the curtains partially around the bed in case the other man returned, hoping the tinny screech of the grommets against the pole would wake Mr. Dobie. Then I stood looking at him in the pale green light.

I wanted to cry. If he kept on sleeping, I was afraid I would cry. What a sight for the poor man. To open his eyes and see my face dangling above him, pale, leaking tears and mascara out of frightened eyes. With that wide white cap (bristling with bobby pins but never dead centre as it should be) looking as if it would spring off my head. One straight strand of my limp brown hair had fallen out of my bun; I felt it on my neck; its split ends lay like a whisk broom inside my collar.

I was wasting time. Efficient use of time is efficient patient care, Miss Love. I vacillated. Should I wake him? Or go to the next patient on my list? Or walk out of the room and keep on walking, down the hall to the elevator, to the main floor, and out the front door?

Was I sleeping? he asked.

Mr. Dobie, I said. I'm Miss Love.

Luff?

Love.

My eyes started to sting. I picked up the pot of aluminum paste and pretended I couldn't screw the top off. With no resistance at all, the lid turned and came off in my hand. I placed it bottom up on the newspaper I'd spread on his bedside table. I took up the spatula and stirred the thick aluminum paste. I stirred and stirred, then lifted the spatula. Mr. Dobie watched with me as the silver substance massed then slid off into the pot. Not silver really, that colour, something between silver and lead. Pewter. The liquid and the solid never mixed completely; no matter how much you stirred, the solid swirled heavily in partial suspension.

I set the pot down and began to peel the gauze off his cecostomy. I opened a bottle of solvent and started to unstick the bag from his abdomen. The smell was — the smell was. Enough to shock out, for a moment, all other sensory perception. Mr. Dobie turned his head to look out the window at the brick wall of an adjoining wing and other windows.

The considerate nurse distracts the patient if he seems embarrassed. In conversation, she may glean information useful to her understanding of his medical history, Miss Love.

I cleared my throat. I said, I heard you had TB.

Yes.

Oh now what? My eyes smarted and filled with tears. I knew my face was red.

I was in the san two and a half years, Mr. Dobie said. Finally checked myself out. Left without doctor's permission. He looked at the ceiling for a few moments, then grinned. Are doctors still gods? he asked.

Pretty much, I said. I blinked and the wetness splashed out onto my cheeks. I'm sorry, I said. My nose was going to start running any second, and my hands were busy with the bag.

Mr. Dobie pulled a Kleenex from the box on his bedside stand

and held it out for my nose. I took a quick look past the green curtain to the door, then leaned my face forward like a snot-nosed kid. I thought, If Mrs. Thompson could see me now.

My wife needed me, Mr. Dobie said. That was back in the Depression. It was hard for her to be alone, hard to run the farm by herself. The weather got to her, the heat, the dust, ruined crops. She wrote to say she was thinking of moving to British Columbia.

You have a light touch, he said. I was painting the paste around the hole, trying not to touch the scalded skin, trying more to stroke the air above his skin.

It wasn't only the weather, of course, he said. We had a new baby. A son.

I lifted the spatula again over the pot. I liked the aluminum paste; it made me think of the word *molten*.

Is that stuff mercury? Mr. Dobie asked.

Aluminum paste, I said. I think it should be called quicksilver, the way it piles up and slithers out of shape again. It seemed I couldn't stop myself from saying things like that. It's like making plans, I said. You think you've got your life planned, then you don't.

That's right, Mr. Dobie said.

I set the spatula down, put the lid on the paste, and squeezed cement for the new bag around the hole. Putting the bag on, I accidentally tugged at the swollen red roll of skin that formed the cecostomy. I dropped the bag. Mr. Dobie drew in his breath and his stomach muscles clenched. I'm sorry, I gasped.

Not at all, he said.

While I was cleaning up, wrapping the old dressing and the putrid full bag in the newspaper, he asked if I was going to watch the moonwalk that evening. I thought about asking you earlier, when we were talking about mercury, he said. It reminded me.

Then you forgot about it, I said. When I hurt you.

Don't worry about that. You know, he said, you'll have to get used to hurting people. You're just bound to do it once in a while.

And then he said, I had a great nurse in the san. He had a fond, faraway look in his eyes and I thought immediately: He loved her. And I raised my eyes and looked with him into the same distance he was looking into while he spoke, and I saw her, I genuinely saw her, as clear as day. She had dark hair and lovely fair skin and those dark blue gorgeous eyes that go with that colouring and her hair went out like a dark cloud under her cap, and she was tall and slender and vital. He was telling me something she used to say to him, something wise about the way a person lives their life. She was a fine young woman, he said. She was just fine.

I went back to residence and lay on my back on my bed. My throat had a big lump in it. I looked around my room. It had been mine almost a year, ten days less than a year, I calculated. I looked up at my window, to the left above the bed; it was the old-fashioned sash kind you had to heave open, and you were not allowed to call down to your boyfriend from it at night, though no one could stop you from looking out into the restless trees. Such a little room: one chair, a desk, a dresser, and a bed. Like a nun's room. And it was supposed to be a calling, nursing. I knew that it should be. I knew there was no use being a nurse if you couldn't be a great nurse.

It must have been about three-thirty. The student nurses came off the wards at three to give them time to do classwork. That day most of the girls were in the lounge, where there was a TV. Lying on my bed, I had a crazy idea that I would go back onto the ward and talk to Mr. Dobie, ask his advice. He had such an endearing smile. His smile said: There is sadness and happiness, there is sickness and health. It was like the wedding vows — not pretending all would be fine.

Neil Armstrong, I said to myself. If somebody said to him last week or last year: Write an essay or quit, what would he have done?

But I'm me, I said. Even in own head, my voice sounded petulant.

It's your life, Mr. Dobie said.

What if I make the wrong decision?

It's still your life, Mr. Dobie said.

And then I saw her again, standing in front of me all starched and efficient. Not a hair out of place. I saw her in her starched uniform, the soul of efficiency, like a fine tall, spiky Scotch thistle in a field of lesser weeds. Starched and perfect, no not one hair out of place. No wispiness to that dark cloud, no wrinkles in that uniform, no runs in those stockings, no scuffs on those shoes. Your hair Miss Love. (Sigh.) And the way you *walk*. You walk down the hall, Miss Love, looking *dozy*. Do you know what I mean by *dozy*, Miss Love? You look like you're in another world, a world far away, Miss Love, a little tiny faraway world of your own. You drift down the hall with your eyes unfocused and an inane *grin* on your face. You *drift* down the halls on this ward, Miss Love. And do you think it inspires confidence — in your co-workers, in the patients — to see you like that?

A regular sparkle on the wards, was she, Mr. Dobie? I said.

I was still wearing my uniform in case my decision was to go and see Miss Tuba, the head of the nursing school. I climbed off the bed, bent to peer into the dresser mirror, and lashed my cap to my hopeless hair. I blew my nose and took a deep breath. And went to see Miss Tuba.

Afterwards, walking to the residence for the last time, wearing that uniform for the last time (and even my cape, I remember, and I loved that cape, how it billowed out navy blue around me making me feel heroic), I considered going up to the ward to say goodbye to Mr. Dobie; he was such a gentleman. But I was finished with all that.

Sometimes still, though, in dreams a door bursts open and a bunch of girls in white fills a hallway, fifteen or twenty of them, they come striding toward me, all their unbanded, virginal white caps in a cluster like gulls lazily lifting their wings, about to take effortless flight.

I can't be one of you, I whisper to torment myself. But I am dry-eyed, hot. I am resolute now. Long ago I had my little cry.

Karen

We call him Leonard. Do you know where you are, Leonard?

No doubt he's in many places at once, only part time in this hospital, more of the time in the past. Especially and recurrently, he's in a snow-filled valley. Or so he tells me. Outside in the freezing winter. A young nurse is pushing his bed over the snow.

All the nurses are young now, to Leonard, and not one of us offers to push his bed through a snow-filled valley. None of us has much time to talk about a snow-filled valley or acknowledge the existence of any place or time outside this hospital right now. We're short-staffed, as usual. To get the job done, we have to behave as if other places and times and other selves have not only ceased to be, but have left no trace and might just as well never have been. Even our present lives outside the hospital are discarded when we walk in through the hospital doors. If you watch us, you'll see: we work as if we're in a dream. We never look past what's in front of our eyes. One body today, another tomorrow. We try not to forget the names.

Leonard is one of the few patients the nurses in ICU can even imagine they've come to know. He's been in and out of here for weeks now. We try to joke with him, keep his spirits up. It's easier for everybody — you can walk while you talk — when you keep the tone light.

We tell him the scores of games. Detroit is his team; the Red Wings are still in the series. Leonard tells us he learned to square dance (Oh the moon shines bright on pretty Red Wing) with a girl who had two silver teeth, front and centre. Not a puck but a baseball bat did that, wielded by her brother, and not in a game.

Then he's slated for his fourth surgery this month, to tackle the bladder problem they can't seem to fix. All the banter we have time for doesn't eliminate his fear. He has a leaky heart valve and he's eighty-eight. We had to defibrillate him and intubate him after the last two surgeries; he's asked us not to do it again. It's not death he's afraid of, it's what we're going to do to him to prevent him dying that has him scared.

She had no sense of rhythm, Leonard says. He's just coming out of the anaesthetic, and has no idea he's back in intensive care and ten or more hours have passed since his last conversation. He's doing okay, according to the numbers, but he's looking grey.

Did you say something, Leonard?

That little girl with the silver teeth, he says. Aluminum paste, he says. It was just the colour of that little girl's teeth.

Later he tells me he can remember the time his mother broke a thermometer; he can see the thermometer fly out of his mother's hand, her wrist still snapping, and when it hit the wall and broke in two, he saw the mercury spatter and bead on the kitchen linoleum and run like live things with an instinct to unite.

I was lucky that time, he says.

You were lucky, Leonard? When were you lucky?

The cecostomy, he says. Lucky it was only . . .

Temporary.

Yes. That was lucky.

It was like one of his mother's stockings on the floor, still rolled in its sealer ring, he says. But moist and red raw. Ugly thing, he says.

Then he starts to get anxious, he starts coughing, sputtering, and his heart's going arrhythmic and I pick up his hand and my thumb leaves a print near his thumb, so I call the house doctor and we get him more morphine, increase the diuretic and bronchodilator and he calms down. But every time he wakes up, he's so apprehensive, he can't breathe, his rhythm changes, so we sedate him again.

By the time I come back to work the next day, nearly every limb and every orifice of his body holds a tube. There are two ivs in his left arm and one in his right, there's the central line into the external jugular vein, and the arterial pressure line in his groin, and the drain out of his abdomen, and the urinary catheter. He's lost the nasogastric tube that went to his stomach via his nose because he's on the respirator and his jaw is taped tight around the endotracheal tube that forces air down into his lungs. In the night they had to shock him and do CPR. Two of his ribs are broken. He is unconscious. He is sweating and swollen and grey. And his son is on his way.

There's someone here to see you, Leonard.

It's me, Dad, the man says.

Leonard's son has flown to Regina, rented a car. He is a man of at least sixty, but ICU makes innocents of everyone. He leans over his father's bed, looking right at Leonard's face, trying not to see all the tubes going in and out of the old man's body, trying not to notice how many machines the tubes are hooked up to, and especially not to hear the beeps he can't decipher anyway.

I've booked time off, Leonard's son tells me. My company owes me weeks of holidays. We're standing one on each side of Leonard's bed.

I've rented a car, he says. Thought I'd drive out to the old farm, take a look around, and out to the san; you know, my father was a patient there a long time, during the thirties. I've never been out there myself. Thought I'd like to see the place. When do you expect him to wake up?

He's in critical condition and heavily sedated, I tell the son. And if he wakes up, he won't be able to talk because of the ventilator tube. I don't mention the pain of breathing with those broken ribs. I ask if he's the only next of kin.

Yes, he says. My oldest sister died last year, and the other lives in New Zealand. My mother died years ago, so there's only me.

I probably won't be here when you come again, I let him know. My shift is up tonight and I'm off for four days. I tell him I've been his father's nurse for weeks now, and I think his father wouldn't want to go on like this. We keep him sedated, I say; whenever we try to bring him out of it, he chokes, his blood pressure falls, his heart goes crazy.

I should have come earlier, he says. Can you wake him one more time?

Do you want us to do that?

We stand there looking at Leonard, listening to the ventilator hissing. It doesn't even look like him, Leonard's son says.

I tell him about one time I roused his dad, one time he was coming out of anaesthetic, and I said: Do you know where you are, Leonard?

Apollo 11, Leonard said.

Apollo 11? Is that where you are, Leonard?

No. Not me, he said. I'm no Neil Armstrong.

Leonard's son and I share a chuckle.

He says, I think we'd better let him go.

I tell him I'll arrange for him to talk to Leonard's doctor. We walk out of the room together. I say I can see he loves his father.

Yes, he says. Just that.

And before I go off shift, I've got the No Code order and a verbal order from the house doctor, so I hit the silence button on the ECG monitor at the desk and I give Leonard the morphine and turn the ventilator down and all the time I talk to him because hearing is the last to go. I hope you heard your son today, Leonard, I say. He liked how you said you were no Neil Armstrong. I'm glad I remembered to tell him. It was like you to say that, with that laugh in the words, but you know while I was standing there with the two of you, I had a picture of you cruising down the ladder of the lunar module.

It's the truth, and when I start to tell him what I imagined, I see him again. In that cumbersome spacesuit, slow-motion stepping onto moonscape, bending down to retrieve a rock sample, behind him the horizon so close and so much blackness beyond that rim, I want to call out to him not to step back. He bends down, down, his hand reaching to that white surface, but now he can see it isn't moondust, it's snow.

Talking to someone while they're dying can make you a little fanciful, but what the hell, it's a comfort. Maybe to the both of you. I sit there beside him watching his heart rhythm slow, his blood pressure fall. Then, as gently as I can, I extubate him, put his teeth in, bring his hands on top of the blanket, and turn the lighting down. And I'm really happy — I am so very happy — that I thought of snow, that I remembered that was where Leonard wanted to be.

Connie Gault is a Regina writer of plays and fiction. Her plays have been produced across Canada and include Sky *(Blizzard Publishing, 1989),* The Soft Eclipse *(Blizzard Publishing, 1990), and* Otherwise Bob *(Scirocco Drama, 1999). She has had two collections of short fiction published, most recently* Inspection of a Small Village *(Coteau Books, 1996) which won the City of Regina Book Award, and her stories have appeared in many anthologies, including* Celebrating Canadian Women *(Fitzhenry & Whiteside, 1989),* Best Canadian Stories *(Oberon, 1996), and* The Writer's Path *(Nelson, 1998).*

THE JIMI HENDRIX EXPERIENCE

It's the summer of 1970 and I've got one lovely ambition. I want to have been born in Seattle, to be black, to be Jimi Hendrix. I want a burst of Afro ablaze in a bank of stage lights, to own a corona of genius. I ache in bed listening to "Purple Haze" over and over again on my record player; the next night it's "All Along the Watchtower." I'm fourteen and I want to be one of the chosen, one of the possessed. To soak a guitar in lighter fluid, burn baby burn, to smash it to bits to the howl of thousands. I want to be a crazy man like Jimi Hendrix.

What I didn't know then is that before my man, Jimi, flamed his guitar at Monterey, he warned the cameraman to be sure to load plenty of film. This I learn much later, after he's dead.

It's not a good time for me; my father moves us to a new city when school finishes in Winnipeg; all I have is Jimi Hendrix, Conrad, and Finty. I don't know what I am doing with these last two, except that with school out for the summer I lack opportunities to widen my circle of acquaintances. Beggars can't be choosers.

Finty I meet outside a convenience store. He introduces me to Conrad. There's not much wrong with Finty; born into a normal family, he'd have had a chance. But Conrad is a different story. Finty proudly informs me that Conrad's been known to set fire to garbage cans and heave them up on garage roofs, to prowl a car lot with a rusty nail and do ten thousand dollars' worth of damage in the wink of an eye. He's a sniffer of model-airplane glue, gasoline. That stuff I don't touch. It's impossible to imagine the great Jimi Hendrix with his head in a plastic bag. Occasionally, I'll pinch a little grass from my big sister Corinne's stash in her panty drawer, have my own private Woodstock while Jimi looks down on me approvingly from the poster on my bedroom wall. I tell myself this is who I am. Finty and Conrad are just temporary way stations on the big journey.

Conrad scares me. His long hair isn't a statement, just a poverty shag. His broken knuckles weep from hitting walls; he's an accident willing itself to happen. The only person who comes close to scaring me as much is my father, a night janitor who works the graveyard shift in a deadly office complex downtown, midnight to eight in the morning. A vampire who sleeps while the sun is up, sinks his teeth into my neck at the supper table, goes off to work with a satisfied, bloody, grey smile on his lips. As far as he's concerned, there's only one lesson I need to learn — don't be dumb when it comes to life. I hear it every night, complete with illustrations.

I'm not dumb. It's my brilliant idea to entertain ourselves annoying people because that's less dangerous than anything Conrad is likely to suggest. The same principle as substituting methadone for heroin.

The three of us go around knocking on people's doors. I tell whoever answers that we've come about the Jimi Hendrix album.

"What?"

"The Jimi Hendrix album you advertised for sale in the classifieds in the newspaper."

"I didn't advertise nothing of any description in any newspaper."

"Isn't this 1102 Maitland Crescent?"

"What does it look like? What does the number say?"

"Well, we must have the right house then. Maybe it was your wife. Did your wife advertise a Jimi Hendrix album?"

"Nobody advertised nothing. There is no wife any more. I live alone."

After my warm-up act, Finty jumps in all pathetic with misery and disappointment like I've coached him. "This isn't too funny, you ask me. Changing your mind at the last minute. I promised my sister I'd buy your album for her birthday. A buck is all I got to buy her a lousy secondhand birthday present, and then you go and do this. We had to transfer twice on the bus just to get here."

"His sister's got polio, mister." I tilt my head like I can't believe what he's doing to the poor girl.

Conrad says to Finty, "I got fifty cents. It's yours. Offer him a buck and a half. He'll take a buck and a half."

"I ain't going to take anything because I don't have no Jimmy Henson record. I don't even own a record player."

"I've got thirty-five cents. That makes a buck eighty-five. He *needs* the album for his sister. Music is all she has in life," I tell the man.

"She can't go out on dates or nothing," Finty says, voice cracking. "It's the wheelchair."

"Look, I'm sorry about your sister, kid. But I'm swearing to you — on a stack of Bibles, I'm swearing to you — I don't have this record."

"Maybe you've forgotten you have it," I say. "Does this ring a bell? Sound familiar?" And I start cranking air guitar, doing "Purple Haze," no way the poor wiener can stop me until I'm done screaming hard enough to make your ears bleed.

One afternoon we're cruising the suburbs, courtesy of three bikes we helped ourselves to from a rack outside a city swimming pool. Conrad's been sniffing. You can feel the heat coming off the asphalt into your face when you lean over the handlebars to pump the pedals. This is steaming the glue and producing dangerous vapours in Conrad's skull. Already he's yelled some nasty, rude remarks at a woman pushing a baby carriage; now he's lighting matches and flicking them at a yappy Pekingese on somebody's lawn, driving the dog out of its tiny mind. The lady of the house is watching him out her front window, and I know that when she lets the drapes fall closed it'll be to call the cops.

Conrad is badly in need of structure, a sense of purpose at this particular moment, so I point to a bungalow across the street, a bungalow where every shrub in the yard has been trimmed to look like something else. For instance, a rooster. I definitely recall a rooster. It's easy to guess what sort of person will live in a house of that description. Prime territory for the Jimi Hendrix experience. Finty and Conrad are off their bikes in a flash; no explanation needed.

There's a sign on the front door, red crayon on cardboard, Entrance Alarmed. Please Enter at Rear. The old man who comes to the door is dressed like a bank manager on his day off. White shirt, striped tie, bright yellow alpaca cardigan. He's a very tall, spruce old guy with a glamour tan, and he's just wet-combed his white hair. You can see the teethmarks of the comb in it.

"We came to inquire about the album," I say.

"Yes, yes. Come in. Come in. I've been expecting you," he says, eyes fixed on something above my head. But when I turn to see what's caught his interest, there's nothing there.

"This way, this way," he urges us, eyes blinking up into a cloudless sky. For a second I wonder if he might be blind, but then he begins herding us through the porch, through the kitchen, into the living room, pushing air away from his knees palms out like he's shooing chickens. Finty and Conrad are giggling and snorting. "Too rich," I hear Conrad say.

The old man points and mutters, "Have a seat. Have a seat," before he evaporates off into the back of the bungalow. Conrad and Finty start horsing around, scuffling over ownership of a recliner, but it's already a done deal who's going to end up with it. Like the big dog with the puppy, Conrad lets Finty nip a bit before he shoots him the stare, red little eyes like glazed maraschino cherries left in the jar too long, and Finty settles for the chesterfield. Big dog flops in the recliner, pops the footrest, grins at me over the toes of his sneakers. "Right on," he says.

I don't like it when Conrad says things like "Right on." He's not entitled. He and Finty aren't on the same wavelength as people like me and Jimi Hendrix. Conrad would just as soon have been asking people for Elvis Presley albums if I hadn't explained that the types whose doorbells we ring are likely to own them.

Finty is into a bowl of peanuts on the end table. He starts flicking them at Conrad. Conrad snaps at them like a dog trying to catch flies, snaps so hard you can hear his teeth click. The ones he misses rattle off the wall, skitter and spin on the hardwood floor.

I'm wondering where the old guy's gone. My ear is cocked in case he might be on the phone to the police. I don't appreciate the unexpected turn this has taken, the welcome mat he spread for us. I'm trying to figure out what's going on here, but there's this strange odour in the house that is worming into my nostrils and interfering with my thoughts. When I caught the first whiff of it, I thought it was the glue on Conrad's breath, but now I'm not so sure. A weird, gloomy smell. Like somebody's popped the door on a long-abandoned, derelict fridge, and dead oxygen and stale chemical coolant are fogging my brain.

I'm thinking all this weird stuff when Finty suddenly freezes on the chesterfield with a peanut between his thumb and middle finger, cocked to fire. His lips give a nervous, rabbity nibble to the air. I scoot a look over my shoulder, and there's the old man blocking the entrance to the living room. With a rifle clutched across his chest.

Conrad's heels do a little dance of joy on the footrest.

The old gentleman pops the rifle over his head like he's fording a stream, takes a couple of long, plunging strides into the room, and crisply snaps the gun back down on a diagonal across his shirt front, announcing, "My son carried a Lee-Enfield like this clear across Holland in the last war. He's no longer with us. I thought you boys would like to see a piece of history." He smiles, and the Lee-Enfield starts moving like it has a mind of its own, the muzzle sliding slowly over to Finty on the chesterfield. One of the old guy's eyes is puckered shut; the other stares down the barrel straight into Finty's chest. "JFK," he says. Then the barrel makes a lazy sweep over to Conrad in the recliner. "Bobby. Bobby Kennedy."

Some nights I turn on the TV at four in the morning when all the stations have signed off the air. I like how the television fizzles in my ears, how my brain drifts over with electric blue and grey snow, how the phantom sparkles of light are blips on a radar screen tracking spaceships from distant planets. Similar things are happening in my head right now, but they feel bad instead of good.

"Get that out of my face," Conrad orders him.

The old man doesn't move. "I could feel John and Bobby giving off copper right through the television screen. Lee Harvey could feel it and Sirhan Sirhan could feel it. I think, as far as North America goes, we were the only three."

Conrad squints suspiciously. "What kind of bullshit are you talking?"

"And you," says the old man, voice rising. "You give off copper, and so does your friend by the peanut bowl. Chemistry is destiny. Too much copper in the human system attracts the lightning bolt. Don't blame me. I'm not responsible."

There's a long silence. Conrad's heels jitter angrily up and down on the footrest.

"Do you understand?" the old man demands. "Am I making myself clear?"

The question is for Conrad, but I'm the one who answers. I feel the old man requires something quick. "Sure. Right. We get it."

He sends me a thoughtful nod as he lays the gun down at his feet. A second later he's rummaging in his pockets, tearing out handfuls of change, spilling it down on the coffee-table top like metal hail, talking fast. "Of course, there are always exceptions to the rule. Me for one, I'm immune to the thunderbolt. I could walk clear through a mob of assassins with a pound of copper in my belly and no harm, no harm. Untouchable." His fingers jerk through the coins, shoving the pennies to one side. Suddenly his neck goes rigid, his tongue slowly pokes between his lips. A narrow, grey, furry trough. He picks up a penny and shows it to each of us in turn. Presses the penny carefully down on the tongue like he's sticking a stamp on an envelope. Squeezes his eyes tightly shut. Draws the penny slowly back into his mouth and swallows. We watch him standing there, swaying back and forth, a pulse beating in his eyelids.

Conrad's had enough of this. "Hey, you!" he shouts. "Hey, you, I'm talking to you!"

The old man's eyes flutter open. It's like watching a baby wake up.

"We don't give a shit how many pennies you can swallow," Conrad says. "We're here about the album. The famous album."

"Right, the album. Of course," says the old man, springing to the footstool, flipping up the lid.

"And another thing," Conrad warns him, winking at me. "Don't try to pass any golden oldies off on us. Troy here is a hippie. He's got standards. You know what a hippie is?"

"Yeah," says Finty, taking heart from Conrad. "You know what a hippie is?"

The old man drags a bulging photograph album out of the footstool, drops it on the coffee table, sinks to his knees on the hardwood beside it. You'd think it was story time at Pooh Corner in the children's room at the library the way he turns the pages for us.

The pictures are black and white, each one a snapshot of a road under construction. All of them taken just as the sun was rising or setting, the camera aimed straight down the highway to where it disappears into a haze of pale light riding the horizon. There are no people in any of the pictures, only occasional pieces of old-fashioned earth-moving equipment parked in the ditches, looking like they were abandoned when everybody fled from the aliens, from the plague, or whatever.

Conrad grunts, "What the hell is this?"

"An example of the law of diminishing returns," the old man answers, dreamily turning the pages. "In a former life I was a highway contractor. Unrecognized for my excellence."

"How come there's nobody in these pictures?" Conrad wants to know. Pictures without people in them don't make any sense to him.

"Oh, but there is," the old man corrects him. "Identify the *person*. I think it's evident who he is, although there has been argument. If you would confirm his identity, it would be very much appreciated."

Conrad and Finty peer down hard at the snapshots. As if there really might be a human being lurking in them. After a minute, Conrad irritably declares, "There's nobody in any picture here."

"He fades in and fades out; sometimes he's there and sometimes he's not. But he's very definitely there now. You'll recognize him," the old man assures us.

By now Conrad suspects the old man is pulling something, a senior citizen variation on the Jimi Hendrix experience. "Oh, yeah, I see him now. Jimi Hendrix peeking around that big machine in the ditch. That's him, isn't it, Finty? The nigger in the woodpile." He jabs Finty in the ribs with his elbow, hard enough to make him squeak.

"Wrong. The person in question is definitely in the middle of the road. Walking towards us. Look again."

This only pisses Conrad off. "Right. I ain't stupid. Don't try to pull this crap on me."

"Please describe him," the old man says calmly.

"Here's a description for you. An empty road. Get a pair of fucking glasses, you old prick."

"So that's your line." The old man's voice has started to tremble; it sounds like Finty's when he talks about his sister in the wheel-chair, only genuine. "Just a road. Just an *empty* road." He stabs his forefinger down on the photograph so hard it crinkles. "You, sir. Describe him," he says, turning to Finty.

"Huh?" Finty looks over at Conrad for help. Conrad's eyes are slits, glassy with the glue oozing out of his brain.

"Knock, knock. Who's there?" The old man's finger taps the photograph urgently, bouncing like a telegraph key. "Who's there? Who's there? Knock, knock."

Conrad juts his jaw at Finty, a warning. "Don't you say nothing."

The old man slaps his knee. "There, you've given it away!" he shouts. "Not thinking, were you? Telling him not to give it away — but that's an admission by the back door, isn't it?"

He snatches the album, shoves it into my hands. Tiny points of chilly sweat break out on his forehead. They make me think of liquefying freon, or whatever gas they pump into refrigerators to keep them cold. The chemical smell is industrial strength. It's coming from him.

"The truth now," he whispers to me. "Tell me what you see."

I feel Conrad staring at me. I hear him say, "Nothing there, Troy. Nothing."

I gaze down at an empty road, scraped raw by grader blades, patches of greasy earth shining like freshly picked scabs. A burr of foggy light bristles on the horizon.

"Just a road," I say.

"But roads don't just happen," says the old man gently.

"No."

"So tell me, who else is in the photograph?"

It's no different from staring into a blank television screen. The snow shifting, forming the faces of famous people locked in the circuitry from old programs. The hiss of static turning into favourite songs, guitar chords whining and dying.

"He's playing head games with us, Troy," Conrad warns. "Fuck him. Fucking lunatic."

The old man leans in very close to me; I feel his alpaca sweater brushing the hairs on my bare arm. "Tell the truth," he murmurs. "Who do you see?"

I hold my breath, and then I say it. "You."

"Yes," says the old man. When he does, I sense Conrad rising to his feet, sense his shadow lurching down on the two of us.

"And my head. What do you see above my head?" the old man coaxes.

"Enough of this shit, Troy," Conrad says.

I look at the picture, the old man's finger guiding me to the pale grey froth on the horizon. He rests it there, the phantom light crowning his nail.

"Light."

"The aura."

"The aura," I repeat numbly after him.

All at once, Conrad boots the album out of my hand, sends it flying across the room, pages flapping. The old man and I dare not lift our heads; we just sit there, looking at the floor, listening to the ragged whistle of Conrad's breathing. It goes on for a long time before he says, "You think I don't know what you're up to, Troy? But you don't fuck with me, man. Just don't try to fuck with me. Just don't."

The old man and I sit with bowed heads, listening to Conrad and Finty pass through the house, their voices getting louder the closer they get to the door. Then it slams, and the old man's head jerks up as if it were attached to it by a wire. Conrad and Finty hoot outside. I listen to their voices fade away, and then I realize the old man is talking to me.

"I knew you were the one to tell the truth. I knew it at the back door when I saw all the generous light . . ." He pauses, touches my head. "Here."

And I'm up and running through the house, colliding with a lamp, moving so fast that the sound of breaking glass seems to have nothing to do with me. Out the screen door, hurdling my stolen bike, clearing the broken spokes, the twisted wheel rims that Finty and Conrad have stomped. I'm running, my scalp prickling with tiny flames, I feel them, the flames creeping down the nape of my neck, licking at my collar, breathing hotly in my ears.

And Jimi, two months from being dead, is out there in front of me, stage lights snared in his hair, a burning bush. And a young road builder is standing alone on a blank, unfinished road, his head blooming with a pale grey fire.

And here I am, running through the late afternoon stillness of an empty suburban street, sucked down it faster than my legs can carry me, this hollow, throaty roar of fire in my head, that tiny point on the horizon drawing me to where the sun is either coming up or going down.

Which?

Guy Vanderhaeghe is the author of three collections of short stories, three novels, and two plays. His short-story collection Man Descending *(Macmillan of Canada, 1982) won the Governor General's Award and the Geoffrey Faber Memorial Prize in Great Britain. His novel* Homesick *(McClelland & Stewart, 1989) was a co-winner of the City of Toronto Book Award. His novel* The Englishman's Boy *(McClelland & Stewart, 1996) was shortlisted for both the 1996 Giller Prize and the 1998 International IMPAC Dublin Literary Award. It was awarded the Governor General's Award, the Saskatchewan Book Award for Fiction, and the Saskatchewan Book of the Year Award.*

Dionne Brand

Tamarindus

Indica

Tamarindus Indica. He sat under this tree every day. A tree perhaps brought here from Africa in the seventeenth century. Probably brought here by his great-great-grandmother. As a seed in the pocket of her coarse dress. Probably held in her mouth as a comfort. Perhaps then germinating in her bowels. How the tree came to stand in his path he really did not know. And if it had been his great-great-grandmother, she would have brought a silk cotton tree, its high wing-like buttresses webbing out in embraces. His great-great-grandmother, however, had not passed down into memory, but he had heard that silk cotton blew all the way here from Africa and that is how he thought of any ancestry before Marie Ursule, who was his great-grandmother.

This tree grew daily in purpose. It was brought; set down in his path. Or perhaps he was fooling himself again; fooling himself that any piece of the world could be arranged with him in mind; fooling himself that he had a specific heading or that he was in the middle of all actions, important.

He sat on the ground under the tree's shade each day. He had counted leaves made of fifteen pairs of leaflets, rarely more, sometimes less; fifteen pairs of leaflets as small as the nail on his baby finger. Smaller. He was noticing minute things. A small piece of blue glass between his bare callused toes, a piece of gazette paper gone black which he used to insert in his shoes. The flower of *Tamarindus Indica* smaller still and pale yellow not enough for a show; all the show was later, in the pods he mashed open that looked like some brown jam but were sour.

He sat each day after his walk in the burning sun, the sun heavy on his back as a sack he carried. The sun was a burden and a relief in the wood he had grown of his life. *Tamarindus Indica*. Finally shading him from the stout relentless sun, which always proved too much for him in the end.

And so the next day his walk would have to start all over again. And he would have to sit there under the feathers of *Tamarindus Indica* and count how many leaflets on this leaf, how many leaves on this branch, his face in a stroke-like sweat and his penance unpaid. He wished the tree did not stand there, as much as returning from his walk he longed for its shade. Because if when he saw it he felt relief then that meant he had not done with what he owed, and if it were not there it meant he would not have the relief to fall under it and recover to do his penance over again.

It was a fitting tree to hear his confession and take his penance, since such a tree must have come in his grandfather's cheek or in his broken toes. More native to India, such a tree would have travelled this way. Yes. Such a tree which had seen to it that it did not wash itself away in water or tears but waited until it was spat out from his grandfather's mouth or passed from between his legs; its seed an indigestible stone, when someone finally collapsed on this shore. This was the tree, *Tamarindus Indica*, from which he had to beg a forgiveness to which he had no right.

Misconduct! he mumbled to himself, sweat and the sun ironing what was left of his black suit to a shine. Misconduct! The man tell me to clean his knife, get his water, clean his clothes, dig the pits. Misconduct! So is not me and he climb the hill on Damieh together? Is not his foot in mud just like mine? Why he tell me to shine his boots, clean his knife? I not tired too? Force march back to Jericho, one whole day and the fever fighting me in the desert and I must get his boot when we both sit down. I must dig shit pits. Who more misconduct? The man have no mind! I poorly with the fever coming and he need his clothes clean.

Misconduct my ass, he mumbles each day to the *Tamarindus Indica* since no one else will hear him. No one wants to listen again to the story and anyway all who knew it have passed away and those who remain think that he is off his head.

It is dry and hot the morning they rout the Turks on Damieh Hill, the unexpected cold at night chills him, his leg wrappings seem meagre and the paper in his boots rank. He has been cold ever since he left home. He hasn't known whether to take his boots off and rub his toes or leave them hurting in his boots. But all turned to unimportance when they received the order and the knowledge that the Turks were trapped between their lines and the assault was to ensue. The Second West India Regiment, posted in Palestine for the past five months doing labour services, advanced up the hill like real soldiers at Damieh.

He had come all the way here to serve the mother country, Great Britain. After all the official entreaties by the governor of the island, whose impassioned letters to the colonial office assured them of men, though of colour, willing to fight for Great Britain. Men who were young and strong and of intelligence no matter their skin. And he was one of them, marching and doing their aimless drills across the parade grounds in case they were needed. And he was not feeble like the Indians all sent back not fit. He was in his physical prime, boarding the ship first to Great Britain then to Palestine. Him. Private Samuel Gordon Sones of the Second West India Regiment–Foot.

When the Second West India Regiment–Foot first disembarked at Liverpool, he had kissed the ground, taking a handful and putting it in his pocket. He felt the wet remains of it hit his thigh as he moved up the hill with his regiment at Damieh.

War! he roars under the *Tamarindus Indica*. War. I went to war for them. Misconduct my ass. But most days he just does his penance without a word because the sun is so hot it doesn't take a word. Breath has to be rationed, and besides it is nobody's business what his penance is for. It is between him and the *Tamarindus Indica* and the furnace of a sun that makes his skin weep.

When he returned in disgrace, he looked at himself in the mirror and said to his own face, "You is a English man? Take that in your arse then." He put on his black English suit with its vest and his white shirt with its stiff starched collar, his black English shoes and white socks; he tightened his tie to his neck and set out to walk the length and breadth of Culebra Bay, beginning at precisely eleven-fifty and ending at one-thirty back at the tree. He chose the time when the sun is most fierce, only this could burn away his shame and loathing.

He showed himself no mercy. His collar ate into his neck and he did not carry a handkerchief to sop his brow. Now the suit is frayed. For the first few years he had bought a new one every year, but thinking after a while that this was vanity and why his sin was not expiated, why each year he felt more and more criminal, he'd worn the same one now for nine years, patching where it needed it for decency and leaving the sun to iron the sweat and dirt into the seams. He had grown thicker, more dense than the young man who had climbed with hands and feet up the hill at Damieh, slower than the young man who had shot into a fleeing Turk and, pausing in shock, was swept up by shouts and the running frightened inhuman screams of the Second West India Regiment, under the terrified command of Captain Michael De Freitas.

It is not that he hadn't noticed little by little or that he did not know his place and yes he would be humble in that place. Yes sir was not a hardship. Yes sir, no sir. That was the result of his birth. But a man could rise. A man could strive. And he had been let into the Second West India Regiment, proving that men of colour were improving their situation and would be repaid for their duty.

It was the public contingents that he was let in and they were just for Blacks and Indians but no matter, his mother had said, a man could rise above all this. His mother had encouraged him to think himself a man above what Black men thought they could be in those days.

His mother, Augusta, was above what a woman could be. She managed his birth and the world and managed to make a son who would rise above himself. Augusta Sones built a parlour up on the roadside, selling fried fish and sweets, doing washing in the back of her shack and so little by little built up her son and put shoes on his feet and sent him to school. Whenever Sones, his father, came to pull teeth with his pliers she took a few shillings from him and tied it in a knot and put it in her bosom, then lifted her dress, bent over her washtub so that Sones would give her some pleasure for herself until the next time he passed through.

In her ninety-sixth year Bola had laughed loud in her delirium when she heard that her grandson, Samuel, was going off to war. Rocking on the verandah, her eyes blind, her body as robust as when young, her face collapsed around her gums, and her hair patchy and balding, she laughed big and rippling as if she had heard something fantastic and absurd.

He had been afraid ever since he was a boy when he came home and she would grab him and go through his pockets like a bullying child looking for candy. And she would slap him if he didn't have any and when he did she would steal it and tell him not to tell. Then she would go back to her rocking, rocking, endless rocking and all alone talking to herself, then every now and then she seemed to catch up precisely with whatever conversation was going on around her. He felt that she could read his mind when he was a boy.

Her chair was in the yard near the clothesline and she would rock there after sweeping the dirt clean, leaving lines from the broom crossing themselves and making arrows and swirls, and he would play around her drawings destroying her lines and brushing her feet with his stick. He did not know what to make of her.

Senseless, his mother said, senseless; she had lost her senses and he was not to interfere with her. And so, like someone who had his senses, he provoked her, happy that there was an adult whom he could mistreat until she reached for him and grabbed him to her and rode the rocking chair on his toes and looked him square in the eyes, her own eyes emerging from their glaucomaed grey and said when he screamed, "Don't cry. When you're wicked you can't cry. Who will hear you?"

He left her alone after that, playing far away and glancing towards her every now and again to see if she was about to attack or if she was still there, sitting in her chair rocking in the middle of nowhere, the dust swept clean around her, her occasional pointing at the sea, her internal conversations lifting her arms in delight, and mumbling, her sometimes singing, "*Pain c'est viande beque, vin c'est sang beque . . .*"

So when he heard her laugh as he was going off to war dressed in his khaki breeches and leggings he spun around forgetting that she was still alive. His face contorting in worry. He felt an urge to pick up a stone and fling it at her, but her old warning that if you hit your mother in life your hands will remain in the air in death and you would not fit into your coffin, that old warning stopped him. "Old Ma, shut up!" he screamed instead.

He was twenty when he went away to England in the year 1917, and twenty-one when he returned in disgrace. Sent back for misconduct. He had spent another two years in the military jail at St. Joseph, suffocating in the hot dome half-buried in the fort's hill. They let him out as if they had forgotten him. He heard a steward wondering aloud at who he was and what he was doing there. He had been so quiet stewing in his own flesh the whole time, the steward had not noticed him. When he was released he lingered outside the jail for many hours not knowing his direction, then walked home to Culebra where his grandmother still sat in her centuries and his mother already dead of consumption.

"Waiting for you, boy. Your mother gone." Bola precise when she was lucid.

"Gone where?" he asked, refusing her meaning.

"Gone where people does go, where else?" she said as if he was stupid. Then she went back to her rocking and he to the small shack and the roadside stand to weep. Late that evening he noticed her stillness in the chair still rocking and went to give her food. Her body was stiff, her face strangely had only now fallen into its age and Samuel Sones for all he cared was alone in the world. If he had not shouldered Bola's own coffin onto a bullock cart and made his lone procession through Culebra Bay, past the flame trees, halting at the tamarind tree in recognition, and taken her coffin out to sea himself, he would have believed his eyes when he returned and found her rocking in the swept dirt.

"Waiting for you," she said again when he arrived home after her funeral. "Your mother gone, *oui*. She not strong, she catch cold easy."

He ignored her ghost; he did not trust her confidences and went about his business and she continued her rocking and her searching for the breath of whales. She lived her life as she'd always lived it, swimming and loving and birthing children, sending some off in the ocean and off in the world and keeping some.

"Englishman," they began to call him in Culebra Bay, out of admiration that he had been abroad and in the Great War, and behind their hands in derision as he had been sent back for misconduct. He explained nothing, and some malevolence visible in him told them not to ask or laugh when he was present. But as if asking them to be cruel he began wearing his English suit everywhere. To market, to garden, to drink, to the river, to stand in the roadside stall reduced to a few dried-out provisions from Augusta's usual plenty. He stood there in his suit offering weevil-eaten flour and ants-aquefied sweets left there since his mother. Once or twice he tried to sell a fish that he caught but he had become so belligerent that no one came to buy. As if inviting their scorn he didn't speak to anyone personably. He was abrupt, formal, and dismissive. A man inviting ridicule and determined not to have any comfort.

This tree, which was hard and brown, whose fronds he remembered for stinging childhood beatings he received from Augusta, he hated and loved because it gave shade, because it forgave him and punished him for being an Englishman.

He had had it in mind to disappear into the English countryside with a milk white woman. To stand like a man who was on the edge of a book page, overlooking a field and a milk white woman. She was in a small book he had borrowed from Captain Michael De Freitas when they were both small boys and De Freitas lived in Abyssinia down the road from Culebra Bay in a big house with his mother and father, and De Freitas shoved a school book through his iron fence for Samuel Sones to notice him. Sones left off rolling a tin can to snatch the book like a jewel. She would have a blue ribbon in her hair and wisps of hair across her face — he had seen her in that reader, a milk white woman going a-milking in the English countryside. Or he had it in mind to find someone called Mary. "Oh, Mary, go and call the cattle home, and call the cattle home across the sands o'Dee." Yes, twice, call the cattle home and call the cattle home.

But he had seen no milk white woman when he finally arrived in Great Britain, and no countryside. He had heard only men barking in another language and all he was aware of were his ears trying to understand. His only sense it seemed was his hearing because he did not want to make a mistake and his other senses were already overwhelmed. His eyes overwhelmed by smallness where he had experienced greatness, his mouth overwhelmed by rations, and his nose overwhelmed by the stench of other men sweating their fear.

The events of it, the actual events and what things looked like, he could not remember. The moment they were loaded again onto the ship at Liverpool headed for Palestine he became senseless. He was just part of a senseless mass of physicalness. He lifted his body like others, he ate like others and he dressed like others and he wanted to do that because if he thought for a moment about himself alone he became weak, his chest and arms would sweat and his mouth turn dry and stink.

Washing linen and cleaning latrines, digging trenches and refilling them, and running to the beck and call of anyone with less colour than them, the Second West India Regiment was sent to Palestine and Sinai for labour services along with other Black soldiers from the other islands. Anyone, with less colour than they, could spit and they would have to clean it up. Their encampment smelled of night soil and disappointment.

One night he wrote home to his mother, "We are treated neither as Christians nor as British citizens but as West Indian 'niggers' without anybody to be interested in us or look after us." The letter arrived but his mother never opened it, nor could she read it if she had, but she kept it nailed to her stall, pointing to it and telling everyone of her son, the soldier, in the Great War.

The others in his battalion wanted to fight. They quarrelled each night about the backbreaking work they were doing yet not allowed to do combat against European soldiers because of their colour. He grew smaller and smaller inside. He wanted to go home. He wanted to get through the days.

When they were called up to fight the Turkish troops on the other side he sank on his bunk sweating and thanked God that it would not depend on his own will to move but the surging upswell of the regiment, the sheer energy of these men wanting to be a credit and to prove the British Empire wrong.

He could never remember what really happened then. They routed the Turks on Damieh Hill and even that he was told. His body was so liquid that events fell through him. The only thing that he remembered was the stunned Turk whom he had shot by mistake and felt wicked after. All he could remember was a body trying to give in and the steep climb and the mud or dust he could not say what. Whatever it was he was burdened in it and his boots were wet and hot and his toes itchy. He did not think of himself as a person any more, and his plans to return with stories of his heroism were taken over by his fear.

After the battle they marched for days towards Jericho and a fever made his remembrances more blurry. His nose was running and his eyes felt like blisters and he wanted to sit down. Sit down in his yard where his mother combed his hair and his crazy grandmother sat rocking in another world. And someone kept pulling him up every time he tried to sit down. Someone kept barking at him and by now his hearing was gone too and his head wrapped in his shirt as they used to do it when he was a child and got an attack of fever and delirium. They would soak him in bay rum to sweat his fever and wrap him in cloth and put him to lie in a warm corner of the room and he would hear rain and he would hear night and he would hear the wind as if they were breathing. He would see the flame tree dappling on the curtain as the sun was falling. And he wanted to cry into his mother's lap but they kept pulling him up and making him walk.

Once he lay down, hearing feet pass him by, stumbling against him, and he turned his face to the ground and licked the dirt of the road and realized he wasn't home but on the road to somewhere where something should be waiting for him and he hurried to his feet and kept going. Feeling thin in his clothes but suddenly invigorated he pushed forward, jostling other men in many stages of pain.

Tamarindus Indica. The tree under which the remainder of the world passed him by. He did not see the arrival of his cousin Cordelia Rojas by small boat from Venezuela. He didn't see her, with her small grip and her hair pulled back severely, walk up the beach to begin her new life, going towards the shop that now took over all of his mother's business. He would not have known her anyway, her grandfather was only a rambling song in his grandmother's mouth.

Four years later, in 1929 when they sank the oil well Magdalena five miles away in Abyssinia and the spout of oil could be seen and felt in Culebra Bay, he did not look up; when the warm black spray rained on Culebra for two days and fear that the uncapped well would explode spread, Sones sucked his teeth in derision. The transformation of cocoa pickers to oilfield workers made no

impression on him, not even the emptying out of Culebra Bay
to Abyssinia in search of money and modern houses. In the
years to follow, the deaths by fire and mishaps in the oilfield
and the growing worker unrest did not concern him. The strike
of 1937 passed him by. When the policeman was killed and the
army marched on Abyssinia and Culebra Bay to quell the rioting
workers he found himself in the middle with a bloodied head
among bloodier ones only because he was walking to his tree.
Even the lashes he received from the soldiers, their bullwhips
whipping left, right, and centre, didn't disturb him. He waded
through them to his tree, his suit dripping blood. "War," he
said. "War."

Small years and then decades passed him. The whole march of
villages to Port-of-Spain and San Fernando looking for work,
when he did not notice that he was now alone. And the importa-
tion of workers from Grenada and the small islands, and the
migrations to the Panama Canal and all who did not return from
there. He sat impassively as boats ran aground on Culebra coral.
In the deluges of water he saw fishermen disappear, he saw storms
and four hurricanes between 1939 and 1952. Through all of it he
made his way to the tree that had also withstood what was
immaterial.

Him. Private Samuel Gordon Sones. Next to his name in the
war registry was "Sent back for misconduct." Not "Unfit." "Unfit." "Unfit" as written against the names of Indians but "Sent
back for misconduct."

De Freitas. De Freitas was a minister in the government now,
a minister of water. And Samuel Sones had thought of killing
him many times in the years since. But in the end of every plot he
made, he ended up with himself to blame. He ended up with that
stinging moment of recognition of his colour and his dreams.
". . . Because who send me to them people' place? Who send me
to be in their business?"

He had trusted De Freitas ever since he had first seen him. A
lonely boy just as he. A lonely boy behind an iron gate, whose

loneliness Sones took for friendship but was really envy. Envy that
Sones could walk about on the road in his bare feet rolling a
discarded can if he wanted and Sones could kick a rag with other
boys and Sones could take a stick and whack puddles of rain water
collected in ditches after rain fell. And though Sones envied De
Freitas's iron gates and his orderly flower garden and his crisp
clothes and shoes even when it was not Sunday, De Freitas loved
and envied the way Sones could turn away from the gate to some
other child calling him and break into a gurgle of a laugh forgetting De Freitas standing there.

But Sones trusted De Freitas, if only because De Freitas had
shown him his book and therefore another life, and given him a
round orange marble to play with. If only because he spent as
many curious hours sitting against the fence peering in at De
Freitas's world of silence as De Freitas spent looking out at
his. There at the fence he grew to know the real value of things.
Those reflections coupled with his mother Augusta's dissertations
guided him. "I didn't lift up my skirt for you to be a old rab. I
didn't suck salt for you to come out like the rest. I e'nt come out
of the gutter for you to put me back here. I e'nt stand up on the
street whole day selling nuts for you to sell nuts too. I e'nt buy
you good clothes for you to jump in canal with them. I e'nt
make you for you to dead on the street on me. I e'nt make you
for no knife fight. I e'nt make you to get kill I e'nt make no
ragamuffin. I e'nt make no criminal. I stand up over scrubbing
board for you to make bad? I stand up over hot stove? I take the
meat from my mouth, I deny myself, I walk barefoot . . ."

In the endless stream of Augusta's tongue, which always began
in "I" as if she was God, Sones saw more and more what he
wanted to be. And what he wanted to be was De Freitas, who had
a father who owned a cocoa estate and leased land to the foreign
oil company and a mother who always smiled, a mother who
spoke harshly only when she called him from the fence away from
Sones, a mother who when Sones observed her, unaware of him
hovering at the edges of the road, played with De Freitas and

laughed with him and gently held him, a mother who could afford tenderness and who was not washing, ironing, selling; a mother under whom he, Sones, could be a boy without anxieties, a boy who did not have to amount to much but who could simply with the effects of his shade glide into manhood as if it were his skin and his island.

When Augusta noticed her son's friendship with the De Freitas boy she encouraged it, sending Samuel with a cloth-covered dish of mangoes or pomme cytheres or pomeracs for the boy. Hoping the De Freitases would throw a little kindness to her son. She made Sones dress up to go talk with De Freitas, she asked him constantly what they spoke about and if the De Freitases had invited him in behind the fence yet. Sones became uncomfortable and didn't always go to meet De Freitas but sometimes shared the mangoes with his other friends running past De Freitas's house only waving at him. He showed De Freitas how to pitch marbles, he digging in three holes on his side of the fence and De Freitas doing the same on his, they sucked mango seeds white and sometimes De Freitas would sneak out a pretty tin of wafers which Sones ate not wanting to eat because it would spoil the prettiness of the tin. They often stooped together against the fence in a friendship sweetened by green plums, sweet candy, salty tamarind balls, joints of sugarcane, pulpy cocoa seeds or velvety chenettes, rocking on their heels enjoying the tastes on their tongues like an unspoken world.

De Freitas went away to big school in Port-of-Spain and Sones saw only glimpses of him when he came home, taller and leaner and more and more reserved, every July. The last time they talked through the fence they were fifteen and there was not much to talk about. Sones knew that De Freitas was expected home given that it was the end of the school year so he lingered along the street in front of De Freitas's house until he saw him and De Freitas yelled, "Aye, boy!" out of habit before realizing that perhaps he had nothing to say. Sones hurried over to the fence smiling and they both stood there awkwardly for some moments.

Then Sones said, "Well, anyway, boy, I gone," and took off in a brief confused sweat.

Sones finished the elementary school in Abyssinia, walking the five or six miles each morning and afternoon. When he was done with that there was nowhere to go except helping the teacher to clean the blackboard and standing in front of the class taking out the talkers and those who moved their fingers from their lips when the one teacher was absent from the classroom. Augusta didn't want him helping at the roadside shop, he, she said, was not made for that. Only on Saturdays she made him stand there counting people's change out loud so that she could show people what a bright son she had, and when the roadside stall was crowded and he was warming to the numbers she would tell him loudly and chuckling, "Rest your head, child, rest your head now. Go and lie down. All your book-studying and you still want to help your poor mother out. All you see what a good child I have?"

When Sones saw De Freitas in his uniform in 1916, he adored him. He wanted a uniform just like it. He read slyly to his mother from the gazette paper that men were being mobilized for the war, hoping that she would let him join up. "But people does dead in war!" Augusta told him and cut the talk short. Sones pined away to go to the war and sat sprawled in front of the roadside stall looking like a "rab" who was going to turn into a no account, until Augusta relented.

He'd seen De Freitas's face when they were flying into the flanks of the Turkish troops. It was as frightened as his. He was certain that his own face he would not recognize, nor would he know what feeling was passing over it. He had tried to convey some sympathy and he was sure that De Freitas acknowledged him, remembered him as the boy who used to pass by and play with him. But the next day and the following on the march to Jericho, De Freitas was as cool as any other officer. De Freitas had received his commission joining up in the merchant and planter contingents, the whites. It was a shock to see Sones and that same look of sympathy as if he was still behind his iron fencing and Sones on the outside, free. He avoided Sones until they arrived at Jericho.

Sones was among his group, their dehydrated bodies struggling for one more foot of ground, he himself, officer or not, was weak with exhaustion. He went over to the group, they tried to stand up straight. Pointing to Sones, he said, "Soldier, fill these!" handing Sones a string of officers' water canteens. "When you're done come back and get the boots."

Any soldier in the regiment would have understood the orders and those beside Sones understood, any soldier would have moved quickly to comply but Sones stood there drooping and dumbfounded. The others became uneasy when Sones did not move and one of them made an effort to rouse him. Sones brought his eyes to De Freitas's, lunged at him, knocked him down with a ragged bruised fist, then fell on De Freitas in exhaustion.

Lovers passed him. *Tamarindus Indica.* Some who liked his fine suit, some who wanted to take it off him, some who only wanted his baby because as dour and disagreeable as he was he used to be handsome. Some thought that he had money when he used to change his suits each year and even after he stayed in the same one they took this as the eccentricity of people with money under their mattresses. Lovers lingered, walking slowly past him at his stall or calculating the time that he made his walks, waiting at the bench under the tree dressed in yellow or pink, in red polka dots or white cambric, and smelling of violet water. These passed him long before he came to resemble something filthy under a tamarind tree. His cuffs frayed and gluey from mopping up every liquid that came out of him. And even after that some thought that maybe they could fix him up like a house or a water tap, brush him down like a horse because they knew that he would be faithful. Some thought that they could fix up his roadside stall and make a go of it. Some even thought that they could get used to his ghost of a grandmother rocking in her chair. But they all failed. He was filled with so much self-loathing every time he remembered the Second West India Regiment, he tried to root out that small place inside him that had led him to it. Root out that small pain that never grew any bigger but that was like a tablet of poison. He had knocked De Freitas down. It wasn't an insult that he could just pass off. Yes, he had knocked him down and had wanted to kill him right there and then. Yet killing him would not have been sufficient because the man insulted him and he understood that the insult would stay with him no matter if he knocked De Freitas down or killed him. And he understood that it was his fault. All of it. He deserved it for pushing himself up and thinking that he was more than he was.

He sat there through another world war and he crowed for the enemy. In August 1940, when the Germans tried to cross the English Channel and the Luftwaffe bombed London nightly, Sones was gleeful. *Tamarindus Indica.* He walked back and forth to this tree through the sweep of nationalist ideas and speeches towards independence from Britain, the lowering of the Union Jack, and the lifting of the blood and the earth. He sat through small children stiffly starched and sweating in the hot sun waving the Union Jack to the motorcade of the vanishing queen. None of that could soothe him. He had already disappointed himself too much, nothing could repair him. He laughed at the speech-making; he knew that in the end it was not grand plans that ruled the world but some petty need of some individual, some small harassment made things go bad.

He could have picked a flame tree, cooler and at least colourful, an orange one or a red one; he could have picked a Poui, again indescribably coloured and soft when the petals fell; he could have picked a mango tree, Rose or Julie, sweet at least, the fruit and the smell would have calmed him, but, no, he had chosen *Tamarindus Indica* with its sour fruit and spindly dry branches, its unnoticeable flower, and its dusty bark. He didn't move from the tree now, because some days he just couldn't make the walk or some days he thought that he had already done it. Some days he in fact did the walk many times.

He grew flabby and thin at the same time, like an old man does.

Fidgety and narcoleptic at the same time. Dropping off to sleep and jumping up remembering his way again. From where he sat he could hear clearly his grandmother laughing in another century. And he wished that he could go back before that laugh. That laugh that had filled him with uncertainty and nervousness and opened a dread in him. And he wished that he could return to the time before that laugh, just before he came home with the news that they were going to the war, because before that he was a young man in his stiff starched khaki pants and shirt; a young man who could have stayed home and married a girl and made many children and yes he remembered . . . well, he recalled . . . He recalled nothing. Nothing but the hope of going to Great Britain, going home to the mother country. He recalled nothing but the plans he had made right away when he touched De Freitas's reading book, when he kept it and thumbed the pages smudgy. And that was his departure, and the laugh of his senseless grandmother.

Dionne Brand has produced acclaimed volumes of poetry, stories, and essays. She won the Governor General's Award and the Trillium Award for her latest volume of poetry, Land to Light On *(McClelland & Stewart, 1997). Her first novel,* In Another Place, Not Here *(Knopf Canada, 1996), was released in the U.S. by Grove/Atlantic Monthly Press and in the U.K. by Women's Press, and was a* New York Times Notable Book of the Year. *Italian rights have also been sold. Her second novel,* At the Full and Change of the Moon, *from which "Tamarindus Indica" is taken, will be released in 1999 in Canada by Knopf, in the U.S. by Grove, and in England by Granta.*

Bonnie Burnard

EVENING AT THE EDGE OF THE WATER

C lose to perfect. An August evening at the edge of the water with the comfort of the cottage behind her in the grassy dunes, the pretense of Jack's mystery novel open beside her on the tartan blanket, and a heavy, low-slung glass of very good Scotch to drink. And all alone.

She had asked for this. They'd packed up the kids and the car after a supper of fresh-picked corn from the stand on the highway, and then she had kissed and hugged them all good-bye, double-checking their seat belts, checking the twins particularly, pulling hard on the straps that secured their car seats in Jack's Lincoln. Jack had already done this himself, and he sat at the wheel frowning, throwing her a look that meant to say: Relax, for God's sake. In thirty-two years of marriage the workings of Jack's still oddly handsome face had not so much changed as intensified and evolved, and her reading of that face was by now as close to precise as you could get.

This weekend, bringing the four kids out to the lake, had been their birthday gift to their daughter Jenny, who was back home in London now after a decadent weekend with her husband,

Matt, at a posh hotel in Toronto, waiting for the safe return of
her exhausted children. She'd called just when they were sitting
down to the corn and she had wanted to say her thank-yous to
them both, had asked to speak to Jack to thank him directly. But
the formal expression of her gratitude was unnecessary. You could
hear it clearly in the way she said "Mom," in the way she said
"Dad." She had not always been so grateful a child. And neither
had her brothers. Although everything was better now.

Jack had warned that their sons would be expecting the same
thing, the same sweet relief of a child-free weekend, and he'd
wondered if it was really that good an idea anyway because the
two of them were, as he liked so much to say, past their prime.

But she'd had it in the back of her mind to hire the Beaudry
girls to help, both of them, and that's what she had done. The girls
were just the right age, maybe eight and eleven, and they had come
over from their own cottage right after breakfast each morning to
get the kids into their bathing suits and take them down to the
water, smearing them with sun protector, surrounding them with
their toys and gear, keeping them more or less occupied until nap
time and then again until supper and marshmallows toasted over
a quick bonfire in the pit and finally an early bedtime. All day
long the screen door had banged shut a dozen times in any given
hour, and the big table had been covered with playing cards
and crayons and storybooks and colouring books and pop bottles
for some complicated, not entirely successful, experiment with
water and food colouring and baking soda. And on the floor, wet
sand, lovely, small sandy footprints that were still waiting for her
up there.

She'd paid the Beaudry girls generously, as they and their
mother had assumed she would. Money was that one thing that
made being a grandparent so much easier than being an energy-
enriched parent. No one would be able to tell her otherwise, not
now that she'd seen both sides of the equation.

She took a small sip of Scotch and convinced herself that Jack
would be all right driving into London with the kids in the car.

Women did this all the time, and anyway they were so deliriously pooped, so played out, she guessed that they'd be asleep by Ravenswood, every blessed one of them. Zonked.

Reassured, she placed the glass of Scotch beside her on the blanket and reached up under the frayed, purple sweatshirt for her breast. The unrestrained, summer-free breast was full and heavy in her empty hand, the skin smooth and warm, already lonely.

Her fingers, practised instruments now, searched deep to find the marble buried in her flesh. "Come to me," she coaxed, "you little black-hearted misery."

She leaned back to lie down on the blanket, to look directly up at the blue sky, which rolled like a player piano with the continuous, drifting rhythm of stretched-out clouds. Lying flat made most of the legitimate flesh of her breasts fall away, back down into her body. Lying flat made the thing bigger, easier to locate in her otherwise normal tissue. This solid core, this hard little bastard bullet, had not yet been touched by any other hand and it had not yet been given its official name.

Her appointment was for Thursday afternoon and she'd told Jack please to come back to pick her up Thursday morning. Not Wednesday night, Thursday morning. She had cut three days and four nights out of their lives, for herself, her own treasured, terrified self. She'd watched Jack ask himself why she wanted this, and what husband wouldn't, but he had not asked her the question.

She knew what was coming. Mammogram, ultrasound, biopsy, which sounded godawful but apparently did not hurt, waiting, an MRI, and still no discomfort there either, only the imperative to lie absolutely still, which she could do, then more waiting, surgery, waiting, radiation, and finally, if it had to happen, chemo.

She knew what she knew because in the past four years both her best friend, Heather, and Jack's sister, Sandra, had been down this road. After three years fighting, Sandra had dropped off the dreary road into the black ditch of death. "Black ditch of death"

— Sandra's own choice phrase from the time when she still felt
an obligation, still had the energy to try to make herself at least
a bit entertaining to the people who loved her.

The surgeon had initially removed a good chunk of her breast
and a year later they'd taken it all off and then they'd taken the
other one and then it was just chemo cocktails and the daily
concoction of hope diluted with Sandra's rendition of courageous
acceptance. And many, many good months, she'd said, some of
the best months. Sandra had been fiercely anxious to play the
role of trooper; she had worked hard to accept whatever came her
way, whatever was offered up as love. "I don't want to go badly,"
she'd told them. "All of you will have to remember, so your job
is to help me not go badly." At the end she said that she had
watched her death changing people. Certainly more than her life
ever had.

Two of Sandra's kids had sought and found a temporary peace,
a way to be wise and kind; two of them had been awkwardly,
sometimes stupidly, brave; one of them had crashed, hard. They
had all learned it too soon, the thing they should have got twenty
or thirty years to learn.

Near the very end, watching his sister, Jack had been unable
to touch her. He could visit her hospital room only briefly and
then come home to lie in bed and cry. That's how Jack had
changed.

Sandra's ashes were out in the deep blue lake, poured there by
her five children. They had crowded one misty morning into
Jack's outboard bowrider, the oldest, Candace, a sleek thirty-year-
old woman in cut-offs, hugging the elegant urn, carrying it across
the sand down to the boat. Birth control available in all but the
earliest of their reproductive years and still five kids for Sandra.
Some days it had looked like she'd done a wise thing, some days
not. Her husband, Richard, who had been fun, just so damned
much fun, had predeceased her by seven years, had gone before,
as the old aunts liked to say, his body fouled with stomach cancer
and then signed over to science.

Because Richard and Sandra's kids did not want to carry on with joint ownership of the cottage, she and Jack had made arrangements to buy them out. But most of them, the ones still in the province, turned up once or twice each summer. Came back to the deep blue lake that held their mother's remains. *Remains.* There was a word.

Heather had got a better shake. Found earlier? Who knew. But found and Heather sliced open and the thing popped right out of there fast and then the healed flesh cooked to a simmer with radiation to kill off everything, good and bad, that thought it might like to reproduce itself.

"No garden," Heather said, "no weeds."

Although from the outside you would have to say that her breast still looked almost exactly like a breast should look. Heather had sat on this beach on this blanket last summer and not very discreetly pulled down the top of her bathing suit to show off what she had left, which was a surprisingly substantial amount. The scar a straight, narrow, bumpy line of tougher tissue, like a rugged back road falling from the edge of the nipple, which was large and rosy pink, down to the dark crevice between her breasts. The crevice had glistened in the afternoon sunlight, damp with sweat.

Jack had been sitting above them in his beach chair reading the *Globe and Mail* and he'd only half heard what was being said, only half glanced over, and then he'd turned away quickly at the sight of the rounded flesh. Heather had not missed this, Heather missed so very little, and when she asked him if he'd turned away repulsed or aroused, and that was simply straight-up Heather, no huge surprise there, he'd answered, "Let's just say not repulsed."

"Right answer!" Heather said. "Prizes," she said. "Another beer for the man." And she'd reached into the beat-up cooler he'd brought down with him from the cottage.

Before she tucked her breast away she'd rubbed it gently with the palm of her open hand, as if she had a kitten living there inside her bathing suit. "Hurts some," she'd said. "Sometimes.

Although I don't find it ugly. Nor apparently does the man who pays it such fine attention."

Later in their bed, with Heather gone home to her own cottage five miles down the lake to cook dinner for her breast-attentive husband, Gus, who played eighteen holes every Sunday morning and then slept the afternoon away, she'd grilled Jack, of course. They had long been in the habit of double-checking each other at the end of the day, testing out fabrications or evasions, which were usually only social, and necessary. He'd frowned and turned to face her. "Whatever year we are in," he said, "whatever era this is supposed to be, I am not going to lie here and talk to you about another woman's breast." Which meant he had been aroused, or ready to be, that the quick glimpse of Heather's private flesh had done what private flesh is meant to do.

"How nice," she'd said, peeling off her nightie. And she did think it was a fine thing that Jack had not lied, that he had not felt forced to lie. Although she wondered if he would have, for her sake if nothing else, because Heather had been her friend for longer than forever.

It was always a question. Jack wouldn't leave her, of course; in their thirty-two years he had never thought of leaving her and he would not be doing it now. She could be sure he'd never wanted out because she had always kept a cautious, wifely watch on his contentment and, more to the point, because he wasn't anything close to that kind of man, he had never been the kind of man who would compromise himself for his own imagined happiness. But how much imperfection, how much ruin, could a lusty man be expected to embrace? A tenderness? A scar? An amputation? Could an extremely robust man be aroused by something that no longer existed? Could anyone? And how did you express yourself without the friendly release, the calm of middle-aged lust, that not even slightly dangerous love?

Mounting Jack, she'd asked, "Would you have lied?"

"I would have lied," he'd said, reaching up to fill his hands, easing her into place. "I promise you."

She sat up straight again on the blanket. Sitting up or standing gave her normal tissue a chance to surround the thing, to bury it, suffocate it, smother it. Kill it.

She had not had a mammogram for two years, which, given what she knew, was just monstrously stupid. But four years earlier she had created for herself a framed, moving picture, a fantasy of three grey-haired women sitting together in a really good restaurant in the city, herself and Sandra and Heather, their grey hair a pact from their thirties, their histories not exactly shared but told and known and remembered, their temperaments complementary, easy in the huddle. In her picture, they had to order a quick lunch because they were busy women who had just recently come into the wondrous thing they called free time and what a thing it was. You could work again, for money, you could take one philosophy class or an entire degree, you could develop a new kind of usefulness and offer yourself up. You could discover what you had to give, decide what you had earned the right to take. Three standard-issue, busy women sitting in a very good restaurant and what were the chances that even two of them . . . ? Let alone three?

She wondered if the mammogram she'd soon be having would hurt more than the usual quick, severe pinch now that she carried within her something that might not want to be flattened. For years she had followed the advice of the young technician, who recommended she take a Tylenol beforehand, had taken two in fact, one for each, but this next session might be an entirely new experience.

She wondered too if squashing it like that, or even touching it, finding it again and again and worrying it with her fingers, might cause some horrid, minuscule bit to break off and float away, to go looking for a new, more peacefully secluded home in her lung or her liver or her bones.

Shit. Oh, buckets of shit.

She stood up off the blanket to climb the long sandy slope to the cottage. Halfway there she remembered Jack's mystery and her empty glass, came back for them scolding herself, impatient with forgetfulness. She walked up through the grassy dunes, in through the screened porch, past the mess left behind by two full days of wildly healthy kids. Only their own bedroom was tidy. Jack was just a naturally tidy man, even more so as he aged.

She stripped standing on the rag mat at the foot of their bed and pulled this season's new black bathing suit, which was still a bit clammy from her afternoon swim with the kids, up over her hips. She bent forward slightly to settle her breasts, to ease them comfortably into the sturdy black cups. She hiked the straps over her shoulders, pulled the sweatshirt back on, ran her fingers through her hair to subdue it, and grabbed a towel from the bathroom. Passing through the kitchen, she stopped to pour herself another Scotch.

Down on the beach again, she bent to set her glass on the smoothed-out centre of the blanket and tossed off the sweatshirt. She walked across the warmed sand toward the water as she always did, with the towel slung around her neck like an athlete's towel, an old habit from her brief time as a competitive swimmer, when she was a very young woman, before she knew Jack even existed. The sound of the waves breaking on the sand, that sound which could not in any way be replicated, not on this earth and certainly not in any uterus, refreshed and calmed her, in equal measure, in absolute equal measure.

Although the kids' castles had not been entirely obliterated by the water's action on the sand, they had been depleted; they would certainly have been a disappointment if the kids had still been here to see them. Their trenches, which they'd dug deep with kitchen spoons following her own sketched-with-driftwood sug-gestion of long wide arcs and complicated twists and turns around the castles and then a dead-ahead channel down to catch the spill from the delicate shoreline waves, had been filled in, washed almost smooth. Their trenches were almost invisible.

The sun was only a foot above the water. Blue-red tonight. Gorgeous.

She dropped her towel on the last dry sand. The Warrens two cottages down were swimming off their raft now, the teenagers anyway, and she assumed that they would see her walking into the water. If she went under, which was not probable, she liked to hope that one of them might take the trouble to pause from his horseplay to notice, to ask aloud, "Where's Mrs. Hart? I just saw her a minute ago and now she's gone. And her towel's still there." And then, very loudly, "Hey!" They were good kids, boys all of them, with an endless summer supply of young male friends, which made their constant presence on the beach some days a bit of a headache. But they'd grow out of it in time, soon enough. Nearly all men did.

Lining up her approach with the sun's reflection, which had laid itself down in a broad, fiery path across the easy rolling surface of the water, water like this always in her mind a large, deceptively relaxed muscle, she wondered why she had never once coveted that colour. The one colour that she loved more than any other, that soaked warm through her skin on even the coldest winter afternoons, right through her triple-glazed kitchen window in the city. She had chosen sweaters trying to catch the colour of a flower just barely remembered from someone's fall garden, chosen shoes to match a stone. Why had she never tried to wear a sunset on the water?

Past her knees now, the clean chill of the lake bolting up through her muscles to her brain, her hands reaching down to cup the cold water, to splash her long arms and her broad shoulders, past her thighs, getting ready to extend her arms and lower her body completely, to swim hard out to the third sandbar. She spoke again to her little black-hearted misery. "You and I are going swimming," she said. "It will feel shockingly cold, and you won't like it. You will discover that I do lots of things you won't like."

She swam only briefly, out to the third sandbar and then across the water away from the Warrens' raft toward the casino and then back and then in again to the shallower depth, where she could get her footing. Standing with the water just below her breasts she took a few minutes to catch her breath and then she bounced up off the smooth ridges of the lake bottom sand and dove under to stand on her hands again. As she had that afternoon, to entertain the kids. It was her trick. She was the grandma who could stand on her hands in the lake, who could hold her legs dead straight above the water, her calves tight together and her toes pointed hard. She was an expert.

She came up out of the handstand and floated for a few peaceful minutes on her back, the lake a soothing, softly lapping ring around her face, the low sun warm on her skin, the sky much clearer now, almost free of cloud. "You little fucker," she said. She had not once in her life said this word, not until that moment in the lake. She had never even thought it. Not a bad word, she thought, now.

She stood in the water and turned to walk in, the lake strong against her thighs. Pushing to shore, she believed that she was content to be alone. She believed that she was glad she had asked Jack to leave her behind, that it had been a reasonable thing to do, a useful thing.

Believing, she looked up to see a small figure sitting on the edge of the tartan blanket, hugging her knees. It was the youngest Beaudry girl, Rachael, yes, Rachael was the youngest. She was waving now. Sitting on the blanket waving. And what did this mean?

She shook her arms and legs hard. A long time ago, before the kids were born, Jack had told her she came out of the water like a dog, like a sleek black Lab. She picked up the towel and brought it to her face, tucked her grey hair behind her ears. The girl hadn't moved. She walked across the sand to the blanket.

"Hello, Rachael," she said.

"I've been watching you," Rachael said. She looked at the glass of Scotch and quickly looked away, as if she had counselled herself not to do that. "You are never supposed to swim alone," she said. "It's not ever okay to swim alone." Her disapproval took the breath away.

"Oh," she said. "Yes. That's right. That was foolish of me." She shivered, rubbed her body hard with the towel, pulled the sweatshirt over her head. She lowered herself to the blanket and picked up her glass. "I won't be able to sit here long in this wet suit," she said, taking a drink.

"My mom said Mr. Hart took the kids home," Rachael said.

"Yes, he did," she said. "Home to their mother."

"How come you didn't go?" Rachael asked, getting up on her haunches to brush sand off the kicked corner of the blanket and smooth it out again.

"I'm going to stay on for a few days," she said. "Sort of like taking my own private holiday."

"My mom's done that," Rachael said. "She just needs to get away from us sometimes. Desperately."

"Desperately?" she asked. She was seriously cold now. She would have to go up. "I think I have to change out of this bathing suit, Rachael," she said, pushing herself to her feet, bending to grab the towel and the still almost-full glass of Scotch.

"Okay," Rachael said. She leapt up quick as lightning and stepped back into the sand to gather the blanket, dragging it off a few yards to give it the best, hardest shake she could.

"Here," she said. She dropped the towel, nestled the glass in its folds. "Let me help you."

They stood the distance of the blanket apart, gripped two corners each. They shook it hard, snapped it clean, turned their faces away from the flying sand. "Good enough," she said and then they folded the blanket hand to hand and hands together and hands together again. "You've helped your mother with a sheet or two in your time," she said.

"Yes," Rachael said, pleased to have this recognized. She hugged the blanket in her arms and turned to lead the way up to the cottage. "I'll come with you," she said. "I can stay for a while."

"All right," she said. "You can keep me company for a few minutes."

Rachael placed the blanket squarely on a Muskoka chair in the screened porch and when they were inside she walked directly to the big table, which still held the plates from supper and the dish of melted butter and, piled high on the cottage platter, all the gnarled cobs of corn, dancing with flies. At the far end of the table a crowded disarray of books and crayons and bottles sat pushed together in a heap. "I'll put everything back where it belongs," Rachael said, already reaching for the crayons, slipping them one by one into their flip-top box. "And then I'll sweep the floor."

"You don't have to do that," she said. "Cleaning up was not part of the deal."

"I know," Rachael said. "But my dad says if you want to get somewhere in your life, you always have to do a bit more than people expect." She stood stock-still, threw her head back, and laughed hard at what she'd just said, the sound she made so deep, so full of stark confidence, that it could only be called a belly laugh.

"Yes," she said, thinking, Oh, Rachael, you laugh so nicely. "I suppose that's true, isn't it?" She excused herself to go into the bedroom.

She kicked off her suit and used the towel to rub the sand from the folds of her body. She stepped into fresh panties and old jeans and pulled on one of Jack's T-shirts, and then she went out the kitchen door to pin the towel and her bathing suit to the clothesline on the back porch. When she came in, Rachael was carrying dinner plates two at a time from the table to the kitchen, placing them in a careful pile on the counter beside the sink. To explain herself, she said, "You don't ever scrape and pile plates at the table because it's too noisy."

They got things put away and Rachael swept all the floors while she started the dishes in the big porcelain sink and then Rachael swept the floors again in the opposite direction, pushing down hard on the bristles of the broom.

When they were finished, after the dishes had been dried and stacked into the pine cupboards and all the floor mats had been taken outside and thrown over the clothesline and whacked a few times with the broom and the table had been wiped and dried and covered with a pretty cotton cloth she'd dug out of the pantry under the stairs, Rachael said yes, thank you, she would like some lemonade. But then she'd better go home.

They took their glasses of lemonade out to the screened porch, Rachael curling up on the swinging couch, looking out over the wide, sunset lake with her legs tucked up under her bum and finally not a word to say. And then she said she had to get going and in seconds she was quietly gone.

It was very good indeed to have the cottage returned to normal. Two hours' work had been reduced to little more than half an hour. She decided she would pick something up for Rachael when she was back in the city, maybe something for her hair, which was long and golden white, streaked summer blonde by the sun. It would probably stay streaked well through the autumn. Her hair was established now. By eight or nine you had the hair you would always have.

She went inside and stretched out on the old sofa, picked up the television remote. She felt clean and nicely tired. She went through the channels twice and then stopped clicking at three young guys and one older woman who were talking with a confidence she found despicable about security in retirement, mutual funds, the danger of being distracted from your plan by short-term ups and downs in the market.

She pulled the crazy quilt over her legs and decided that what she wanted was to get herself far, far away. Maybe France, maybe Australia. What she wanted was secrecy. She did not look forward to needing them, and she would, she would need them all very soon. She was just on the brink of it. And the people who cared for her would deliver in spades, each of them separately, differently, nobly. Each of them changed, diseased by her disease, by her, and with no chance for escape. This was no gift, this need.

The knocking on the door, its insistence, brought her up from sleep quickly. It was dark, inside the cottage and out. The windows were tall black squares and the air around her jumped

with the flicker of shadowed images from the television. Peter
Mansbridge was reading the news and her hand was cradling her
breast. Her sleeping hand had been nursing her sleeping breast.

She threw off the quilt and walked through the kitchen to turn
on the porch light and open the back door. Rachael had changed
into her pyjamas. They were black and white, clean white cotton
with dozens of small black cows, each of which had a dialogue
bubble attached to it, jokes or something, although the print was
too small to read from any distance. She was holding a switched-
on flashlight under her chin.

"Did you forget something, honey?" she asked.

"I thought you might want to come down to watch *Mir* with
everybody," Rachael said. "It's orbiting. It's supposed to be going
over us in ten minutes." She waited only a half-second for a reply.
"The *Mir* space station," she said.

"Oh," she said. And then too quickly, "It's good of you to ask
me, Rachael, but I don't think I can." She was remembering her
own repeated advice to Jenny and the boys, particularly to Jenny:
Always say no because it's just a lot easier to go from no to yes
than it is to get yourself back from yes to no.

"Why can't you?" Rachael said. She seemed to be looking
around the kitchen for the reason. She was inside now, although
not far. "You might never get another chance. That's what my dad
said. He said us kids would have lots of chances, but you older
people likely wouldn't." She started to rearrange the magnets on
the fridge door. She was making the Big Dipper, giving herself
time to think of something more to say, something helpful to her
cause. "He said the men on *Mir* are in a bit of trouble."

"I like your pyjamas," she said.

"They were my sister's," Rachael said, twirling once. "And now
they're mine."

She decided she could more easily put a stop to it tomorrow,
when she had some energy, enough energy to do it carefully.
"All right," she said. "Let me get a jacket on."

They walked together down through the dunes to join Rachael's parents and the Warrens and several other families at the water, most of the adults grouped in fold-up lawn chairs, talking quietly. As soon as he saw her, Dick Warren got halfway out of his chair to offer it but she waved him down, shook her head, said she was fine because she wouldn't be staying that long. People said hello, said they'd noticed she'd had an unusually busy weekend, laughed gently. The lake had changed; it was rougher, the shoreline waves higher, breaking harder on the sand. One of the Warren boys, maybe Geoffrey, she knew they had a Geoffrey, was describing some of the constellations, directing everyone's attention to the most easily recognized configurations of stars. He was still in his bathing suit and he pointed with a beautifully muscled arm, and used the Latin names: Orion, Ursa Major, Ursa Minor, Cassiopeia. Watching him, she decided that he understood exactly what he was doing, that he was eager to add his own beautiful body to the night's attractions.

Rachael's sister and her brothers were sitting on the sand around their parents' lawn chairs, leaning on their legs, their faces already lifted to the sky. It looked as if Rachael was not going to join them. She stayed close, just a little in front, stood with her small arms crossed as if this space station owed her something, a vision, an experience, a wondrous something to remember for the rest of her long life. In the dark moonlight at the edge of the water the white field background of her pyjamas glowed a bright, shocking white. That's why the cotton had looked so extremely clean when she was standing under the light on the porch. It was fluorescent. Impossibly, if the men on *Mir* could look down through their window on the world and see this beach in Southern Ontario, in Canada, in the northern hemisphere of the spinning blue earth, it would be Rachael who would catch their attention. "Right there," one of them might say. "Right there," pointing from the impossible distance. "A girl glowing on that beach, waving like mad."

She leaned forward, her hand on Rachael's shoulder now, but only lightly. "I have something difficult to tell," she whispered. "I think I might practise on you."

Rachael turned around fast, her hair a golden drift against her cheek, her big eyes filled with fearless, shining expectation, her arms still locked across her chest and her narrow shoulders squared against the night. "Me?" she asked. "Now?"

Bonnie Burnard's first collection of short fiction, Women of Influence *(Coteau Books, 1988), won the Commonwealth Best First Book Award.* Casino and Other Stories, *a second collection published in 1994 by HarperCollins (a Phyllis Bruce Book), was shortlisted for the Giller Prize and won the Saskatchewan Book of the Year Award. In 1995, Bonnie Burnard received the Marian Engel Award. Her first novel,* A Good House, *is forthcoming with HarperCollins.*

Leo McKay Jr.

THE
WEDDING
RING

She's going to leave me," Jeff says. He looks at his wife, Bev, who is sitting across the table from him. She has taken off her wedding ring and is rolling it around the rim of her Heineken can, smiling tauntingly at Jeff. The bar is crowded for a week-night. A band of men with long hair and scraggly beards stands on the stage smoking cigarettes and playing guitar blues. The tables nearby are occupied, but Jeff and Bev are here by themselves. No one is listening to them and no one is watching, but Jeff is speaking in the third person, calling Bev "she."

"She's going to leave me," Jeff says.

There is a ring of cigarette ash around the hole in the top of the beer can, where Bev has dropped two or three butts since they have been here. Her wedding ring pings off the raised lip of the can as she jiggles it. Now and then it comes close enough to the hole to knock some ash down into the can.

"She thinks this is funny," Jeff says, but he knows that the wild smile on her face is a cover. She is as afraid as he is. They have come to the edge of something.

They are sitting against the back wall of the barroom, far

enough away from the stage that they can hear each other when they speak. The room is dark and smoky. At the bar is a group of men in blue coveralls who have just lost their jobs at the tire plant. The big layoff was all over the papers this morning. The men are drinking heavily. Now and then they send up a roar that drowns out the band. One of them stands up at his stool, swaying violently back and forth, waving his arms and shouting angrily at his friends. The bouncer is standing across the room from them. He is leaning against the wall by the fire door, his back straight as a nail in a board, watching the men in coveralls at the bar. He is a young man in an emerald golf shirt. His hair is long and parted in the middle. His chest is as large as two men's chests and his waist almost as thick as his chest.

"I don't know what she thinks," Jeff says.

"Will you stop!" Bev shouts. She bangs the bottom of the Heineken can on the table. The ring rises from its lid, turning slowly in the air. It lands with a clink in an unused ashtray, and Bev casually picks it out and replaces it on her finger. "*She* this! *She* that!" She takes the ring off again and places it on the first knuckle of her index finger, dangling it over the beer can.

"*She she she she she she she.*" Jeff cries. "She wants me to stop calling her she." He picks up the pitcher of draft from the table and pours his glass full, then takes a drink.

Bev has the ring in her right palm. She closes her fingers loosely over the ring, then shakes her hand with the ring inside, as though she is about to roll dice.

Jeff moves his hand quickly in her direction, and she leaps away from it, as if she thinks he is about to strike her. But he is pointing at something behind her. One of the men in blue coveralls at the bar, a man with a shaved bald head and a big purple tattoo at the top of his neck, has gripped the man beside him in a headlock. In a single swift motion, he turns his friend around. With a forearm, he sweeps the bottles and glasses from the surface of the bar and slams his friend's forehead against the bar's edge. He pulls his friend back, and is winding up for a second swing

when the bouncer clamps onto him from behind. The bald
man wiggles madly and curses and spits at the bouncer, but the
bouncer holds the man against his chest and squeezes him until
he stops wiggling. He shifts the man over to his left arm. The
man's friend's forehead is split wide across. Blind with blood,
the cut man gropes with his hands out before him, a scalded
expression on his face. The bouncer puts the bleeding man under
his right arm and wades across the barroom, carrying the two
men at once. A waitress holds the fire door open, and the bouncer
steps sideways through the door with both men.

The barroom is now in an uproar. A bartender and two
waitresses are mopping up blood and beer. A third waitress is
running a grey-and-black vacuum over broken glass. Two men in
blue coveralls remain at the bar. They look at each other and look
at the staff cleaning up the mess their friends made. They stand
up from their barstools as though they are going to help, then
they sit back down.

"Where will all this end?" Bev says, shaking her head signifi-
cantly. She picks up her beer can, empty but for two or three
cigarette butts, and looks into the hole in its lid with one eye
closed, as though she is looking through a telescope.

"There's supposed to be a no layoff policy at the tire plant," Jeff
says. "A lot of people believed in that. Even people who didn't
work there."

"Galileo," Bev says. When she takes the beer can away from her
face, there is a ring of ash around her eye. "I don't even know who
Galileo is," she says, wiping at the ash with the heel of her hand.
She thumps the can on the table and leaves it there. She holds her
wedding ring up between her thumb and index finger and regards
it at arm's length, as though it is a rare coin. She brings the ring
in close to her eye and looks through it at the room, scanning
back and forth, top to bottom, coming to rest on Jeff.

"Ask any fifteen-year-old Japanese kid who was Galileo," she
says, her lashes catching on the ring, folding backward as she blinks.
She drops the ring into her palm again, shakes it in her loosely

closed hand, then slips it through the pull-top hole in the lid of the beer can. The ring lands with a clank on the can's bottom.

Jeff lays his arms on the tabletop and rests his forehead on his arms.

The band is still playing, though they look somewhat confused by the commotion that has just taken place at the bar. Their guitars churn through the smoke-filled air, the drums sound off the walls. Suddenly, the music stops, seemingly in the middle of a number. "Fifteen-minute break," one of the band members says through the sound system, and the band disappears backstage.

Jeff looks up and sees the bouncer coming back in through the fire door. He is alone. Jeff thinks he looks bigger than he did before, as though he has eaten the two men he left the bar with. His shirt is darkened with blood. He takes measured steps toward the two men in coveralls who remain at the bar. He lays his arms across their shoulders and talks to them in a way Jeff knows is meant to quell any further unrest. He would be asking the men if he could expect any more trouble. And from the way the men in coveralls are shaking their heads and showing their palms in gestures of reason and reconciliation, Jeff knows they are apologizing to the bouncer for the behaviour of their friends.

The bouncer steps around to the other side of the bar and exchanges a few words with the bartender and two waitresses. Then he disappears through a door.

Jeff stares down into his beer. Bev picks up the beer can with her wedding ring in it and shakes it back and forth so the ring clanks around inside.

"This has me scared to death," Jeff says. He stares down through his beer glass.

Bev rattles the ring in the can again, and Jeff looks up suddenly. "Come on, now," he says. "Cut that out."

Bev smiles to see him react and rattles the can tauntingly.

"Come on," Jeff says. "Enough."

She holds the can out to him and jangles it. When he makes a grab for it, she pulls it away, just beyond his reach.

"You think this is funny?" he says loudly. He stands up and reaches over to grab the can. She pulls it away from him. He grabs her wrist and brings it close to him, but she switches the can to her other hand.

"This isn't funny," Jeff says. He slumps dejectedly back into his seat. Bev sets the can back on the table in front of her.

The bouncer comes out of the back room wearing a clean shirt. He smiles at the staff behind the bar and lays a friendly hand on one or two shoulders as he makes his way back to his spot near the fire door. In a few minutes the band comes back out onto the stage. The members pick up their instruments, light cigarettes, and begin playing again.

Jeff hears a loud bang and looks up to see that the fire door has been thrown open, slamming into the wall behind it. The bouncer turns around surprised. A shotgun blast charges the air. A flash illuminates the bouncer and part of the wall behind him. The bouncer's left arm and shoulder light up red with blood. He grabs at his wounds bewilderedly, then slumps to the floor. The bald man with the tattoo on his neck comes into the room, the butt of a short-barrelled, pump-action shotgun braced against his shoulder.

"Jesus, God have mercy," says Bev. She crouches down beneath the table. She pulls at Jeff's leg for him to join her on the floor. But Jeff is spellbound. He cannot take his eyes off the purposeful movements of the man in coveralls. The man no longer appears drunk, and he marches straight to the bar, where he shoots out the clock behind the counter, pumps his gun, and blows out the glasses, bottles, cups, and plates on their shelves against the wall.

The music has clanged to a stop. The musicians dropped their instruments as they scrambled for cover. Guitars lie face up on the stage, humming and jangling, whistling in a wall of feedback. A noise rises from the people inside the bar, a human noise of fear. Workboots slam the wooden floor as those near the door, whom the gunman has already passed, scramble outside into the parking lot.

The two men in coveralls who were sitting at the bar walk slowly backward, past upturned tables toward the abandoned stage. Their mouths are open. They are shaking their heads. One of them, the taller of the two, begins speaking to the man with the shotgun. "Benny. Benny," he says. "Jesus, Benny. Jesus." Benny holds his gun at waist level and points it at one of his friends, then the other, as they make their way across the floor. "Benny. Benny," says the one who has already spoken. Suddenly, he breaks and runs, skittering across the room, tripping over upturned tables, sliding on broken glass.

Benny raises the shotgun and fires. The pellets whack into a wooden pillar. He pumps the gun and shoots again. A splat of red flashes on the back of the running man, and he falls to the floor.

The other man has put himself on his knees before his friend, begging for his life. Soundlessly, he moves his lips to these words: *Please, Benny. Please, Benny.*

Benny lowers the barrel to the man's forehead and squeezes the trigger. He has forgotten to pump the gun and nothing happens, not even a click. Appearing angry for the first time, he turns the gun around and grips the barrel like a baseball bat. He winds up and smacks his friend across the back and ribs with the gun's stock. When the man rolls over onto the floor, writhing and moaning, Benny silences him with a blow from the butt end of the stock.

Beneath the tables and booths around the room's perimeter, dark forms of huddled people shift and squirm and emit nervous whimpers. The wall of feedback from the abandoned guitars on stage has risen to a high-pitched whistling from the amplifiers.

Benny pumps the gun to fill the chamber and steps to the centre of the room. He crouches in a defensive stance with his gun at his hip and slowly turns about on the spot, sweeping the room's outer edges. When he sees Jeff, their eyes meet in a clear gaze. Jeff tries to move. He tries to bend his knees to duck below the table. Benny has his gun pointed directly at him. Beneath the table, Bev has a hold of Jeff by the leg and is pleading with him in a whisper. "Jeff, please get down."

Benny turns up the corners of his mouth in an odd smile. The tattoo on his neck is a pattern of lizard scales that are detailed enough to appear to be growing out of his skin. He drops to his knees, squares the butt of the gun at the base of a wooden pillar before him, takes the end of the barrel between his teeth, and leans forward onto the trigger.

What followed was more or less predictable. People slowly came crawling from beneath tables, crying like babies at what had just almost happened to them.

Sirens rose slowly in the distance and built to a deafening volume as lights flashed in through the window from outside. Police and ambulance attendants rushed into the bar, around the barroom, in and out the door with empty and full stretchers.

The bouncer was alive, at least when the ambulance attendants reached him. "He's breathing," one said to the other. They rolled him onto a stretcher and took him out the door. The man Benny hit with the rifle butt was unconscious and broken up. Benny and the friend he shot in the back were dead on the scene.

The police cordoned off the building, and no one was free until after questioning. Everything in the barroom was broken and bloody and shot full of twelve-gauge pellets. Jeff and Bev sat at a small round table, staring at each other. Two policemen, one in plain clothes asking questions, the other in uniform taking notes, slowly worked their way through the witnesses. When their turn came, Jeff and Bev answered the man's questions, the officer in uniform wrote down their answers. Then they were free to go.

The next day, they both took sick days from work and slept in until ten o'clock. Unable to speak and unable to eat breakfast, they stared at each other, stared at the floor, drank their coffee, and listened to the radio show that used to be "Morningside." There was a short mention of the shootings on the national news at twelve o'clock. Three people killed, the news reader said, but she did not say who the third person killed was, the bouncer or the beaten friend. It was almost one o'clock before Bev realized she was not wearing her wedding ring.

"My ring!" she said in the middle of the regional weather.

They got into the car and rushed down to the bar. The front entrance was locked, the window boarded up. They went around to the back door and let themselves in.

The bar's owner was a short, dark-skinned man with thick curly hair and a dark shadow of stubble on his face. He was dressed in green work pants and a plaid shirt. As Bev and Jeff approached him, he was emptying dirty, soapy water from a galvanized bucket into a sink behind the bar. One of the waitresses who had been there the night before was standing behind the owner with an identical bucket full of identical water. Jeff explained what had happened. "It was a Heineken can," Bev told them. The waitress led them to the back room, where empty cans were kept in transparent garbage bags. With the help of the waitress, Bev and Jeff went through each bag, shaking the Heineken cans first, then the other cans.

"How about the bouncer and that other guy?" Jeff asked at one point.

"Very serious," the waitress said. Tears welled in her eyes. She shook her head, but did not say which of the two had died.

When they had gone through all the cans, they started in on bottles, even though they knew that the ring had been in a can, and it would not have fit into the mouth of a bottle.

They worked until their hands were covered with sticky, stale beer and their clothes were wet and smelled boozy. The owner gave them a flashlight from under the bar, and they carefully searched every square centimetre of the floor.

"Did anyone see anything while they were sweeping?" Jeff asked.

"We vacuumed," the waitress said.

They opened the custodial closet and rolled out a grey-and-black wet/dry vacuum. They opened the drum of the vacuum under a light and spread a big orange garbage bag on the floor beside it. When they dumped the contents of the vacuum onto the bag, broken glass rattled and crunched. A small cloud of dust rolled over the heavier debris and settled on the carpet beside the garbage bag. With a blue Rubbermaid dustpan, they dug into the pile of refuse, then sifted each panful over the drum of the vacuum, poking through with their fingers to get a good look at every bump and protrusion.

When they had gone through everything that came out of the vacuum, they gathered the corners of the orange bag and dumped what remained on top of it into the drum. The waitress clamped the top back on the drum and vacuumed the carpet near where they had been working.

The owner set four cups of black coffee on a table in a corner that had been thoroughly cleaned. When he and the waitress and Jeff and Bev sat down, the waitress lowered her face into her hands and began to weep. The dark line where her hair was parted showed that the bleach was growing out. The owner patted her gently on the shoulder.

"That such a thing would happen!" he said. He shook his head slowly in disbelief.

"So much for the no layoff policy at the tire plant," Jeff said. He did not know whether he was serious or trying to make a joke.

Bev fingered the place where her ring used to be. "Maybe it's . . ." she said. She looked around the room.

When their coffee cups were empty, they sat looking down into them.

Leo McKay lives in Maitland, Nova Scotia, a tiny village on the Bay of Fundy. His first book, a collection of stories called Like This *(Anansi, 1995), was a finalist for the Giller Prize. He is a former editor of the literary magazine* Prism International. *Aside from being a writer, he is a husband, a father of two small children, and a teacher. He is currently at work on a second book, a novel.*

Monique Proulx

BANANA
CHAUDFROID

TRANSLATED BY MATT COHEN

What comes first, the water or the ice?

What falls from the sky is water, what arrives on the ground is ice. But before it falls from the sky? Before the sky, in what form does the water hide?

Before the sky, there is nothing. Between the water from the sky and the ice from the earth there is us.

Gabrielle has positioned herself to get the panoramic view, at the place where the boulevard cuts the park in two, near where she lives. It's the only thing to do: to stay still and look. The city gleams like a razor blade. Everything has turned sharp, crystalline, petrified. She no longer recognizes the trees. They were naked and impoverished, now suddenly they are covered in diamonds. She no longer recognizes the five o'clock traffic. The roaring horde has been transformed into a convoy of skidding jalopies starting and stopping all over the place. There are no more traffic lights, at least those that exist swing lifelessly at the ends of their cables, struck down by some unknown illness.

Where are the police? Where are the trucks spreading sand? Disorder reigns supreme, magnificent disorder. Those who dare to walk, walk towards their fall. A man in front of Gabrielle does a complicated somersault and ends up stretched out on the sidewalk. Two laughing teenage girls cling to each other until they go down together. A crystalline music accompanies all these improvised dances, the music of rain solidifying on trees, cement, cars, people's stunned heads. Gabrielle's clothes are already crackling like armour while she gets going again, walking one small step at a time like an old lady, putting her feet down flat, her body relaxed and centred, no kicking up the heels. When chaos erupts that's what it's for, to make you relearn the simplest movements, to bring back the care and the intensity that were there at the beginning, to remind you that if human beings walk upright, unlike animals, it was not a small victory in the evolutionary journey.

Turning at the corner of her street, Gabrielle laughs with delight. The maples in front of her place are no longer trees but pillars of glass thrusting, all their branches phosphorescent, towards the sky and the polar gods. But under the glass cathedral are bustling mice who do not have the soul for contemplation. Gabrielle sees three of her neighbours engaged in a noisy fight with the ice that is paralyzing their cars. The usual tools being useless, one is banging a hammer on his Honda's windshield, another is using an axe to free the wheels of his Pathfinder. Gabrielle holds back her giggles. Too bad they don't sell flamethrowers at the corner hardware.

Why? Why is it so urgent to go commit suicide on impassable roads? Why fight against reality when it finally comes to surprise us? Why not, finally relieved of the burden of doing, stay inside drinking hot chocolate, forget about schedules and appointments, take time to pet the cat and contemplate the ice-covered trees?

That's what she says to Francis. On the other side of the Atlantic Ocean, he's preparing to fall asleep in his Parisian night. Why don't people like to live, Francis? Why are we fighting for nothing,

Francis? By way of response, the telephone sputters. She says that she'll take pictures for him of the cathedral maples tomorrow morning in the light of the sun, and that it will be the most beautiful thing she has ever given him. He says that she is the most beautiful thing, and with those words, which aren't bad as an ending, the connection breaks off, leaving her smiling on this side of the Atlantic.

All evening she tries to write, but nothing wants to come. As the ice keeps beating against the window, irritation worms its way into her. The telephone rings but she doesn't pick it up. When it is time for the news, she doesn't watch. Why write instead of taking pictures? Why be infatuated with Francis instead of someone from her own country who would be in her bed with her right now? She puts a roll of film in her camera, for the next morning, when the sun will light up the maples.

The next morning there is no sun in the maples.

The same musical drizzle as the night before, as the night before that, breathes its cold breath on everything it meets, and creates ice, more ice, translucent ice that has grown much thicker than before and is gradually masking all colour.

It could still be called beautiful. But from the window it's clear that the beauty is contrived and is on the verge of turning ugly. The maples are being crushed by their makeup and now look like kitsch monuments to which ornaments keep getting added and added. Enough. Time for the artist to stop.

Gabrielle turns on the radio. She immediately comes upon a news bulletin describing a catastrophe. The catastrophe is happening in this very place, in her city that is safe from everything, and if the trembling voice of the broadcaster is to be believed, this catastrophe is the worst of the century. Gabrielle smiles skeptically and turns on the television. There too is a news bulletin when there shouldn't be one, and the news readers' commentaries strike the same apocalyptic note. And moreover, there are pictures that lend the abstract words a naked and irrefutable truth.

Gigantic hydro breakdown. Gabrielle sees the chaos of the downtown stripped of its traffic lights, its computers, its businesses,
the lights of its skyscrapers. Buses are ramming into trucks, the
city's bridges are jammed with stalled traffic, people are raging
as they get out of their immobilized vehicles. *A million house-
holds without electricity.* Gabrielle envisions neighbourhoods she
knows, gone numb in the darkness. She learns that she is living
in an unaffected zone that is protected from this gangrene thanks
to the fact that it is supplied by underground cables. *Record
amounts of ice.* Layers of ice thicker than mineral wool surround
the wires, the trees, the poles, the houses — everything that lives
in the open air. A woman who is not Gabrielle's neighbour
shatters her windshield with a hammer —a flame-thrower would
definitely have been the safer choice — and twenty-two pedestrians are laid out on the lacquered sidewalks. *Three thousand
fallen pylons.* A kilometres-long parade is shown of the massacred
pylons, ten-ton metallic creatures twisted and crumpled, brought
to their knees like little paper things casually knocked down by a
playful King Kong.

And it's not over yet. That's what the television announcer
repeats several times, looking Gabrielle straight in the eye: it's not
over yet, it's not over yet, the worst is still to come, more freezing
rain is forecast, the power breakdowns can't be repaired for days,
weeks, the whole city is caught in a sandwich between the warm
air above and the cold air below, and this sandwich is not moving.
Galvanized by the word *sandwich*, Gabrielle stands up. She is
hungry and immortal images are waiting for her outside. She goes
out, her camera slung from her shoulder, a half-chewed croissant
in her mouth.

The trees. First of all her maples, their crystals all gleaming, a
little thicker than yesterday, inclined towards the street like
old-fashioned actors taking a bow. She photographs them straight
on, in profile, with her wide-angle lens, with her telephoto lens,
sudden movements almost making her fall a thousand times.
Click click. The neighbour from across the hall is watching her

through the window, clearly disapproving. Gabrielle takes her picture. *Click.*

Next, the park beside her house. The closest parts are condemned, totally covered with ice. But it doesn't matter. From a distance, the view of the whole is amazing, an enchanted forest in the sparkling country of the star fairy. Every now and then Gabrielle is surprised by a huge noise, the sound of splitting trunks and branches, and that reminds her, in the time it takes to feel a twinge of sorrow, that the crystalline splendour of these trees is not without cost and what she is admiring is exactly what is hurting them. Then the twinge is over. *Click.*

To Francis she describes everything: the chaos, the noise of the trees, the panic, the paralysis, the missing light of hope. At the end of the line he is silent, then he says: "You seem to like it." "It's interesting," she says. She hears her own voice, sharp, on the defensive. "It's a very interesting thing," she repeats weakly.

Very interesting. That evening, a barbecued half-chicken cooling on her knees, she devotes herself to the television and the special bulletins that keep unloading their cargo of striking images late into the night. There were the pylons, there were the broken-trunked trees, now there are the people. They flee their unhealthy lodgings, they desperately seek electricity, they crowd into schools, recreation centres, improvised shelters fed by generators. This is what refugees from a rich country are like. They have no bundles of clothing on their heads, they carry very little with them, they hope to be furnished with what they need immediately. They are worried about the budgie they left behind. "I can't sleep without two pillows," an old woman says worriedly. Gabrielle takes note of everything. An objective witness is required.

At dawn she is woken by an explosion, a bomb, the sound of the world ending.

The century-old maples have just split in two beneath the weight of their icy beauty, and now they are lying in the street, spread out over the broken windows of cars. Glued to her window,

Gabrielle is trembling with disbelief and sorrow. If the giants are starting to fall, what will happen to the others?

She goes to get her camera. Her hands tremble as she focuses on the shattered kings.

So it's war. So this is how war feels. Terribly alive.

Under their elegant garments, rich countries wear tattered underwear.

Gabrielle is forced to change her mind. The ice-storm refugees aren't among this country's wealthy. They cram into the shelters, now multiplying, because no other solution is available — not staying in a hotel, not staying somewhere else in a comfortable guest room. They sleep on army mattresses on the floor, five hundred bodies laid out side by side, crowded together in a closeness that grows more nauseating as time goes by. They receive free food and they are even entertained in the evening thanks to artists who come to do their best for them. Each shelter has become a micro-city, with its thievery, its petty crimes, its neon lighting, its stifling atmosphere. A blind old lady has had her boots stolen. Two children have been attacked by a pedophile. In one shelter a gang was spreading terror and had to be chased out. Most of the people in these refuges are either very young or very old, and they live on the edges of the city, where the electrical breakdowns are the most disastrous. For weeks they will have to live in concrete enclaves like well-nourished domestic animals. They lack no essential. No one dies from not washing every day and having no privacy. No one.

On the other hand, people do die from staying in their frozen bed when it is minus twenty outside, people do die from refusing to be close to each other. For several days now, the mercury has fallen dangerously low, and the army and police are checking every house without electricity to evacuate those who were previously unwilling to leave. And that's where the images become the most unbearable, that's where the underwear of the rich country, shown in prime time, is the most shameful. A whole race of secret indigents are presented as a spectacle, solitary individuals whose existence had gone unnoticed, without official status, without winter clothes, without the ability to understand English or French, a race of people who have been waiting for the heat to come back on for days, hugging their dogs close, who cry and struggle as they're led by force into the monster of heated civilization.

The prime minister makes a brief and dramatic television appearance. He says that the shelters aren't an ideal long-term solution and asks his well-off fellow countrymen to open their doors and their hearts.

These words, which sum up the essence of human goodness, stun Gabrielle. She drops her notebook and pencil. She tries to phone everyone she knows, to make sure they are all right. Everyone she knows has electricity or is staying at a hotel, or has already found somewhere comfortable to stay. Everyone she knows, like her, is one of the privileged. Didn't she realize that?

There remains coming to the aid of everyone she doesn't know.

"You would do that?" says Francis, astonished, from the other side of the Atlantic. "You would take in strangers?" The tone of admiration in his voice is like a wind that sweeps away all of Gabrielle's last doubts. The next day she borrows her neighbour's hammer and axe to free her vehicle, and she sets out towards the farthest and most populous shelter.

It is outdoors that the true texture of the disaster can be felt. The disaster isn't swarming with powerful images like on television. The disaster is uniformly grey and cold. An icy sleep has descended forever onto the deserted roads, into the abandoned houses. The soldiers and the hydro workers are the only visible survivors, struggling in the midst of struck-down trees and hanging cables. Over the sixty kilometres of her journey, not a single hydro pole has been spared, and Gabrielle drives past their great fallen bodies with the strange sensation that she is accompanying them in an old-fashioned and interminable funeral procession. Sometimes she stops her car on the shoulder to take a picture. *Click.*

The survivors are hiding here, in the huge rooms with apple green walls that used to be for recreational functions, back in the carefree era of electricity. There's the section used for sleeping, the section that serves as a cafeteria, the amusement section. At first sight it could be a gigantic, overcrowded holiday camp, dominated by children crying and the warm smell of bodies. Those who aren't children are sitting down and waiting for something to happen. But their blank looks leave no room for ambiguity. Some refugee camps are more miserable than others, but they are all prisons. Gabrielle doesn't dare take pictures.

The two women in charge of receiving people look at each other when Gabrielle makes her offer: she will take in two or three people at her place — a young family, for example — for as long as necessary. "You aren't the first," one woman says unenthusiastically. "We have a list of offers that long." "No one's happy here," says the other, "but no one wants to go live with strangers."

Suddenly a young woman, using the boy in her arms to clear her way, bumps into Gabrielle.

"Me, I want to get out of *this place*."

Gabrielle has never felt so much anger in a voice.

Paula, Wayne, and Roger are at Gabrielle's place. Wayne is Paula's son. He is ten years old. He has overlarge ears and his veins can be seen through his skin — which is transparent, as though it hasn't been completed. He is agitated, with adult tics like rubbing his eyebrows and chewing his lips. His laugh is also adult, especially when he tells, for the third time, the story of what provoked Paula's most recent burst of anger and precipitated their departure from the shelter, the story of the man who put his hand in his pants.

Paula is pregnant and exhausted. She smokes Rothman cigarettes. She knows she shouldn't. She says she knows she shouldn't each time she lights up a new cigarette against the previous half-smoked one. She would have a pretty face if she smiled more often. Her most intolerable recent memories, aside from the attack against the boy, are the snores of her sleeping companions. "Three hundred pigs groaning at the same time," she says, glancing at Roger and incriminating him along with the rest.

In real life Roger is a welder. He isn't Wayne's father, but he is the father of the baby growing in Paula's belly. He is big and fat with beautiful blue eyes that flee confrontation. He is terribly embarrassed to find himself at Gabrielle's house. This evening Gabrielle would know nothing about him if it weren't for Paula's acidulous interjections. "Roger doesn't like to talk," Paula confesses about him, and Roger has to agree.

They eat in front of the television, which is on. The television is their common glue, the free zone that ceaselessly reminds them why they are together. Otherwise the situation would be too strange, untenable. Between two questions from Gabrielle and two sentences from Paula, the television talks and wipes away the silences, like at a family party where a cousin who tells jokes rescues the evening from boredom. Except that the television doesn't make jokes, it shows how the disaster, instead of resolving itself, is growing worse, how the functioning part of the power grid is breaking down from the overload, how the city and its surroundings have just been declared a disaster area.

Gabrielle takes in these new signs of the apocalypse with a slightly distant curiosity. The centre of the world is no longer out there, it is right here, along with these uncomfortable guests who need to be comforted. She exists only for that purpose. She offers them a second helping of spaghetti, which they decline, she hurries into the kitchen to prepare dessert. She has worked out simple menus for days to come, familiar cooking so they won't be frightened. How many days to come will she be able to bear? If she were asked that question right now, she would reply truthfully that it's all the same to her, she'll cope one day at a time.

She brings in the bananas chaudfroid. This is a very simple dessert. You cut open an unpeeled banana lengthwise, stuff it with butter and brown sugar, put it in the oven until the sugar melts, then when this small banana boat has turned black you take it out, drench it with rum which you set on fire, add vanilla ice cream. Repeat as many times as there are guests. Eat right away.

They eat. They eat in silence, in a silence of extreme contentment rather than embarrassment. The television disappears. The strangeness of the situation disappears. Nothing remains but this taste of being very young, a transparent taste of the world's beginning, when the taste buds first encounter the explosive wonders of life, the smooth, the melting, the warm and cold together. "That's good," Roger says. "Oh yes, it's good," Wayne says. Paula gives Gabrielle her first real smile. "Why did you make that?" she asks. "To help," Gabrielle replies humbly. The two women keep smiling — and it continues for several minutes, a gaping breach through everything that separates them.

When the evening is over they retire to their own quarters. Gabrielle has given them the living room, the biggest room in the apartment, with its sofa bed, a futon, an old television with which they can follow the nighttime wanderings of the ice storm, and a priceless view of the street and the fallen trees. They have closed the door. They aren't asleep; when she listens closely Gabrielle can hear their whispers mixed with the television.

"It's going well," she sums up for Francis from her bedroom, which has been turned into an office and a multi-purpose refuge, her mood still sweetened by that devoted loving warmth that has filled her all evening. "They are intimidated but they're doing very well." "Is she pretty?" Francis asks. Suddenly there is a howl from the living room, followed by more howling that reaches all the way to Francis, on the other side of the Atlantic. Gabrielle abandons the telephone and cautiously approaches the living room.

The door is open, and then Wayne seems to be thrown out of it, almost into Gabrielle's arms. Paula follows, clothed in a long T-shirt that conceals her round belly.

"The little shit," she is fulminating, "everything he says is a lie! The horse's ass!"

"What . . . ?" Gabrielle tries.

"It isn't even true that someone felt up his bum! . . . He made it all up!"

And since Gabrielle's stunned expression shows she doesn't see why this is bad news, Paula adds despairingly: "If he hadn't lied, we never would have come to *this place*. Don't you see?"

Incapable of anything further, she goes right back into the living room, leaving Wayne in the hall beside Gabrielle. Her voice still reaches them, muffled and discouraged. "Horse's ass."

Another, weaker voice, Roger's, says something soothing, and gradually the silence returns. Gabrielle looks at Wayne, frail and awkward in his crumpled pyjamas. Without looking at her he rubs at his eyebrows. All the children she knows are nice looking and spontaneously attract caresses. This one belongs to a different species. Just the same she places her hand on his head.

"Is it true you like doing that? Lying?"

For a moment he is immobile, paralyzed by the touch of her hand.

"They're not lies," he says. "They're stories."

He frees himself from her hand.

"She must have cooled off now," he adds, in his adult voice.

He goes back into the living room. Before closing the door he looks at Gabrielle, then he slams it loudly, as though he was throwing her out.

Horse's ass. You shouldn't even consider calling your child a horse's ass, even when you're tired. Nor should you call him Wayne, especially in that dragging nasal voice that sounds like a moan. W-aaaaay-ne. A horsy neighing. Gabrielle doesn't sleep. She remembers a childhood story in which a little horse — or was it a pig? — called Poony fell in love with a kite. She laughs quietly. She searches inside herself for that warm, melting feeling, the unshakable compassion that had gripped her so strongly the last two days, but she doesn't find it.

The city is an island. The bridges that link it to the world have just closed because ice falling from the structure is a threat to cars and trucks. The city is a prison.

Generators are needed.

The food supplies come in more slowly. Nonetheless, citizens are asked not to stockpile in order to prevent panic buying.

Water is rationed until further notice. What remains in the reservoirs is no longer drinkable.

Generators are desperately needed.

Fifteen people have died of asphyxiation because they used camping equipment as heaters. Ten others have died of hypothermia because they avoided the army patrols and stayed in their icy beds.

Fifty thousand trees have been mortally damaged.

Five hundred thousand animals have frozen to death because they were domesticated and under the care of humans without generators.

It has been sixteen days without sun.

The international community is being begged to send generators.

"What's a generator?" Wayne asks.

Their daily routine is centred on the television. Their daily routine becomes more and more like a bad television serial in which there is much drinking of coffee and no action. Paula has made herself a place on the sofa, in front of the small screen. She doesn't budge, except in the morning when she goes to wash and to eat the breakfast that Roger makes her, and in the evening when she goes to the other television and eats the meal Gabrielle has made. The rest of the time she is stretched out lifelessly, the telephone in one hand and a cigarette in the other. She talks to friends and relatives who stayed "there," in the disaster zone, she talks with them about the disaster and the television commentary about the disaster, and she always ends her conversation by asking them what they ate for dinner yesterday.

Also she cries. Now that happens behind the closed doors of the living room and Gabrielle can hear only the high notes of her voice when she loses all control. It's always about Wayne. The horse's ass.

It's true that Roger doesn't like to talk.

He has a silent agreement with Gabrielle. He gives her a little money for the food and she isn't arrogant enough to refuse it. He takes care of the breakfasts and he washes all that she leaves him in the way of dishes and pots and pans. Without a word. To spare him the painful threat of her conversation, she leaves him alone in the kitchen while he's working. Afterwards he goes right back to Paula in the living room and closes the door for privacy, even during the day. When he forgets to close the door, Gabrielle sees him holding Paula in his arms and singing her country-and-western songs while she sniffles, like a little girl who is being consoled. Roger has a beautiful voice, perhaps because he doesn't talk.

What exactly Wayne does is unknown. Gabrielle sometimes sees him kneeling on the living room's parquet floor, playing noisily with plastic toys. Or he stares at his mother while she talks on the telephone. He doesn't cry when he gets shouted at. *Poony.* Maybe he's been ordered never to leave their new family territory.

It's not the way Gabrielle imagined. "It's perfect," she tells Francis. "They leave me alone. I can write."

Except that she isn't writing anything.

She had imagined that disasters must break down all barriers and that they would end up united, united the way humans ought to be to confront the end of the world.

She has never felt so alone as she does with them.

Alone, her camera slung over her shoulder, she is walking downtown, walking towards the fissured skating rink that the downtown has become. It is so cold that the frost from her breath follows her like a ghost. As she goes forward, civilization recedes. She hears police sirens, the sounds of broken glass, the growl of tires trying to pull themselves out of the ice. The only visible living beings are furtive silhouettes coming out of buildings with packages and suitcases; fat rats fleeing the dying city.

Such devastation. Such devastation cannot be photographed.

She walks down the middle of streets, climbing over branches and tree trunks. In the uniform half-light the blind skyscrapers can hardly be seen. How long can a skyscraper stay standing when it has no reason to live? She imagines the downtown skyscrapers crippled and smashed in like the metal pylons, the universe of offices reduced to a pile of rubble being carefully sifted by archaeologists a thousand years from now, here and there fishing out a broken computer, a secretary's chair, a piece of a telephone. Suddenly she steps on something that she crushes. It's a Christmas wreath that fell from a store window. Her heart jumps, as though she has crushed a living being.

Go back, go back home, her instincts tell her.

Home. At home, from the moment she comes in, there is the smell of cigarette smoke that has soaked into everything forever, and the deafening sound of the television. And the three of them, silent and drowned in the afflictions that are pouring out from the news bulletins, silent but terribly present.

She wants to say to them: Go away, please go away. Instead she sits down beside them, in the warmth of the electricity, and she watches the small screen with men crying because they have lost everything — their apple trees, their cows, their sugar maples, the slowly ripened fruit of their lives.

That day she is inconsolable when she talks to Francis. Francis, ice does come before water. Ice is the true nature of water, Francis. One day everything will be covered by ice again, even the chestnut trees of Paris. Ice will cover over the dust of our miserable bones, Francis, how could we have forgotten? Everything will go back to ice, it's the universal plan, everything will go back to ice because everything comes from ice, the vast frozen nothingness, do you understand, do you understand what I'm telling you?

He doesn't understand. He says: "My poor sweetie, you're exhausted." He says: "Come here, get on a plane and come here right now." "The airports are closed," she sobs. She hears the tinkling of his cup of coffee and she imagines the tapping sound of his heels, just moments ago, on the dry pavement, on that other side of the Atlantic where it is warm and the trees are already preparing to bud. She finds that unbearable. She hangs up.

Hanging up she sees Wayne's head, with its big translucent ears, framed in the doorway where it stays without moving like a moose's rack.

"What do you want, Poony?" she asks without thinking.

"Nothing," he says.

He doesn't leave.

"What did you call me?"

"Poony," Gabrielle repeats, but in a different voice, a voice welling up with an affection that surprises her.

He reddens with pleasure. What he'd been wanting to say finally comes out. "Do you have skates?"

The iced-over paths of the park, the gleaming and unusable sidewalks, the wide, sweeping, closed boulevards, it is all theirs, the whole city is their city. They have rediscovered why ice exists. Ice exists so they can fly like the wind where before they walked heavily through ordinary life. Ice exists so they can rediscover their angels' wings and use them far from the cramped enclosures and skating rinks, fly freer than astronauts. Even wearing Gabrielle's old skates that are too big for him, Poony knows how to skate backwards and how to jump over the sidewalk chains. Gabrielle knows how to fall down without hurting herself. This grey January afternoon they are so rejuvenated by laughing that they are barely ten years old between them. Gabrielle takes pictures of Poony.

"I don't want to go home," he begs in his child's voice.

When, just the same, they finally do go home, his hand spontaneously finds Gabrielle's.

"I want to skate again tomorrow," he demands.

"Of course," Gabrielle says.

"I want to eat banana show-offers," he also demands.

"Banana show-offs?"

"I want to stay with you, even when the electricity comes back on," he says in his adult voice.

That's the day Gabrielle falls in love — without knowing whether it's with the magic to be found in the midst of despair or with the little boy with sticking-out ears, or maybe just with childhood. She falls in love with an image of Wayne that slowly dissolves, like a mist, because the next day he leaves. The next day they don't go skating again because Paula, Roger, and Wayne move to a brother of Paula's whose power has just come back. They go almost as quickly as they arrived. Gabrielle hardly has time to kiss Poony on the cheek before he is in his uncle's car, not at all upset to be leaving her, excited by the activity, excited and a liar. Paula, on the other hand, gives Gabrielle a long hug, holds Gabrielle against her, against her living belly, and this unexpected embrace shocks Gabrielle and she feels she has been abandoned at the entrance to a fabulous country that she hasn't had time to visit.

Who is Paula? Why is she Paula instead of someone else? What is the source of her sorrow, her anger? Who is Wayne's father? What will Wayne turn into when he grows up? Gabrielle spends hours exploring the deserted living room. She finds used tissue, a plastic astronaut, disgusting full ashtrays. She doesn't find any answers to the questions she didn't ask.

And then she calms down, her sorrow eases. So many people are coming and going, closed around their secret treasures, so many treasures everywhere that can never be touched. It is a miracle that she had access to a bit of each of them, a very small bit.

On her dresser she puts the picture of the ice-covered maples, erect in their splendid agony. And right beside it the picture of Poony. The red ears, the curved skates, very small but with a big feeling, the feeling of a happy little king in his kingdom of ice. His temporary kingdom, because the ice is starting to melt again.

All over, houses are starting to have power again. January is starting to slide normally into February again. Gabrielle is starting to write again. And the ice is starting to melt again. Again, this time, the ice is melting. For how long will it melt? Until what millennium?

That's what she asks Francis, on the other side of the Atlantic. "For how long will the ice melt, Francis?" And right after: "What would you think about us having a baby, Francis? . . . I mean, one day? . . ."

From the other side of the Atlantic there is a silence, an opening into which might come something very cold, something like black ice. So she adds, right away: "I mean, some day, maybe some day . . ."

Monique Proulx was born in Quebec City and lives in Montreal. She has published two short-story collections, Sans coeur et sans reproche *(Québec/Amérique, 1983) and* Les Aurores montréales *(Éditions Boréal, 1996), and two novels,* Le Sexe des étoiles *(Québec/ Amérique, 1987) and* Homme invisible à la fenêtre *(Éditions Boréal, 1993, and Éditions du Seuil, Paris), which was awarded the Signet d'Or Prize and the Québec/Paris Prize. She has also written award-winning screenplays, including adaptations of* Le Sexe des étoiles *and* Homme invisible à la fenêtre *(to be released in 1999).*

Matt Cohen has published more than twenty books, including novels, collections of short stories and poetry, and books for children. His novel Last Seen *(Knopf Canada, 1996) was shortlisted for the Governor General's Award for fiction. His most recent novel is* Elizabeth and After *(Knopf Canada, 1999). He has translated three of Monique Proulx's books,* Invisible Man at the Window *(which was nominated for the International* IMPAC *Dublin Literary Award),* Sex of the Stars, *and* Aurora Montrealis, *all published by Douglas & McIntyre.*

Mark Jarman

Burn Man

on a

Texas Porch

Men who are unhappy, like men who sleep badly, are always
proud of the fact.
— *Bertrand Russell*

At fifty everyone has the face they deserve.
— *George Orwell*

Propane slept in the tank and propane leaked while I slept,
blew the camper door off and split the tin walls where they
met like shy strangers kissing, blew the camper door like a safe
and I sprang from sleep into my new life on my feet in front of a
befuddled crowd, my new life on fire, waking to *whoosh* and
tourists' dull teenagers staring at my bent form trotting noisily in
the campground with flames living on my calves and flames
gathering and glittering on my shoulders (Cool, the teens think
secretly), smoke like nausea in my stomach and me brimming
with Catholic guilt, thinking, Now I've done it, and then thinking, Done what? What have I done?

Slept during the day with my face dreaming on a sudoral pillow near the end of the century and now my blue eyes are on fire.

I'm okay, okay, will be fine except I'm hoovering all the oxygen around me, and I'm burning like a circus poster, flames taking more and more of my shape — am I moving or are they? I am hooked into fire, I am hysterical light issuing beast noises in a world of smoke.

To run seems an answer. Wanting privacy, I run darkest dog-bane and daisies and doom palms, hearing bagpipes and whistling in my head, my fat burning like red wax, fat in the fire now. Alone — I want to do this alone, get away from the others. I can't see, bounce off trees and parked cars, noise in my ears the whole time.

The other campers catch me and push me onto a tent the blue of a Chinese rug, try to smother me, but soon the tent is melting, merrily burning with me while everyone in the world throws picnic Kool-Aid and apple juice and Lucky Lager and Gatorade and ginger ale and ice cubes and icewater from the Styrofoam coolers. Tourists burn their hands trying to put me out, *extinguish* me.

My face feels like a million white hot rivets. I am yelling and writhing. One of my shoes burns by itself on the road.

Where does my skin end and the skin of their melted tourist tent begin?

At some point in this year of our Lord, I began to refer to myself in the third person, as a double: Burn Man enters the Royal Jubilee burn unit, Burn Man enters the saline painful sea. Burn Man reads every word of the local rag despite its numerous failings, listens to MC5 on vinyl, listens to Johnny Cash's best-known ballad.

I am not dealing with this well, the doctors tell me. I am not noble. They carried me in the burnt blue tent, a litter borne from battle, from defeat on the fields of fire and disassembly lines and into three months of shaking, bandaged pain. Your muscles go

after you're burnt, but if you pump iron the skin grafts won't
stretch over the larger muscles. Skin is your cage.

Once straight, now I'm crooked. I lack a landscape that is mine.
A doctor shone a light at the blood vessels living in the back of
my retina. I saw there a trickle-down Mars in a map of my own
blood: twin *red planets* lodged in my skull.

As a nerdy kid in horn-rimmed glasses, I haunted libraries, reading
about doomed convoys in WWII, Canadian sailors burnt in the
North Atlantic or off icy Russia, Canadian sailors alive but
charred by crude oil burning all around them after U-boats from
sunny Bordeaux took down their tramp freighter or seasick cor-
vette — circular scalp of sea on fire and flaming crude races right
at them, so eager, enters them, fricassees their lungs and face and
hands, the burning ring of fire come to life on the Murmansk run.

I can't recall what happened when the burnt sailors moved back
into the non-burnt world, crawled back home above Halifax's
black snowy harbour or the sombre river firs of Red Deer, the
saltbox houses of Esquimalt.

No war here; no peace either. Only the burn ward's manic protracted
nurses sliding on waxed floors and the occasional distracted doctor with a crew of rookies whipping back the curtain, the gown,
jabbing me to see if I'm done like dinner. Sell the sizzle. Door
blows off the rented camper, spinning under sulphur sun, and I
too am sent out into red rented sunlight, your basic moaning
comet charging through a brilliantly petalled universe.

I was on a holiday in the sun, a rest from work, from tree spikers
and salmon wars, from the acting deputy minister on the cellphone fuming about river rights, water diversions, and the botched
contract with Alcan. I was getting away from it all, resting my
eyes, my brain.

I had left the cellphone sitting like a plastic banana on the
middle of my wide, Spartan desk. I was working on my tan, had
a little boat tied up dockside — plastic oars, 9 HP, runs on

gas-and-oil mix. I rested my skin on the sand-and-cigarette-butt beach. I lay down on a pillow in a tin camper. I caught fire, ran the dusty leaves and levees of our campground, alchemy and congress weighing on my mind.

Back home in my basement, a 1950s toy train circles track, its fricative steam locomotive emitting the only light in the room, swinging past where a slight woman in a parody of a nurse's uniform does something for Burn Man, for Burn Man is not burnt everywhere, still has some desires, and the woman doesn't have to touch anything else, doesn't have to see me, has almost no contact, has a verbal contract, an oral contract, say.

"Cindi: Yes, that's me in the photo!" avows the ad in the weekly paper.

Cindi can't really see me, except for the toy-train light from my perfect childhood, can't make out my grave jerry-built face. I can barely see her. She has short, dark, hennaed hair that used to be another colour. I imagine her monochrome high-school photo. Dollars to doughnuts she had long hair parted in the middle, a plain face, a trace of acne. No one sensed then that Cindi would become an escort pulled out of the paper at random and lit by a moving toy train and red-and-yellow poppies waving at a big basement window — mumbling to me, I have these nightmares, every night these nightmares.

I explained my delicate situation on the phone — what I wanted, didn't want.

Good morning, Cindi, I said. Here's my story, you let me know what you think.

She coughed. Uh, I'm cool with that, she claimed.

So Cindi and I set up our first date.

My escort dresses as the nurse in white, her hands, her crisp uniform glowing in the rec room. All of us risk something, dress as something: ape, clown, worker, Cindi, citizen, *cool with that*.

Here's an ad I did not call: "FIRE & DESIRE, Sensuous Centrefold Girls, HOT Fall Specials, $150 per hour." I didn't call that number. I don't live in the metro area. I'm not one of the chosen.

Once, maybe, I was chosen, necking on the Hopper porch, that stunning lean of a Texas woman into my arms, my innocent face, our mouths one. Perfect height for each other and I am pulled to another doomed enterprise.

The iron train never stops, lights up my decent little town, its toy workers frozen in place with grim happy faces, light opening and closing them, workers with tin shovels, forklifts, painted faces. God gives you one face and you make yourselves another. My nurse is too thin. I like a little more flesh. I wish she'd change just for me.

My slight Nurse Wretched carries my cash carelessly and heads out to buy flaps of coke, or maybe today it's points of junk for twenty or thirty dollars (her version of the stock market), scrutinizing different receptor sites to clamp onto, an alternative brand of orgasmic freeze and frisson, and she forgets about carrot juice and health food, any food, forgets about me, my eyes half-hooded like a grumpy cat's, eyes unfocused and my mouth turned down and our shared need for death without death, for petit mal, tender mercies.

Cindi is out this moment seeking a pharmacy's foreign voice and amnesiac hands and who can blame her?

Some people from my old school (*Be true to your school*) fried themselves over years and years, burned out over dissolute decades, creepy-crawling centuries.

Not me. Ten seconds and done, helter-skelter, hugger-mugger. Here's the new you handed to you in a campground like a platter of oysters. An "accelerant," as the firefighters enjoy saying, was used. Before, I could change, had nine lives. Now I have one. O, I am ill at these numbers.

In the hospital not far from the campground, I cracked jokes like delicate quail eggs: You can't fire me, I already quit. Then I quit cracking jokes. The skin grafts not what I had hoped for, didn't quite fit (*Why then, we'll fit you*). The surgeons made me look like a wharf rat, a malformed Missouri turtle, a post-mortem mummy. Years and doubt clinging to her, the nurse with the honed Andalusian face tried not to touch me too hard.

At first how positive I was! Eagerly I awaited the tray with the Jell-O and soup and fruit flies, the nurse with the determined Spanish face carrying it to my mechanical bed. I overheard her say to another nurse, No, he's not a bigot, he's a bigamist! Who? I wonder. Me? My aloof doctor? Does he have a life? If only we could duplicate the best parts and delete the rest. A complicated bed and her arms on a tray and her serious expression and unfucked-up skin and my hunger and love for a porch (*I spied a fair maiden*), for the latest version of my lunatic past.

I spill Swedish and Russian vodka into my morning coffee now (rocket fuel for Rocket Man) and, blue bubble helmet happily hiding my scarred face, fling my Burn Man motorcycle with the ape-hanger handlebars down the wet island highway, hoping for fractious friction and the thrill of metal fatigue, hoping to meet someone traumatic, a ring of fire. I re-jetted the carburetor on my bike, went to Supertrapp pipes — wanting more horses and torque, wanting the machine to scream.

Before I became Burn Man, the Texas woman kissed me at the bottom of her lit yellow stairs, porch dark as tar, dark as sky, and her cozy form fast leaning against me, disturbing the hidden powers, ersatz cowboys upstairs drinking long necks and blabbing over Gram Parsons and Emmylou (*One like you should be / miles and miles away from me*), impatient taxi waiting and waiting as we kissed. I had not expected her to kiss me, to teach me herself, her mouth and form, her warm image driven like a nail into my mind, her memory jammed on that loop of tape. (Such art of eyes I read in no books, my dark-star thoughts attending her day and night like a sacred priest with his relics.) In that instant I was changed.

Now I'm the clown outside Bed of Roses, the franchise flower shop beside the dentist's office on the road to Damascus, the road to Highway 61. On Saturdays I wave white gloves to passing cars —

dark shark-like taxis, myopic headlights like yellow cataracts — and helium balloons with smiley faces bump my wrecked and now abandoned mouth. (*Where have all the finned cars swum to?*)

Pedestrians hate me, fear me; pedestrians edge past by the bus-stop bench where the sidewalk is too narrow; pedestrians avoid my eyes, my psychedelic fright-wig. I want to reassure them: "Hey, dudes, I'm not a mime. Different union."

Burn Man must have his face covered, bases covered. I'm different animals. In the winter nights I'm the mascot Mighty Moose for our junior hockey team down at Memorial Arena. You may recall TV heads and columnists frowning on my bloody fight with the other team's Raving Raven mascot. All the skaters were scrapping, Gary Glitter's "Rock & Roll Part One" booming on the sound system, and then both goalies started throwing haymakers. I thought the mascots should also duke it out — a sense of symmetry and loyalty. I banged at the Old World armour of that raven's narrow, serious face, snapped his head back. Hoofs were my advantage.

Later we went for a drink or three and laughed about our fight, Raven and Moose at a small bar table comparing notes and bloody abrasions, hoofs and talons around each other, shop talk at the gin bin.

"Don't fuck with me," rummy beard-jammers and balls-up bean-counters snarl at every bar on the island, as if they alone decide when they get fucked over. I could advise them on that. I didn't decide to have the camper blow to shrapnel with me curled inside like a ball-turret gunner.

They hunker down at the Commercial Hotel or Blue Peter Marina or Beehive Tap or Luna Lounge thinking they're deep, thinking one ugly room is the universe's centre because they're there with flaming drinks by the lost highway, clouds hanging like clocks over the Japanese coal ships and the coast-guard chopper and across the water a distant town glittering the green colours of wine and traffic.

Like an idiot I sit and listen to their hyena patter, their thin sipping and brooding and laughing. Sometimes I'm still wearing my clown outfit while drinking my face off. Why take it off?

Friday night a man was kicked to death in this bar. In that instant, like me, he was changed, *his* memory jammed on a loop in a jar of wind, living the blues, dying.

At my front door a rhododendron sheds its scarlet bells one by one. A dark blue teacup sits on the rainy steps, looking beautiful and lonely, and there's a bird in the woods that sounds like a car trying to start.

One Sunday session a man lifted his golf shirt to show me his bowel-obstruction-surgery scar. His navel shoved four inches to the left. He didn't mind getting fucked over — in fact, he guffawed gruffly at his own wrecked gut. We're so pliant, I thought, prone to melt, to metal, to a change of heart, to lend our tongue vows.

I who loved the status quo. I'm different animals now. New careers in fire and oxygen, careering and hammering through the dolomite campground to fall on your tent, to fall on my sword. Flame created me with its sobering sound. Wake up, flame whispered in my ear like a lover, like a woman on a porch, like a muttering into cotton, a rush to action.

Here's a haiku I wrote in the hospital for the woman on the Hopper porch.

Lawyers haunt my phosphorus forest
I was bright paper burning in a glass gas-station ashtray
Owning old cars is like phoning the dead

I might have to count the syllables on that baby — I believe haikus follow some Red Chinese system. The Texas woman plays a gold-top guitar, never played for me. She sings in a band doing Gram and Emmylou's heartbreaking harmonies. You narrow the universe to one person, knowing you cannot, knowing there's a price for that.

I want to be handsome more than anything else now that it's impossible, now that I'm impossibly unhandsome, and there is a certain hesitation to the nurse's step at my door, a gathering in of her courage, a white sun outside hitting her skin.

Before I caught fire in the campground I golfed with a smoke-eater from Oregon. Mopping up after a forest fire, he told me, he found a man in full scuba gear lying on the burnt forest floor. Crushed yellow tanks, mask, black wetsuit, the whole nine yards. At first he thought it was a UFO alien or something like that. Scuba guy was dead. Recently dead.

They couldn't figure it out, how he got there. Finally some genius decided he must have been diving somewhere and a water bomber scooped him right out of the ocean and dumped startled scuba man onto the forest fire.

The smoke-eater from Oregon on the golf course swore this was a true story, but then I'm in England, a little seaside cottage in ugly Essex, my Thatcherite uncle snoring, and what starts off this American cop show on the telly? A TV detective talking about this scuba diver found in a forest fire. Then a month later a neighbour I bumped into at 7-Eleven insists it actually happened to him on Vancouver Island near Central Lake by Port Alberni. Water bomber scooped the diver out of the big lake, not the ocean. Now I don't know what to believe. Everyone keeps telling me the same false true stories.

The toy train runs and Cindi shows me a photo of herself as a little girl in a little bathing suit at the beach (*Yes, that's me in the photo!*).

Cindi cries, points at the photo: Look. I look so happy! Once she was happy. Now she has nightmares. Cindi lights a cigarette, says she wants to see real icebergs and lighthouses before she dies. Then she says, I dreamed the two of us travelled to Newfoundland together, and it was so nice and calm; not one of my nightmares. Cindi also dreamed I killed her. She says, When I die, no one will remember me, and tells me it must be her period coming on, makes her emotional. I decide mixed messages may be better than no messages at all, though I feel like the palace eunuch.

Cindi spends half her day looking for matches. Cindi struggles with her smoking, as if it takes great planning to get face to end of cigarette; she seems to move her face rather than move the cigarette. Cindi says, Nothing attracts police like one headlight. (*Do you know why I pulled you over?*)

At the tavern by the rushing river, men said things to me in my clown suit, my eunuch suit, thinking they were funny. They were deep. The waitress knew me from my previous life, gave me red quarters for the jukebox. She trusted my taste, trusted me once at her apartment. She wore deliberately ugly plaid pants and her wise face looked just like the Statue of Liberty's. With the bar's red quarters I plugged honky-tonk and swing B-sides only. The B-sides rang out, sang their night code to me alone: Texas, kiss, lit stairs, a world changed.

The old boys in the Commercial Hotel had been drinking porch-climber, watered-down shots of hooch, emptying their pants pockets, their bristle heads.

We watched a man kicked directly to death. Strangely, it was an off-duty police officer who had stopped another officer for drinking and driving and refused to let him off. The drunk driver was suspended from the force, from his life. Then guess who bumps into who at the wrong bar?

The night alive with animals, the whole middle-class group taking some joy in the royal beating, displaying longing, bug-house excitement, wanting to get their feet in like mules kicking, believing it the right thing to do. He was struggling. I don't think they meant to kill the policeman with their feet, but it was a giddy murder, a toy in blood. They busted his head and eyes and busted his ribs and arms and kidney and returned to their drinks, expecting him to resurrect himself of his own power with his swollen brain and internal bleeding. Then the ambulance attempting to dispense miracles, a syringe quivering into muscle. It was fast. I stood fast. I stood shaking in my suffocating clown suit and they returned to their drinks and sweaty hyena hollering, their "Don't fuck with me, Jack," their legions and lesions and lessons and their memories of twitching creations face down in the parking lots of our nation.

I can wait. Wait until they pass out, then punch a small hole in the drywall under the electrical panel and pour in kerosene, my accelerant du jour. I will run before the doors blow off.

Nothing happens, though, because I feel immediately moronic and melodramatic, dial 911 outside, and firefighters are on top of it lickety-split. The doors don't blow, their faces don't fry or turn to wax. I fly away on my rare Indian motorcycle with a transplanted shovelhead engine and Screamin' Eagle calibration kit. No one new joins my Burn Man Club. Burn Man is alive and the unyielding moral policeman is dead, his family in dark glasses at the bright graveyard.

O, how our sun smiled on me, breezes blew softly in the dappled leaves over the low-rent beach and my head touching a cool pillow. I napped and the propane fire snapped my skin, remapped me. I twisted and travelled in beautiful lost towns and low registers of postmodern western wind from the sand hills of Saskatchewan.

I am a product of light, of hope.

I still have that shy desire for the right fire to twist me back just as easily to what was: to milky youth and a mysterious person falling towards me on a Texas porch with her tongue rearranging hope in my mouth. Under oak trees by the river the Texas woman put words in my mouth, secret words pushed in my mouth like a harmonica. *Her temple fayre is built within my mind.* Perhaps God will have mercy on me in my new exile.

The right fire. Doesn't that make sense?

Like corny cartoons and television shows — amnesia victim loses memory from blow to head, but a second blow makes it right, fixes it all right up, no matter what.

Instead I rise Saturday a.m. with TV cartoons, set up a supper-time date with Cindi, climb inside my mask and clown suit like a scuba diver, like Iago on Prozac. For what seems a fucking century, we wave white gloves at you (*Drowning, not waving*), wave at blind drivers passing Bed of Roses and the helium balloons — gorgeous ivory moons and red planets *bump-bumping* my skin, trying to enter the hide of Burn Man's teeming serious face, trying to push past something difficult and lewd.

Ours really is an amazing world. Tristan falls in love on a Hopper porch, but Isolde loses faith in a Safeway parking lot, Isolde takes the magic bell off the dog. And a famous scuba diver rockets like a lost dark god into smoking stands of Douglas fir, into black chimneys burning.

Mark Jarman has published a novel, Salvage King, Ya! *a herky-jerky picaresque (Anvil Press, 1997), and two short-story collections,* Dancing Nightly in the Tavern *(Press Porcépic, 1984) and* New Orleans Is Sinking *(Oberon Press, 1998). His stories have been shortlisted for the Journey Prize, the National Magazine Award, the Western Magazine Award, and the Pushcart Prize Anthology, and were included in the 1997 and 1998 editions of* Best Canadian Stories *(Oberon). He is the editor of the short-story collection* Ounce of Cure: Alcohol in the Canadian Short Story *(Beach Holme Publishers, 1992). In 1998 he won the Playwrights' Union of Canada's International Monologue Competition.*

Lynn Coady

PLAY THE
MONSTER
BLIND

Drinking

The father was drinking again, in celebration. John said he remembered being three, tooling around town in the green station wagon with fake wood on the sides, watching his father drink. He would drink and visit his friends, at their homes or at the boxing club. He would pull into the driveway, pause to smile at John, take a quick couple of swallows before reaching over to unbuckle the boy. And he would hoist his young son inside to show him off, both of them pink-cheeked. John showed her a picture of himself then, his little hands tied inside a pair of enormous boxing gloves, his father perched behind him, holding them up to take aim at a smiling, sweaty man in trunks.

John was strapping then, and he was strapping now. One of the first things the father told her was that they used to have to pin John into three layers of diapers, he was such a big eater. It was obvious he and the old man were close. The second evening after she and John arrived, she stayed inside doing dishes with the

mother and saw the two of them sitting out in plastic chairs on
the lawn facing the shed with rums in hand. The mother said,
"That should keep him happy for a while," and the plastic chairs
sagged and quivered from the weight of men. The father was built
all of hard, stubborn fat, but John was just big. They sat quietly
torturing their lawn chairs together. John had told her he used to
be fat. He was very sensitive about it. In high school he stopped
eating and started taking handfuls of vitamins, which made him
thin and absent-minded, but his mother stopped buying them
and he had no choice but to go back to eating. In university he
just gave in to everything and ate and drank until he ballooned.
Now he was approximately in the middle, a big man with a thick
beard. When he was fourteen, his father had him collecting UI
for all the dishwashing he had done at the family restaurant,
because the workers didn't know any better from the size of him.
She had thought, when she met John, that he looked like a
lumberjack. He wore plaid shirts and workboots whenever she
saw him in class, not because it was fashionable, and not fashion-
ably, but because it was what he wore. She learned where he was
from and imagined they all must dress like that, that it must be
a very welcoming place, rustic and simple and safe, like John
himself.

When his sister showed up, pasty and in leather pants despite
the August swelter, the first thing she said to him was, "Hey,
you fat shit." Bethany knew that they had not seen each other
in a couple of years. He reached over and grabbed one of the
sister's wrists. Her knees buckled at once and effortlessly he
turned her around, already sinking. Then he grabbed the other
wrist and held them together in one large paw while guiding her
face first to the kitchen floor, using her wrists as a sort of steering
apparatus. Then he sat on her.

"Pardon?" he kept saying.

"You fat bastard."

The father sat nearby, laughing. The mother saying, "Johnny,
Johnny, Johnny, now," as she tried to move around them to the

stove. Bethany and the sister were exactly the same age. She felt she should have something to say to her.

When the brother arrived, he at once began to beat and contort the sister in the same way, as if this were some sort of family ritual. She railed at him as he pulled her feet up behind her to meet her shoulders. While John just used the sheer force of his bulk and his size, Hugh, smaller and wiry, was a dabbler in the martial arts. He said he used to box, like his father, but got bored with all the rules. Now he was interested in something called shoot fighting, which scarcely had any rules at all. He knew all sorts of different holds and manoeuvres, some of which he demonstrated on the sister for them. When he was finished — Ann yanking herself away, red-faced and hair awry and staggering towards the kitchen for a beer — he darted at John, head down and fists up. John responded in the way Bethany had seen him do at bars whenever drunken men, maddened by his size, ran at him. The strategy was to reach out his big hands and simply hold the opponents at bay until they got tired and embarrassed.

Bethany thought of herself as an easygoing person and tried not to be nervous, but she and John were going to get married, and she knew that the family was striving to be civil in a way they were not used to. John kept cuffing his sister in the head whenever she said "goddamn" or "cocksucker" and quietly saying: "Dad," when the father did the same. Bethany and the sister tried and tried to talk to each other, bringing up woman things like belts and shampoo. She knew that the sister worked in theatre in Halifax and lived with a man who was thirty-five, and everyone was disappointed in her but hoped she would soon turn her life around. It was touching the way the family spoke of Ann when she was out of the room. The father, overwhelming his armchair, ponderously clinking his ice cubes and turning to John.

"What do you think, me boy?"

"Well, who knows, boy."

"She's getting by," the mother would say.

"But for how long?"

"We'll talk to her at some point," John promised. The father was always turning to John and waiting to hear the right thing, and John always seemed to know what it was.

Hugh and Ann presented themselves as allies, of sorts, against John's authority, even though they fought with one another more furiously than they did with him. They rolled around the living room, knocking over lamps and bothering the mother's nerves as she complained from the kitchen, and John would come in and bark at them to smarten up. They would call him a big fat fruit and he would sit on them both, the sister on the very bottom of the pile. At one point she looked up at Bethany, blood vessels throbbing to burst in her face, and squeaked, "Can't you control him?" Which Bethany lightly laughed at.

When the parents went to bed, the four of them sat around the table drinking rum. She'd never had so much rum in her life. She liked spritzers, which John said were for pussies. John tried to talk to his brother and sister about the father. How the drinking bothered him.

"It keeps him in good cheer," said Ann.

"You two don't remember how he used to get. I remember how he used to get."

"Maybe he's too old to get that way now."

"It bothers Mum's nerves."

"I think he's been dandy," said Ann.

"Just because he's not yelling at you all the time doesn't necessarily make it fine and dandy."

"I disagree," said Ann.

Hugh said nothing, waiting for the conversation to turn to sports or parties. Bethany noticed how jolly Ann looked when she said she disagreed with John. She thought, once or twice, that John might grab his sister's head and slam it into the table a couple of times. Ann looked capable of disagreeing with John in her sleep.

Hugh never seemed to bother getting into a conversation with his brother. He merely lurked in corners, behind chairs, waiting for an opportunity to get him in a paralyzer hold, but John would always shrug him off like a summer jacket. Hugh showed some of his holds to Ann, who in turn tried them out on her mother, but the mother complained loudly about her arthritis.

"Hugh said they're not supposed to hurt — they just immobilize," the sister protested, chin digging into the mother's head.

"Well, they do. Get away before I clout you."

Ann released her mother with much reluctance, sorry to lose the fleeting power. The mother had just stood there politely the whole time. She probably could have broken out of it if she had wanted to. Like everyone else in the family, she was bigger than Ann.

Ann wore combat boots with her sundress. The father made fun of them, and the mother wanted to know if her feet didn't get overheated. Bethany felt sorry for Ann, because when they all were sitting around the picnic table eating lobster, Ann couldn't open hers but wouldn't ask any of them for help. Bethany finally passed her a cracking utensil under the table.

"I never used to eat lobster until last year," Ann explained. "It grossed me out. Then I decided I want to be the kind of person who'll eat anything she's given."

"She won't eat the pickled alewives," said the father through a mouthful of roe.

"Don't count as food," said Ann, sullen. Hugh was sneaking up behind her with a lobster that had not yet been boiled alive.

Boxing

They would pick up the uncle and the bunch of them, some in the father's car and some in John's, were going to tour around the trail, staying in cabins and eating in restaurants and swimming at beaches. This was the father's gift. John told her that doing it was important to him and she would have to have fun. She was surprised he would put it this way, because she was looking forward to seeing the island. She was worried about being in the car with the father, however. At the airport after they arrived, he made them stop at the duty-free liquor store and purchased an armload of tiny bottles of Crown Royal. Once they were in the car, he handed one to each of them and said: "Slug 'er back, you two. The vacation has officially begun." Bethany had never drunk straight whisky in her life and had no idea how to respond. She looked at John for help and he took the bottle from her and dropped it into her purse.

"Can't be into this on the road, boy," he said smiling and blinking ahead of him.

"Ach, I'd need fifty or so of these before anything good started happenin'."

"Let me drive, boy."

"No, we can't have you drinkin' and drivin'."

"I don't need to drink."

After scant argument, the father declared, "Betty, it's just you and me!" turning around in his seat to beam at her. "My God," he added, "did you down yours already? Well, good boy yourself."

So the father sat in the backseat with her the whole way, making jokes that John was their chauffeur and kicking his seat and telling him to step on it while Bethany watched the innumerable veins road-mapping his nose and cheeks begin to glow as if filling up with lava. She was terrified of everything. They were on a stretch of road where one sign after another read things like: "Jesus Is Coming!" "Prepare Thyself!" "Repent! Saith the Lord."

All the way to the house, he told her about boxing. He rhymed off one boxer after another, not famous boxers like Muhammad Ali, but ones from, as he said, nearby. Men with names like Sailor Dave and Fisher MacPhee and Ronnie the Dago. He said he had met more than a few of these fellows in the ring, and could tell her something about the style of each if she was interested. The Dago, for example, was a smart fighter, a thinking fighter. Always went in with some kind of strategy. Archie the Rigger, however, had nothing going for him but a hard head and had the record to prove it. Fisher was the prettiest of fighters, floated on air. Sailor Dave was like a goddamned bull, just an ox. The father went on and on in this vein. He handed one little bottle after another to her, so that when they finally got out of the car, her purse clinked and sloshed.

"Johnny," the old man pronounced, holding the kitchen door open for her. "This is a goddamned good girl right here." He went to bed almost at once, and so they sat up and had cornflakes with the mother.

The sister very much admired Bethany's luggage as they loaded up the car. She marvelled at it, it was so nice, so much that Bethany was embarrassed. John intuited this and kept making jokes that some people had moved beyond Glad bags and cardboard.

"It would never even occur to me to have bags like that," Ann persisted, and finally John told her to shut the hell up and she told him to kiss her rosy red arse and he strode over to her and picked her up and placed her, barely able to squirm, in the trunk of the car and then held the hood down, not completely closed, until Bethany told him for Pete's sake to let her out of there, and Ann, who throughout the performance had not made a sound, flung one bare leg out and then the other and hopped away like a crow. Hugh stood by looking pensive, as if he wished he had thought of it first.

Hugh himself was a strange one, because although he had gone to university, he spoke with an insanely nuanced accent that was nothing like the rest of the family's, and he wore an Expos cap just perched on the top of his head, but when she asked him what he did for a living, he replied that when he was not "partying his hole out," he worked with computers. Bethany asked John about it later on and he said, "Oh, yah. He's the brain. Straight A's. Could have done anything he wanted." What he chose to do was teach courses at the vocational school and help people around town with their systems. He didn't go anywhere after university because, he said, all his friends were here. "Friends're pack a retards," John once remarked. And after a few days Bethany began to realize that Hugh didn't own any shirts except T-shirts with sayings on them. He sat around in T-shirts that said things like: "I'd rather push a Ford than drive a Chevy," and "It's not how deep you fish, it's how you wiggle your worm!"

After the mother, the uncle was the one she felt most comfortable with. They picked him up at the group home where he stayed in Port Hastings the night before the trip. Bethany knew in advance that he was Mentally Handicapped, and having this foreknowledge made her calm about meeting him, far less nervous than she had been about the rest. It was good to have a label, something her mind could scrutinize. It was good to have an idea what to expect.

Lachie was his name, and she found him delightful. He reached out one hand and wished her merry Christmas as she shook it, and then he extended the other to wish her happy Easter. He puttered away, then, announcing: "There now! He knows Betty!" to all present. For the rest of the evening he sat in a chair in the corner of the living room and raised his eyes every once in a while to ask if it was time for cornflakes. Bethany felt at home in the chair beside him. Now and again he would show her the fingers of his right hand to let her know that he'd been nibbling at the nails. Apparently this was a great pastime of his, much frowned upon by the rest of the family.

"Breaks his nails," he remarked more than once.

"Tch. Isn't that terrible," Bethany answered.

Lachie would smile back and reach over quickly to poke her in the cheek with a ragged fingertip before reclining again.

"You kick his arse if you catch him at that!" the sister yelled from across the room. Lachie plunging both hands into the tucks of his armchair and closing his eyes.

The fat hung off Lachie in an unpleasant sort of way, like it wasn't quite a part of him, something that had to be strapped on in the morning. John said that his grandmother had spoiled him from birth, heaping his plate and feeding him entire pies, and

Lachie had never done anything but follow a few cows around on the farm for exercise. Now he had arthritis in his knees and he could hardly walk any more. John said that was how he would be if he let himself go, how would she like that? He said it was in the genes.

"Your sister's a bone rack," Bethany pointed out, "and she looks more like your uncle than you do."

"She had the anorexia all through high school," John explained, dismissive and also somewhat grudging. "Sees the nutritionist once a week."

"All she talks about is eating," Bethany said.

"I know."

"What about Hugh?"

"Works out every day," John said with a bit of contempt, because anyone could see this with one look at the chest beneath the T-shirt slogans.

At the dinner table the father congratulated Bethany for her fine appetite, unaware that she was eating so much only because she was afraid of offending him.

"Get Betty some more potatoes, Annie. Jesus Christ, she's wasting before our eyes."

"Do you want more potatoes, Betsy?"

"Ummm . . . sure."

"She doesn't want any more, Dad."

"She just said she did, for the love of God!"

"Quit forcing food down the woman's throat."

"Well, Jesus Christ, I'll get her the potatoes if you're not up to the challenge," said the father, practically spreading himself across the table.

"No, no, no! I can get them for myself!" Bethany exclaimed, horror-struck.

"There now," the father said, emptying a greyish steaming mound out of a Corningware dish and onto her plate. "Some of us know how to be civil to a guest."

"You're making her sick," said Ann.

Bethany was a big eater most of the time, however, and went to bed in only slight discomfort, having eschewed the evening's cornflakes ritual. She asked John if he thought she needed to lose weight and he said who gave a shit one way or another. He would not have asked her to marry him if he thought she was a tub of lard. It was being around Ann and the mother that made her feel that way. The mother said having her "nerves on the go" all the time was what kept her skinny, and Ann, meal-obsessed, hopped about the kitchen a pale crow, swallowing the occasional morsel. John had said that he and Hugh had teased her about being fat all throughout their childhood. Now John would wrap a hand around one of her thighs whenever she passed by and squeeze, feeling for meat. "Get in the kitchen and eat a tub of ice cream or something, ya stick," he'd say, thinking he was being kind. And Ann would smile as if she was thinking it too.

Swimming

Lachie couldn't get his clothes off fast enough. Scarcely had she put the picnic cooler down than his shirt was in a heap on the sand and rolls of white flesh sprouting the coarsest of black hairs gave salute to the sun and the ocean. The sight of so much exposed skin caused her to reach instinctively for a bottle of sunscreen. She tried to hand it to him, but the uncle was busy unbuckling his pants and muttered, "No, you put it on me. He can't get his pants, can't get them." She waited a moment to see if any of the family would come down the path before finally squirting a little onto her fingertips and trying to apply some to Uncle Lachie's shoulders, but he had the pants around his ankles and staggered out of her reach. Then he regained himself, muttering about the ocean, and yanked off his swimming trunks on top of everything else. Bethany said calmly to the uncle, "Put on your trunks, Uncle Lachie. You need to put your trunks back on."

Lachie protested vigorously for a good minute or so. Bethany thought it strange that he did not actually defy her outright, trundling away, a white blur against the blue sky like a walking snowman. Finally she just said: "You can't go swimming without your swim trunks, Uncle Lachie," like it was the most logical thing in the world, and he gazed meditatively down at the shorts for a bit before hauling them back up about his hips and plunging towards the Atlantic. Bethany wished there had been someone around to witness the crisis and her unexpected competence. At that moment, Ann appeared. Struggling with a cooler and in a polka-dot bathing suit with moulded bra cups that must have belonged to the mother in 1968. She lingered beside Bethany for the briefest of moments before taking in the sight of Lachie. White like a plump cloud had fallen directly out of the sky and now bobbed free and independent with the waves.

"Lord lifting Antichrist, he'll fry like a pork rind!" she hollered, seizing the sunscreen out of Bethany's hand and giving chase. Bethany could see that he was seated up to his belly now, and seemed to be looking down at the point where the water divided him up.

Eating

The father drank too much at dinner and made the waitress cry. She wouldn't come back to the table, and John had to get up and walk across the restaurant and talk to her and talk to the manager. She watched him standing there with them, grinning under his beard, gesturing in an open and accepting sort of way with his enormous hands. The girl was being charmed by him, and the manager was being charmed by him in a different manner. She knew how he was charming the waitress, because she had been charmed like that too. How a big man like that could grin so open-handed and vulnerable. He could take your head between those two hands and pop it like a zit, but he was decent enough not to do that, not to even remind you that he could. Everything about his demeanour said: I am just a great big guy with a drunk dad and a new fiancée and nobody wants to feel like this, so let's not. It was brave of him. It was exactly what made him so good.

Pretty soon the girl was laughing with tears still in her eyes and John was laughing and picking her up from the ground with a bear hug that made her shriek and laugh even harder. She could not have been more than seventeen, and was in love now. He sauntered back to the table, his mouth pursed in a comical sort of way.

"A little thing out there called PR," he said to his pink, smirking father.

"A little fucking thing called incompetence in the workforce," the dad shot back. "If one of my girls had ever pulled any of that kind of shit back when I was running the Bluenoser — "

"Boy, boy," said John. "Jeez, eh?" He went on making inarticulate noises of comfort and reprimand. The father made noises of declining outrage and increasing shame, as his awareness of the situation grew. But she could see that he wasn't going to acknowledge it, blustering about incompetence all throughout dessert and, while waiting for the bill, about teenage girls with earrings in their noses instead of their ears, where God intended them. Blustering all the while but now drinking out of his water glass instead of the other one, which was poised beside the wreckage of his meal. Bethany could tell he hoped to bluster until he was blustering on a different topic, one that made everyone more comfortable and jovial. Blustering wittily and cheerfully, no longer blustering at all — a benevolent father regaling the family with priceless and innumerable anecdotes from a rich and varied life.

The sister puked for what seemed like hours. Bethany in an agony because she thought she should go and see if she was sick, but on the other hand, John had said she used to be anorexic, and she knew that this was what anorexics sometimes did after big meals. It was an impossible situation. It was almost dawn, and she and John and the sister had made a deal — that Bethany would sleep with John for a little before slipping through the bathroom that joined their rooms and crawling into Ann's bed. This being the arrangement the parents would be expecting when they arrived from the other cabin to make breakfast. But now it was getting light and Ann was still in there, puking away, and Bethany was in an impossible situation. John snored.

Lying there angry, it took Bethany a couple of seconds to realize that the retching echoes from the bathroom had ceased. The bedroom was now almost fully illuminated, and she flung the blankets away, completely awake, deciding she didn't care if Ann knew she had heard her puking or not. When Bethany didn't get a good night's sleep, it did terrible things to her body. It gave her indigestion, made her cranky and intolerant, red-eyed and snippy. She had to catch a good couple of hours in Ann's bed before the parents stormed in wanting to take pictures and see them splashing around in canoes.

"Uhg," said Ann as Bethany crawled in beside her.

"Are you okay?"

"The dreams I was having!"

Bethany wasn't going to pretend she was stupid. "But you were throwing up, Ann."

"Before I was throwing up," Ann said. "Sick dreams. It has to have been the scallops. Sometimes my stomach doesn't welcome the shellfish."

"Hm," said Bethany, in a way she hoped sounded as if the explanation had been accepted and the incident forgotten about in almost the same moment.

"Ohg," moaned Ann some moments later. "Did you ever dream that you were where you were?"

"I don't know what you mean," Bethany said around a yawn.

"You're not supposed to dream about being where you are. It's not natural. I'm not supposed to be dreaming about being in this cabin with all of you. In my grandmother's house. Or in school, or in Halifax or something, somewhere I've never even been. Nobody dreams literally, for Christ's sake."

"What were we doing?"

"Oh, God, it was horrible. We were just doing all the things we've been doing all along," Ann moaned. She was snoring not five seconds later.

Driving

They drove another few miles, on their way to still more rented cottages, which the father made a point of repeating all through breakfast he hoped would be much more amenable than the ones they had spent the previous night in.

"No TV, no radio," he kept saying. "Nothing but four walls and a goddamn bed. I can haul a cot into the closet at home, if that's what I want. Charge people fifty bucks a night to use it."

"It's a cabin, boy," John said. "You're supposed to sit on the porch and watch the sunset. What do you need a TV for?"

"It's the principle of the thing. What if it rains? What if there's a ball game? Beds not fit to piss on — I can see plain as day that poor Betty didn't get a moment's sleep. I should have complained. I should have complained at that goddamn restaurant, and I should've complained the moment we showed up here. Reservations two jeezly months in advance and this is the best they can give us."

"You did complain at the restaurant," Ann reminded him, looking around to confirm that no one else was going to do it. "Don't you remember?"

"To the manager, not to that young one. Poor girl didn't know what I was talking about."

"You might have thought about that before you called her a useless twat."

"Well, goddamnit, I was mad!"

"Leave it now, Ann," said John. Bethany was beginning to see that this was the way they commenced most mornings. John saw her understanding this.

"All I wanted," rumbled the father, "was a good dry chip.

That's all I wanted. What do they bring me? Potato wedges! What the Jesus? Greasy old potato wedges with some kind of crap sprinkled all over them. That's not chips. I asked for chips. I just wanted a good dry chip! Not that gourmet crap swimming in Christ knows what."

"Well, it's done with now."

"Well, I'm not letting them get away with that shit."

"Good, then, boy."

"You have to let them know, Johnny. You can't just let them keep on with that kind of shoddy service."

"All right."

"You have to remind them — I'm the customer. I'm payin' your salary. You need me. I don't need you." The father seemed to whisper to himself for an instant, as if imagining some outlandish response, and then turned to Bethany and smiled suddenly. "You just ignore me, Betty," he said. "John here's the family dip-lo-mat. We'd get kicked outta where-all we went if the dip-lo-mat wasn't around."

"I guess to God," said John.

"I'm just an old boxer," said the father, manoeuvring his bulk from the confines of their picnic table. "I hit people. Don't take mucha the dip-lo-mat for that." He chuckled, moving off to examine the workmanship of the cabin's front step. Intermittently they heard quiet exclamations of disgust from his direction as they cleared away the breakfast things.

He wanted John and Bethany to ride with him to Dingwall because he felt as if he wasn't spending enough time with them. He told the mother to take the car with the other two. The mother announced that she would have to drive, then, because Hugh was a maniac and Ann had always been too stubborn to learn, and they couldn't expect her to go for very long because her nerves were bad. The three of them chewed at each other for a bit, but Bethany got the feeling that they were pleased to have been thrown together — a day off from the father's gruff bullying and the more genuine authority of John. Lachie didn't care either way.

"Come on, come on, come on," he kept saying, watching them load the baggage. "Ding Dong. Going Ding Dong now."

They stopped at a look-out point, and Bethany climbed out of the car before the rest. In every direction she turned, she could see nothing but dark, fuzzy mountains. The ever-present ocean was nowhere in sight, and it disoriented her. She didn't know if this was beautiful or not. The green mounds sloped upward uninsistently, and then came together in dark, obscene valleys that reminded her of the creases in a woman's flesh — her own. Reminded her of sitting naked and looking down at the spot where her stomach protruded slightly over her thighs. She didn't like how these low mountains were everywhere, their dark rolling motion completely uninterrupted by a view of water or patches of field. John suddenly moved past her and jumped up onto the wooden railing, framing himself against them.

"Get down. John, get down. Get down now," she said.

"What? Take my picture!"

"Get down," she hissed, queasy at the sight of him poised there, ready to disappear into one of the dark creases. Meanwhile, Lachie refused to get out of the car to look. She could hear the father's persistent cursing as he tried to yank him by the hand, then coming around to the other side of the car and trying to shove him out the opposite door. Lachie remained where he was, however, unmoved and only a little irritated with the father's proddings. All he wanted to do was go, to drive in the car. "Come on, come on, come on," he said, and "No, no, no." With their arms around each other, Bethany and John watched him easily resist the father. Bethany was thinking that John could probably go over there and lift him out, but she hoped that he wouldn't. By this time the father was laughing with frustration. He said that they were going to stay there and see the view and Lachie could drive the friggin' car to Ding Dong all by himself if he wanted to go so badly.

The rest of the trip, the father told her the story of Archie "Fisher" Dale, a fine boxer he knew out of the Miramichi, "who some people called Tiny because he was such a little fella — in fact, his manager had wanted to bill him as Tiny Dale, but Archie would have none of it. In actual fact, he wasn't all that small — five-six — but smaller than what you'd usually see hanging out at the boxing clubs and what have you. Well, this one — you wouldn't find yourself taking him too, too seriously to look at him — I mean, some of the fellas you'd see at those places were like Johnny here, great big bastards, and a lot of them figured they could fight simply by virtue of the fact that they were bigger than anybody else. But that's not always the case, you know, and there's nothing more pathetic than seeing some big lumbering bastard getting all tangled up in his own legs trying to keep up with some little lightning rod like Fisher himself, who lands you a good right cross before you even see him in front of you."

Because, except for height and mass, this little fella had it all. John's father had never seen a fighter so well equipped for greatness. He fought single-mindedly. He often appeared vicious, but he never actually got angry — to get angry at your opponent was just foolishness, the quickest way to spot an amateur. He was fast, he was graceful, he had arms like steel cords lashed together, but for all that grace he was tough. You could just hit him. He didn't care. John's father and Fisher Dale would go drinking downtown in Halifax, and after downing a few, the little prick would just grin at him with his gap-filled mouth and say, "Hit me, John Neil. Hit me a good one, now." Well, John's father was never one to oblige in this respect, but there would always be one or two fellas nearby just chompin' at the bit to take a poke at Fisher Dale. You couldn't drop him. You just could not drop him. He'd weave and teeter, blood pouring out of his mouth, and by Jesus that grin would never leave his face. "Hit me again, why don'tcha?" was all he'd say.

"What would he do that for?" Bethany asked, genuinely mystified.

"Because," John's father told her with very precise enunciation, to give the statement weight, "Fisher was crazy as mine and your

arse put together. Everywhere except the ring. He was Albert jesus
jesus Einstein in the ring. The drinking, you know. What it does
to some people. Archie Dale was such a one.

"This is the saddest story I know," the father reflected, after
having paused for some time. "Now that I think of it. What that
boy couldn't have done. And he was one of the hardest working
in them days too. The stamina. Fight in Halifax one night, under
one name, hop on the train right after for one in Yarmouth or
somewhere, callin' himself Wildman Dale or some such thing.
You could fight only a certain number of matches in them days if
you wanted to keep your licence, but the more ambitious and
greedy of the bunch — Dale was both — would just hop from
town to town, fighting under different names. Sometimes he'd go
ten, fifteen fights a week. Outlandish, if you knew anything about
the circuit. I could never go more than five.

"You know, the only time he had the boozin' under control was
when he was fighting that way — hopping from town to town,
sometimes going two a night. Kept him busy, kept him focused.
See he wasn't the type a fella could just fight a couple times a week
and then head down to the tavern for a couple of beers with his
buddies waiting for his manager to call about the next one. It was
all or nothing with Dale. That was his problem right there. If
he stopped fighting, he started drinking; it had to be one or the
other. Manager shoulda just kept putting him up against one guy
after another till he dropped dead of a brain clot — least he
wouldn't've ended up a drunken failure."

"What happened?"

"What happened was that he got caught; they found out he was
fighting illegally like that, and he got his licence suspended. And
howls just went up all across the country, you know, with the
gamblers and everything, because the boy was on a streak — he
was winning every match he fought. He'd pounded me long ago,
I don't mind telling you, not to mention pretty near every other
fella on the circuit, and his manager was talking about taking him
over to the States. But that was that — suspension for a month."

"That's not so bad."

"Ach, no. Most boys'd take their winnings and go off on a tear. Well, that's what he meant to do at first, but, like I said, with Dale it was all or nothing. I went downtown with him the one night, we drank ourselves stupid, and the last I seen of him" — John's father began to heave and shake at this memory —"he was chasin' a cop down Gottingen Street at four in the morning. He was chasing the cop! Somehow he got his nightstick away from him, and he was chasing him down the street waving it around his head like a lasso! Cop hollerin' to beat hell."

"So what happened to him?"

"That happened to him. Like I said, it was the last of him I seen. Never fought again, I can guarantee you that much. Disappeared into the night."

"You saw him again, Dad," John's voice came from the driver's seat. It was as if he was repeating something by rote.

"Oh, yes, wait now, I did see him again. Eight or so years later, in Inverness of all places, walking home from a square dance. This little frigger in a trench coat shuffling towards me with great deliberation, you know? I didn't know who it was, some queer or something, I was getting ready to pop him. Well, isn't it Fisher Dale. 'John Neil!' he shouts. 'Whad'llya have?' Then he yanks something from the pocket of his trench coat" — the father began to act out the role of Fisher Dale now—" 'A little puck a whiskey? Or' " — reaching into his other pocket with the opposite hand — " 'a little puck a rum?' " The father shook and heaved and gasped. He repeated the gesture a couple of times for effect, the yanking of one bottle out of the right-hand pocket upon the word *puck*, and then another from out of the left. It was like Lachie wishing her merry Christmas and happy Easter in succession.

"This is all he has to tell me after eight years," John's father finished, jovial and refreshed from the story's telling. "Ah — Jesus, though. Lord save us if it wasn't a shameful waste of a beautiful fighter. Just a beautiful little fighter."

John told her later that he told that story to everyone. It was

his favourite story. She would hear it a hundred more times in the
upcoming years, he said. In the meantime, the road rose and sank
like a sea serpent's tail. Every so often they would come around a
craggy bend, after miles of nothing but the low, fuzzy mountains,
and all of a sudden it would seem as if the whole of the Atlantic
Ocean was glittering before them, so big it eclipsed even the sky.
And then the road would sink lower and lower imperceptibly,
until they were trundling through some infinitesimal community and she'd see grey, half-demolished barns with black letters
spelling CLAMS painted across the roofs and little stores with
Pepsi-Cola signs from the early seventies in the windows, the red
in the logo faded to pink and the blue now a sick green. She went
into one of them to get lemonade and ice cream bars for everybody, and the woman behind the counter was not nearly as
friendly as Bethany had been expecting. The woman had a little
girl sitting with her back there, and every time the little girl did
something other than just sit there the woman would bark,
"Whad I tell ya? Whad I tell ya?" at her — oblivious to Bethany's
presence — so the little girl would place her hands at her sides
and arrange her legs and sit chewing on her lips until the fact of
being a child got the better of her and she would once again reach
for something with absent-minded curiosity. Then the woman
would bark again.

"You've got a lovely place here," said Bethany, and the woman
regarded her with terror. She thought Bethany was talking about
the store, and not the island, and therefore must be insane. She
added, "This is my first visit," to make it more clear. The woman
looked down at the little girl, as if hoping to find her trespassing
again so that she could yell at her and ignore Bethany. But the
girl was being good, so the woman ignored Bethany anyway, a
confused and queasy look taking over her ruddy, mean face. "Six
sevenny five, wha?" she said. Bethany gave her a five and a two,
hoping she had understood correctly. She gathered up her ice
cream bars without asking for a bag and staggered out the door
and into the sunshine, cowbells clunking rude music behind her.

Fighting

She ate barbecued baloney for the first time in her life. John was trying to convince her it was a delicacy of the area as he slathered Kraft sauce onto it, splattering the coals. She kept telling him in a low voice not to lie to her, to quit lying to her. She made her voice low because if he was telling the truth, she didn't want the rest of the family to know she hadn't believed it.

"Listen here," he kept saying. "You haven't lived until you've scarfed a good feed of barbecued baloney."

"Shut up," she said, giggling and looking around. "Liar." She saw that Ann was nearby, sprawled in a sunchair and drinking a beer. She had probably heard everything, and so Bethany took a chance and looked seriously at her for confirmation. Ann smiled and raised her eyes to heaven. She turned back to John.

"I knew you were lying!"

"What?"

"Ann says you're lying."

"Ann's not gonna get her share of barbecued baloney."

"Quit teasing the woman," said Ann. "You're always teasing her. How long do you think she'll put up with it before she kicks your arse?"

Bethany smiled at Ann. They were getting somewhere. Most of the time the sister had seemed too high-strung even to talk to, but Ann had started taking long, slow draughts of beer early in the afternoon, and now her movements were easy and fluid — nothing of the crow remained. She had been in the sunchair most of the afternoon, letting the sun burn it out of her while the rest of them played badminton and lawn darts. Her smiles became slow and amused instead of fleeting and anguished. Bethany sat on the grass beside her every once in a while to drink a beer of her own, and together they would holler insults at John about whatever he happened to be doing at that moment. Hugh came over and capsized the chair at one point, but Ann simply rolled away from it and fell asleep a few feet off in the grass.

They must have eaten the red, charred flesh of every beast imaginable that evening, and the lot of them sat exhausted in chairs they had pulled up around Ann's chair as if she had become some sort of axis during the afternoon. The father's face was the same colour as the meat they'd consumed, and bloated, and he blinked constantly as if a breeze was blowing directly into his eyes. While Ann had relaxed herself with slow, sunny draughts of beer, the father had done the exact opposite — disappearing without a word at steady intervals throughout the day to shoot rum in the kitchenette, the imperative of it seeming to make him more and more anxious. She knew he was doing that, because she had stupidly kept asking, "Where's your father got to? Isn't it your father's turn? Where's your father?" until John finally had to tell her. He said this was the only way the father had ever learned to drink — like a teenager taking swigs at a dance. He'd never sipped a cocktail in his life, much less enjoyed a beer during a fishing trip or something. John said that his father had never understood the purpose of beer. He didn't see the point of an alcoholic beverage with so little alcohol in it. Why something should take so long to do what it was intended to do.

"He's an alcoholic," said Bethany, epiphanic. They were walking along the beach when he told her this.

"Oh, Christ," John said then, letting go of her hand. "You don't know much." It hurt her feelings, but she didn't tell him.

On the path back to the cabin, they saw the father coming towards them. The sun had set moments before and their eyes were used to the dark, but the father's weren't. They saw him first, walking with great clomps, his arms stretched out in front of him like Boris Karloff in *Frankenstein*. Bethany remembered hearing that in *Frankenstein*, Boris Karloff had stretched out his arms before him like that because the filmmakers had at first wanted the monster to be blind. They never followed up that aspect of the story, but they kept the footage of Karloff playing the monster blind anyway, and that was why the enduring image of Frankenstein ended up being this clomping creature with his arms stuck out in front of him. The problem was that this was what John's father looked like coming towards them — a frightened, blind monstrosity. John made a sound beside her, before speaking to him in a loud, fatherly voice. She almost thought she'd imagined that sound. It could have been mistaken for a brief intake of air. But it hadn't been that.

"Jesus, Jesus, Jesus, boy!" was what John said. "You stumbling around looking for someplace to take a piss or wha?" Bethany jumped at the "wha." High-strung like the lady at the store.

The father tittered, focused in on their dark outlines, and came forward, blustering jokes about getting lost in the raspberry bushes. He had just wanted to talk with them on the beach, he said. Was he too late? Were they on their way back?

"We'll have another walk," said John.

"No, no. Betty's tired. Are you tired, Betty?"

"No, no." So they headed back to the beach.

She couldn't remember what he said. She pretended to be enthralled with the moon on the water. The truth was, the old man was incoherent. She could hear John mm-hmming in response to him. It seemed as if he had something very important to say, a zillion different things, none of which he could keep straight. He said that they were blessed. He said that they were lucky. He said that he would help them. He said that family was the only important thing. He kept saying that he was old, and that life could be difficult. He said wouldn't it be nice if people sometimes understood each other. Nobody had ever come close to understanding him in his godforsaken life. But at some point he'd decided that being understood wasn't as important as being good. So just because nobody gave a shit about him and had no respect for him and thought him a foolish old bastard — he'd decided that wasn't what was important.

"Boy, boy," John kept saying. "You need to get to bed."

At the cabin they shared with the brother and sister, they found Hugh and Ann locked in violent combat, the worst Bethany had seen so far. Laughing hysterically, Hugh with a giddy and unrelenting "Huhn! Huhn! Huhn!" and Ann with an ongoing, high-pitched shriek. John was not in the mood for it. There was a broken glass on the floor and a lamp on its side. Hugh was trying to manoeuvre Ann into one of his paralyzer holds, but Ann was resisting heroically. Bethany had never seen her quite so nimble — just as he managed to position his arm about her throat, or somewhere equally critical, she would slither away as though greased. "I've uncovered the secret!" she kept shrieking when she could speak. "I've uncovered the secret!" And Hugh would gasp, "Shut up! No, you haven't! Shut up! No, you haven't!" — so that for an instant, Bethany thought there must be some hideous secret about Hugh that Ann was threatening to reveal. But Hugh was laughing too hard for it to be that. He seemed to be hysterical with disbelief that Ann was suddenly able to wrench herself out of his every grip.

"Settle the fuck down!" John was shouting.

"You just move . . . " Ann sputtered, near to the point of being too winded to speak, "where he moves." She dove around her brother and jabbed a fist into his solar plexus, Hugh howling with pain and laughter. "You just move" — she threw her hands into the air and brought them down onto his ears — "with the hold! You move *with* the hold!"

"Shut up!" Hugh roared, holding his ears as if he couldn't stand to hear it. Giggling and panting, she scrambled for a phone book to defend herself from his next onslaught. John stepped forward and wrenched it out of her hands and hit his stampeding brother with it himself, which stopped both his laughter and his forward momentum at exactly the same time. Ann flew across the room, but might have caught her balance if not for staggering against an end table, which propelled her, arms like windmills, into Bethany, who caught an elbow in the mouth.

All night she lay wriggling the tooth with her tongue, tasting for blood. Everyone was deeply upset with Ann, but Bethany didn't care. She could hear them in the next room yelling at each other. She could hear Ann crying like one betrayed and broken-hearted.

Tomorrow, Bethany thought, she would have to go up to her and assure her that she was all right, that it wasn't her fault and all that. But she didn't feel like doing it at the moment. Hugh had given her a 222 that he had been carrying around from the time he sprained his wrist, and now the pain had transformed itself into torpor. But she didn't feel as if she could sleep. She just wanted to lie in the dark, away from the bunch of them.

Ann kept whining that it wasn't fair, whining and sobbing. "Just because you guys can beat up on anybody you want without actually hurting them!" she was saying. Then John crawled into bed and issued almost a formal apology.

"Everybody's fuckin' drunk," he sighed afterwards.

"I know."

"Well, again, I'm sorry."

"Again, it's all right."

She could feel him picking up a handful of her hair and pressing it into the centre of his face. "I'm lucky to have you," he said. "I don't tell you that enough — I know it."

Bethany wriggled her tooth and felt pleasure at the sudden bit of power. She smiled involuntarily, separating her split bottom lip and receiving a thread of pain. Perhaps she would be angry. Refuse to say another word. Keep him up all night with worry, her very need for him in question.

Lynn Coady is a Vancouver-based fiction writer from Cape Breton whose novel Strange Heaven *(Goose Lane Editions, 1998) was shortlisted for the Governor General's Award for fiction. She is an award-winning playwright, and in 1998 won the* CAA *Air Canada Award for most promising writer under thirty. Her short-story collection, of which "Play the Monster Blind" is the title story, will be published in 2000 by Doubleday Canada.*

Elisabeth Harvor

Down with
Heartbreak

Dim snowy Sunday, muffled and slushy, the boys still asleep.
Unless they were only pretending to be asleep so that they
wouldn't have to come down and be polite to Ilsa. Kay was feeling
the need to escape from her, too, and when she could hear the
final flops and ticks of the dryer coming to the end of its cycle
she hurried down the stairs to the basement. I'll just stay down
here and fold laundry, she decided. Fold laundry and take my time
folding it. Smooth out every sleeve, every pocket. But it was
not to be: she was just scooping out the first soft armful of hot
clothes when she heard the phone start to ring. She ran up the
stairs to take it, but as she was running she could already hear
Ilsa's shrill voice anxiously crying, "Whom should I tell her is
calling, please?" *Whom?* thought Kay, her heart indignant, Oh,
please, Mother dear, please do not put on grammatically incorrect
airs with my friends; and then as she was on her way back into
the kitchen she was greeted by Ilsa's urgent "It's a *man*." And only
then did Ilsa tell her his name: "William Lindstrom."

"A voice from the past." Kay said this almost in a whisper as
she carried the basket of warm laundry over to the counter next

to the stove. Then she came back to accept the phone from her mother.

"Hello?" she said warily.

"A voice from the past," said William Lindstrom.

Kay could feel herself flush. How could he possibly have heard her? She had spoken so deliberately and carefully low. She said, "William." And then, "Are you in town, then?"

He was, but only for a day and a half, two days, and could she meet him tomorrow for lunch?

"Absolutely. That sounds terrific."

"You sound a bit constrained."

Did she? She had tried so hard to sound modulated, warmly calm. But she decided to say, "A good idea might be to talk that over tomorrow at lunch."

Ilsa was over at the stove by this time, rubbing at its chrome knobs and dials with a pinkish damp cloth, doing a poor imitation of a woman deeply lost in her thoughts.

"Does this mean that the voice that answered the phone belongs to your mother?"

"I believe so," said Kay.

"Is she right at your elbow, then, listening in?"

"Actually," Kay told him, "it's a favourite spot."

William's voice had a smile in it that told Kay (while telling her where they should meet to eat) that she was really quite good at this sort of thing. And she herself thought that she wasn't at all bad at it.

"And what favourite spot is that?" Ilsa called out to Kay in her in-the-swim voice after Kay had hung up the phone.

"The restaurant where I'm to meet William Lindstrom for lunch."

Ilsa came over to sit down next to Kay. She had changed from yesterday's slacks and shaggy silver sweater into a sporty doe-coloured suede windbreaker and the beige linen culottes of a faculty wife. "Tell me about him," she said. "Is he handsome?"

"Extremely handsome," said Kay. "Big. With fair hair and a

reddish-gold beard. Swedish. Or half-Swedish. Almost a giant. But a friendly giant. He's got a lot of charm too, and he's also intelligent . . ."

"And is he a considerate person?"

Kay said yes. "A really fine and thoughtful and considerate person."

"What sort of work does he do?"

"He's an engineer," said Kay. And then she told Ilsa that when William was still living in Sweden, he used to lecture at a technical institute in Eskilstuna. "In his free time he's also writing a book."

"Oh," said Ilsa, in a dead voice. And Kay knew why: Ilsa had been enraged by a story Kay had written, in which a character suspiciously like Ilsa had put in a not very appealing appearance.

"A book he refers to as his Nazi novel."

"Are there Germans in it?"

"No," said Kay. "Academics."

But Ilsa didn't smile.

Upstairs there were footsteps, the sound of the flush. Kay reached two pottery mugs down from the cupboard that was cantilevered out over the sink. "In fact," she said, "after Eddie and I split up, William used to come over here all the time. He put up the storm windows for me and he helped the boys fix their bikes."

Ilsa said, "He's keen on you, then," and Kay replied with invented conviction, "Yes he is." But she hadn't seen or heard from him in more than a year. She didn't even know if he and Gunilla were still together. They had split up at least once and then reconciled again. So it was in a spirit of pure mischief that she now said to her mother, "The boys are awfully fond of him too, they call him Sir Will —"

"But after a time he moved away, I gather."

"Yes. To Thunder Bay."

"You must tell me more. Is he romantic?"

The tea could have been steaming hot iodine, it was such a fine tincture against the rust-pocked grey glaze of each mug's interior.

Romantic? Kay wanted to say to her mother, Who the hell cares? She wanted to say, Personally, I hate and despise romance and every single hypocritical thing that goes with it. She wanted to say, You really do believe that love is men saying they love you and bringing you rings and flowers. She wanted to say, But of course, darling Mother, you are a strategist and a stock-taker, like all romantics. She also thought of how romantic Eddie's courting letters to her had been, and of how he had called her not only darling but dearling, and not only dearling but dearlingest. "Romantic enough," she said. "Romantic enough for *me*, anyway . . ." But then she decided: Enough is enough, joke's over, and so she said to Ilsa, "But what he is most of all is an excellent father. And an *almost* excellent husband."

Everything in Ilsa's face shifted at this — the quizzical happiness was instantly kicked away and locked up. Her pale eyes became even paler, and colder. You led me on, her eyes said. "I hope you won't have anything to do with him, then."

"To do with him? Do you mean not even have lunch with him?"

"Don't you be saucy, Kay. You know very well what I mean."

Kay wore her long black coat to the restaurant to have lunch with William. The place they had agreed on was close to the War Memorial, a tall and old brick building, painted a matte black and with a lot of brass rails and greenery in it.

A trembling old waiter led her down a shallow flight of steps to a pew so deep within the leafy but churchy interior that it was close to the big sunny windows at the building's back end. The tobacco leather upholstery and the table's tablecloth — a dull maroon linen — also gave the alcove a churchy and ugly look.

No sign of William, and after a few anxious minutes Kay got up and pushed her way past the pink door at the back of the dining room so she could check herself out in one of the hallway's tall mirrors. Her glasses had a tint that was a glamorous plum. She took them off, put them on, took them off, peered at herself with and without them. Without them she looked like a shell-shocked lily. Still, Ilsa's visit hadn't been a terrible visit as visits go; it had only left Kay feeling the usual — a little destroyed, a little superior. They had even managed not to have one single big scene. The worst moment didn't come till the very end, out at Uplands, when the look that Kay had spent Ilsa's whole visit trying to avoid was diagnostically turned on her — a look that seemed to be powered by an irritated pity as Ilsa began to tug at Kay's shirt collar and bat at her coat sleeves. Kay had stood at the big windows in the lounge, watching to make sure that Ilsa's plane really and truly did fly away. Then the wild dash home to change out of her workshirt and jeans. But the only really special thing she'd put on was her Indonesian belt. It had plum colours in it, plums and maroons and tropical browns. It surprised her how much they were in harmony with the depressing decor out in the dining room.

And then back in her alcove again, still waiting for William, she wondered if she should ask him about Gunilla. How she was. She didn't think so.

William arrived at the restaurant at ten after one. Even seen at a distance across a roomful of diners he was like a breath of fresh polar air — looked, in his big parka, like an Arctic explorer.

Kay waved to him, a tiny restaurant wave, and he shouted her name as he made his way towards her across the crowded room. When he reached her, he told her she looked fabulous. She had no idea if he really meant this or if it was only the sort of thing that he shouted at women every day of his life. No, no, she wasn't being fair to him; his eyes — he was watching her while pretending not to as he was taking off his parka — were thinking a lot they weren't telling. And his hair was no longer combed down in shining bangs, either; now it was wiry and combed back and had gone partly grey and looked damp, as if he'd just showered.

"Sorry I'm late." He laid his parka down on the pew beside him with a noisy, healthy rustle of chilled nylon. "Usually I'm William the Prompt, but today I got a call from a client just as I was on my way out of my hotel."

Kay smiled up at him. His calling himself William the Prompt made her think of the children in *To the Lighthouse*, of how they had been nicknamed after the kings of England: the Ruthless, the Fair, the Red, the Wicked. He could be the Red, thought Kay. "But wouldn't punctuality be a sad thing to be revered for, down through the ages? Wouldn't you rather be remembered as William the Wicked?"

William smiled at her, still flushed from his walk. "The forecast said snow, but you'd never know it, it's so cold and bright out."

"I know!" Kay shivered. "The glare." But in fact in here the glare didn't seem like a glare at all; the sun was pouring so warmly in through the tall windows that she could smell it on the silky backs of the linings of all the fur coats. She smiled at William again and said, "So."

"I think we should have wine," William said.

Their waiter arrived with their menus. William ordered veal Parmesan. Kay ordered the shrimp curry. William ordered the house wine. Their waiter was already beginning to go bald, but the rest of what Kay could see of his body was amazingly hairy. Dense black hair, soft as fur, was even growing in the shells of his ears. An ape, but a gentle ape. He collected their menus with his great hairy hands. "Very good, monsieur. Very good, madame."

After he'd swung off through the greenery to go back to his kitchen, Kay turned to William. "Imagine being rich. It would be like being teacher's pet at school."

"How so?"

"The way you'd be praised every minute of the day for no reason." She pantomimed the waiter collecting their menus. "*Very* good, Master William. Very *good*, Mistress Kay."

William sat back and studied Kay with solemn affection. "I've missed you," he said.

Kay said, "It's really good to see you again too, Willie." Which struck them both silent until William asked Kay about her eternally unfinished novel. But by the time they were eating salads that made Kay think of health-food restaurants (musky odour of woodlot rising up from broken-off chunks of raw mushrooms), they were talking about D. H. Lawrence. William couldn't understand how any woman could admire him. "The man was just such a total fascist — so what if he was the one who scrubbed the floors and baked the bread because Frieda couldn't be bothered to learn her way around a kitchen? — the guy was just such a tiresome autocrat. Such a pest, really." He was taking excited little sips of his wine. "Pedantic hedonist," he said.

"I like that," said Kay. "Pedantic hedonist." She drank down the rest of her own wine. "Speaking of fascists," she said, "how's the Nazi novel?"

"Gone into hibernation," William said. Then the conversation was jumping from one topic to another. Kay's job at the Arctic Institute. The music scene in Thunder Bay. Rachmaninoff. A recent holiday weekend William had spent in Chicago. The main course had arrived by this time, and strings of cheese were hanging in Parmesan ligaments from William's cubes of veal as he forked them into his mouth. He talked, chewing, swilled down his veal and potatoes with great gulps of wine. He was a bear, a great dancing medieval bear with an iron napkin ring chained to one of its ankles, and as the wine was warming Kay's throat and breasts, William's chest began to seem very warm to her too — broad and healthy and Swedish and with a bear's healthy layer of fat on it, beaming out a great hibernating bear's pleasant warmth. How pleasant all this was anyway — the food, the wine, the sun on the silky backs of all the fur coats, William talking; he's the sort of man, Kay decided, who can sit and rub one side of his chest as he talks — he was rubbing it now, in concentric circles over his heart — and you'll never think it is self-centred, you'll only think it is warm, and she recalled a conversation she'd had with him the spring after Eddie had moved out. They'd been sitting on the floor of somebody's summer house out in the Gatineau Hills, and Kay could still recall the selective fever of the fire's burn down the length of one arm, on her throat, and the chill from the flagstones too, in front of the fire. A chill that had seemed both medieval and suburban as it had penetrated the thin cotton of her long skirt until she'd got achy and cold all along one thigh. And then one of William's partners, a man named Stan Sadri, had come over to join them and had stood, head bowed, listening in. Finally, he had hauled off his tie and started to draw the point of it slowly up and down Kay's bare arm. She had smiled up at him, but she'd been too naive to understand that he was wanting to see her alone. She felt ashamed of this now, remembering how Stan Sadri — not giving up, or at least not giving up immediately — had flirtingly walked the point of his necktie in a slow, weak-ankled dance up and down her shy arm.

As if he were psychic, William now began to speak of Stan Sadri. "He's gone. Out to the West Coast. He was planning to come and work with me in Thunder Bay, but then changed his mind." The man he'd got to replace him was definitely gifted, but well on his way to becoming an alcoholic. "Basically, the man's a masochist," he said.

Kay speared a leftover wedge of tomato and a small section of lettuce shell with her fork, shoved them over to a lake of vinegar and oil, moved them around and around in it. After a small silence, she said, "I think I might be a masochist myself."

"Really?" William studied her with a thoughtful, diagnostic gaze that seemed to be incubating a satisfied belch somewhere deep inside itself. He wouldn't have thought so, he said. He looked at her with careful attention. "You don't mean whips and handcuffs, do you?"

Kay could feel herself flush. She said she supposed one thing could lead to another. "But I hope I don't." And then she almost airily added, "I think my cravings lie more along the lines of . . ." But here she decided not to go on. There was no law in the world that decreed that she was obliged to finish such a sentence.

"Along the lines of . . . ?"

"William the Prompter," Kay dubbed him. But she knew that above her waylaying smile, her eyes were uneasy.

William gazed seriously back at her. "I think I would prefer to be William the Conqueror," he said.

"It would only be an anticlimax if I told you."

"Try me," he said.

Kay shook her head.

"*Tell* me."

How did they ever get into this mess? They were talking about nothing, they were talking about Stan Sadri, and in anxiety Kay planed her hair back from her temples as if she planned to experiment with it in some way. Do it up in a twist or a top-knot. But then all at once it seemed flirty *not* to tell him, a kind of tease, and so very fast she came out with it: "Being spanked."

William gave her a long look of appraisal. Or perhaps he was only appraising himself, his own proclivities. "I could spank you," he said in a voice that was wonderfully low, for him.

Kay shook her head. "I wouldn't let you," she told him.

But now their waiter was coming to take away their plates. The silence even lived on a little after he had lunged away with his tray.

"You wouldn't let me?" By now William was looking unhappily alert and a little hurt. He picked up one of Kay's gloves and pulled at each of its long leather fingers. "Strange words," he said. "Strange words, coming from a masochist. Why not? Why wouldn't you let me?"

It was a question that asked more than the question it seemed to be asking, and on that account Kay knew it had to be carefully answered. So that even before she'd only half-finished answering "Because it wouldn't suit you," she knew it was the wrong answer.

"Why wouldn't it suit me?"

She didn't want to say, Because you're not emotional enough, and so she said, in a neutral voice that she could already tell she'd be regretting, "Because you are too nice, William."

"I am not too nice." Now he was definitely offended. And quite rightly so. What a frightening debacle this whole conversation was turning into, and all because the man who'd taken over Stan Sadri's job was on his way to turning into a drunk.

"Word of honour," said William. "I am not nice."

Kay was feeling more and more remote from herself. She whispered, "I believe you. Really."

"We could go back to my room right now and I could spank you. What a lovely way to spend an afternoon."

All around them civil servants were cracking open new conversations, their laughter coldly happy, forceful. Kay couldn't help wondering what they would think if they could overhear her conversation with William — a conversation that just had to be, in its own careful way, wilder. She shook her hair and, with it, her smile. "No," she said. But her no seemed to have come out in a warm-sounding moan. "I can't. I have an appointment with my dentist at a quarter to four —"

"Where's that?"

"On Bronson."

"I could drive you there — it probably wouldn't take more than fifteen minutes. More likely only ten. We could go down to my hotel right now." He glanced at his watch and Kay was struck by his persistence — and what was persistence at a time like this but bravery? — and she felt ashamed of herself for having (however unintentionally) led him on.

Their waiter was back again, holding a tall pink plastic menu close to his chest and smiling a smile that said: My dear monsieur and madame, I am here to entice you. But they both shook their heads to cake and coffee, and once they were alone again Kay wondered if William was taking her refusal of dessert for acquiescence and, wondering this, she began to feel a peripheral vaginal tickling — nothing deep, more like a physiological equivalent of the giggles — and when William looked up at her and asked, in a voice as low and seductive as the Devil's must be, "Are you tempted?" it did seem to Kay that the only decent and humane response would be to whisper yes.

But once they were out in the cold air, and after a moment of nervous but half-amused doubt, she asked, "Why *me*, William?"

She had thought he might say something light but flattering like "Good God, woman, how can you ask?" but he surprised her by saying, "Because I trust you."

She slid an arm through his, but then could feel from the tension in him that her hand was too wifely, and so at the first traffic light she withdrew it and used it to pull up the hood of her coat. It was starting to snow lightly — an early spring snow, fine as dust but with pin-pricky stings in it. "I'm feeling a bit anxious about this."

"Don't be." And then he told her that he'd been wanting to go to bed with her for years. It added to her nervousness to hear him say this — it made her even more afraid of being a disappointment to him. He didn't haul up his own hood. The snow was falling onto his hair and making the ginger haze of his beard sparkle. He said that the last time he was down here, he was sure it would work out. "But you were very into masturbation back then."

"I was?" She blushed in the cold, pretending not to remember, although she could recall it all quite clearly enough. They were at a Sunday afternoon party out in the Gatineau Hills, and she'd propped herself up against a pile of cushions on a sofa over by the longest row of windows while William (wearing an unbuttoned denim shirt over his black bathing trunks) was sitting on a rocking chair facing her, leaning towards her as she'd extolled the virtues of sexual self-reliance. Pleasantly tipsy, they had traded slogans. Kay remembered liking one of William's (No Body Like Dis Body), but the only one of her own she could now recall was Onanists' Coalition: Down with Heartbreak.

They came into William's hotel to find it crowded with the baggage and cries of a group of women who were all dressed alike, in ham-pink plaid skirts and monogrammed blazers. Members of a bowling team, possibly, or a choir. William had to wait behind a crowd of them over at the registration desk to ask for his key. Kay crossed the lobby to the smoke shop, to give herself something to do. It seemed to her that the women in the blazers were

all incredibly happy, away for a few days from husbands and
children; she could hear their excited voices calling out to each
other, nicknames and last names, while she was trying not to
notice the way her back had gone slick with almost nauseated tiny
terrors. She tensely splayed all her fingers inside the silk privacy
of her long coat's deep pockets. Did William understand that no
spanking was to happen? She had the feeling he did. Or perhaps
she only hoped so. She would have to know someone very much
better than she knew William, she thought, for that to happen.
But wasn't the truth simply that he would have to be a different
someone? She looked up and saw that the clerk was expecting her
to buy something and, rattled, she bought a magazine —but what
was she buying? She didn't even know, some mindless slick thing
— and once she was on her way back across the lobby to join
William again she was convinced that the only decent thing to
do would be to make her eyes go blank so that he wouldn't see
how much they were carrying an imploring announcement of
what she would (and would not) do with him.

William and Kay rode up in the elevator with the blazered
women, but the moment they'd all crowded into the little mir-
rored box they all seemed to become so instantly demure that they
stood gazing down in mass sorrow at the toes of their shoes. And
although it was a relief when the whole team of observers trooped
out on the floor below William's floor, Kay could still feel the
presence of a ghostly audience rising up beside them, their invisible judges. If she had been with someone she loved, she didn't
think she would have had this sensation of being watched, but
with William she felt watched.

And then up in William's airless beige and grey room, William
was the one who did the housewifely things: turned on the
lamps whose gold-papered lampshades were the size of parade
drums; drew closed the heavy hotel drapes; turned down the dull
brocade bedspread that looked as if it had been stolen from a tiny
royal bed in a museum.

Kay sat down in one of the armchairs to undo the buttons on

her pale silk shirt. She could feel the nervous damp in her armpits. William was over on the far side of the bed by this time, unknotting his knitted black tie, and when he got his first glimpse of Kay's breasts in their skin-coloured brassiere, he moaned, and Kay hated herself for deciding that his moan sounded like a moan that had been moaned many times before, in many hotel rooms, but she couldn't lie to herself, she was feeling very detached.

William came over to her then, to pull off her high boots. He pulled off the first one, but the second was a tighter fit and he had to rock it heel to toe to pry it off her foot. So much gallantry made Kay feel awkward, a child, and when they stood and right away started to kiss she could feel the relief of not being exposed to his reading anything more in her eyes.

"*Bed*," groaned William when they stopped to catch their breath, and he pulled her over on top of him as they fell back onto the Javexy sheets and they continued to kiss skilfully, deeply, passionlessly, at least until William whispered that he had a condom. "Are you afraid of the plague?" he whispered, and when Kay responded in the accent of Greta Garbo in *Ninotchka* but also with what she was sure was an uneasy smile in her eyes, "I am afraid of *everythink*," they laughed in deep unison, as if she had just made a brilliant, ironical joke.

After he had rolled them over so that he was on top, William raised himself up on straight arms to look down at Kay. Like a god gazing down at — what? scenery? his own creation? "Don't go away," he whispered, "and that's an order." And then he hitched himself up into sitting position, sat on the side of the bed like a father, smoothed Kay's hair back from her right temple so soothingly that for a few moments she became a child again, a child in bed with a fever. "I'll be right back," William told her.

Kay listened to the sound of the faucets: one discreet blast, then another. She was still feeling stupidly drugged from the wine, and so had to push herself to shunt herself out of her jeans, unhook her brassiere. Her breasts, released, felt warm and fat; her sense of their fatness was the first thing that seemed faintly hopeful. She could hear William starting to brush his teeth and prayed he would use enough toothpaste for the two of them. But the industrious, hopeful sound of the brushing was also making her feel edgy and so it was a relief when the bathroom door opened and he came into the dim room towards her, his erection solemnly bobbing.

Tenting the sheet up for him like a wife, she could feel how cold his tongue was in the wine-warmth of her mouth, and his breath was cold too — a cool peppermint breeze high up in slippery mountains — and the kissing meant nothing, just as before, and they made love as competently as any married couple on a Saturday night and afterwards William stayed lying heavily on top of her, telling her funny stories. Kay felt bathed in his sweat. She felt clamped to the bed by his moist Nordic weight. But at the same time, she kept stroking back his sweat-dampened hair and kissing him along his salt-beaded hairline and rubbing her nose in the scratchy and salty bush of his beard as if she wanted him never to leave her. And in a way she did not; it was deeply consoling to be pinned down by such a warmly breathing-in, breathing-out heaviness — and in particular by such a breathing-out heaviness that it would now and then make William's belly go tight as a drum. In the meantime, his lips were kept busy grazing her eyes and mouth — little licks and kisses — although now and then he would make a quick detour to dip down to lick the little hollow at the base of her throat. A sweet feeling, and one that made her feel abundant and useful, as if she'd been turned into a salt lick at the edge of a forest. William had another story to tell her too: On his first night in Chicago he had slipped his contact lenses into a glass of water on his bedside table, and later that night, overcome with thirst but not quite awake, he had drunk them. They exploded with laughter at this, and their laughter made Kay recall a former neighbour of hers who always baked sugar cookies for her boyfriend's lunch box, but who one night decided to surprise him by baking a family of gingerbread men with genitals on them. "And the delicious thing about the boyfriend was that his skin was almost exactly the same colour as a gingerbread man's."

William stretched, held his arms straight up in a yawn, then said, "But to go back to this spanking business again: Were you ever spanked as a child?"

"No," said Kay.

"Were you ever threatened with a spanking?"

"More or less constantly."

William lowered his arms to fall into a conductor's gesture. "So there we have your answer then: You're still waiting."

Kay smiled into his shoulder, again aware of how much she still didn't want it to happen. Not here, not now. She whispered, "William, I'm going to be late for my appointment, we'll have to go," and they both sat up, and then, under cover of hauling on their clothes in the curtained dark, were able to avoid reading in each other's eyes revelations of pointlessness.

On the way to the dentist's, William began to sing the praises of Gunilla and his three daughters, and when he slowed to a stop for the traffic crosswalk that led from the university to the park bordering the eastern side of the highway, and a strong-looking blonde in a short dark plaid coat and thigh-high burgundy boots came striding in front of his car, he turned to look after her and then to say to Kay that there must be more goddamn beautiful women in Ottawa than in any goddamn city in the whole god-damn Western world.

Kay couldn't speak, at least not until she understood that William was only warning her not to be so naive as to fall in love with him, and when they reached her dentist's glass tower and he said in a low voice, "Listen, it was lovely," she was convinced that he was above all anxious to hurry off, be gone, blue-at-the-gills William. But she needed to say one more thing to him: "Will you write about this?"

He smiled a smile that said, "I'm centuries older than you are." But then he said: "No, I won't."

Kay felt spared, then, from some great humiliation. At least until he said, "But *you* will."

They both laughed at that, but as Kay was getting out of William's car he told her that their little dialogue had actually already put in an appearance in a novel he'd read years ago. "And I've been waiting all these years for someone to ask me what you just asked me."

But he's wrong, Kay decided as she hurried away from him along the strip of pavement leading to a tower that was equipped with drills and picks and other miniature and glinting instruments of torture, the very last thing in the world I would want to do is write about this.

Elisabeth Harvor is the author of the award-winning poetry book Fortress of Chairs *(Signal Editions, 1992) and three story collections, including* Our Lady of All the Distances *(HarperCollins, 1991) and* If Only We Could Drive Like This Forever *(Penguin, 1988). An earlier version of "Down with Heartbreak" was a recent finalist in the* CBC *Literary Competition. Harvor's fiction and poetry have appeared in the* Malahat Review, Prism International, *the* New Yorker, *and many other magazines and journals. Her new book of poetry,* The Long Cold Green Evenings of Spring *(Signal Editions, 1997), was shortlisted for the Pat Lowther Award, and she has twice won the League of Canadian Poets' National Poetry Prize. Her most recent book of stories,* Let Me Be the One *(HarperCollins, 1996), was a finalist for the Governor General's Award.*

Kent Nussey

SUMMER

Hicks didn't really think about the hornets in the bathroom until Sperling phoned with the story about the man who'd died after swallowing a bee. It was an awful story, the sort that Sperling told well. He began with the ceremony at city hall, where he, Sperling, had presented the mayor with the cement-fondue bust of a long-dead city father. Certain descendants of the latter had endowed the new library, and the city had commissioned Sperling to create his likeness as a weighty token of appreciation to the family. A great crowd of local swells had turned out, and afterwards most of them had adjourned to one of several garden parties around town to continue the celebration. Sperling himself had attended a different party from the man who swallowed the bee, but he described the lushness of the summer afternoon and his surroundings in a way that made it easy for Hicks to imagine the setting in which the other man had perished.

Sperling said, "These parties were going on at wealthy homes all over town. Everyone was dressed up and drinking tea from china cups or choosing canapés from long tables that glittered in the sun."

When he mentioned the victim's name, Hicks recollected meeting the man at some lecture at the high school. He'd been introduced to Hicks as a professor at the university, and although their exchange was brief, the man was memorable for his English accent and suave, slightly haughty bearing. In fact, Hicks had immediately disliked the other man's ruddy complexion and his full head of silver hair, swept back Peter Lawford style, shaggy on the collar. As a mere high-school teacher, Hicks had sensed vague condescension from this figure, and when Sperling reported how the bee had dropped into the teacup, how it had lodged in his handsome throat, Hicks had to laugh.

"God," he said. "What a flukey way to go! What an ignominious death!"

Then he remembered the hornet he'd killed in his downstairs bathroom just yesterday while he was shaving. It was the second one this week. He hadn't thought much of it at the time: he was looking in the mirror, applying sweet lather to his face, when he saw movement in the glass, something swooped above his ear and veered towards the electric light. He followed the angry whine and stalked it with a magazine, the same magazine he'd used to kill the first one a few days before.

On the other end Sperling was silent.

Hicks said, "Christ, what am I laughing at? A hornet took a shot at me in the bathroom the other morning. Imagine swallowing one of those buggers."

"Bees are bad enough, but hornets . . . Do you know where they're coming from?"

"Coming from? Outside, I guess. I think I've seen them around the flowers in front."

"If you're seeing hornets you probably have a nest," Sperling said. "You should take a look around. They make nests almost anywhere."

"That's all I need," Hicks told him, and at that point Sperling asked after his mother, who was in hospital in a different city taking chemotherapy. She'd fought off the first attack with similar medicine a year and a half ago, but the cancer had come back and now they were feeding an altered formula into her veins. Two weeks ago he'd gone to visit her in the hospital and he'd been shocked at how thin and jaundiced she looked; though her spirit and intelligence never wavered, for the first time it struck him that she might not win this one. He sat beside her bed while the potent liquids dripped from a small bag into the tube in her arm. When he kissed her forehead there was a sweetish chemical smell, oddly poignant in that it was not unlike the familiar scent of her skin, but somehow mingled with the essence of her disease. Somehow the therapy, the prescribed antidote, had become the very scent of her self and her sickness.

After he hung up the telephone he went outside and inspected the short strip of roses and flowering bushes in front of the house. His mother had planted them on a visit several years ago, just before she got sick. He recollected taking her a tumbler of iced tea, the floral print on her small white glove that gripped the glass, the way she drank it down, squinting through her trifocals as if it hurt.

As he looked at the roses, Hicks felt another stab of guilty fear for laughing at the bee story. That was courting bad luck, bad karma, for sure. But there were no hornets to be seen. Only a yellow butterfly fluttering from blossom to blossom in the twilight.

Next morning, as he stood in the living room behind the big picture window, Hicks definitely saw hornets circling the bushes just outside. In the full sunshine of morning he could plainly see them coming and going around the flowers. He had business at school that day, but in the evening he put on a pair of shorts and looked in the bathroom downstairs. Kitty-corner to the sink, inches beneath a framed painting of palm trees, a waist-high door led to the storage space under the house. On a hunch he turned on the light and opened the door. He had to squat and shuffle, occasionally dropping to hands and knees to move through the damp, musty space. He clambered over a garden hose, pushed aside empty beer bottles and an old kitchen chair. In the dim illumination from the bare bulb between the rafters he recognized a box of text books he'd bought in graduate school. The cement floor was cool and dank, almost slippery under his bare feet and knees; tiny semi-transparent spiders ran away from his hands when he paused on all fours to peer through the murky light. Awkwardly, following his hunch, he moved towards the far wall at the front of the house. He stopped and listened. From behind him came a sound like electricity singing in the light fixture. He was thinking something was not right in the wiring back there when the sound changed pitch and rose in volume as if there'd been a power surge. From his crouch he strained to look over his shoulder. The low-wattage bulb seemed to be alive; it seemed to vibrate and hum with crazy energy. Hicks thought he saw particles of raw energy leaping around the bulb, swirling the darkness around it like a strobe light. He turned towards the light and the first hornet came at him, looping out of the gloom on malign instinct. It swerved up to his face and he fell backwards batting at it. Trying to rise, he saw five or six more, activated by the light, zigging and zagging towards his exposed head and arms and legs. He yelled and scuttled crabwise towards the open door. The hornets circled the bulb and glanced off his knees. Hicks flailed and scrambled; ahead of him the rectangle of friendly light beckoned from the bathroom. He rolled to his belly and lurched up, banging his head on a rafter. With the drone in his ears, he propelled himself towards the light. Hands and feet skated away on magazines and newspapers. He swore and ducked, and with one more effort launched himself into the bathroom. Skidding on his haunches, he whirled and slammed the door. Braced against it, legs splayed on the cheery Congoleum, he could hear the hornets hurling themselves against the door. Through his panting gasps he heard the faint *tick, tick, tick* of hornets battering the other side.

"Christ!" he said, rising slowly beside the sink. He touched the wound on his scalp, had a thought, and frantically shook the baggy legs of his shorts. Satisfied, he drew a breath and looked in the mirror. There was blood in his hair. He stepped around the corner into the laundry room, where the shelves above the appliances were lined with aerosol cans and pump bottles. The bug spray was behind some other cans that clattered to the floor as he grabbed at it. Back in the bathroom, he crouched and tried to hear whatever was behind the door. Slowly, he opened it a few inches, waited, then proceeded into the storage space on two knees and one hand, the other at the ready with the insecticide.

Two hornets banked out of the shadows side by side and tilted towards his head.

With two deft squirts he shot them out of the air.

Avoiding their still-squirming bodies, he pushed forward. Somewhere up there, he knew, the nest was waiting. Probably between the wooden ceiling and the cement-brick wall. Another hornet flew straight from the flank; he twisted and nailed it on the second blast. He would have to be careful they didn't slip behind him. Careful he didn't get trapped. He peered through the ill-lit space to the far wall. Now he heard the humming, as if the entire wall was alive with voltage and pain, as if the foundation was infected with a vein of pure torment and outrage. The shadows seemed to shift towards him. He hesitated on his knees and brought up the can. The hornets uncoiled out of the dark and rippled towards him in broken waves; he fired, ducked, and fired again. One got in close and he rolled on his shoulder; they swarmed the light bulb and peeled away like tiny torpedo planes dive-bombing a battleship. He shot them out of the air in twos and threes; he fired wildly and shuffled backwards, gasping the heavy poison. He had a brace lined up in his sights when the compression failed, the nozzle wheezed lightly, and he realized the can was empty. Instantly they were on him. Hicks threw the can and clamped his mouth just as one grazed his lip. He turned and scampered into the light and slammed the door. One dazed hornet came through with him. Hicks tracked it from his sprawl, reached for the magazine by the toilet, then slapped it from the air and flattened it on the floor with one explosive wallop.

Without turning off lights or putting on shoes, he rose from the basement and went outside into the backyard. He stood there in the waning daylight and spat the chemical residue from his mouth. The lawn was vivid green, alive under his feet. Small nameless bugs swam around the green-laden branches of the birch tree that stood between the house and the hedge.

It was early July, high summer, a season that promised to go on forever.

That night, on the phone, Sperling said, "I don't know, man. I'd let sleeping dogs lie. I'd just leave that nest alone, assuming one's in there. Be like the Jains."

"The what?"

"It's a Hindu sect that won't kill bugs. These guys go to incredible lengths to avoid stepping on ants or spiders. All life is holy to them. All creatures their brothers."

"I've got nothing against bugs," Hicks said. "I like bugs. But this bunch could kill me."

"All the more reason to leave them alone."

"Yeah, but they could take over the house. It's like they're eating it from the inside out."

Sperling hesitated. "That reminds me," he said. "When I was a kid there was an abandoned house in our neighbourhood. No people had lived there for years, but the house was inhabited by millions and millions of bees."

He went on to describe it as one of those old frame dwellings on an overgrown lot, the sort of place that kids can't stay away from, although the appeal of this one was also its particular hazard.

"If you crouched near a broken window you could hear them whining in there like a power plant. You could feel them buzzing in the walls. The place was famous for miles around. One day Jimmy Feller actually went inside. His old man kept an apiary and owned all the protective clothing. So he and Jimmy suited up and checked the place out, top to bottom. They said it was like walking through an enormous beehive. The bees had infiltrated every inch of woodwork and the walls were rotten with honey. Honey oozed through the wallpaper. If you pulled on a plank, honey dripped out. Not long after that the bees swarmed and left the house in one huge cloud. For no good reason, one summer afternoon the entire colony lifted from the house, darkened the sky, and moved on. I saw them from three blocks away. It was like a blimp made out of bees, sailing slowly out of town."

"Jesus," said Hicks.

"Jimmy Feller was a hero for a while," Sperling said. "A few years later his old man was stung to death by his own bees. Funny, I haven't thought of them in ages."

When Hicks finished talking to Sperling, he phoned his mother in the hospital. She'd just completed one cycle of chemotherapy and felt not too bad. She reckoned it would hit her next week. That's the way it worked, she said. Next week she'd feel it. Hicks said that he was sorry she had to go through this again. Maybe it wouldn't be so bad this time. With some luck, the new formula would be easier on her.

"I know I'm not young," she said. "To some folks seventy-five seems like a ripe old age. But I'd like to stay for a while longer."

"Don't worry," Hicks told her. "I have a feeling you'll be able to. I have a hunch your time isn't up yet."

He promised to visit her soon and hung up. For a moment he stood beside the phone in the kitchen, scowling at the floor. He could feel the scowl on his face. Then he opened a beer and drifted downstairs: he leaned into the dark bathroom and listened. He took a drink. What was he listening for? What was he thinking, inclined towards the dark and the small door that opened to the deeper dark at the heart of his house?

A summer curriculum committee kept Hicks occupied at school for the rest of the week, but more than once, in the mornings, when he poured himself a glass of carrot juice, he swore the liquid tasted of pesticide; at odd moments during the day the taste would recrudesce on his tongue, sometimes accompanied by a strange hitch in his gut, on his left side, just below the ribs. Not exactly a pain, but rather a tightening, as if a section of his vitals was being pulled taut from end to end.

For these several reasons he didn't meddle with the hornets until Saturday, when he was mowing the lawn. As he pushed the electric mower near the bushes and flowers below the front window, four or five of them rose and hovered in the midday sun. Hicks clearly saw them slip from a crack in the foundation. The snarl of the machine seemed to enrage the insects, then become the very sound of their anger. Hicks had just enough time to note their exact point of exit from the house before he dashed for safety. Later, in the evening, he crept back to the bushes and located the crack. He picked up a small chip of porous wood from the base of the roses and fit it into the opening. His general logic was that the hornet colony, unable to forage for nutrients, would slowly perish from want of same. He supposed there'd be a day or two he definitely must not open the door in the downstairs bathroom, but it made more sense than going after them with more poison. He made sure that the wood chip fully blocked the hole, then he went inside.

Before he went to bed he phoned his mother. There was still no definite word on whether her treatments were working. She tried to sound brave, but a note of exhaustion came into her speech.

"I can't believe I'm losing another summer to this disease," she said. "All winter I looked forward to the good weather, and now I'm more sick than ever. You have to get out there and enjoy it for me. Make sure you don't miss this one."

Hicks promised he wouldn't. He told her that the roses were blooming beautifully, extravagantly, and that he'd bring her some next time he visited.

That night he lay in bed wondering about her cancer. He was thinking there was some connection between his own life and her illness. He was thinking there was something he could do, or there was a way he could think, and live, something private and special that would have positive repercussions on the physical level miles away in his mother's hospital room. He was not religious in any orthodox or doctrinaire way, but he was her son, their blood-link was strong and he felt there was a way that he could *be* — a mode of clarity within himself — that would rally the higher forces on her behalf. The more he thought about it, the more certain he felt that if he could order his thoughts, if he could order the contents of his heart and connect them with his thoughts, he might earn a point in the ultimate scheme of things. If he could find and enter that mode, he might save something he loved.

Next morning, as he stood in the downstairs bathroom running the electric razor over his face, he tried to remember a dream from the night. He and the professor who had swallowed the bee were serving on a committee together, and whenever Hicks tried to speak the professor blocked his motion with a superior remark or put-down that left Hicks choking with frustration. But the rest of the dream was lost. He seemed to recollect that it ended in light, in transcendence, but the only part he could definitely remember was being thwarted by the dead professor. Lost in thought, he held the razor beside his face until he seemed to hear something through its steady whine — a noise like another razor going just behind him, or the sound's memory in his brain occurring simultaneously with the actual buzz in his ear. Hicks turned off the razor and rested his hand on the knob of the small door to the storage space. He felt the faintest of tremors, as if a current were running through the door to his hand. He could feel the power, the compressed fury he had made by stopping the hole in the foundation. They were going mad in there, searching for a way out. He imagined them buzzing and bumping into each other in the musty darkness, madly exploring every nook and crevice, pushing upward, ever upward and outward against the limits of this house. From the laundry room he brought a beach towel and wedged it against the minuscule space between the Congoleum and the door. Then he took another look at himself in the mirror, turned off the light, and went upstairs.

The telephone rang just before he caught his cab to the train station. Sperling said he wanted to check in; he asked Hicks about the hornet problem. Hicks explained his latest strategy.

"I don't know," Sperling said. "You can't just plug the hole and think you've beaten them. They'll go crazy down there. God knows how long they'll last."

Hicks heard the taxi in his driveway and he told Sperling he'd call him soon.

"Give my best to your mother," Sperling said. "And don't worry about those hornets."

On the train Hicks contemplated Sperling's warning. He felt panicky, off-balance, on the verge of chance disaster. When he entered his mother's room she was fast asleep and utterly still. The other bed was vacant and Hicks drew a chair close to hers. Shrunken and small, she was wearing her glasses and her own pyjamas. Behind the trifocals her eyes were shut; her lips came together as if they'd been gravely and serenely sealed. He could barely discern her breathing. But as Hicks leaned closer, her eyes opened clearly and she smiled and said, "Hi!" with a delight so genuine his heart jumped. For the rest of the afternoon and through the supper hour he stayed with her, talking and helping her eat. Tomorrow was her last round of chemotherapy.

"After that they should be able to tell if it's working," she said. "If it isn't, I'm not sure what comes next. Their bag of tricks might be empty after that."

"Don't give up," Hicks said. "We're not at that place yet. Not yet."

His mother shifted her head and looked at him.

"But is this any way to live? I feel like a chemical dump. I can smell it through my skin." She blinked and gazed at him. "Tomorrow they'll hook me up and run that stuff into me again, if they can find a vein that hasn't been burned out. It would be worth it to get another year or two of life. That would make it worthwhile, I guess."

Hicks squeezed her hand. He said, "I think you'll get it. There are other tricks left in the bag. There are still things we can do here. I really believe that."

After they said their goodbyes, as Hicks stood to leave, he glanced through the window that looked out over the city's parkways and vast municipal lawns. In the distance, high over the trees and green and streaming cars, a hot-air balloon hung in the pale blue sky. His mother had always been fascinated by objects in the heavens — strange aircraft or satellites or just the evening star — and he raised her bed so she could see.

Her eyes widened behind the varying depths of her glasses.

"Oh, it looks like something," she said. "It looks like a cross, or a butterfly. Doesn't it look like a butterfly?"

The balloon above the gondola was supposed to be a giant maple leaf, but Hicks had to admit that at first glance it might be a cross or a butterfly. At first glance it might be either of those things.

Riding the train through the night he thought about how small and fragile his mother had seemed. He thought about how her talk had been bright and calm, the voice and words so at odds with the wasting body. More than ever he believed that he was not helpless, not without recourse, in defending that body. He felt the proximity of death intensely; he knew that he was riding a series of events, events that might or might not be foreordained, through a specific darkness, an ultimate mystery that pressed the panes of his consciousness like the summer night that contained the lit carriages of this train. He felt certain that there was a mode of heart, a cast of mind, that extended to a sacramental act that might alter the course of these events, if only temporarily. That death would eventually triumph, he never doubted, but in his heart he was convinced that his very acceptance of this fact put him in the position to make a deal. For him, this summer, higher powers were in play — powers that supplanted and overrode the quotidian rules of his regular days. Through some connection of blood, or love, or even a vaguer element he might call faith, he was riding the night train with his mother, and if he found that mode of clarity, if he faced death without denying its final authority, he might demand one more cycle of life for her, one more set of seasons that would end in a different summer.

Far down the night Hicks awoke with a sluggish start. All was silent, the room dark, but he knew that something in or around the house had jarred him from sleep. The luminous clock on the dresser said three-ten. He got up and parted the curtains: the sky beyond his backyard held a peculiar bluish light, like the spread of a premature dawn. Something was happening. Something real was happening in the large outer world, and something in his house. Looking out at the strange blue pallor, he felt a leap of connection with the distance. Someone had told him that the terminally ill often die at three in the morning. Doctors and nurses had commented on the fact.

He went down to the kitchen and turned on a light. Now he was sure that he actually heard something. Below him, in the basement darkness, there was a noise of agitation, like particles of darkness colliding wildly, darting and colliding in a madness to escape. He placed his palm against the wall to feel the vibration rising from the dark.

Turning lights on as he moved through the house, he put on a hooded sweatshirt and some heavy sweatpants; in another closet he found sneakers and high white socks. He tied the sneakers and tucked the sweatpants into the socks. Down in the laundry room he found the paper mask that fit over his nose and mouth and an old pair of paint-spattered sunglasses. He donned these and drew the hood tight around his face. A flashlight sat beside the tall new can of bug spray on the shelf. With the flashlight in his left hand, the spray can in his right, he went into the bathroom.

He stood in the half-light from outside the room and looked at his peculiar image in the mirror. But after all, this is what it came to. Taking action. Blundering into the dark space, for better or worse. Through the cinched hood and the low door he listened for the dark buzzing in the storage space. He wasn't sure if he heard anything now or not.

He crouched and opened the door and breathed the stale dampness. A chemical taint lingered. It was like crawling into the dank
mouth of a tunnel, a familiar space that had become the domain
of an enemy. He proceeded cautiously, taking noisy breaths
through the paper mask. At what he guessed was the halfway
point to the far wall he stopped. He brought the spray can to the
ready and turned on the flashlight. For the first time he saw the shaggy
nest plastered between the foundation and a ceiling beam. Turning the light towards the floor, he noticed the curled bodies of
dead hornets around his knees, casualties of the first skirmish.
Can the dead ones sting? He should have thought to wear gloves.

As he brought the light back to the nest, the first live hornet
flew out to meet him. He brought it down on the second shot.
Unlike the other can, which produced a mist that functioned like
scattershot, this spray came out in a long, concentrated stream
that made it harder to hit the insect in flight. A few drops
spattered the nest. Hicks heard them distinctly against the papery
material that bulged on the cement. Through his tinted lenses the
nest looked alien, almost unnatural, like something that should
be growing underwater or in outer space. He heard the low
current running through its inner labyrinths, as if it were out-
raged or profaned by the drops of pesticide.

From his crouch, the flashlight trained on the nest a scant yard
away, he perceived individual hornets separating from it, dropping drowsily and veering suddenly into the flashlight beam,
following it towards the source. Hicks ducked and fired as they
droned over his head. He sprawled on the clammy cement floor,
rose on one elbow and squeezed off four shots that soaked into
the nest. As he fired the hornets grazed his covered arms and head.
One smacked against the paper mask over his mouth and went
into a sick dive in the thickening air. They were homing in on the
flashlight, funnelling down the beam faster than he could pick
them off. He fired and rolled, bobbling the flashlight and clutch-
ing the can. They fell around him, wriggling on the cement, some
regaining altitude with tiny sputters like prop planes coming out

of a stall. And still they poured out of the nest, groggily attacking the light. On his knees, trying to shoot them on the fly, he realized he couldn't see. Hot needles pierced his wrist; he heard the flashlight clatter to the floor as he clapped the stung hand to his chest. He tore off the glasses and tried to retreat. He understood that he was in it now; he was deep in the blind current where the essences battled; he was in the black cell where things were decided, finished or reborn, and with a desperate twist he half-turned and fired wildly in the direction of the nest until he was certain he'd drenched it, while his hand was stung again and again. The lit flashlight on the floor plied the dark like a phosphorescent vein through shifting green seas. As he shuffled backwards he realized the mask wasn't filtering the heavy air. His lungs were on fire; his brain teetered towards oblivion.

"Save me," he said. "Get me out of here."

He followed the flashlight beam towards the open door. He seemed to be pulling himself hand over hand from a black hole, a darkness that scorched his brain and smothered his will. On hands and knees he entered the light. His bare palms registered the smooth white floor and he kept going, blinking through the chemical perspiration, crawling onto the carpet beyond the next doorway. Retching, he felt his ribs scrape his lungs, he felt something in there ruined forever. He leaned his head against the worn plaid couch where slowly, slowly, the darkness bled away, the room levelled, and he pressed a finger to the raised white welts on his inner wrist.

In this way he bought his mother another year of life.

Kent Nussey has published two short-story collections, In Christ There Is No East or West *(Quarry Press, 1992) and* The War in Heaven *(Insomniac Press, 1997). His essays have appeared in* Brick, *the* New Quarterly, *and* Quarry *magazine. Currently he is at work on a novel tentatively entitled* The Big Golden Book of the Universe. *He lives in Toronto.*

Janice Kulyk Keefer

DREAMS:
STORMS:
DOGS

I.

Sogno di Sant' Orsola: Vittore Carpaccio. Venezia, Galleria dell' Accademia

There's a strange woman in that bed, hand cupped to ear, listening hard to her dreams. My bed, I'd know it anywhere, though I've never clapped eyes on it before. The bed I was born for, no matter what my husband says. And for once he'll have plenty to say, hunting me high and low, through all the dizzy-dazzle of this gallery, gold blinds and marble stairs. Not that he'll ever find me — I've given him the slip but good. Even if he trots down a hundred corridors and opens a thousand doors, even if he runs smack into this room, no bigger than a broom closet next to all the others, he will never find my hiding place.

The bed of my dreams.

To start with, it's got a velvet canopy.

No.

To start with, it's a bed for one. Not that it's a small bed, a single bed. There's lots of room in this bed, but not for him. No husband's body beside you, hairy-chested or sleek, feet like fish on a marble slab or two warm piglets rooting up to you. None of that. It's a bed for one dreamer, and the one that dreamer dreams. It has a canopy, like I said: nothing flim-flam flighty, but dignified — ambassadorial, you might even say. Red like blood; deep, not dark.

The colour of the heart,
that pulpy bridge where all
the rivers end and start.

I'm in this city under duress, I want to make that clear. Flattened like grass under a roller. I had no part in wanting or planning this; my husband's taken me hostage here. I said that if we had to go, I wanted a bus tour, but he wasn't having any of that. A bus tour with all my girlfriends to come along: Emmie and Erna and Gert and Sal and all the others, hundreds and thousands, the whole pack of them. At least I'd have someone to talk to when he gets his brooding spells, which is all he ever does get up to nowadays. And they pick the restaurants for you, and the hotels, and every minute of your time's accounted for. You don't get a chance to feel strange, your shoes gone slippy-slidey so there's no place you can plant your feet and fold your arms and say you'll never budge. No occasion, you have no occasion at all to wonder if the person next to you, sleeping beside you and eating across the table from you all these years, is more of a stranger than the driver of the bus, who'd be friendly at least, thinking of the tip you might squeeze into his palm.

My bed has columns: sober, not spindly. Tassels hanging from each little lap of the canopy — *lap* is the only word I can find for them. Lap as in dewlap: upside-down bells; or yes, like breasts flappy as tea towels hung on the line. The woman in my bed has no breasts at all, to judge from the coverlet — you can see her feet bob up towards the end of the mattress, but nothing at all where her breasts should be. *Breasts* sounds so runaway, marshmallowy. *Bosom's* better — except that women don't have bosoms any more. We don't even know how to pronounce the damn word.

This strange woman sleeping in my bed may have no breasts, but she makes up for it with all that hair, braided like egg challah on the top of her head. Yellow hair, like Katie Maguire's, Katie sitting beside me on the bus, grades one to six, Brookvale Consolidated. Slipping me holy pictures, swearing that if only I prayed hard enough to her Blessed Virgin my hair would jump overnight from black to gold. I prayed so hard the roof of my mouth got blisters, but my hair stayed black as coal and poker straight, even in my dreams.

This bed of mine is mounted on a platform, so it's like a stage; there's a small white dog keeping watch beside a pair of slippers, so you could hightail it out in an emergency. The pillow's big and round: not hard, but solid. Which is for the best: more headaches are caused by soppy pillows than the world gives credit for. I myself favour a pillow tough as a telephone directory, and I've never woken up with an ache in my head all my years as his wife, now officially forty-five and the achievement of a lifetime, so to speak.

We never fight at home, it's only because I know we never fight that I agreed to come here in the first place, and what should happen but we're daggers drawn? Right here in the picture gallery, him gawking in front of painting #11,001, expecting me to follow like a dog on a leash, but I said no. It was time to move on, we'd seen more than enough already, all I wanted was to sit down someplace snug and snap my eyelids shut. But he kept on staring at that picture, staring and staring, the whites of his eyes near swallowing their yolks. And the more I tugged at him to go, the tighter he held on, not a word would he say till what could I do but up and run? Find my way back here, taking the shortest cut you could imagine. Back into bed, covers pulled tight, hand cupping my chin, and my sleeve squoze-up like an accordion.

That creature coming in with a bit of greenery, snapped from the garden hedge, I'll bet — no way that's her husband. Not her twin sister, either, in spite of those skirts and all that golden hair spilling shoulderwards, like it's falling down a flight of stairs. Not her sister, not her husband, but a combination plate: that's to say, a lover. That's how I'd describe the lover I never had: close as a sister; strange as a husband in skirts.

Lover-boy — there's an expression for you. We used to talk that way, the girls and me, coming off shifts at the hospital. How's your lover-boy? Hiya, lover-boy. But this stranger here, coming in through the door to that golden dreamer on the bed — no way to tell whether it's boy or girl, what's hiding under those skirts. I haven't a clue what's going to happen when they meet, the sleeper in my bed, the stranger rushing through the door and dropping not so much as a golden hair on the carpet. Every night of my married life I've picked up his socks, his shirts, and underwear from the floor where he throws them, though the laundry hamper's not a foot away. Every night, year in, year out. That's what I'd look for in a lover: someone who needs no clothes, or never needs to take them off.

And I'm looking for a lover — why else would I have come all this way, to a place I never wanted let loose from his head? The city of love, romance thicker than the letters in alphabet soup. Thinking I just might, at the end of it all, find my lover here, boy or girl, hair like egg challah or coal dust, it doesn't matter which. Just so I find what it is I dream about and can never remember once I wake. Rolled up beside the bars of his blue-striped pyjamas. Never able to remember, though I'm whacked out with dreaming; hardly the strength to pull the curlers from my hair.

No time for dreaming when he courted me: no time for courting, either, just bim bam and next thing you know the knot's tough-tied. On account of the war, and so few of the boys coming home, you grabbed who you could get and were grateful. He kissed me some, but we never once held hands. And here we are now, in the City of Love, and what do I get but waterworks instead of fireworks. And all he can do is complain: *Everything's gone, changed, spoiled.* Nothing's what it used to be however many donkey's years ago he says he came here. Our first night, he tries to get up at two in the morning: get up and walk around to see if that's when the city combs its hair the way it used to, dresses in the old, familiar style. I say no dice, no deal, no way I'm letting you loose, no way you're lugging me out of bed — and such a pitiful excuse for a bed you never did see, more like a camp cot squared, so you toss and turn all night and all the time he's lying beside you staring at the ceiling and won't say a single word. So what have I got out of this escapade, his coming back to someplace I've never been before? What but the chance to give him the jump and land tucked up in the bed of my dreams.

Waiting for my lover, the one who's waited for me, day and night, all these mortal years. This stranger rushing in with just a few ferns, all the roses having jiggled out into this canal or that, he was running so fast to find me. When I get home and they ask me what I brought back for a souvenir from this trip of a lifetime, I'll say, A bed. The dream of a bed, and me, alone, asleep, my lover rushing in, all golden hair and shining skirts. That's what's made the whole damn fuss worthwhile. Come to this city, of all places, with a husband who turns out to be madman, or a madman who turns out to be your husband. Can't even sit down to a meal without having walked ten miles past every menu pasted to a window, never the right window, till my stomach's meaner than a snake tied up in knots.

Maybe he's noticed I'm gone; he must know something's up, even if he doesn't know enough to follow me. Maybe he's run right out, past the ticket booth, all the way to the post office we passed on our way down. Thinking I'll be lining up for stamps, sending home foggy shots of gondolas, mouldy straw hats. And just when I get to the counter, just when I'm fishing for pennies through the ticket stubs and lipstick tubes in my purse, he'll jump out of nowhere and hand some funny money to the girl behind the counter. Putting me back in my place, which is penniless and always has been.

First thing I'll do once we get home is start saving up. Every red cent I can get my fingers on. Salt them away till I can go with a whole apronful to Angelo's Carpentry and say, Make me a bed, on a platform, with a canopy and little lip-laps hanging down, a bed with room for no one but me and whatever I'm dreaming. And when it's done, I'll just lie myself down, and never get up again. Of course, I'll leave the door wide open for that stranger to slip in. Sweet and swank and quiet, so that little dog asleep beside my slippers doesn't even bat an ear.

II.

Egregio Signor, Gentile Signora

I would like a room for the nights of 12–16 May, for my wife and myself. We stayed at the Albergo Marinara on our honeymoon, forty-five years ago, and it would be a great pleasure for us to return. I wonder if we might have the same room we stayed in before: number 12, overlooking the little street with the garden opposite? I realize that this may be an impossible request, and that much may have changed over the years — nearly half a century! — but your kind cooperation in this matter would be greatly appreciated.

III.

La Tempesta: Giorgione. Venezia, Galleria dell' Accademia

No matter how long you look, there's no figuring it out. Who they are, what's between them; whether they even know one another. Or notice the storm breaking over their heads: sky bruised by cloud and split by lightning; sky green as grass and deep as drowning.

The way she has to twist to hold that lump of a baby on her lap. To keep an eye on the soldier standing on the left fork of the lightning, spying on her nakedness. Her whole body gone lumped and clumsy, the way it does when you know someone's watching you and you're in no state to be seen. Naked, except for a petticoat round her shoulders: naked to the rain and cold and dark.

That soldier, onlooker, whoever he is. Why doesn't he jump across to where she's sitting, help her up off the ground? Why doesn't he get them to a place of safety, her and the baby?

Crossing the bridge, we saw a beggar, a man who looked like a soldier, though he wore no uniform. He was all alone; the cardboard square he held up said he had a wife and child in that place where all the bombs had fallen. He had no obvious disfigurement: no missing leg or arm or war wound visible. Perhaps he was mute. Perhaps, like me, he's one of those men who can never come out with a single thing to say when it matters most. But the sign didn't tell us why his wife and child were still in that terrible place and why he was here; how he would get back to them, if he intended to. Whether he was, in fact, no husband or father, but a soldier who'd picked up a gun and killed someone else's wife and child. And so I gave him nothing, and we walked on, into the picture gallery, right into the thick of this summer storm.

Stopping here, in front of this soldier, this woman nursing her baby; stopping and looking together. Under my lids I could feel her eyes; I thought she was looking through mine, until she turned to me, saying, "What are you thinking?" An impossible question; not a question at all, I can see that now. And all I had to do was open my mouth and say something, anything, just to reach across that split she'd opened in the sky. But I could only stand and stare with my mouth shut tight, as if language were a sealed room and I'd used up all the oxygen.

Always her back towards me as she slept. In the red, narrow light of the mosquito lamp her body was a cloud salted with dark stars. You can't pray to a mosquito lamp: it burns differently than the candles in churches, candles in small red jars. No matter how long we let the lamp burn, there were always mosquitoes, blurred planets circling and settling; we would awake each day with yet another stitch of poison in our skins.

We met so soon after the war that we were still in uniform: a nurse, a soldier. We met in one of those sudden, heavy rains that come from nowhere and slick even the spongiest marble. Running from two different directions towards the same shelter: a canopy of vines over a small table set outside a restaurant. Her hair thick with rain, but spilling red-gold around her face, so bright I could look at it only through her reflection. A lamp lit under her skin, burning its way right through the glass. I could tell her none of this, I made no mention of her beauty, though it lapped against everything I thought or felt, then and ever since. Night after night I've lain awake wondering what I could have done, how I could have kept her from turning away as she did; from walking into the rift opened by a storm, and vanishing. I searched for her everywhere, down every street and square, and all I found were my own footsteps. Not a lane or alleyway here that doesn't curve back on itself, and find that self changed past knowing. Five days now, walking from morning past midnight, and never taking the same route twice. Never finding the little square I'd stumbled on that night, watching her face in the window, so clear, so beautiful that face, I would know it anywhere.

The little square with a church on one side and a restaurant with tables spread under a roof of vines. The place where we met, where we'd agreed, if ever we were separated by the crowds, to come and wait for one another. Sitting up late each night, the candles dyed green by the vine leaves overhead, and then her skin, her hair, under the mosquito lamp: a cloud, a sun, red-golden. And suddenly the sky's split by lightning; the earth tears open and you fall, you keep falling farther and farther from the one person who called out the life left in you, who made the skin dance over your bones.

Coming back from the restaurant last night — the wrong restaurant, like all the others — we lost our way and stumbled into the fish market. Flakes of marble, gills, scales all licking up the light the moon was throwing down. We were alone, except for a small white dog that seemed to know exactly where it was going. It had no collar or muzzle, as most of the dogs here do, and it carried, instead of a bone or brandy cask, an empty plastic bottle, the kind you see floating where the yachts and motor launches dock.

I wanted to follow that dog, I knew he'd been sent to me. He was carrying an elixir in that bottle, something so precious it was invisible. If only I'd called out to him; if only I'd knelt down on the stones where she must, just once, have passed; if only I'd beseeched him. But again, I couldn't speak — I couldn't move, even to put my hand out, to show him I meant no harm and could be trusted. If I had, would he have given up even a few drops from his bottle so we might have found each other, come home at last, together?

Would I have returned to the hotel, carrying flowers I'd found on the way — geraniums thieved from a pot, roses sprung up from cracks in sheer marble? Pushing open the door to our room, would I have found her right there, in our bed, under the red roof of the mosquito lamp? Asleep, her hand cupping her ear, listening hard to whatever it is she dreams: lightning, silence, the opened sky.

IV.

In the end they find each other: husband, wife. Somewhere outside the picture gallery; exactly where doesn't matter, since in this city every street's a hiding place and a discovery.

They are footsore and forlorn. This is their last night here, they are heading home tomorrow, everything will go back to the way it's always been. They are hungry as well as tired. This time he lets her choose a restaurant and doesn't even shake his head at what she settles on: a scattering of tables on the lip of a major canal, diesel fumes cutting whatever bouquet your wine may offer, whatever freshness still hugs the bread on your plate. Waiting for the food to come she kicks off her shoes and kneads her small, puffed feet. As always, he says nothing, pulling the bread to pieces, rolling them between his fingers, making eggs or stones, she can't tell which and it doesn't much matter.

The food is overpriced and the waiters contemptuous. She keeps her eyes fixed on her husband's shirt and tie, anticipating how, in a few hours' time, she will crouch down as she's done every night for the past forty-five years and pick them up from the floor. She sits with her elbows on the table, staring through him at the motor boats chugging down the canal, as if expecting them — only one would be enough — to dislodge a stranger, someone proffering the remains of a bouquet. She would follow that summons to the ends of the earth — she's come this far already, hasn't she?

He stares at his plate as if the smears of tomato sauce were half-digested hieroglyphics. His glasses like a slide trombone on the end of his nose, the veins at his temples a code someone's forgotten to keep tapping out. He doesn't look like a man on holiday, but like a man in mourning: not for what's been lost, but for something he's never been able to find. Someone told him, once, of an ill-matched couple who'd come to this city for their honeymoon; how the bridegroom had turned from the body waiting for him in the close, heavy bed. Turned and opened the shutters instead, falling into an endless pillow of green water.

They have eaten their appalling meal in silence. She knows as well as he how badly they've been cheated by the cook, the waiters, the city itself, which has only tantalized them, giving them nothing at all to keep for their own. She never did find a postcard of the bed of her dreams, and she is already forgetting the details of the canopy, the number of braids looped round the dreamer's head, the colour of her lover's skirts. All she remembers with any vividness is the small white dog guarding the bed — and dogs like that you can find anywhere.

He is thinking he deserved to have her turn on him and vanish. Four nights and five days of Rachel: forty-five years of Leah, lying like a bolster in his bed. Squat, stubbed Leah, her golden hair the product of a false elixir. Yet even she has tried a disappearing trick, though she hadn't the skill to carry it off.

How had he let her out of his sight, even for a moment? How had he let it happen, Rachel turning into Leah? All because he could not reach out his hand, utter a word, any word, when it most mattered?

Distress, despair, division — when all of a sudden a storm breaks out. Two couples, natives of this place, are walking their purebred dogs, and the dogs, one of them ridiculously small, the other the size of a pony, rush at each other and begin, frantically, to copulate. Their owners leap to separate them before worse comes to worst. But the harder they yank on the leashes, the faster the animals stick, their legs skewed, strained, rigid as marble. Tears and curses from the lady attached to the small dog's leash; silence from the owner of the pony as he listens, terror-struck, for snapping sounds. Until one of the superbly discourteous waiters runs to the dogs, lifts them in their agonizing pas de deux, and throws them into the canal. Whereupon a miracle occurs, as much a miracle as if the thick, filthy water had turned clear as glass. For the dogs leap apart and up onto the pavement, flapping the water from their coats. Their owners seize them and stomp off, each in a different direction, trailing dogs and abuse in their wake.

They've been staring at this piece of street theatre, the husband and wife: they are transfixed. The suddenness of this storm, the abruptness of its resolution, the possibilities opened and extinguished before their very eyes have entered them like electricity, singeing each branch of their blood. Without a word, they shoot their hands across the table, grabbing one another, holding fast. So fast they can never shake free, no matter how many mazy streets they must turn down to get to their hotel, no matter how many cues for vanishing they give to one another.

The waiter, approaching with the bill, makes no move to part them.

Janice Kulyk Keefer is the author of several works of poetry, prose, and literary criticism. Among her awards are first prize in the CBC *Literary Competition and the National Magazine Award;* Under Eastern Eyes *(University of Toronto Press, 1987), her study of Canadian fiction from the Maritimes, and her novel* The Green Library *(HarperCollins, 1996) were both shortlisted for a Governor General's Award. Her most recent publications are a memoir,* Honey and Ashes: A Story of Family *(HarperFlamingo, 1998),* Marrying the Sea *(Brick Books, 1998), a collection of poetry, and* Two Lands, New Visions *(Coteau Books, 1998), an anthology of contemporary fiction from Canada and Ukraine, co-edited with Solomea Pavlychko of Kyiv, Ukraine.*

Lise Bissonnette

DRESSES

TRANSLATED BY SHEILA FISCHMAN

It ought to be worn with patent-leather pumps, a string of pearls, and most important, with your hair in a coil, the kind that ripples halfway down the back as it comes undone.

I had high-heeled shoes in a matte, smoky grey-black, harlequin glasses, a rhinestone necklace, and hair as straight as we imagined the nuns' would be under their coifs.

It crossed my mind to throw myself into the water; I tried in vain to feel the urge. On the wire hanger with its scrawny shoulders, the little black dress murmured a call to sin. We'd see.

It had been sewn miles away from the boarding school, during the Christmas holidays. I'd been allowed to choose a Vogue pattern, something my mother consented to only for grand occasions, but on this one we were silent. There comes an age when we pass from taffeta to soft crepe; I wanted it to be dark, she merely warned me not to iron it on the right side, that would make the seams shiny. The hem stopped just below the knee, the sleeves at the elbow, the only fullness was at the bosom, where it was draped over as yet non-existent points. At the last fitting my brother had whistled. The legs, he said, weren't bad.

But now, standing at my bedroom closet, Michèle was gazing at it with the pout of a connoisseur. She'd been dealing with boys for a long time now and if I was able to stand up to her, it was through literature. Jean-Jacques Rousseau was on the Index; I could quote him word for word. Borrowed from the Ottawa library, from which they no longer dared ban us, his *Confessions* under my pillow was considered to be the first licentious book to reach our dormitory. I also claimed to know the loves of Claudel and I invented some for Charles Péguy. I impressed the readers of *Seventeen*, including Michèle, who got along fairly well in Latin too.

My black dress was declared to be too sober. It's true, I didn't dare tell anyone where I'd got the image. That of the wife of Yousuf Karsh, a hieratic beauty I'd brushed up against late that fall. The city was so boring in those days that even Churchill's photographer attended the Jeunesses Musicales concerts. I did mental dictation as I listened to the pianists, an odd little habit that took the soul out of Chopin and left me free to observe this high society among whom she stood alone. So white in her black silk that you could hardly see the pearls around her neck. At intermission, I saw her lean her head towards a man whose chin disappeared into his cravat, a layer of softness for a voice entangled in its accent: "Vould you come mit me to see ze artist after ze concert?" She had the remarkable power of not responding, or of responding so briefly that it seemed she hadn't. I wanted to be long, lithe, and unattainable.

Michèle decided otherwise. Of course I'd wanted this black dress so someone would touch me, while she wanted to correct the faint melancholy of this basic garment, which actually looked rather feminine. In English, and passing ourselves off as a pair of hotheads from Hull, after lengthy explorations we bought first the red shoes and then the matching bag. There was no money left for a perm, but we did that at home quite successfully. Glasses

were unthinkable, a myopic gaze being in any case more flattering, and she was going to lend me the earrings and necklace of
fake gold I turned out to be allergic to.

On the evening in question, she found a man with dark hair
and a friend to take us to the Club Chaudière. I wasn't ugly; a
cross between a poodle and a bluish Siamese cat, I felt vague and
strong. "You're more sensual than I am," Michèle decreed, promising herself that she'd borrow the dress the following Saturday.
We claimed we were going to the movies, a double bill that the
chaplain pretended to check on.

The boy was as inane as Péguy would have been at a *bal musette*.
He had thick lips and a kiss curl, and he was a compulsive
hand-holder (his was damp). Nothing could have been longer
than the drive home, complete with the ritual of the backseat
Michèle had warned me to go along with.

I came across as a future nun while I dreamed of wantonness in
soft crepe. I thought of jumping in the water, I searched in vain
for the desire to do so.

Spring came to me on Ste. Catherine Street. A slenderness under
woollen clothes, a warm glimmer on a motorbike, an evil thread
of violin music through the window of a Tourist Room, dust in an
ambulance's wake. I didn't intend to feel provincial for very long.

It was still dark as shopkeepers pushed their displays into the
middle of the sidewalk, series of dresses all the same except for
the colours in the pattern, hung crowded together on racks, with
a piece of cardboard at one end where "$5.00 each/chaque" was
written in felt pen. Surrounded by the smells of plastic and of
sour winter, squashed into a cupboard where half a mirror jutted
out over some packages, I tried on one that moved like daylight
itself. Green spangles were woven into the grey weft, the neckline
was round, the sleeves short, and the waist was barely caught in
the plastic belt, a thin twist in the same green.

Straight and without a fold, it fell like jersey, and it was.
Mid-season, I thought, listening to myself in silence. It's fluid,

jersey, you grow taller when you pour yourself into it, and its two consonants rub against your skin. You feel like Michelle Tisseyre entertaining in her garden on the first evenings that aren't so cool. "Shall I bring you a sweater?" "No, perhaps another few drops of port." And the man's arm brushes against your shoulder as he pours. There'll always be time to go inside.

I felt as if I were twenty years old; I was dismantling the pleasure of it in advance.

The little man with the moustache was keeping an eye on both the sidewalk and the boutique; he saw none of my beauty, which was camouflaged by a winter coat once more when I paid. The jersey would be for other eyes, that very evening.

The bag was light, so light, as far as the corner of the street. For there are limits to frivolity and I had five dollars less for the unexpected — a bookstore that was also displaying its wares in the sun. I spent a long time leafing through the pamphlets published by Éditions du Jour, they were blaring rages unknown in my Ottawa-area boarding school. The door was open and I worked up the courage to go inside as far as the first section of shelves, which disappeared into the half-light of noon. The book-seller was affable and I was terrified by his voice, that of an examiner in search of brilliant students. "You're studying philosophy at your age? Nonsense, I imagine." I hadn't said a word and he was confirming the limits of Thomism, an insight that struck me as original.

It cost me a dollar and twenty cents for the brand-new paper-back edition of *The Situation of the Worker*, Simone Weil's journal of her days as a factory worker, a double volume with a red-and-black cover, blood and night. Henri Tranquille had just sold me my first book worthy of the name, and entrance into the world of women who had rebelled, which would lead me later to the world of both George Sand and Rosa Luxemburg.

But I certainly wasn't there yet, though I was in fine form, with my book and my dress in my bookbag. At 101 St. Joseph Boulevard West, I was the last of the regional representatives to take my place at the table where we were to discuss secularism and the Parent report on Quebec's education system. Though at school you couldn't shut me up on the subject, which I used to harass a professor of pedagogy, I would be silent in the presence of the boys, some of whom were about to meet with the minister, Paul Gérin-Lajoie. I would write the press release, however, which only *Le Devoir* would run, abridged: "Through its president, the Presse étudiante nationale (PEN) declares that democratization of the education system must be the primary objective of any reform."

I was thanked as they left the premises for their dinners in Outremont. The only people still there were middle class, the Gestetner operators and stamp-lickers, ready for the night on the town they'd been promised for months. I relinquished Simone Weil and my woollies, the dress clung tenderly — jersey is uncrushable. Jersey for jazz, jersey for the knee offered under the table. To a skinny boy whose blue eyes were looking elsewhere.

Peel Street, second floor, the trumpet blasting into the piano, the beer as bitter as it was illegal at my age. And I plunged forever into the atrocious solitude of a woman who wanted to be one and wasn't. For what the skinny blue-eyed boy saw all around were Juliettes in black sweaters, black skirts, and black stockings, their hair as straight as the very notion of despair, sooty lashes, souls in hell. My green spangles caught in my throat, and my short sleeves undressed me roughly. The sun was totally out of fashion. I spent hours and a night suffering from the springtime that I'd misread so badly.

On the bus home the next day, Simone Weil taught me about detachment from material goods. In vain. I'd felt as if I were twenty years old, and I had dismantled the pleasure of it in advance.

"You aren't going to wear that for making free love!" Rose-Aimée's cry came not from the heart but from the throat. A fluttering of nerves, hers were fierce and accustomed to scandal. As usual, she was speaking as much to the ceiling as to me, with that way she had of pushing both instruction and morality with her chin, of holding high the tablets of the law. Of all of us, she was the only one who had a boyfriend, a deathly pale member of the Catholic student movement with whom she actively practised purity and preached about it so, she made us loathe it.

Facing the closets we were emptying in preparation for packing our bags in June, she finally encountered evil elsewhere than in sermons. Displayed before her was a long nightgown in which a young woman could die a martyr or live condemned to hell: it was a question of what I might have had in mind when I chose it: deep pink percale, with the bodice cut from a piece of lace crocheted by a grandmother I'd never known. Cream and satin was the ribbon that snaked its way through the lace to cinch the empire waist, and the wide pleats fell like those of Josephine de Beauharnais or St. Cecile, patron of music, depending. Rose-Aimée obviously suspected me of designing this wonder and having it made for purposes other than elegant sleep, especially since I'd never worn it. But she was mistaken. I'd wanted it for no particular reason, for an image, to bring beauty into the tedium of the dormitories.

Still, I was about to wear it for the first time, finally. I'd recently met a young man whose natural shyness went well with my desire to be done with regional activities. His name was Roger, I forgave him for it, and in his slow way of moving one could sense the necessary aptitude for practising existentialism. He was long and pensive, with blue-green eyes and a pianist's hands. During meetings he drew. At the movie he stroked my fingers, on the street his fingers brushed my neck, and he said all kinds of intelligent things about the futility of the world. He'd introduced me to his mother, a mistake. Her enthusiasm had put a little too much colour into the shades of grey where we were silent about our feelings.

He had the use of an apartment that belonged to a friend of his in Montreal, where I was going the next day for a final meeting before the summer holidays. He would be alone, he'd take care of the wine, cheese, and candles, we would eat and sleep there, just the two of us. Not another word had been said. But never was a lace-topped pink nightgown so appropriate as for this occasion. The whole dormitory was in on the secret, and with the exception of Rose-Aimée they all agreed. "Don't forget perfume," Michèle had fussed. She lent it to me with a new reverence. She didn't know any boys who had the use of an apartment; I was the first one to cross that particular threshold.

As for free love, you'd have had to be warped to threaten me with it. There were still so many kisses to discover before I got there, so many acts to perform, so many murmurs to commence. I felt nothing but impatience for a window open onto the noise of Dorchester Boulevard, for a pink gown that moves all down its length, for the bitterness of the wine, for the silence we'd flow into before nightfall, and its hours that would be what they would be. We would open them one by one.

And so there I was at seventeen and a half, draped in pink, drinking Spanish Iago, and chatting about Auguste Comte. I'd become acquainted with him at the same time as with Roger, who considered him to be the spiritual father of Jean-Paul Sartre, and I nearly fell genuinely in love with this long, lean boy buried under his words, who bestowed them on me without vanity. We talked about everything except ourselves, even as we moved closer together in the low armchair that we never dared to abandon for the big bed in the next room. I was excited enough to palpitate a little, I would have untied a ribbon, perhaps I did so just before he finally told me into my hair that his heart was strange and a stranger. He traced the lace with his finger: "I love a boy, this is his place, I can't leave him. . . ." His cheek was hollow in the lamplight, his body tense. Was he expecting to see me slip away from him, outside this place, outside of us? But I was filled with contentment. The night passed serenely now, I was fascinated by this man's confession, I was penetrating much deeper than I'd expected into the forbidden, I could put off the decisions of my body, which wasn't serious because it was seventeen years old.

At dawn we went to the mountain to watch the sunrise. The mosquitoes were preparing for a humid day and real summer. We stretched out in the short grass, I imagined us upright and impossible like Tristan and Isolde, who slept with a sword between them.

Roger disturbed the arrangement when he put his hand on my stomach; he was as free now as he was chaste, he could touch a girl.

That was what brought a bellow from the policeman on horseback who was passing by, he drove us from the earthly paradise with words as religious as those of Rose-Aimée. To him I owe the long kiss that my false lover placed defiantly on my neck, love was as free as the air that was gilding both man and beast, we laughed, we were hungry. Life was going to be irresistible.

Lise Bissonnette is the author of two novels, Following the Summer *(Anansi, 1993), which was a finalist for the Governor General's Award for French fiction, and* Affairs of Art *(Anansi, 1996). Her short-story collection,* Cruelties, *was published by Anansi in 1998. From 1990–98 she was the publisher of the influential Montreal newspaper* Le Devoir. *Currently she is the director of La Grande bibliothèque du Québec.*

Sheila Fischman, Canada's pre-eminent translator, has translated more than eighty books and has won numerous awards. She is a two-time winner of the Felix-Antoine Savard Award from Columbia University and of the Canada Council translation prize. Her translation of Michel Tremblay's Bambi and Me *was awarded the 1998 Governor General's Award for translation. Sheila Fischman has translated all of Lise Bissonnette's fiction.*

Michael Winter

THE

PALLBEARER'S

GLOVES

Martin says, I've seen a man walk a wire forty feet up.
I've never seen that done live, I say.

He follows me, balanced, along the curb. Arms out, foot in front of foot.

And there was a half-alive gorilla, he says.

Half-alive?

Well, there was a man inside dressed up.

Martin says, You've got nice-from-behind legs.

I turn. What about the fronts?

Bony, he says. Bony as Daddy. And then he says, You know what? Daddy smells bad. But it's not him. It's what he spits up.

I lift him onto my shoulders. Martin says that Daddy had shown him where the hair was falling out. And new tufts like goose fur were underneath. He says the whole house had smelled bad and it stayed bad until after Daddy had been gone two days.

The bald man in grey pyjamas, with a strange new thinness in his hips. On his right side, the only way he could lie without the lung coughing. They had opened his ribs and left the lung in.

Bruce had said, It's me, Gabe.

I could recognize his voice.

You got a good view.

Oh, terrific, he says. Trees. All day trees.

And it was trees. A sea of deep green with no deciduous for colour. It was fall and there would have been colour.

I brought you a photo.

Bruce studies the photo of Martin. He springs it between his fingers. Martin was doing things he hadn't seen. Dressed for kindergarten. There were the cherry and birch around their house, turning. Then his body gently shook. His large eyes closed tight.

He says, I'm sorry about this.

Bruce. It's okay.

I take his hand. I have never taken his hand. I have, but we were very young, crossing a street.

I say, You must be terrified.

No. Not terrified. It's terrible.

I hold the hand tightly. There is a laxness in the tone of the muscles. He lifts himself to spit in a plastic bucket, and I see the staples on his chest. The pyjamas from Mom. His spit smells of sharp chemicals, a clear liquid that had flowed into his arm a week before. They use this stuff, he'd said, grinning, in chemical warfare.

I ask if there's anything I can do. Anything.

He says, Ann doesn't visit enough.

Junior arrives from Florida. He brings his girlfriend, Carol. I greet them at the airport.

Hiya, Gabe, she says. Wow, Junior, your family all this tall?

She hugs me hard. She seems proud of me. As if Junior had something to do with how I turned out, which is probably true.

We wait for their luggage. And stretched out on the carousel is a six-foot-tall stuffed Sylvester. For Martin.

Junior: Hey, they broke his neck.

Carol: His neck is all wonky.

On the way into town Junior holds Sylvester's neck and turns the head out the window. He says, Look, Sylvester, guardrails. *In* the city. Man, we're back in the sticks.

I say, You want to go to Signal Hill?

No, Gabe. Straight to your place. No, stop in to Butcher's.

I drive down to Water Street. Butcher's is a strip club that Junior used to work in. Carol says, I'm staying for one drink.

The bouncer takes Junior's hand in an arm-wrestling gesture and Junior says, They're with me. In a booth Carol leans over her drink and, while Junior is talking to the bouncer, says, We're married. She says this as if it's something she was not supposed to reveal but, against Junior's wishes, had no intention of not telling me.

She says, Junior wanted to stay down there and apply for a green card. So I said, Honey, let's get married. And we got married. But he doesn't want you all to know because, he says, we married for the wrong reason. But we love each other now, don't we, honeybun?

She grabs him around the waist and he leans reluctantly.

Junior: Mom'll be really mad if she finds out.

What do you mean *if*?

He nods a find-the-right-moment nod.

The bouncer gives Junior a playful punch on the biceps.

The next day I take them to the hospital. We bring a pineapple. I realize too late that I haven't prepared Junior well enough. Junior sinks a little at the knees.

Hi, bro.

June.

I cut the top and heel off the pineapple, then slice it vertically like a pie. Carol introduces herself. I hand around wedges of pineapple.

Bruce: This is the way to eat pinochle.

Junior: You growing sideburns?

Bruce: Only hair I got.

I have told Junior to talk, to entertain. He goes: I gave Carol a few driving lessons, Bruce. She said, Junior, one hand on the wheel. I'm used to driving with my knees, see. Fifteen years of driving with my knees. But she wants one hand. This is Disneyland, not Newfoundland. And then she doesn't like how I'm passing. I tell her, You need momentum, Carol. You can pass anything if you got momentum. You flow through traffic. But she says, You're getting too close. So I slow down. Then there's two-lane passing. And she says okay. And I look at her. I had momentum back there, but now I got no momentum. You want me to build another cylinder on the head of your block? And then, on a curve, I take this Porsche. For a joke. Porsche doesn't like that. Comes right back on a straightaway, zipping. And I say, Oh, yeah you're fast, buddy. You can take a little Tercel on a hill with my wife and the dog in the back and a fifty-pound bag of blue potatoes over my shoulder. Oh, yeah, you're speedy.

Bruce: Your wife.

Junior raises a finger to his lips. We have been withholding information all our lives.

You got a good place down there?

Oh, yeah, Bruce, nice. There's cockroaches with wings. I let the reptiles go; they're too hard to hit with a towel — though I've killed a few with my blowgun. Nailed them to the ceiling, but Carol doesn't like that, do you, Carol. Junior pauses. And you're going to a good place, Bruce.

What's that?

You're going somewhere good.

Another pause.

You mean heaven.

Yeah, heaven.

I'm not going to heaven.

Yes, Bruce.

I'm going there, but not now.

He clasps a hand around the bone in his thigh. He says: Gabe thinks I'm going to live a long time.

You are, I say.

Junior rubs the seam at the side of his jeans. He says, Does Ann have a lot of wood? I'm gonna get her a massive turkey for Christmas. Is the house well-insulated? You can take off one of the outlets to check.

Bruce closes his eyes and smiles. Think I can have a piece of that turkey?

And then Ann and Martin arrive, Martin with no shirt on. Ann calm. She hasn't seen Junior in, what, five years? Bruce, quickly: It's been three. We were together before Junior left.

In the hallway Junior says, That's it, Gabe. I'm quitting smoking.

Junior and Carol fly to Corner Brook to be with Mom. And then they drive in together in Junior's old Cordoba. He took it off blocks and drained the cylinders of oil. Junior: We were in a gas station, Gabe. Mom was looking in the coolers, she doesn't want a coffee. Orange crush, she says. Ooh, cream soda. *Red* cream soda. So I take her, tender like, by the shoulder and say, Mom. You don't get out much, do you?

Junior tells her Bruce is on the way out. His head has shrunk, his eyes are goggly, and he's got no legs. Mom is clenching her ears. It's as if the muscles in her temples are seized shut.

Bruce the oldest but still a young man, just forty-two. He still has a quick look in his eyes. I say, Do little exercises. Lift your legs, Bruce. You've got to get your strength.

But I cough, Gabe. It saps me.

I've been visiting every day. I sit in the blue chair and read from my journal, from stories I'm writing. He asks if I'm interested in him and I say of course. That it's all down, everything. He says he's keeping a diary. He's writing down his life for Martin.

When they move him to the palliative care unit his spirit improves.

You can open the window here, he says.

And the Waterford River. There are houses and traffic. With

the window open, the city is with him in the room.

In the hallway is a large stained glass, he says. And the nurses coddle you. They bring poached eggs in ceramic cups.

It's here that his family has come for the last time.

Ann had this plan. To have Bruce home for an afternoon. So he could admire the outdoors through his windows. She'd rent a car. But Junior doubted it.

It would probably kill him.

But he would have that afternoon.

I know that's all he wanted. One afternoon in the light of his living room. A little medieval music on the stereo, the soft juniper. Martin coming home from kindergarten with his recess box and the two Ziploc baggies. His knapsack with gym sneakers and a colouring book. The sneakers too small so he wears thin socks. A boiled egg with toast cut into soldiers. The couch and the cat and a strip of the bathroom if you turn your head. The stained deck with some split birch for the woodstove.

Junior: Bruce thinks he's going to get better.

What else can he think.

He can be realistic.

You can't be realistic. Death isn't realistic.

We drive to Ann's. Over the moonscape of rock near Avondale. The sun punches through and lights up a knoll here, a valley there. The burgundy blueberry bushes, small bowls of grey ponds. If I were to make a film, I'd have a scene here.

At Ann's. I hear Mom say about a book: If I was interested in it at all I would have been very impressed.

We walk around the pond. Junior notices that a thin film of ice has just caught over. I ask him why water sinks as it gets colder, but rises before freezing. He says there is no good reason for it. It's one of the reasons he believes there is a God.

Looking at the canoe in the dark. Martin: It looks blue, but I know it's green.

Junior: If it's blue, it's blue.

Junior's wife cuts Martin's hair. And then Ann's. And then Mom's and mine. I've got a weight line in back. Carol does the New-foundland accent and Ann does the Florida. Martin says, Carol's favourite saying is Don't you just hate that?

Ann is shaking a cast-iron pan full of hot Italian sausages and onion. Carol cuts up three tomatoes they've brought from Mom's garden. Garlic and crushed chili. The sausages spit and cry. I put on water for pasta. Martin watches me lay plates in the oven to warm.

Mommy, he's cooking the plates.

Carol says, Everything with meat in it is really different between here and down there.

Junior: Fat. Fat content. Down there ham is laced with fat.

Ann says she's glad they've come now. There's no need, she says, for you to visit after.

Mom: It's all bullshit anyway, what they'd be saying at his funeral. Because it's not the truth, is it.

Junior: I'm coming when he dies. I'm coming both times.

Junior and I paddle to the island. We take it slow to slice the ice. I have to spot for rocks. It's Bruce's canoe. The ice splits like torn paper. Junior takes a beer, which he balances on the floor of the canoe. Bruce, he says, wouldn't cut the trees here because he wanted to look at them.

He's a man of beauty.

He says, What do you think of Carol?

She's great.

She's a little fat, don't you think?

I think she looks great.

And I don't like how she treats me in front of Mom.

Junior. She's funny and she's strong.

She's got two kids in Tampa, did you know?

I hadn't heard that.

He says, We've been fighting. She'll go back now and strip the apartment down and move back to her mother. I know it.

I hear him glug the beer and toss the bottle. It smashes the ice and bobs.

I need a challenge, he says. I got a Honda CRX. So small I wouldn't survive in it. I killed a vulture with a .357 Magnum. Big guy. Fucking around with my pork chops. He was trying to swoop down on them. One shot, poacher's rule. If you shoot twice, warden can tell, he can echolocate you.

When I hear this, it sounds like: He can electrocute you.

I'll come home for three weeks, Gabe. In November. The van is my safety net. If I fall I got the van.

On the paddle back he shows me the J-stroke.

Have you told Mom yet?

No, Gabe. I was gonna tell her and then she whispered to me — she'd been eyeing Carol — she said no matter where I am she'd come to my wedding.

Junior leans back against the gunnels and stares at the sky. Out here you get the stars. He says, I live between two bodies of water, Gabe. You got to come down. Gulf of Mexico and the North Atlantic.

The North Atlantic?

Yeah, Gabe. Atlantic is still the north, even in Florida. I drive east after work, in the dark, and there's lightning. And in behind the lightning there's an orange atmosphere. From the sun. The sun has sunk but the light's still there, banking off the clouds in the dark. That's the best time of day, driving home in that residue.

Ann is making tea. Junior is finishing a box of beer and eating out the fridge shelf by shelf. He wants a cigarette terribly. My mother has her legs up on the couch. She is reading scripture. Martin in bed.

Ann says she had woken up to Bruce struggling. He couldn't get enough air. The ambulance service coating the tops of trees with orange light. And now it's been sixty-one days. Ann says she knows. That some people find her behaviour callous: They can't believe how I'm treating Bruce. Your husband. Bring him home, they say. They visit and wait for their cup of tea and cake. Their sandwich and a dill pickle. They sit right where you are and demand service. And I have to work and take care of Martin and drive into town and visit Bruce and boil a kettle for them while they sympathize and tell me what a loving wife would do, what they would do for poor Bruce. Well, shag them.

Mom looks up from Romans. She says, The trouble is you have no past. This kind of thing you expect to happen in your sixties. And by then, you've stuck by the person. You nurse them through anything because of that past. Bruce got sick too early.

You're saying I'd do more if I was seventy.

A sudden hatred overtakes us. Ann: And I suppose you'll be writing all this down, she says. Colder than a witch's tit.

I have never heard her use this tone.

Mom: You could see how besotted Bruce was. When Ann said she'd marry him. He called me once and I said, Well, Bruce, you've got yourself a woman there. I hope there won't be any complaints. And he said, No, Mom, I won't complain. That was six years ago. And when I saw him at the hospital and asked how he was he said, quietly, I've got no complaints. I know he was thinking about that. He never forgets those things.

Ann, relenting: You must write about the things that you love.

Junior's eyebrows go up and he nods to me. It's midnight now and I follow him outside. At the woodpile: Gabe, zip zip?

Junior holds Ann's chainsaw.

Quit it.

Got to, Gabe.

You'll wake Martin.

You don't want to help your sister-in-law?

You don't know what I do.

I know you don't zip wood.

I don't do a lot of things.

You don't paint her house.

I'm scared of heights.

Just a little, Gabe. Hold the logs. Just stack for me.

Sorry.

Afraid of wood in general?

I don't like the pace you set.

You don't like to get it done quick.

I like to enjoy my moment with the wood.

Yeah, Gabe, I can see that's your whole problem. You like to enjoy a moment with the wood. A little station break with your meal ticket. Gabe, you got to do things quick. Get in, get out. Don't fuck around in there. Speedy man. Points are dirty.

Junior starts scraping at the plug with a screwdriver.

I say, The moment is all we have.

You've got the future. The whole fucking works in front of you.

Me: I thought you were a moment-by-moment kind of man.

Moments, yeah, moments. But I got a plan, Gabe. I got the future. Right here. Junior taps his head with the screwdriver.

I tell him I have a hard time believing it. There's no future for Bruce.

Oh, but that's unfair. That's unusual. He's what you'd call a worst-case scenario.

I'd call him my brother. Dying.

Oh, so he's dying now.

I never said he wasn't.

Funny, thought I heard it.

All I ever said was that he looks to me like he's getting better. That he's a young man. He's putting on weight.

That's water, Gabe. He's bloated. He's a dead man.

Well, perhaps it's not the best thing to tell that to his face.

Junior lays the chainsaw on the woodhorse.

You saying I told him that?

You told him he's going to heaven.

I said, You're going to a good place. I did not say, Bruce, you're a dead man.

I get the phone call in the small hours. It's still dark.

This is Joan at the palliative care unit? I'm afraid Bruce's taken a turn.

I drive under a full moon, eating an apple. The quiet, empty, blue city. I clomp down the dark corridor in heavy boots on the red tiles. I didn't realize how loud the boots were. Joan intercepts me. She says, You just missed him.

In the hot room he is lying on his back. The first time I've seen him on his back in months. Just a small yellow lamp on. His feet and kneecaps poking up the white sheet. His eyes are open. His head hot and I can hear breathing, except it's from the man across the hall.

I help Joan peel the art off the walls and we drape the art over his legs because there is nowhere else to lay it. I sit with him until Ann comes.

Ann: What do you think?
  Me: Put the white shirt on him. And the tie.
  Ann: He never wore ties.
  He wore slacks with sneakers.
  He's not going to have any shoes. And he never wore underwear.
  Ann, you've got to have him in underwear.
  He doesn't have any. He had raggy old pairs. I think he expected me to get him some and I never did.
  Let me get the underwear.

Ann is drinking brandy from a Mason jar as Ed Chafe plays guitar with his left foot resting on his right. Bruce is laid out in his white Edwardian shirt. Junior talking to Harold Drover about polar bears: the only animal that will stalk us as if we're just another animal, like seals. Harold: Yams are the only food you can live on. Martin asks why guests get fed first. Mom: They wouldn't come if they were fed last.

I am a pallbearer, along with Arnold Chubbs and Ann's two brothers and Mike Pierce and Harold Drover. Junior was asked, but he said he was too tall to carry it. We wear white cotton gloves. Martin wants a pair. I say, I'll give you mine when we're done.

I need a lift and the hearse driver says I can go with him. So it's me and Bruce and the driver in the hearse, cruising to Conception Harbour. Bruce in the box between us. The sky low and dark and sad. There is no wind and the sea is some calm, the driver says. Hasn't seen it so flat in ages. All the colours of the woods thrown into the harbour.

I guess you do this a lot, I say.

Oh, yes, he says. I know this road well.

There is a shoe streak of dog shit on the church steps, and not much room to get through. The hushed, full church. I am surprised there are people. Ann drapes a sheet over the coffin. Junior holds Martin as she does this. Martin a little bored, but he stays quiet. Then he walks proudly around the pews to his friends. There is a young minister, the pews are full. I'm surprised by the numbers and it makes me feel some kind of hope. Hope had gained ground on desolation.

We carry the coffin out of the church as the pews sing "How Great Thou Art" and I can hear Mike Pierce sobbing behind me at that surge of music and the poet Andy Meades I see his hand with a big black stone ring. Andy takes my gloved hand and holds it as we walk down the aisle with the coffin and that song, which is a powerful, positive song, a strong song with all those voices in it. We carry him out to the car and drive to the cemetery, which overlooks the blurred hills of Avondale. There is a brown horse in a field and the gravediggers rest beside a backhoe and a truck. The pallbearers stand around the grave and Ann places a dry shaft of golden wheat on the coffin. The head undertaker lowers the coffin on a hydraulic system operated by his shoe. I watch the pallbearers tug off their gloves and lay them on the casket as it sinks. I do the same. When the lid is flush with the surface they stop and cover it with green felt.

I say to Ann, No one takes pictures at a funeral. She says she'd noticed that and wished someone had. Of Martin playing around the new tombstones and of the pallbearers' gloves. Andy Meades says he thought about taking a camera but didn't know if it was proper. Junior mentions the spectacle of past funerals, of horses with black plumes. The sky had cleared and it's warm and sunny. Bruce's given us a good day, our mother says, smiling.

We walk out to Ann's brother's house. Patrick. We eat white triangles of sandwiches. Junior leans over to check the legs of a black chair. He says, A Windsor chair. You know how old this is, Gabe? It used to be green. It would have been used on a porch. It was painted black when Queen Victoria died. There are no squares, he says, on a good chair.

When we leave, Patrick says: Now don't be a stranger — and don't be a fixture either.

Martin puts his legs over my ribs. I can feel his short breaths. The lightness of him balanced on me.

You're Daddy.

I'm not Daddy.

Pretend you're Daddy.

What would Daddy do?

He would snuggle right in.

I take Martin one night a week. We have supper, then read and it's bedtime. The first time he threw up and I asked him about it. He was embarrassed. He'd tried to cover the vomit in the sheet. He'd made a little pocket of it and tucked it under the pillow. He said he'd woken up and didn't know where he was. He didn't recognize anything and that had scared him. And he wasn't that fond of supper and up it came. I said, You want to get in with me? and he said, Of course.

You're my favourite uncle.

And you're my favourite nephew.

He kicks. I'm your only nephew.

He asks where Daddy is now. I say, He's in God's book. Martin says, Is he in heaven? Is he with Mrs. Tuft and her knitting socks for all the angels? I say, He's in God's book, and when God remembers everyone you'll see him again.

We watch a videotape that I took with Bruce on the ice of the pond. The audio was broken on the camera so it's just pictures. Bruce and Ann walk out on the ice, about halfway out, their backs slightly bent, testing its strength. They do an impromptu dance. Bruce is wearing a navy Russian coat and a fur hat. His beard. And he starts the dance. Or perhaps the camera prompts it. Or maybe it's Martin urging them. But they waltz over the pond with Martin chasing, falling, and you can almost hear Martin's screams. The next frame jerks to black and then it's me and Bruce on the ice. We stand looking at each other, our feet still. Our breath in steady blue puffs. Martin, you can tell, is telling us to dance. But we box. We shadow box over the ice, just like when we were kids, feinting. And Ann loses interest in us as she finds a juniper bare of needles covered in silver thaw. You can see the camera's indecision and then choice. The camera pans off the boxers to study that dormant, glittering juniper. And you know that Martin is somewhere below, someplace screaming for the men to dance, grabbing at their bare hands.

Michael Winter is the author of Creaking in Their Skins, *a collection of stories published by Quarry Press (1994), and of* One Last Good Look, *a collection forthcoming (1999) with Porcupine's Quill. He is a former fiction editor with* TickleAce *magazine in St. John's, Newfoundland, and now lives in Toronto, where he is at work on a novel.*

Greg Hollingshead

BORN
AGAIN

It wasn't until the boy heard the scuff of a shoe on the concrete porch above him that he could feel the defeat in the slump of his body against the bottom step, and this feeling of defeat was why when he heard his father sniff, he heard disapproval. Except his father only ever sniffed when he had caught a whiff of something or did not know it but was getting ready to sneeze, which he would do with tremendous violence, in a fan of chunks and spray, and just as the boy was pulling in his head, he caught it too: the swamp chalk fragrance of river mud.

"Breeze from the south," his father said.

The boy's eyes rose to the toes of his father's shoes, protruding now over the edge of the porch. They climbed his father's trousers and his white shirt to the planes of his face and did not follow his father's gaze — southward, down the street — but continued to rise, to the fall of his father's hair against his forehead and beyond, to the grey sky. The flood was receding, the kids were in school again, he could practically hear the bell, the scrape of the desks, but not his desk, because he couldn't go back yet, was sick now, in the care of Mrs. Told next door, until five-thirty, when his mother would arrive home exhausted from work and collapse on the chesterfield with a magazine and a cigarette and coffee for the half-hour she would put the vegetables on to boil, the ones she had peeled and sliced and covered with salted water this morning while having her first cigarette and coffee before she left for work. And she would say, "What is it now? Could you let me catch my goddamn breath for one second?"

The father came down the steps. "Stand up," he said.

The boy pushed himself to his feet.

The father held back the hair to study the crusted infection. He let go and rubbed the boy's scalp. "It's pink eye. You'll be fine. You'll stick around and play, or something. Just not with the Told kid. What's his name?"

"Darko."

"Darko. He's getting too old for you. . . . I almost said, 'And too weird,' but what's weird? And don't go down to the river."

"Why's Darko weird?"

The boy's father looked at his watch. "Maybe when you're older."

"I'm older now."

"So are we all."

As the father descended the front lawn to the sidewalk and started across the street, the boy watched him — the long arms, the back-turned thumbs, the predatory lope — and when the father had disappeared into the poplars that lined the lane to the mills, the boy sat down on the step. He straightened a leg and looked at his foot in its sneaker, angling it left and right. He did the same with the other. It was clear to him that he did not have the advantage of his father's feet, which resembled the bound feet of Chinese women, compressed in a vise heel to ball and then talced until the spider veins faded to white. Feet so broad and high that the tongues of the father's shoes were no match for the gap created by the hump of the arch. Feet so short from being high-arched that the empty toes of the father's shoes curled like the toes of pixie boots. The foot in the sneaker

at the end of the boy's leg was not like his father's. It was not a
foot you would never think capable of carrying anyone any
distance at all and yet in stride with the other fast-moving,
homing in on its destination, eating the miles, while high above,
the eyes moved in their sockets famished and wary. The father
believed that a man should bear himself erect and bow his head
to no one and to nothing. He had no patience with the servile
future he saw in the boy's hunched shuffle, and when they walked
together and the boy, his eyes downcast, stooped for a nickel or
a four-leaf clover, the father would stop talking, and when the
boy straightened with the discovery in his fingers, his eyelids
would start to flutter, and then would come the cuff across the
back of the head.

Later in life the boy believed that on this morning, as he sat
alone on the step and watched his father walk to work, he first
came to consciousness, first became aware of his own awareness,
an inner eye opened and this was himself. Except by eleven he
was too old; he must have been conscious before this. More likely,
the agitation of his emotions as a result of not being in school
with his friends but at home in the care of Mrs. Told, the woman
he loved, threw up a mental picture of himself at his desk, and
this picture threw up another, of what he was doing instead —
sitting here on the step watching his father walk to work — and
it was the double exposure of this second picture by its difference,
first from the other, of sitting at his desk, and second from the
actually doing it — actually sitting here on the step — that fixed
it so vividly in his memory (while others faded) that however
conscious he was at that moment, the unfading vividness of the
memory came to require an explanation, and dawn of consciousness seemed more likely than most.

But first time or not, the boy on the steps that morning understood that the back-turned thumbs, the high-arched feet, the
predatory lope, did not belong to him but to another, his own
father, yes, but not him, and as he looked out at the world —
the houses on the other side of the street, the trees over there,

the sidewalk, the lawn — all of it was strange to him, but more than strange, hulking and sullen, puffed with resentment, that he should ever have considered any of it part of himself.

"Your suffering eyes," Mrs. Told murmured, holding the boy's face between her hands as she examined the infection when he came to her back door for his lunch.

He nodded, or tried to, and then he dropped his gaze to the perfect crimson disks of Mrs. Told's toenails in her pink sandals. At night as he was falling asleep he would levitate through his bedroom wall and across the driveway and through the bedroom wall of Mrs. Told and stretch out on top of her as she lay naked in her bed sleeping or waiting — he liked to think waiting. This was why as he turned from her to climb the steps to the kitchen his mind was in confusion, and why when he heard her say something behind him he did not know what it was, and must have glanced back as he groped for a kitchen chair and then was about to sit down before he realized that someone was already sitting at the table, and this was Darko Told.

The boy froze.

Mrs. Told was now in the kitchen too. "After lunch," she said, "it is necessary for me I run errand."

Darko was using both hands to make robotic overcorrections to the direction of his face. When he had got it just right, he unleashed a smile so brilliant the boy was forced back.

"Run?" Mrs. Told was asking. "Errands are *run*? I *run*? Or is *run* like engine runs, or person runs business?"

The boy glanced around miserably. "I guess so," he said.

"This is guesswork? You surprise me."

When the boy turned back to Darko, Darko's eyebrows had lifted as if he too were surprised, but not really.

"You will be with him in meantime after you will eat," Mrs. Told said.

Again the boy glanced around, this time to see which of them she was talking to, though he knew it made no difference. She had gone back to preparing their lunches. He sat down. He hadn't played with Darko Told since last spring.

Darko was beautiful like his mother, but his hair was white gold, whereas hers had the crop and sheen of a mahogany helmet. Darko's hands were flat on the table. "How are your eyes?" he asked. He was probably home with a cold. His voice was deeper than the boy remembered it.

"Good."

"Tell no one, but I am in strong health also. After lunch we explore flood damage."

"I can't," the boy answered quickly. "My dad said."

Darko may have hesitated, and then he said, "Okay with me."

The boy could not tell if Darko was agreeing or objecting.

Lunch was pink meat piled between thin crescents of black bread. The black bread was a new experience for the boy, a wild sour ferment. Sharing the plate with the sandwich was the biggest dill pickle he had ever seen. The pickle was so big that it insisted on the identity of pickle and cucumber. The sweating, warty torpedo in its puddle of green juice might have been something harvested from the bottom of the sea.

The boy looked at Darko, who leaned forward, confidential. "After lunch I show you pictures of my father."

The boy had seen most of them before. They were pictures of a handsome man of wealth and leisure, a sportsman perhaps, who faced the camera boldly, like one whose life had been in large part devoted to pleasing that instrument. They were taped into a small album that Darko kept behind the taller books in his bookcase. A habit of mental timidity made conclusions difficult for the boy, but he did wonder why they were not like regular photographs but cut from magazines.

"He's alive, right?" he asked, trying to be casual but instead was shocked to sound so tactless.

"Yes. He lives in New Mexico. Testing fighter jet."

They were standing in the Tolds' backyard. While they were

eating lunch and later sitting on Darko's bed looking at the
pictures, the clouds had passed, and the sun was now blinding.
The boy was shading his pink eye, aware of the dampness of his
pocket against his leg, from the pickle, which was still there.

"He visits often," Darko added, with a long blink. "But his
work is done in secret. He must fly here under cover of darkness."

The boy's head was bowed at an angle into his hand. In that
attitude he nodded.

"Come with me to back field," Darko said.

"I can't, my dad said." When the boy took his hand away, Darko
was looking at him.

"Not river," Darko said carefully. "Only far as back field."

"I can't," the boy said again, and now he didn't have the courage
to look at Darko at all.

"Too bright in back field," Darko offered.

"Yes . . ."

"Fine. We do something not so interesting, therefore. Here, in
shade."

"No, I have to stay in our house, alone. My dad said."

Darko didn't say anything. And then he said, "He is dangerous
man, your father, I think."

The next morning the father and the boy, whose pink eye was
better but still infectious, walked south in order, as the father
said, to monitor the situation. He meant the flood. The street
they lived on, and were now walking down together for the first
time that the boy could remember, was separated from the main
residential grid of the town by a hydro right-of-way. There was
just the street running parallel to the power line, a concession
road really, and the miscellaneous churches, halls, businesses,
and houses that had built up along it over six decades. Most
of the buildings before they reached the highway were familiar
to the boy because this was his weekday walk.

Once they had passed the school and not long after it the
highway, they crossed to the middle of the street and made their

way among parked cars and through a gap in a low wall of sandbags and across fifty feet of muck and flood garbage to the edge of a sheet of brown water, where the passing branches and scraps of wood made slow revolutions. On either side of where the boy and his father stood, the double column of houses did not end but like the street simply descended into the water, the next house a little deeper in than the one before it, the current rearing back gently from each upstream surface in a low standing wave. The flood was receding, but the river was still half a mile wider than it should have been. The farthest house had water to the tops of its ground-floor windows and a high-water mudline partway up the roof.

This moment too would stay with the boy. What most impressed him was how easily the river had undone the human function of these buildings, how easily it had reduced them to useless cisterns, out-of-place obstructions to the flow, and maybe it was his state of mind from yesterday, but as he gazed out over the brown expanse it seemed to him that the pretensions of human life amount to empty dreams that will soon be swept away.

The father's thoughts must have taken a more positive turn, for he placed a hand on the arm of the sightseer beside him, a crewcut man in a blue suit, and said, "Nothing beats a good flood. If we could count on one a year, this would be a new world. Look what the Nile's done for Egypt. Or ask yourself: What would Babylon be without the Tigris and Euphrates?"

The sightseer chuckled and shook his head as if delighted to have been addressed from the ranks of the harmlessly insane. But the boy had often noticed how difficult it was for people with little experience of his father and only an immediate context for what he was saying to recognize when they were being casually tormented.

The father put his hand on the boy's shoulder. "I guess you'll remember this," he predicted, or advised, in a voice intended also for the ears of the man in the blue suit. More quietly, he said, "*Keep your head up or you'll be fitted with a neck brace.*"

After a few more minutes of looking out at the water, the father volunteered to help load sandbags onto a flatbed truck, and the boy — who could barely lift the one sandbag he tried — walked back home by himself. As he passed the school he could hear the kids. He looked at his watch, it was lunchtime, and it came to him that this could be his daily walk. It was not, not today, and yet someone watching might reasonably assume that it was. And this possibility (that someone watching would get what he was doing wrong) threw up a picture of himself walking home for lunch, and this picture threw up another, of what he was doing instead — walking home from the flood with his father — and as a result he must have gone conscious again, or something like it, because the buildings and the fences and the telephone poles and the trees and the roadway and even the broken and heaved sidewalk under his feet rose up once more against him, and it seemed to him that these things knew that he was not with them, that despite having just seen what the real world will do to human dreams, he had not changed, was intractable perhaps, committed in a stubborn, wilful way to himself, to that inner eye and its secret dreams and fabrications, and the dread he experienced as he continued walking was one he had known at least a little bit every day for as long as he could remember but never with a weight and darkness like this.

A few days later the boy was sitting on the chesterfield leafing through one of his mother's magazines when he spotted a familiar face. "Hey, here's Darko's dad!"

"You're kidding," his mother said. She came quickly from the kitchen, wiping her hands on a dishtowel, looking to the front window.

The man in the picture seemed to be arriving at an event of some kind, mounting broad steps. He was wearing a collarless jacket. The boy held up the magazine. "In here."

His mother turned from the window and looked at the maga-zine, but only briefly. "I don't think so," she said.

"Why isn't it?"

"Because . . . look. " She pointed to the caption. "Read. It's an actor. Mickey somebody. One of the Mickeys. Whoever he is, Darko's father is not, believe me, a Hollywood actor named Mickey. He'd be more likely to be the mouse."

When the boy's mother returned to the kitchen, he closed the magazine and slipped it carefully into the wire rack alongside the chesterfield. And then he sat for a long time with his fingers tracing the braided iron handle of the rack, and when he looked to the window, in his mind's eye the brown water was jetting in through the crevice between the sash and the frame and pouring in a sheet over the sill. After that it started up the pane.

On Saturday the boy planned to walk down the street to a puppet show at the Orange Hall, but his parents had been out late the night before and were not getting up, and finally he slipped into their room.

From under the covers his father held out a one-dollar bill.

"It's free," the boy said.

"Free puppet show, my ass. Take it. I'll want the change. Keep your eyes open. Be home for lunch."

The boy nodded and left the darkened bedroom and the sour animal odour of his parents' sleep.

There was no admission charge, but his father was right. With no warning, in what should have been the third act, Punch turned into Jesus. Suddenly the tree Punch had climbed was a rough cross, the Devil whacking at him with a sword was Pontius Pilate, it was not Judy but Mary wringing her little mitts, and when the show ended, the children were called to line up at the front of the hall to witness that they had taken Christ into their hearts.

At first it was easier to stay put and think about something else, because this was what everybody was doing, but the puppeteers, a husband-and-wife team or perhaps brother and sister, like midget actors, like children themselves, children with weary, calculating eyes, had exploded from behind the puppet theatre to preach and exhort and challenge and work very hard, and before long the trickle of kids with unreadable faces on their way to the front of the auditorium was an exodus, the balance tipped, there were more kids standing at the front than sitting in the audience, and the challenge became how to remain invisible without leaving your seat.

For the boy this was the stuff of bolt-up-in-terror nightmare. Old habits of self-effacement normally kept him off adult radar; he could come and go without detection. But the kids filing to the front like lambs were leaving behind lost sheep, individuals the puppeteers had made it clear they would go to the wall to redeem. Whether this was because every sheep soul is infinitely precious unto God or because a lost sheep seen to prefer its condition will sow doubt in the herd mind, they did not say.

Cautiously the boy looked around. None of the other holdouts were kids he had any respect for at all, whereas up at the front Darko Told — one of the first to defect — kept half-turning to show him the crossed fingers behind his back, and by other surreptitious contortions and facial gestures, saying, The sooner you get up here, the sooner we all go home.

And then the boy felt one of the puppeteers try to catch his eye and saw a glance pass between her and her partner, and he knew that it was all over for him.

In a dream he rose to his feet and walked to the front and took Christ into his heart.

Exactly what happened next the boy could not have said, but soon enough the last holdout — Ricky Wolitzer, the notorious arson — had come sloping up from his seat to stand with one hand in his pocket, fiddling with his lighter, through a marathon of homilies and prayers and vows designed to seal off every route of psychological escape. But finally it was over, and the boy was nearly crushed at the exit, then went stumbling down the steps in the bright sun, looking to the others for a sign, and right away he could see that none of them had changed. Not the dull, conventional ones, who had failed to change not because Christ was already in their hearts but because they would automatically assent to anything anybody told them was virtue, and not the ones he could actually talk to, though not at this moment, because they were in a frenzy of punching and chasing each other and throwing themselves into piles of screaming bodies and otherwise doing everything they could to convince each other that they had put the low manipulation of the puppeteers behind them. In that whole crowd the only eyes available to the boy's were Darko Told's, and what startled him about them was how keen they were to know what they were seeing in his.

Suddenly then, the kids were gone, dispersed, the boy was walking alone, and it was a different street again. It was not the street of his weekday walk, and it was not the one he had walked after monitoring the flood with his father. This was because he now had Christ in his heart, as witness to all that passed there; Christ who had died for our sins and by the radicalness of that sacrifice had been enabled by His Father to forgive even the boy's. And lifting his eyes once more to the larger world of the street, the boy saw what had happened: Christ's mercy had extended even to the roadway and the trees and the buildings and the passing cars, and these things had been emptied of all resentment against him and now stood diminished, in the plain, dumb ineloquence of what they were: road, trees, buildings, cars. Features of the world here below, either to the Glory of God or to the Pride of Man, it was as simple as that. And the real world offered no further complaint or threat against him, and he stumbled on, weeping tears of gratitude beneath the loving gaze of his Merciful Redeemer.

When he reached home his parents had just got up and were making their breakfast.

"Where's my change?" his father said without looking up from the stove. He was cooking bacon and eggs. Instead of answering, the boy held out the one-dollar bill. The father made to glance at him, but he didn't look away. "What's going on?" he said. "Your eyes are worse than ever. Christ, it's been a week."

"I took Jesus into my heart."

The boy's mother looked at his father. It was a look that said nothing at all.

"It's okay," the boy assured them, making a placating gesture with his hands. He meant that he had understood it was a trick, an adult confidence game, but he had gone ahead anyway and things were good, Christ was with him.

At first the father didn't say anything, only put the bill in his pocket, and when he reached out his hand it was not to give the boy — who blinked and pulled back — a cuff, but only to mess his hair. "The Christers get you, did they, son?" he said mildly, and turned back to the contents of the frying pan. That was all he said.

The boy fixed his own lunch while his parents ate their breakfast. Another sign that everything had changed for him was that as soon as he sat down with his peanut butter sandwich, it was not hard at all to ask his father point-blank if Darko's dad tested fighter jets in New Mexico.

"Fighter jets in New Mexico?" his father said. "No." He looked at the boy's mother.

The boy waited.

"Okay," the father said. He rubbed his face. "Here it is. And I don't want you throwing this back at Darko or telling any of the other kids. You know what rape is, right?"

The boy blushed. He did and he didn't. He nodded that he did.

"Well, Darko's father was a Russian soldier in a nylon ski mask."

Here the explanation ended.

"But where is he?" the boy asked.

"Who knows? Dead? Back in Gorodok looking after his mother and sister? In hospital in Minsk with a leg blown off? The new minister of Kickbackniks? Who can say?"

The next day the boy went out into the backyard, and Darko was standing with his forearms on the fence. "Come to back field," Darko said. "I show you."

Reluctantly, but in the knowledge that Christ was his Guide and Protector, the boy followed Darko through the long grass of the Told yard and the thicket of raspberry bushes at the bottom of it and through the kicked-in Told garden gate and out into the back field, under the hydro pylons. There Darko indicated a long curve of fresh skid marks in the grass. "Here last night my father touch down," he said. "To visit my mother and me."

The boy nodded, but he knew that the skid marks had been made by a car. It had woken him up last night as he was getting ready to float across the driveway and stretch out on Mrs. Told. Remembering this part only now, he marvelled that he should have remained so sinful in his thoughts. He took a deep breath. The air had the fragrance of grass juice. "It's from a car," he said. His voice was like a sigh. When he looked at Darko, Darko was watching him. "Drunk teenagers," the boy added.

"You tell me to my face you don't believe when I tell you it was my father," Darko said in a voice of conclusion so inflectionless that he seemed almost amused.

Still, the boy was expecting a blow; his eyelids were fluttering. When it didn't come, he looked sideways at Darko, who was simply looking at him. With God's help, the boy returned his gaze.

Finally Darko said, "Come to river," and started walking.

They crossed under the hydro wires to the rail fence at the far edge of the field and moved down through sumac and matted grass, skirting the clay bluff, to the river flats. There it was harder going, because of the mud, which had dried to a crust but was like gumbo underneath, and it stuck to their shoes. Following Darko's example, the boy removed his own and carried them. They were heavy clumps with canvas handles.

As they passed a bush where scraps of flood litter were caught high in the branches, Darko said, "Imagine standing here and rushing water so high."

"You wouldn't stand long," the boy replied.

Darko laughed. He was trudging on, towards the river channel itself. The boy followed.

The river when they reached it was a disappointment. Fast-moving but no more than a few feet higher than usual.

"Beast has returned to cage," Darko said.

The boy nodded. He was still nodding when Darko said, "So, you are good Christian now?"

"I guess," the boy replied, not taking his eyes off the river. He was surprised to hear himself so noncommittal, and he wondered if he would be like Peter, betraying Christ the first chance he got. "I don't know about 'good,'" he added, trying to appear self-critical, or at least modest, but what he had just said sounded more like a disavowal.

"Those puppeteers think kids are also puppets," Darko said.

"I know."

Darko was stepping out of his shorts. He looked up, surprised. "You agree and still you allow them to have influence?"

The idea, vague in the boy's mind, was that his pact had been direct with Christ, the puppeteers were His instruments only. They could have been anyone, or anything. They could have been Satan himself.

Darko was removing his shirt. He was only two years older than the boy, but his body was tanned and muscular. All summer, like an adult, he had been jogging the country roads, wearing only runners and shorts.

"So why?" he wanted to know. "Why do you let them?"

The boy could not have begun to explain.

"Is it because there is much evil in world, and somehow, any way possible, one must make stand?"

The boy considered this, or pretended to. He didn't seem to be that kind of Christian. "If I can," he said lamely.

But this answer appeared to satisfy Darko, who said, "Okay, I be Jacob, you angel."

The boy didn't understand.

"You know . . . " Darko prompted, smiling. "Wrestle."

"Naw, I don't want to."

"No *naw!*" Darko cried with sudden force, alarming the boy.

"Evil must be subdued, end of discussion! Otherwise, in blink of eye, dark forces take over world! One must fight with full strength of conviction. Otherwise it is all empty, all making believe! One big fucking lie!" As he spoke, Darko was reaching out for the boy, who kept twisting away. "You will need those off," he said, more quietly. "Otherwise at home you have hell to pay. We can wash in river and dry underpants but not clothes."

Very clearly in his mind the boy could see himself walking back across the flats and climbing the hill, but he wasn't doing it. The summer before last, he and Darko had wrestled every day. And though every bout ended the same way — with Darko sitting on the boy's chest, his knees pressing the boy's biceps and his hands pinning the boy's wrists above his head, and sooner or later the boy bawling loud enough to get Darko into trouble, if he could — the next day the boy would be back for more, and Darko never refused him.

"Lift your arms," Darko said.

When the boy's arms went up, his T-shirt flew off and his shorts were yanked to his ankles. His underpants followed to his knees. Hastily, the boy pulled them back up.

"Step."

The boy lifted his left foot.

"Step."

The boy lifted his right foot. He was now clear of his shorts.

"Look at me," Darko said.

The boy looked at him.

"I am proud sinner," Darko said. "Worst kind. What does angel do?"

"Nothing," the boy muttered. He made to reach to the ground for his shirt, but Darko gave him a push and he stumbled sideways. He still didn't have his balance when Darko pushed him again, and this time he fell into the mud. Immediately he scrambled up. When Darko pushed him a third time, an old switch tripped in the boy's brain and he threw himself at his tormentor. He couldn't get him down, but the next time he lost his balance he took Darko with him. And so they were wrestling again, and though Darko was still stronger, stronger than ever, the boy could feel as always the measure of his own strength against that greater strength, his own softness against that hardness, his own clumsiness against that skill. Really the only difference this time was the mud, and it was as deep and slick and warm as heaven, only river-stinking. Heaven on earth, maybe.

Inevitably then, too soon, Darko was sitting on the boy's chest, pinning his wrists above his head, and looking down at him from above. But this time he didn't squeeze the boy's biceps painfully with his knees or pretend he was going to spit in his face, he only laughed and said, "Well, angel. As reward for earnest, though of course futile, struggle, you have honour to witness miracle Cadillac body of winning beast and sinner." And he climbed off the boy and stepped out of his underwear, and when he rose to his full height, his penis sprang up, bobbing a little, and the boy saw that it was rooted now in a luxuriance of auburn hair.

Conscious of sin, he tore his eyes away.

"No, you must watch!" Darko cried. He dropped to his haunches and shot out his right leg. He grasped the kneecap between the thumb and forefinger of his right hand and moved it in a slow circle clockwise, then counterclockwise. The kneecap seemed to be fully detached, free-floating. Like a small thick hub it moved without hindrance, with the mud on the skin stretching to follow it.

"And this . . . " Darko said. Still on one haunch, his leg extended, chin tucked in, he reached his fingers into the hollows below his neck and —with difficulty, because his hands and body were slippery with mud — he lifted the clavicle up and out and set it carefully upon his breastbone. This done, he sighted upward through his eyebrows and said to the boy, "So?"

The boy had heard about this ability of Darko's but had never seen it for himself. He swallowed. "Doesn't it hurt?"

"Hurt is OK," Darko replied. The boy was not sure what he meant. Darko grasped the clavicle and lowered it into place. "Now I show you feat of speed."

Feet, the boy heard.

Darko had risen to a standing position. His penis was angled a little lower now, not so foreshortened, and for this reason it seemed even longer, and possibly broader, than it had a minute ago. Darko was looking to the sky. The boy extricated his eyes from Darko's penis and looked too, squinting painfully. A jet, a sliver of silver. Darko lifted both hands towards it in a gesture of supplication, crying, "Daddy, oh-oh, daddy mine!" sank to a starting-block position, rose up — "*Bang!*" —and took off across the flats. The boy watched through his lashes, his eyes all but shut against the light. Within a minute Darko had reached the foot of the bluff, and the boy was happy to believe with his friend that even slowed by mud he had out-raced the jet. A small figure now, Darko spun away from the embankment with arms upraised and went jolting leisurely, the head of the victor bowed to receive the tear-streaming ovation.

The time he wrestled in the mud of the river flats with Darko Told evolved in the boy's memory into a happy occasion, one of the happiest of his childhood, but the progress to happy took almost twenty years. In the event — or rather, directly after it — what he mainly experienced was guilt, and even something like shame. And this continued for a good two years, two years of anxiety and compunction about this and other acts and thoughts so unconscionably sinful that he was always down on his knees. Every once in a while there would be visitations of grace, tearful convictions of divine mercy, but in time these came to seem only counterweights in the terrible machinery of sin and fear. And then one day he awoke with the sun streaming down on his pillow, and he asked himself, What if Darko had been right about the little puppeteers? What if they were only ignorant carnies, well-intentioned but not to be trusted? What if, in exchange for the world's displeasure, they had merely slipped him God's? The boy had no idea, really, what the little puppeteers had done, but as soon as he was able to think of them as unlikely agents of any plan by God for himself, the world was back, but the difference this time was that just as Darko's had ever been for him, its aspect was kind.

Greg Hollingshead has published two novels, Spin Dry *(Mosaic Press, 1992) and* The Healer *(HarperFlamingo, 1998), and three collections of stories,* Famous Players *(Coach House Press, 1982),* White Buick *(Oolichan Books, 1992), and* The Roaring Girl *(Somerville House, 1995). His work has been shortlisted for the Commonwealth Writers Prize and the Smithbooks/Books in Canada First Novel Award. In 1995* The Roaring Girl *was awarded the Governor General's Award for fiction. His work has been published in several languages and has garnered numerous awards. Most recently, his novel* The Healer *won the 1998 Rogers Communications Writers' Trust Fiction Award. Greg Hollingshead lives in Edmonton, where he teaches at the University of Alberta.*

Lisa Moore

MOUTHS,

OPEN

A woman climbs over me for the window seat — hair like vanilla ice cream, a purple mink. Beneath the fur, a sweatsuit and spanking new sneakers. She's got a paper bag with twine handles. Lingerie. Her fingernails are false and black, an inch and a half.

You raise your eyes from your book. She tears a hot pretzel — the bread inside porous, steaming — and dips it into the tiny container of honey mustard. The dexterity of a lobster. After each bite she touches her nails against a napkin, rubbing carefully under the concave side. A sex worker who flies to Halifax from St. John's for the weekend. What costs as much as a blow job, a carton of red peppers? Mink earmuffs?

We are in Cuba. The lawn sprinkler beside the pool whispering rounds of silver ammunition that pock the sand. A cockroach with an indigo shell. Banana leaves sharp as switchblades. The plastic of my recliner sweating against my cheek. The pool looks as solid as a bowl of Jell-O, a jar of Dippity-Doo. The Italian transsexuals lower their bodies slowly until they are submerged

to the neck, careful of their curls. They have the most beautiful
nipples. I can't take my eyes off their more-than-perfect breasts.

At the kitchen table at home in St. John's. The tablecloth is
gone; the table is red, bright red, and there is the creamer, full of
milk. My hands are on the table in front of me. I want to throw
the creamer. Milk fluttering over your head, a long ribbon of
surrender. It is a huge effort not to give in and throw it. Then my
fist slams.

What is wrong with you, I shout.

I say, Speak. Do you think I'm joking?

You say, I'm afraid of you.

This is the first thing you've said. There have been pauses. I keep
thinking, What is my tone? I vary my tone. We already know the
lines. Do you think I'm joking? (whisper) Speak! (shout) What
the fuck is wrong with you? (monotone) Do I exist? Maybe I
don't exist. (giggles)

But it's reassuring that you're afraid of me. I have been worried
that I don't exist. I don't think I am, therefore.

Just speak. Speak.

You say, I'm thinking of leaving you.

The beach, in a windstorm. I bang my toe on a concrete block
emerging from the sand. Pass a demolished building. A giant slab
of concrete with a painted silhouette of Che Guevara excavated
from the ruins. I stand on tippytoe and put my mouth up to
his giant lips, posing for a photograph. Weeping, sand under
my contact lens, scratching my eye. The wind flicks the tail of my
dress against the concrete slab like a propeller trying to turn over,
resolutely stalled. Everything in Cuba is at a standstill, waiting
for ignition. You wave me out of the picture.

You say, Just Che. By himself.

In the Museum of the Revolution in Havana, a clear plastic Petri
dish containing a sample of Che Guevara's hair and a sample of
his beard. I feel ashamed for pretending to kiss him. Che and

Fidel, wax figures, beating their way through plastic bushes. The glass eyeballs have a yellowish cast. Beads of clear varnish on their foreheads, cheeks. Mouths open, as if they are shouting to soldiers behind them, or gasping for breath. We are here for a conference. You're talking about the revolutionary spirit of Gianlorenzo Bernini, the seventeenth-century sculptor.

We go into a hotel during the downpour for espresso.

You say, Someone else is doing the . . .

You lift your chin towards an open doorway farther down the lobby. A couple is dancing. The patio is a slick of wet slate, and the reflections of a red skirt and the shadows of palm trees are hydroplaning at their feet. Clothes soaked to the skin. A black man teaching a white woman the rumba. A black girl carries a giant armload of canary yellow towels, brilliant against her black, black cheek. She slits her eyes at them. Everything is a ripe pomegranate.

I say, Should we be sleeping together? If you're leaving me?

You say, I don't see why not.

Lightning cracks low over the horizon, stunted like bonsai trees. The espresso is strong. Tiny cups. The chink of the cup in the saucer.

I say, From now on, if I say I love you, I am speaking out of habit.

I wonder what is you. Am I you? What don't I love any more?

Outside, we hold our feet under a fountain that squirts from a stone fish. I watch you hold up your foot. You turn it and the sand peels away from your ankle. I love your foot. That is the only part of you I still love.

I say, I'm going to think of you as a long series of gestures. You are your nose and eyes and mouth and the things you do with them.

You say, Don't forget my cock.

The hotel room smells of a lemon venom: insecticide. You are asleep. I stand on the bed and photograph you. Your arms thrown over your head, warding off the blades of sunlight from the swinging louvred shutters, a fencing match on your naked back. The maid has twisted the white towels into the shape of swans. Two towel swans joined at the beak, as if kissing.

Back in the kitchen, at home, the creamer stops pulsing. The creamer has lost its meaning.

I say, This marriage can be anything you want.

You say, I might be happier without you in my life.

You say, Let's go somewhere. We need a change.

I guess I should read the *Manifesto*. The literary critic who speaks before you at the conference says it is an authorless tract. That Marx repeatedly tried to make it sound as though it came from thin air, or rose by itself from the people, spontaneously. He was willing to claim the bad poetry of his youth that even Penguin didn't want to publish. But the *Manifesto* just was. Just passed through his pen.

Tell me what happened. Did you meet somebody?

The simultaneous translator becomes exhausted late afternoon, breaking down, translating word by word instead of the sense. So each word is encased in explosive consonants, and the meaning picked up later like shattered bullet casings. She is staccato, and then stuck. The people's . . . ? The people's . . . ? She looks around the room hopelessly. Someone offers the word, *struggle*. Ah, yes, The people's struggle. The room explodes with laughter.

In the pastry shop. A young black girl with long black braids, thousands, in a ponytail on the top of her head. Like squirts of oil from a squeeze bottle, shiny blue. She wears a slippery Lycra bodysuit. It stretches over her body like burst bubble gum, bright pink. She gets in line next to you. Her hip presses into the glass of the display case.

There is an older woman with a cane. We are both waiting, this older woman and me. The heat — there must be a lot of ovens

— they keep bringing out bread tied in knots and other shapes. Giant wicker baskets of oily golden sailor's knots. A man stacks them on steel shelves — the girl is talking to you, she is digging a high heel into the tiles and rocking a little. She has full breasts and is very young. She may be sixteen. But she may be younger.

She may be the age of your daughter, fifteen. The girl touches your collar. You are blushing darkly. But you are laughing too. Two sides of the same coin, shame and pleasure.

There is more bread and a blast of heat. You are buying the girl pastries. She is laughing and pointing and the woman behind the counter puts what the girl wants into a white box. The girl hesitates before she points to each pastry. She looks coyly at you each time she touches the glass with her finger, and each time you nod.

But you have become serious now. The girl turns and sees me. Something passes over her face — perhaps embarrassment. This is what I feel: Fuck off, bitch. But the girl is only the age of my step-daughter, whom I love and protect. I am ashamed of the look on my face. The woman with the cane is joined by her friend. They speak a few words to each other and leave.

A moment more, and the woman with the cane returns. She asks: Do you understand Spanish?

I say no.

She says, A little?

A little, I say. This isn't true. What I understand is less than a little, but I know what she will say. She points to her eye and then out — so that I know to look out.

She is telling me to look out. Her hand grips the plastic handle of the cane tight. She does not hesitate or pause as she speaks. She isn't experimenting with tone. She is telling me, Yes, he was flattered. Don't doubt it. He was flattered.

All I want is to be away from her, for your sake. But I am moved that she has come back into the pastry shop to tell me. She says AIDS. I hear it mingled with the Spanish.

Then she leaves.

There is a white statue of a woman with a basket on her shoulder at the end of the pool. Bernini talked about the paleness of marble. The absence of flesh tone makes it difficult to capture likeness. Would you recognize someone who had poured a bag of flour over his head? To compensate, he suggests drawing the face just as it is about to speak, or after it has just spoken. That's when the face is most characteristic of itself. He's responsible for the sixteenth-century fashion of portraits with the lips parted. We are most ourselves when we are changing.

I say, We can change certain things.
   It's not that.
   We can sleep with other people. Is that what you want?
   You say you are making up your mind. You're sorry. You can't explain. It's as much a mystery for you as it is for me.

The man who lends towels and novels is set up in a grass hut with an impaled and glazed blowfish. This man leans on his elbows, chin in hands, and watches the transsexuals. They seem to let their mouths hang open, in a kind of pout. Like inflated dolls who are ready-made for oral sex.
   Before me my cup is very white and the white saucer is on the white table. Espresso. The table shimmers in its whiteness. A fly lands on the rim of the cup. The fly is so blue-black that it makes me think: significance. There is significance here. What is it?
   The fly touches the cup, and the whiteness of the cup becomes whiter.
   You say, You look insane.
   You say this just as I am applying significance to the white cup. How did you know?

In the evening we meet Carl, Jorge, and Johann, from Austria. Carl takes a switchblade from a pocket over his calf. He opens it with an elegant motion of his wrist. There is a bartender working over a pestle and mortar several yards away.

Carl says, You want me to demonstrate? He raises his chin towards the bartender. I see the blade open the white shirt and blood flushing. Carl closes the knife and slides it back into his pocket.

Jorge is studying to be a veterinarian. He picks up the cat that rubs against his leg. The tail under his nose.

Carl says, No animal can pass him without he picks it up.

Johann: And they could kill him; he is allergic.

I carry a pill, says Jorge, or I die like this. He holds the cat's tail in his teeth.

I say, Will you work with big animals or small?

He leans forward. We have finished four bottles of rum and two, no three, rounds of beer.

He says, I want to work in an abattoir. I don't know how you say in English.

I say, But they kill animals there. I thought you loved animals.

These cats will kill him, says Johann, if they break his skin.

Jorge says, It's a simple operation, the gun they put to the head like that. He holds the flashlight to my temple and flicks the light so my cheek glows orange.

And it scrambles the brain, says Jorge, switching off the flashlight. He sits back and his wicker chair screeches unexpectedly. His throat is exposed by a floodlight in a palm tree. It's covered with bruises like squashed blueberries, hickeys. I realize he is much younger than me.

Jorge tosses the flashlight to you. It turns over in the air and lands in your hand with a neat smack.

He says, Why don't you put this in your wife's pussy tonight? She would like, yes? Is big enough?

Everybody laughs uneasily, and Carl changes the subject.

I think: This afternoon I saw one of the transsexuals rest her feet on Jorge's thigh. He cupped her feet in his hand. Her feet were strong and nicely shaped, like meat-eating flowers. I imagine again Carl's switchblade opening the bartender. He may finally get to rest. He's been here since eight in the morning. The

transsexuals are both very tall, with high cheekbones and beautiful breasts. The nipples are beautiful. They have changed so
much. Full lips. Comic-book eyes. Betty Boop. They go topless
at poolside. I've seen one of them riding down the beach at sunset
on a bay horse. A loop of the reins slapping on both sides of the
withers. Sand tossed. You, a long way from shore, you stand.
There is a sandbar, and the ocean comes to your knees. One of
the transsexuals turns a water Ski-Doo sharply, so a white curtain
of surf falls on your shoulders like an ermine mantle.

I shaved your neck before we left St. John's. Shaving cream
like a neck brace holding you, a guillotine. The scrudge of the
razor against your neck and hair, and cream piling. You were
kneeling, and you turned and pressed your face into my skirt.
Smearing the chiffon like a hand wiping condensation from
a window.

I realize I am at a table with four men and a flashlight. I laugh.
The rum is like a time-lapse film playing in my skin. Briefly, I feel
a leaden euphoria. I am most myself now.

We have been given the key to a different hotel room after
checkout so we can shower before the long trip home. The room
is more luxurious. It is dark, all the curtains drawn, and we turn
on a light. We have to shower quickly to catch the bus to the
airport. There is a dresser with a giant dark mirror.

I say, There isn't time.

My breasts flour white where the bikini covered me.

One foot on the bed frame and the heel of my hand on the desk
edge. You stand behind me, gripping my hip bones, the strength
in your thighs lifting me off my feet, letting me touch down. I
watch in the mirror. Your hair is long and wet, stuck to tanned
skin. Mouth opens. I love you.

In the bathroom you open a jar of coconut pomade and put
some in your hair. Pomade that someone has left behind. Another
traveller. Later, in the Halifax airport, we sleep on benches,

waiting for our connecting plane. I sleep and feel the planes taking off through vibrations in the vinyl couch. I smell through every dream the coconut pomade. You smell like someone else.

Lisa Moore was born in St. John's, Newfoundland. She received a B.F.A. *from the Nova Scotia College of Art and Design. Her stories have been published in journals across Canada, as well as in* Coming Attractions 1995 *(Oberon) and* Extremities, *a short-story anthology of the writing group the Burning Rock. In addition to short stories, she has written radio plays for* CBC, *a half-hour television script, and art criticism. Moore's first collection of short stories,* Degrees of Nakedness, *was published by the Mercury Press in 1996. She is currently working on a novel.*

Olive Senior

MAD FISH

This really happened, I swear. I was right there when Radio came rushing up the hill from the fishing beach all out of breath. Radio is our messenger, and he likes to be first with the news. But everyone called him Radio not for that reason but because of his serious speech defect, which made it difficult to understand him at the best of times, almost impossible when he was excited, which was when he had fresh news to tell. This caused him endless frustration, for by the time he'd calmed down enough to make sense to Jeremy, who was one of the few persons who could understand him, someone with a more agile tongue would have arrived to reel off a version of the story and cheat him out of the novelty of telling. Not this time, though. Jeremy and I were about to have our first cup of coffee when Radio burst into the dining room, so excited he couldn't even get out words that sounded like language, just strange inhuman water-filled noises that were wheezing out of him like a drowning accordion. The only word we could make out sounded like *fish*. He said that word over and over, and he wanted us to come, pointing to the beach. Why should a fish on a fishing beach cause excitement? But Radio was so urgent and insistent that we left our coffee untouched and followed him down the hill and across the road.

As we approached, everything on the beach looked so normal that I started to mentally curse Radio for pulling one of his jokes on us, as he liked to do from time to time, for Radio is sort of simple, or so I used to think, though Jeremy never agreed and now I'm not so sure. We could see the fishermen and the higglers standing about in little groups. There were the usual idlers and mangy dogs lurking and the old men sitting under the Sea Almond, where they played dominoes all day. But as we got closer we realized something was not right. The whole scene was like a stage set, with knots of people standing around in tableaux, waiting for the curtain to go up. Nobody was making a sound and those who moved did so in slow motion, as if in a dream. It was as if each one had just received news that a beloved person had died and was still too shocked to take it in. Jeremy and I walked up to the largest group, which was by the boats, and nobody paid us the slightest attention, amazingly, since Jeremy is sort of the village squire and people are always quick to greet him. Now they were behaving as if we weren't there, but not in a rude way; it was as if they were too preoccupied with more important business. Something made us bite our tongues and say nothing too, as if we had also fallen under a spell that had gripped the entire beach, for even the sky, which hadn't shown a cloud in nearly a year of drought, was suddenly turning black and shadows were beginning to fall on the white sand. I actually shivered. Without exchanging a word between us or with anyone else, Jeremy and I turned and went home without a clue as to what had happened. Once inside our house, everything seemed so normal that we went back to having our breakfast, each of us confident that others would arrive with the tale before long.

But amazingly, no one came forward to speak of what happened, that day or any other. And when fragments of the story did surface to corroborate what Radio eventually told us, it was not at all like the stories these people liked to tell, augmented and ornamented and embellished, built up of versions over time. This one was utterly downplayed — deconstructed, you might say — individual elements singled out and spoken about only in terms of *signs, tokens,* and *miracles,* as if people were not so much interested in the story as narrative as in teasing out all the possible permutations of meaning.

Still, those who were there might eventually have come around to talking and laughing about the episode, as these people tend to do with everything else, except for one or two elements. From our fishing beach that day, four men in a car with a fantastic fish had disappeared not only around the bend in the road but totally off the face of the earth. From the minute they drove off, nothing was ever seen or heard of them again. We know this for a fact, for Jeremy's police friends had also heard the story and could verify that a lot of people had come looking for the men, including their relatives. The police would have been happy to find them too, for other reasons, and set out to do so. But all investigations had proven fruitless. As soon as they drove off, the men, the car, and the fish had simply vanished.

There were other repercussions. Big Jake, our most popular fisherman, never went to sea again and spent his days playing dominoes and drinking himself into idiocy. Some said he had lost his nerve, afraid of what he might catch. Others said that from the day he raised his hand against his brothers, they had taken over the boat and banished him from it. It is also a fact that it was the day of the so-called Mad Fish that the year-long drought broke, though the day had dawned with a cloudless sky and — so people said, for I wasn't keeping count, I was so sick of it after a while — rain fell for forty days and forty nights.

But the most miraculous thing of all is that after we returned home that day, ate our breakfast, fed Radio, and calmed him down to that point where his speech, though rough, would begin to make sense, to our astonishment and without any warning, he began to speak beautifully and clearly, as if he had swallowed mercury, and he has continued to speak so ever since.

You won't believe what a change these things have wrought
around here, everyone suddenly so sober and serious. People have
put all these happenings together and taken them for signs and
wonders — *tokens*, they call them — of the end of the world
and such millenarian rubbish. Radio is giving himself airs, refusing to answer to Radio and insisting on being called by his
rightful name of Joshua. He's been given a message, he says, a big
announcement to make, but he's being coy; he won't tell us what
it is until the time is ripe. A lot of people are taking him seriously,
too. Now instead of running our errands and helping around the
yard, he spends his time riding his bicycle up and down and
ringing his bell, making himself all biblical and apocalyptic,
condescending to pop in from time to time to regale us with
the latest news interspersed with wild talk about leviathans and
fishing for souls.

I keep telling Jeremy it's time to get rid of him, he's got perfectly
useless, but of course Jeremy won't hear of it. He and Radio have
been together since they were boys, and Jeremy I suspect has
always found him kind of amusing, as if he provides the yeast for
Jeremy's rather dull soul. Plus, Jeremy is ever faithful and loyal.
That's the trouble with this country: people ignore the big things
and make such a fuss over the little. I don't want to think this,
but I believe even Jeremy, in his heart of hearts, is beginning to
believe that something world-shattering happened that day. I
keep my mouth shut, for whenever I say anything, he rubs it in
that I'm not from here so I can't understand the culture. What
culture? I ask myself. After fifteen years I should have seen signs
of it. I certainly don't see any of it in Jeremy's other planter
friends and policemen drinking buddies, or in the fishermen and
higglers down on the beach. Well, you can judge, for here's the
story as told by our little silver-tongued Radio, a.k.a. Joshua, all
acted out with many dramatic flourishes, if you please. (Though,
for your sake, I have taken some care to render it into a closer
approximation of the English language than Radio so far uses.
I've also taken some liberties to explain certain things in a more

sophisticated way than he did. But I've tried to retain the colour and flavour of how he told it, for that you'll find amusing.)

Picture this, says he. The fishing boat is pulling up on the beach. Big Jake and his brothers and all the little hangers-on hauling on the net, fish spilling out like quicksilver, leaping and spinning, one last jerk and they lying unconscious and silent, as fish suppose to be. But what's this commotion over here? Something jumping and moving as if a big animal just leap off the boat. The first person to get a good look scream and the next one too, and after that everybody dashing around like mad ants, shrieking and pointing. First the boys helping to pull in the net, then the higglers waiting for the catch. What a commotion! Big Jake and the crew haul in this huge fish that is like nothing nobody ever seen before. Gold on top, silver on the bottom, and all the colours of the rainbow in between.

Big Jake and the other fishermen stop what they doing to get a good look at the fish, which by this time launch itself out of the net and dancing around on the ground. Everybody waiting to hear the fishermen pronounce the name of this fish, for they suppose to know every creature in the sea. But when Big Jake and the rest stand there for a long time just scratching their heads and looking like they lost, and people figure out that even they don't know, the wailing and the shrieking break out fresh again. You have to understand — is not just the looks of the fish, for is not a bad-looking fish at that. The problem is that the fish is not behaving like how fish out of water should behave. This fish not just moving, it dancing. A-wiggling and a-moving its tail and spinning and turning and wining, its big body glistening and flashing in the sun.

After a while, everybody quieten down; we just standing there watching this fish. Is like everybody suddenly feeling fraid in the presence of this mysterious creature that land up on our beach. For who can tell if is call somebody call it up, for it have people in these parts can do them kind of thing. Then a man in the crowd call out:

"Wait! Is a dance-hall queen, this."

Everybody laugh, like we get relief, for that's just how the fish stay, like a dance-hall girl in her fancy dress and her tight fishtail sequins like scales, moving her body to the latest wine. So little by little people stop feeling frighten and start making joke.

"Well," one man proclaim, "the only fish I ever see live this long out of water is mud fish."

"Is not Mud Fish this," another one shout. "Is Mad Fish!"

And is true, the fish acting like it crazy; not like a lunatic but happy and don't-care mad, like it drunk. And somebody actually say the word *drunk* — "The fish look like it drunk" — and is like the word set off something running through people mind, for suddenly everything change, is like a cloud passing over the sun, for somebody, I don't know who, whisper the word *cocaine*. And the word pass from mouth to ear until everybody taking it up like a chorus. "The fish drunk with the coke." Everybody know what that mean.

"Coke!" Quick as a flash, the word like a sword slashing at all of us. That word making people jumpy, for the whole coast awash with story bout small plane a drop parcel into sea so boat can pick it up. That is okay, people don't business with that. Is just that sometime the parcel fall in the wrong place — and end up in the wrong hand — and this is what everybody getting excited bout. For it come like a lottery, now. Everybody dreaming bout finding parcel and getting rich overnight. Everybody know is dead them dead if certain people find out. Up and down the coast they hanging out all kind of rumour on their clothesline. Which fisherman can suddenly buy new boat. Which boat disappear after the crew pick up something. Which old lady find parcel wash up on a beach and hide it in her three-foot iron pot, till her house suddenly burn down with her and her three grandchildren lock up inside and no sign of the iron pot in the ashes. Suddenly fishing taking on a whole new meaning; fisherman dreaming of a different catch.

Well, Big Jake is one of them all right, for though up to now he in the middle of the crowd laughing and joking bout the fish (that still dancing like crazy), the minute he hear the word *coke*, is like he turn a different man. Quick as a snake, Big Jake reach into the boat and haul out him machete and start to lash out with it, as if he suddenly gone crazier than the fish.

"Stan back, all a unno from mi fish. Stan back," he start shout.

But people already backing away for his two eye looking wild and he leaping about and swinging his machete left and right. Everybody looking at him in shock, for never mind his size, Big Jake is normally the most peaceful man around.

By now, is like Big Jake and the fish together in a ring, surrounded by the crowd, with all eyes on Big Jake. But is like I can't take my eyes off the fish, for I seeing it quietly moving round in the circle till it come right to where I standing and it stop, just like that, and it left up its head and it look straight at me. I swear. I can see that it not looking too well just now, tired like, as if the life draining out of it, the colours fading away. And is like the fish calling to me, calling me without voice as if is the two of us alone in the whole wide world. Like it pulling me down towards it. And I can't help myself, I feeling sorrowful for the fish that just sitting there on the sand for I feeling the life going out of it as if is a part of myself leaving me. I bend down and reach out my hand to touch the scales and as I bending down, a drop of my sweat fall right on top of the fish and I swear, is like electricity, the fish jump as if it suddenly get life all over again and it look at me, directly at me, and is like it sucking me in — I swear I black out for a minute there for I don't remember nothing more. When I come back to myself I see the fish reach clear to the other side of the circle, leaping and jumping and dancing, its colours bright and dazzling like it just come out of the water.

All this happen so fast that nobody notice; everybody still watching Big Jake. But I feel my finger tingling and when I look I see a little drop of blood, as if I prick myself on the fish, and I don't even think, I put the finger in my mouth. I don't have time to worry about doing something like that after I touch the mad fish, for Big Jake brethren Ernie and Ray take up their machete too and the three of them circling each other with their weapon now, arguing over is who own the fish. You see my trial? The three of them fishing together from the same boat from them born, it belong to their father before he die, and never an argument about who own what fish till somebody mention coke. This is where it reach: the three of them circling one another, getting more and more rile up, and people just watching and nobody doing or saying nothing. The whole thing looking so serious to me, that is when I decide to come and get you, Mass Jeremy, to see if you can talk sense into these people, otherwise is wholesale murder going to happen right here in Whitesands Bay.

So I start push my way out of the circle of people to reach the road and by now, the crowd so big those at the back don't even know what causing the commotion up front, though plenty rumour flying. You know how people like to go on? One lot of people saying: "Three fishermen drown." A woman swearing: "Is whale them catch." Another one say that fishing boat come back with one missing at sea. A set of little children jumping up and down saying is a mermaid. One boy telling his friend that they catch a big fish that vomit up dead body that starting to come back to life, and another saying no, what they bring back is a fish that join together like is Siamese twin. But all the way, too, like is a snake sliding underneath the joking and the laughing, you could hear the buzz, "Them catch the fish that swallow the coke."

And just as I manage to reach the road, laughing to myself at all the foolishness people talking, this big black car flash by with all the windows dark and roll up so you can't see who inside. Then, as the driver see the crowd, him draw brake and stop, and back back right down to where I standing. Ehh-hee now, I say to myself. Every window roll down same time. Four of them in the car. Black dark glasses. Nobody smiling. The people standing by the road who see the play pretend they don't see nothing, but same time you see them start to move away from the road and back to the sea, and you can tell that the word travelling. The driver come out of the car and he slam the door so he can lean against it and fold him two arm across him chest. "What a gwan?" he ask, and you can see him scanning everything with him eyes. But everybody suddenly turn dumb. Not a soul saying nothing till the silence getting dangerous. "Is something them catch, sar," one little boy finally squeeze out, and you can hear the shaking in him voice. Him mother cuff him same time she drag him in to hold him close to her body. One of the men in the backseat of the car lean out of the window and take him finger call to a young girl who standing with a set of young girls who can't stop look at the car.

"Nice queen, what a go on?" he ask her in this sweet-sweet voice. Well, this little pikni so thrill to have a Don calling to her she just forget herself and make her mouth run weh. "Dem find a fish that swallow coke. It don't stop dance yet. Dem seh is dance-hall queen."

Poppyshow! Is how this pikni stay clear back here and know all that? By this time she dying with laugh and trying to step boldly up to the car while her friend them holding on to her skirt to drag her back.

Well! You'd think these fellows drill like soldier every day. For is like with one movement, the three in the car come out and slam the doors with one slam: *Blam*. The driver fall in beside them. Four of them dress in black from head to toe. Then like they practise every move, the four of them straighten them black suit and them gold chain and them shades, then line up two by two and step off down the beach. The crowd part in front of them like the Red Sea part before Moses. People didn't even turn to look, they just sense a deadly force rolling towards them and they move out of the way. I couldn't let this pass, so I fall in behind the men to see the moves.

They look neither to the right nor to the left; they just march forward through the parting crowd till they reach the circle round the fishermen who still quarrelling and making pass with their machete. The four men just stand there, arm fold across them chest, just taking in the scene, not saying a word. It take a little while for the brothers to realize something happening, and as each one of them turn and see the men in black, his face change as if he seeing duppy and everything just drain out of him. Big Jake and his brothers just drop their machete and freeze. Nobody move. People look as if they not even breathing as they watch the four men turn to study the fish. They stand there looking at it for a good long while, then they turn to look at the one that is the big Don and he give a little nod and the four of them bend down one time to take hold of the fish.

Well, me not lying, is like the fish that never stop moving from it come off the boat been waiting for something like this, for the four men don't have to struggle with it too hard; is like the fish allowing them to pick it up, for they manage to hold on to it and lift it without any trouble; the fish keeping quiet except for a little trembling that running through its body now and then.

Still without saying one word, the four men carrying the fish march back the way they come, straight to their car, the silent crowd parting to let them through, everybody pretending like they not seeing nothing. I still following right behind them, so I see when one of them drop his side of the fish long enough to open the trunk, and then the four of them struggle to lift up the fish and throw it in. Then they slam the trunk shut, dust off their hands, straighten their clothes, get in the car, and drive away.

This is the end of Radio's narrative and that is the last anyone ever saw of the car, the men, or the fish, though people swear that even before they moved off, the car had started rocking from some mighty power like thunder rolling around inside the trunk.

Well, there you have it. Make of it what you will. Maybe you can even find some Culture in it. All I know is, from the day the Mad Fish came, Radio got voice and attitude and it rained for a long, long time.

Olive Senior was born in Jamaica and now lives in Toronto. She is the author of eight books, including poetry, fiction, and non-fiction. Her short-story collection Summer Lightning *(Longman, 1986) won the Commonwealth Writers Prize. It was followed by* Arrival of the Snake-Woman *(Longman, 1989) and* Discerner of Hearts *(McClelland & Stewart, 1995). Her poetry includes* Gardening in the Tropics *(McClelland & Stewart, 1994). She is represented in numerous anthologies internationally and has read her work, lectured, and conducted writing workshops in Britain, Europe, the United States, Canada, and the Caribbean.*

Carol Shields

OUR MEN
AND WOMEN

Our Earthquake man is up early. He greets the soft dawn with a speculative lift of his orange-juice glass. "Hello, little earth," he hums quietly. Then, "So! You're still here."

He puts in a pre-breakfast call to the E-Quake Centre. "Nothing much," he hears. "Just a few overnight rumbles."

Overnight what? Really?

He resents having missed these terrestrial waves, but his resentment is so faint, so almost non-existent, that he swallows it down, along with his vitamin C. He should be grateful. So he's missed a tremble or two! What does it matter? The earth is always heaving, growling, whereas last night he'd slept seven uninterrupted hours with his arms and legs wrapped round the body of his dear Patricia, his blonde Patricia, graceful, lithe Patricia, fifteen years his junior, blessed replacement for Marguerite — perpetrator of sulks, rages, the hurling of hairbrushes and dinner plates. Thirty-five years he and Marguerite were together. Their four grown children are almost embarrassingly buoyant about this second marriage of his. At the time of the wedding, last Thanksgiving, two days after a 3.5 Richter scale reading, the kids chipped in together to buy their old dad and his new wife an antique sleigh bed. Actually a reproduction model, produced in a South Carolina factory. Sleek, beautiful. Closer in its configuration to being a cradle than a sleigh.

Now, in the early morning, Patricia is grilling slices of six-grain bread over the backyard barbecue. She has a thing about toasters, just as he has a thing about the instability of the earth. You'd think he'd be used to it after all this time, but his night dreams are of molten lava and the crunch and grind of tectonic plates. As a graduate student he believed his subtle calibrations could predict disaster; now he knows better. Those years with Marguerite taught him that making projections is like doing push-ups in water. The world spewed and shifted. There was nothing to lean against. You had to pull yourself back from it, suck in your gut, and hold still.

His solemn, smiling Patricia is flipping over the toast now with a long silvery fork. Sunlight decorates her whisked-back hair and the rounded cotton shoulder of her T-shirt. What a picture! She stands balanced, with her bare feet slightly apart, on the patio stones, defying — it would seem — the twitching earth with its sly, capricious crust. "Ready?" she calls out to him, skewering the slices of toast on her fork and tossing them straight at his head.

But no, it's only an optical illusion. The toast is still there, attached to the fork's prongs. It's a hug she's thrown in his direction. Her two skinny arms have risen exuberantly, grabbed a broad cube of air, and pushed it forcefully towards him.

It came at him, a tidal wave moving along a predestined line. This is what his nightmares have promised: disorder, violence.

A man of reflexes, his first thought was to duck, to cover his face and protect himself. Then he remembered who he was, where he was — a man standing in a sunlit garden a few yards away from a woman he loved. He can't quite, yet, believe this. "Tsunami," he pronounced speculatively.

"Me too," she whispered. "Hey, me too."

Our Rainfall woman is also up early. She parts her dotted Swiss curtains and inspects the sky. Good, fine, okay; check. A smack of blue, like an empty billboard, fills in the spaces behind her flowering shrubs and cedar fence; she finds this reassuring, also disappointing. Her whole day will be like this, a rocking back and forth between what she wants and what she doesn't. "I am master of all I can stand," her father, the great explainer, used to say. She can't remember if he meant this thought to be comforting or if he was being his usual arrogant, elliptical self.

At eleven o'clock she conducts her seminar on drought. At four-thirty she's scheduled to lecture on flood. Lunch will be a sandwich and a pot of tea in the staff room. They expect her to be there; it would be presumptuous to go to a restaurant — either they feel this or she does, no one's sure. Today someone asks her about the World Series, who she's betting on. "Hmmmm," she says, blinking, looking upward, moving her mug of tea swiftly to her lips. Then, "Hard to say, hard to say."

Her night dreams, her daydreams too, are about drowning, but in recent months she's been enrolled in an evening workshop at the Y that teaches new techniques guaranteed to control nocturnal disturbances. It works like this: in the midst of sleep, the conscious mind is invited to step forward and engage briefly with the dream image, so that a threatening wave of water closing over the dreamer's head (for example) is transformed into a shower of daisies. Or soap flakes. Or goose feathers. An alternate strategy is to bid the conscious mind to reach for the remote control (so to speak) and switch channels. Even her father's flat, elderly, argumentative voice can be shut off. Right off. *Snap, click.* Or transmuted into a trill of birdsong. Or the dappled pattern of light and shadow.

She lives, by choice, in a part of the country where rain is moderate. There's never too much or too little. Except . . . well, except during exceptional circumstances, which could occur next week or next month, anytime, in fact. Planetary systems are enormously complicated; they tend to interact erratically. She understands this, having written any number of articles on the very subject of climate variability, on the theory of chaos. Meteorologists, deservedly humbled in recent years, confess that they are working *towards* eighty-five percent accuracy, and that this thrust applies only to twenty-four-hour predictions. Long-term forecasting, the darling of her graduate-school days, has been abandoned.

There's no way people can protect themselves against surprise. Her father, for instance, was one minute alive and the next minute dead. The space in between was so tightly packed that there wasn't room to squeeze in one word. Or even to imagine what that word might be. Inundation? Release? Deprivation? Pressure? Hunger? Thirst? What?

Our Fire fellow is relatively young, but already he's been granted tenure. Also five thousand square feet of laboratory space, plus three research assistants, plus an unlimited travel allowance. Anything he wants he gets, and he wants a lot. He's gassed up on his own brilliance. And with shame, too. No one should need what he needs, and need it ten times a day, a hundred times a day.

He's a man of finely gauged increments, of flashpoints, of fevers and starbursts, of a rich, unsparing cynicism. Up at five-thirty, a four-mile run, a quick flick through the latest journals, half a dozen serious articles gulped down, then coffee, scalding, out of a machine. This part of the day is a torment to him, his night dreams still not shaken off. (Has it been made clear that he lives by choice in a motel unit, and refuses even the consolation of weekly rates?)

By seven he's in his office, checking through his e-mail, firing off letters that become quarrels or sharp inquiries. Everywhere he sees slackers, defilers, and stumblers. His anger blazes just thinking of them. He knows he should exercise patience, but fear of anonymity, or something equally encumbering, has edged the sense of risk out of his life.

Small talk, small courtesies — he hasn't time. His exigent nature demands instant responses and deplores time-wasting functions. Like what? Like that wine-and-cheese reception for old what's his name and his new wife! Like staff-room niceties. Blather about the World Series. And that lachrymose young Rainfall woman, who keeps asking him how he's "getting along."

Well, he's getting along. And along and along. He's going up, up. Up like a firecracker.

Right now he's doing fifty double-time push-ups on the beige carpet of his office in preparation for one of his popular lectures on reality. His premise, briefly, is that we can touch reality only through the sensations of the single moment, that infinitesimal spark of time that is, even now as we consider it, dying. We must — to use his metaphor — place our hand directly in the flame.

He pursues his point, romping straight over the usual curved hills of faith, throwing forth a stupefying mixture of historical lore and its gossamer logic, presenting arguments that are bejewelled with crafty irrelevance, covering the blackboard with many-branched equations that establish and illuminate his careful, random proofs. On and on he goes, burning dangerously bright, and ever brighter.

Notes are taken. No one interrupts, no one poses questions; they wouldn't dare. Afterwards the lecture hall empties quickly, leaving him alone on the podium, steaming with his own heat, panting, rejoicing.

But grief steals into his nightly dreams, which commence with a vision of drenching rain, rain that goes on and on and shows no sign of ever ending, falling into the rooms of his remembered boyhood, his mother, his father — there they are, smiling, so full of parental pride — and a brother, especially a brother, who is older, stronger, more given to acts of shrugging surrender, more self-possessed, more eagerly and more offhandedly anointed. The family's clothes and bodies are soaked through with rain, as are the green hedges, the familiar woods and fields, the roadway, the glistening roofs and chimneys, inclines and valleys, the whole world, in fact. Except for him, standing there with his hands cupped, waiting. For him there has not been, so far, a single drop.

She's something else, our Plague and Pestilence woman. She's just (today) won the staff room World Series pool — a lucky guess, she admits, the first four games out of four. No one else risked such a perfect sky blue sweep.

"You were an accident," her mother told her when she was a young girl, just ten or eleven years old. "I never meant to have a kid, it just happened. There I was, pregnant."

Unforgivable words. But instantly forgiven. Because her mother's voice, as she made this confession, was roughened with wonder. An accident, she said, but her intonation, her slowly shaking woman's head, declared it to be the best accident imaginable. The most fortunate event in the history of the world, no less.

Our Plague and Pestilence woman married young, out of love, a man who was selfish, cruel, childish. But one day, several years into the marriage, he woke up and thought: I can't go on like this. I have to change. I have to become a different kind of person.

They are thankful, both of them, that their children have been spared the ravages of smallpox, typhoid, diphtheria, scarlet fever, poliomyelitis. Other diseases, worse diseases, hover about them, but the parents remain hopeful. Their histories, their natural inclinations, buoy them up. She dreams nightly of leaf mould, wheat rot, armies of grasshoppers, toads falling from the sky, diseased flesh, multiplying bacteria, poisoned blood, incomprehensible delusions, but wakes up early each day with a clean, sharp longing for simple tasks and agreeable weather.

It was our Plague and Pestilence woman who, one year ago, introduced her assistant, Patricia, to the recently widowed Earthquake man, and this matchmaking success has inspired another social occasion — which occurred just last night, as a matter of fact. A platter of chicken, shrimp, saffron, and rice was prepared. A table was set in a leafy garden. The two guests — our Rainfall woman, our Fire person — were reluctant at first to come. They had to be persuaded, entreated. Once there, they were put, more or less, at their ease. Made to feel they deserved the fragrant dish before them. Invited to accept whatever it was that poured through their senses. Encouraged to see that the image they glimpsed in the steady candlelight matched almost, but not quite, the shapeless void of their private nightly dreams.

Our P and P woman, observant as she is, doesn't yet know how any of this will turn out. It's far too soon to tell.

We can't help being proud of our men and women. They work hard to understand the topography of the real. It's a heartbreaking struggle, yet somehow they carry on — predicting, measuring, analyzing, recording, looking over their shoulders at the presence of their accumulated labour, cocking an ear to the sounds of their alarm clocks going off and calling them to temperature-controlled rooms and the dings and dongs of their word processors, the shrill bells of approval or disapproval, the creaks of their bodies as the years pile up, and the never-ending quarrel with their smothered, creaturely, solitary selves. Limitations — always they're crowded up against limitations. Sometimes our men and women give way to old nightmares or denial or the delusion that living in the world is effortless and full of ease. Like everyone else, they're spooked by old injuries, and that swift plummeting fall towards what they believe must be the future. Nevertheless, they continue to launch their various theories, theories so fragile, speculative, and foolish, so unanchored by proofs and possibilities and so distorted by their own yearnings, that their professional reputations are put at risk, their whole lives, you might say. Occasionally, not often, they are called upon to commit an act of extraordinary courage.

Which is why we stand by our men and women. In the end they may do nothing. In the meantime, they do what they can.

One of Canada's most distinguished writers, Carol Shields was born in Illinois and has spent her adult life in various Canadian cities. She has published nine novels, one co-authored with the Vancouver writer Blanche Howard. Her most recent novel, Larry's Party *(Random House, 1998), was awarded the Orange Prize. She has also published two collections of short stories, three books of poetry, as well as four plays, one co-authored with her daughter, Catherine Shields, and one with the Winnipeg writer David Williamson.* The Stone Diaries *(Random House, 1993) was awarded the Pulitzer Prize, the Governor General's Award for fiction, and the National Book Critics' Circle Award, and was shortlisted for the Booker Prize.*